Edelweiss

Edelweiss

Book One

J.L. Robison

This is a work of fiction. Names, characters, places, and incidents either are the product of the author's imagination or are used fictitiously. Any resemblance to actual persons, living or dead, events, or locales is entirely coincidental.

For information, contact J.L. Robison at joanlrobison@yahoo.com or https://linktr.ee/j.l.robison

First edition
ISBN 978-1-7358382-4-3

Edelweiss Saga

Edelweiss
Winter Iris
The White Orchid
Beneath the Cornflowers

I would like to dedicate this book to all those who helped me with editing, was patient as I spent countless hours writing it, and who took the time to read it after. Thank you!

Chapter One

February 4th, 2013

It filled Jon with excitement. This was what he had spent his entire career working towards, and now he was finally getting the funding he needed and the opportunity to put his theory to the test. After his many realized failures, he could now see all those years of hard work and long hours spent scribbling finally being made into something real. Seeing it as an equation on a piece of paper was only theoretical, but now, soon, he would get to see it become a reality. He had no guarantee that what they would build would be as it was on his equation, but if his calculations were correct, it would be.

While he waited at JFK International Airport for his eight o'clock flight to Heathrow, Jon thought about how tomorrow could change his life forever and possibly the world. He looked down at his hands, noticing they were sweaty yet cold. He always got this way when he was nervous.

The flight was scheduled to arrive at Heathrow at three-thirty p.m., then straight to Cambridge from there. The researchers at Cambridge were anxiously awaiting his arrival, and as soon as he got there, they were to start the work on his project. Jon was sure that he and the entire Cambridge team would work well into the night and possibly into the wee hours of the morning.

"Flight 377 to Heathrow is now ready for boarding," Jon heard on the speaker overhead.

He looked up from the book he was reading to see the people getting up from their seats and forming a line. *Must be zone one,* he thought. He checked his ticket and saw that he was in zone two. He didn't have to wait long for zone one to board. He had only read three pages of his book when they called zone two. Jon grabbed his backpack, threw it over his shoulder, and rolled his small black suitcase to the newly formed line of people.

Oh my God, this is it, this is actually happening, Jon thought as he showed his ticket and passport to the woman at the gate. Once she handed him his ticket stub and passport back, he started down the ramp leading to the plane door. When he stepped over the threshold into the plane, a tightness began to form in his chest. He quickly found his seat, stowed his suitcase overhead, and sat down. His seat was by the window, so he leaned close to it and peered out over the platform where they were putting the luggage in the belly of the plane. Jon watched them toss the bags underneath as he waited for them to take off. It was all he could do to keep his nerves in check. He was having a hard time distinguishing the excitement from the anxiety, both wreaking havoc on his nerves. He hoped his theory would work like the math showed him it would. As long as there was no unforeseen problem or mistake in his calculations, this would be one of the greatest discoveries in human history.

Once the plane was in the air and the captain turned off the seatbelt sign and told the passengers they could now use their electronic devices, Jon turned on his Blackberry so he could go over some notes he had taken earlier. He knew that there would be no sleep for him. The feeling in his chest would see to that.

So many things were going to or not going to happen in the next twenty-four hours. Cambridge already had all the equipment that the group would need set up. They were just waiting for his arrival. There was so much at stake and so much riding on this one moment. He was afraid of failing; the thought of it not working after all his efforts and all the efforts of the other people involved had him worried. Though deep down in his gut, he knew it would work, the real challenge would be finding a human test subject; this would indeed be a strange thing to explain to someone. And an even bigger challenge could arise when the person actually had to go through with what they agreed to do. Someone might think it sounded exciting at first, and in theory, it was, but the real thing could be quite terrifying. The unknown will always be.

Jon looked out the window at the city of London below as the plane descended. He took a deep breath to calm himself. *It's almost time,* he thought.

After the plane landed and Jon retrieved his carry-on bag, he made his way to the luggage claim. He waited as bag after bag went around the carousel before he saw his large black suitcase with the red ribbon tied around the handle and the orange strap fastened around it come towards him. He pulled it off the carousel, and with a suitcase handle in each hand, he headed to customs. He made it through quickly and started the long walk towards the exit, where he was told someone would be waiting to pick him up.

As he neared the glass doors at the front of the airport, he could see a man and woman, both wearing suits, waiting. The man was holding a sign that read *'Jon Tolly'* in bold black letters. Jon pulled his suitcases over to them.

"Hi, I'm Jon Tolly. You must be from Cambridge?"

"We are," said the woman. She held out her hand for Jon to shake. "I'm Dr. Petterson," she said as Jon took her hand. She was a tall, thin woman but petite in stature, with narrow shoulders. She had shoulder-length straight blond hair and dark-framed glasses that mostly hid her large blue eyes. Her grey pantsuit made her look taller, and her dark-framed glasses all seemed fitting for her profession. Her choice of clothing and the way she carried herself told Jon that she was someone who took her career and herself seriously.

"It's so nice to meet you," Jon told her.

No sooner did Jon let go of the woman's hand did the man hold his out. Jon took it, noticing that the doctor had a firm grip, stronger than he would have expected, given his size. The man was also thin like the woman but considerably shorter. He had his shiny black hair combed to one side and wore a pressed black suit. His features gave away that he was of Asian descent.

"I'm Dr. Yug," the man said as he shook Jon's hand. "Shall we get going? We have a lot to do, and I'm sure that Jon would like to get some sleep at some point," Dr. Yug said to the woman as he helped Jon carry his luggage.

There was a black four-door sedan waiting out front for the three of them. Dr. Yug got in the front with the driver, and Dr. Petterson got into the back with Jon.

Jon admired the architecture in London as they drove through the city. He enjoyed how the new, modern London was mixed with the old and how there was a defining line between the two. It somehow made Jon sad, but he wasn't quite sure why.

This was his first time being in Europe, and though he admired every building for its grandeur and beauty, he struggled to imagine how it would have looked in the past. Not too long ago, the city was uniform, as it had been hundreds of years ago, but after the blitz, it would never look the same.

"Are you ready for this?" Dr. Petterson asked.

"I have been ready my whole life," Jon said. "What about you?"

"I have been waiting for someone like you my whole life, someone to come along that knew just how to figure the right things out and had enough faith in themselves to believe that they could do what you have done."

Jon looked at Dr. Petterson in surprise. "Well, we can all share in this momentous occasion together! Just imagine how this will affect our test subject's life. They will never be the same either."

"But how exactly all of this will affect them is going to be the real question," Dr. Yug interjected from the front seat.

"We have to find someone first," Dr. Petterson said.

Jon turned back to the window and continued to watch the city pass by them but noticed they were not heading toward Cambridge. "I thought we were going to the university?"

"Most of the funding is coming from Cambridge, but we have acquired a building just for this occasion. It is about an hour northeast of London in the country. That way, no one will disturb us," Dr. Petterson said.

This somehow didn't surprise Jon.

A little after five, they arrived at what looked like a warehouse sitting in the middle of a field. The car pulled in front of the building and turned the engine off. Jon looked up at the simple structure, a little unsure if it was the right place to be experimenting. He said nothing about his concerns to the others and followed them to the front door of the building. Dr. Yug took out a keycard the size of a credit card and swiped it through a slot in a small box to the right of the door, then punched in a code on the keypad. The door then made a buzzing sound and clicked just before Dr. Yug pulled it open.

"After you," he said to Jon and Dr. Petterson, following them in and letting the door close behind him.

About forty feet down a small corridor was another door they had to go through. Dr. Yug put his hand on a green back-lit pad, and a light went up and down, scanning it. Then it too buzzed like the other door and made a clicking sound. Dr. Yug pulled the door open and held it for them to enter.

When Jon walked into the room, he saw what he figured was the rest of the group waiting in the lab. At the sight of them entering the room, the other scientists stood from their chairs and peered at Jon, curiosity on their faces.

"We have all the equipment set up over here," Dr. Yug said, pointing to the right.

Jon looked to the side of the room he had pointed to; it was a sizable room with only a few windows near the top. To compensate for the lack of outside light, they had the room well-lit with bright floodlights that reminded him of an operating room in a hospital. Jon's eyes widened with delight at the sight that lay before him.

Chapter Two

March 7th, 2014

Just to the right of the door in the room, Jon had first stepped foot in over a year ago was sitting his invention, completely assembled and ready to go. Jon stood in the doorway looking at it, trying to comprehend what he was seeing, trying to believe it was real. It was now something that he could touch, something he could see. No longer was it just numbers from mad scribblings and a diagram on a piece of paper. The thing that was once just an idea was now a reality.

Inside the main room was a smaller concrete room, and inside of the concrete room were twelve medium cyclotron particle accelerators that made up a large circle. When the charged particles accelerated outward, they would collide and then hold to a spiral trajectory by a static magnetic field and accelerate by a rapidly varying radio frequency electric field. The theory was when this happened for an extended period, it would open a portal in the time continuum. The assumption was that if someone were to go through the portal, it would put them in that same spot, but a different time. Now, setting a specific time could be tricky because depending on which frequency they set, the equipment would determine how far back one would go. Getting it at just the right frequency could prove difficult, but they could do it with enough time and patience.

It had taken Jon years to figure out that the higher the frequency, the farther in time one would go back and how much frequency one would need to account for each week, each month, or each year.

"It is ready now," Dr. Foster, the man sitting at the main computer said. "I hope you are ready because none of this would even be possible without you."

Jon was not sure what to say to that. It felt strange being praised so much, so he smiled at him instead.

Dr. Brandt was standing next to a stack of metal animal cages, and Dr. Jensen was at the control panel. These were the people Jon had worked with for the last year to help bring his idea to life.

"Well, let's get started, shall we?" Dr. Yug said as he handed Jon a lab coat with a tag that had his name and a dosimeter that measured radiation exposure.

"Let's do it," Jon said.

"Jensen, let's get the cyclotrons started, then move on to the next step," Dr. Yug told him.

Dr. Jensen started pushing buttons on the control panel, and the cyclotrons came alive. Jon watched in utter awe at what was happening as rainbow-colored light came from the cyclotrons, and after 15 minutes, a black hole opened up before their eyes. They were watching the entire thing transpire on camera safely in another room. Not knowing what would happen when the cyclotrons started up, they figured it was safer not to be near them.

The door to the concrete room where the cyclotrons were was also closed for their protection, just in case. This was the first test, and they had to ensure it was completely safe. The cyclotrons emitted a small amount of radiation over time, and no one would want to be in the room with the cyclotron for an extended period or leave the door open while it was running for too long for fear of radiation poisoning.

"OK, Dr. Brandt, you're up," Dr. Yug said.

Dr. Brandt took a puppy out of one of the metal cages, walked over to the concrete room, opened the door to it, stepped inside, and then closed the door behind him. He cautiously walked to the portal, stopped just in front of it, and looked up at the camera for a second before continuing. He gave a kind of 'here we go' glance. Dr. Brandt put a collar with a camera on the puppy, then picked it back up and extended his arms out, putting the puppy near the portal; his hands shook as he moved it closer. The puppy started squealing and squirming in his hands, so he stopped.

Dr. Brandt looked at the camera again. "What do I do? If I loosen my grip, it will jump out of my hands?"

Dr. Petterson reached over and pushed the button on the intercom. "Put your hands in as well," she said.

Dr. Brandt frowned at the camera. "Seriously, how did I draw the short straw?"

Jon pushed the button on the intercom. "Do you want me to come down and do it?"

"No, I'm already here. I'll do it." His expression turned to fierce determination.

Dr. Brandt turned back to face the portal; he extended his hands towards it again, but this time a little quicker. Everyone watched as the head of the puppy, Dr. Brandt's fingers, and then both of his hands, along with the dog's body, disappeared into the blackness. Dr. Brandt quickly jerked his hands out, rubbed them on his shirt, and then hurried out of the room.

While Dr. Jensen was getting things ready to see if a picture would show on the monitor from the camera on the puppy's collar, everyone looked at Dr. Brandt. He was out of breath when he entered the room with everyone else.

"What was it like?" Jon asked.

"It was strange, like some force was trying to pull me in along with the dog. And both of my hands tingled, so I hurried and let go, and then the dog was gone. I'm not sure if it jumped out of my hands or if it got pulled in by whatever force was there."

They all turned to the monitor to see if anything showed up, but all they could see was black. Then, they saw green flicker across the screen for a brief second, and then it was gone. Everyone moved closer, hoping to see something again. They stood quietly, staring at the screen for what felt like forever, and then, like before, the green was back. They could not tell what it was, but it appeared to be moving around. The camera started getting farther from the green, and they all focused a little harder on the monitor.

"It's grass!" Dr. Jensen yelled.

“Oh my God, it is,” Dr. Brandt said, leaning in closer.

The camera started moving fast over the grass as the puppy ran across a field.

“It survived,” Jon yelled. “Haha, this is amazing. We did it,” he said as he squeezed Dr. Yug’s shoulder and then patted him on the back.

The room erupted with clapping and cheers; there was a mutual feeling of relief that they had successfully gotten this far.

“Now we watch and see if the puppy is in the right era,” Dr. Jensen said.

“What time did you send it to?” Jon asked.

“We think we sent it to eighteen hundred,” Dr. Petterson said. “We cannot guarantee that what we see is the year eighteen-hundred, but if we see horses and carriages and people in different clothing, then we will at least have a rough idea of the century it is in.”

“Why do you think it took the puppy so long to get up?” Dr. Foster asked.

“I don’t know. Maybe it disorients you for a few seconds,” said Jon.

“Well, we know that the possibility is there. You can tell the person who will go through,” Dr. Brandt told Jon.

They watched the puppy wander for over an hour until it finally started to rain. The puppy hid under some trees and whimpered. Dr. Jensen got out of his chair and disappeared through the door that led to the hall. A few minutes later, he returned.

“It isn’t raining outside. It’s not even cloudy.”

“Well, this is a good sign,” Jon said.

The puppy started moving again when the rain stopped, but it was becoming more difficult to see where it was going because the sun was lower in the sky now.

After watching for a while longer, they could see a faint glow of light coming through the trees.

"It looks like a house," Dr. Petterson said.

"It does," Jon agreed.

As the puppy got closer, they could see that they were right. It was a house. A small wooden cabin was only yards in front of the puppy. It ran up to the front door whining and scratched at the corner.

The door opened, and a little boy stood in the doorway. The soft glow from the candles that were behind him shadowed his face. When the boy bent down to pet the puppy, they could see him better. He was wearing a white dress shirt with lace, cuffed sleeves, a cravat, and knee-length breeches over stockings.

"Well, it looks like he could be from anywhere between the early 17th century to the late 18th century," Dr. Brandt said with his head tilted to the side and brows furrowed as he stared at the monitor, observing the boy's attire.

The little boy picked the puppy up and called for his mom. The woman who came to the door wore a solid-colored dress with an apron tied around it and had her hair in a bun covered with a white bonnet. They watched as the boy and his mother discussed the dog. The woman finally told the boy that he could keep it as long as he took care of it and that he was to do all the work himself.

The boy shut the front door, taking the dog inside to his tiny bedroom. "What do you have around your neck?" the boy said to the dog.

He reached for the dog's collar, and then the camera shook. It moved quickly upward and stopped right in front of the boy's face. He squinted down at it, then put it close to his face, obviously trying to inspect it further.

"What a strange thing you wear around your neck," he said to the dog. "I think you might have belonged to witches. We shall not tell Mother. She would disapprove of such things and put you out at once if she knew. We will hide this so no one will find it."

The boy laid the collar with the camera on the floor, and they were now looking at a wall. His arms then appeared in front of the camera. He pulled up a floorboard, picked up the camera, and laid it in the hole. They could see his face for just a second before he put the board back, and everything went dark.

"Wow, this is incredible," Dr. Yug said. "Now, the last step is to find a test subject."

"A witch," Jon said. "That is too funny. How long is the battery life of the camera?"

"It should last for about a week," Dr. Jensen said.

"Why don't we all get some sleep, and then we can start working on the next phase tomorrow," Dr. Yug said.

"Can I give you a ride to your hotel, Jon?" Dr. Brandt asked.

"Yes, that would be great. Thank you."

Jon followed everyone out front once everything had been shut down and lights turned off.

"My car is over here," Dr. Brandt said.

Jon looked over at the grey mini coop he pointed at. "Nice car!"

"Thanks."

Jon slid into the passenger seat, noticing the mess in the car, with empty coffee cups, candy wrappers, fast food bags, and work papers everywhere, amongst other things. Jon wondered how much time Dr. Brandt spent in his car.

"This has to be the most incredible day of my life," Dr. Brandt said as he got behind the wheel.

Jon laughed. "This is the most incredible day of my life. I have dreamed of this moment ever since I was a little boy. I have always loved physics, science, and anything to do with time travel."

"I always did, too," Dr. Brandt said.

After the relatively silent car ride, they pulled in front of Jon's apartment.

"Don't stay up too late," Jon said as he got out.

"I won't, don't worry."

"Well, it looks like when you go home, you just sit in your car and work, or maybe you just live in your car and don't have a home," Jon said, nodding at the junk in the front floor.

"I have a place to live," Dr. Brandt said sheepishly.

Jon chuckled and shut the door, watching the mini disappear around the corner.

When Jon's alarm went off at seven, he pushed the cancel button and lay in bed for a few seconds, looking at his bedroom ceiling, thinking of the night before and all the crazy stuff that had happened. It seemed like he dreamed the whole thing.

After showering, he gathered up all the things he would need for the day, ate breakfast, then went to the lobby of the apartment building and waited near the front by the windows to see Dr. Brandt when he arrived.

Jon didn't have to wait long when he saw Dr. Brandt pull in front, taking a spot behind another car. Jon grabbed his backpack and headed out.

"How did you sleep?" Dr. Brandt asked.

"I slept well enough, and you?"

"As good as could be expected."

Jon smiled as they pulled away from the curb; it would be another long, busy day! When they got to the lab and went inside, they saw that everyone else was there. Jon looked at his watch, and it read seven fifty-eight. *Right on time,* he thought as they gathered in the meeting room around a long table.

"OK, so the first order of business is coming up with a plan to find a test subject, so I thought Jon could start the meeting," Dr. Yug said.

"That's fine," Jon said. He looked at everyone around the table. "Well, last night, as Brandt was giving me a ride home, I thought about how we might get someone to agree to do this. First, I think that if we pay them, it would be more appealing to them than volunteering. Also, we should have people fill out an application for it and perhaps take an aptitude test. That way, we can pick someone we know something about; we can also conduct interviews with the people with the best applications. We could do them over the phone, via Skype, or in person. I want to make sure that we get the best person for the task; I don't want someone who will do something stupid while they are there or be too afraid to stay after they have arrived. I want to know that they can handle it physically and emotionally. I also think it would be good if they kept a journal of their time there, all the things they learned while there, and their experiences. The best way to recruit would be to say that we are offering an internship."

Everyone exchanged a glance.

"That sounds like a good plan. Does anybody else have any ideas that they want to add?" Dr. Petterson asked.

"Why don't we just start with that? We can improve on it while it's in the planning phase," Dr. Foster said.

Everyone sat quietly, taking notes of what was said.

"I'm OK with the idea Jon proposed," Dr. Jensen said finally, as no one else had come up with a better one.

They all went to work on coming up with the recruitment process.

Dr. Brandt was helping Jon work on the application when he looked up from his computer. "Where do we want to recruit from, and what qualities should we be looking for in the person?"

"Well, why don't we start by recruiting at universities? And qualities…" Jon said, lingering on the last word, thinking.

"In what countries?" Jensen asked.

"Why don't we let Jon decide that, too," Dr. Petterson said.

Everyone looked at Jon, waiting for him to say what he thought.

"How about the UK? Since we are already here and seeing how I am from the US, why don't we recruit from there too?"

"I like that idea," Dr. Yug said.

"We still haven't covered the qualities," Dr. Brandt said. "I know we said someone that can handle the situation emotionally and physically, but we can't just ask someone how strong they are emotionally on the application."

"We could ask what their fitness level is and if they have ever been to a psychiatrist or taken medications for depression, anxiety, or any mental illnesses. We probably should check to see if they have a criminal record as well. I also want to call their employer and ask about their work ethics and what kind of employee they are," Jon said.

"Talking to their professors would be a good idea, too," Dr. Brandt added.

"I think asking them to give a brief description of their upbringing would be good to have on there," Dr. Yug said.

"Those are all excellent ideas," Jon said as he jotted them down in his notepad. "Maybe see what class they come from—lower class, middle, or upper. Sometimes that makes a difference in how people act and their decisions."

"Oh, I think their hobbies and where they see themselves in —let's say in five years—should also be included," said Dr. Brandt.

"I like it," Jon said, giving him an approving glance.

"Should we consider if they are married, single, or have children?" Dr. Petterson asked.

"Yes, I think we want them single with no children," Dr. Brandt said.

"Good. I think we have our layout for the application," Jon said. "Let's get to work."

After a week, they had all the information they needed, the countries they would recruit from, and in which areas. They decided on six in the US and four in England. They would do two on the west coast, two in the Midwest, two on the east coast in the US, two in the north of England, and two in the south of England.

Chapter Three

April 3rd, 2014

Eva Abrams enjoyed going back to Provo to visit her family, but it was also good to get back to her everyday life and routine in Salt Lake City. She was attending the University of Utah, and though she had hoped to go a little farther away from home for school, possibly California or maybe New York, she had gotten accepted here and could not pass up the in-state tuition.

She worked at a daycare on the weekend and pulled a few night shifts during the week at the University of Utah Hospital. Neither of the jobs brought in much money, so she applied for financial aid and took out a loan to help with school, and her parents helped with the rent.

She drove her 1997 Geo Metro down Interstate fifteen back to Salt Lake; she had class early in the morning. Otherwise, she would have spent the night. She reached over to turn the heater up but realized it was already on high. The fan in her car was not strong, and the heater never really got hot, but it wasn't even blowing out lukewarm air now. It was an unusually frigid April, and the roads were slick. She kept her speed at thirty and hoped she didn't go off the road. The snow was falling so fast that her windshield wipers could hardly keep up, making it almost impossible to see.

"Why didn't I go home earlier," she said, chastising herself. A buzzing sound came from the passenger seat; she reached over and dug in her purse for her phone with her right hand as she gripped the steering wheel tightly with her left. As usual, it was at the bottom of her bag. She pulled it out, flipped it open, then put it to her ear and held it with her shoulder. "Hello."

"Eva, where are you?"

"Jenny, I'm sorry, but I'm still driving from Provo. I won't be home for at least an hour, maybe longer. The roads are bad, and I have to drive slowly. If I went any faster, I would probably slide off into the ditch."

"Well, that really sucks! Everyone is having a get-together tonight at Michael's house, and I wanted to go, but I didn't want to go alone, so I was going to see if you wanted to come with me?"

"I am sorry, Jenny, I would if I were going to be home earlier. But I will already get home past eleven, provided the roads don't worsen, and I have a class at eight tomorrow, so I need to go to bed."

Jenny made a grunting sound. "Well, that just spoils everything. I guess I'll just stay home, too, then."

"Maybe we can go to the next party if there's one. I know you like Michael and have waited a long time for a chance like this.

You know, you could go without me. You don't need me there to hold your hand. I have faith in your ability to procure a man without my help."

Jenny laughed sarcastically. "No, it's OK, maybe another time. I need a wingman to help me, anyway. Just drive safe, and I will see you when you get here."

"OK, bye, Jenny." Eva closed her phone and tossed it in the passenger seat without bothering to put it back in her purse. She took a deep breath and held it for a few seconds, then blew it out, seeing her breath in the air as she gripped the steering wheel tightly with both hands.

Jenny had been her best friend ever since they met in college. She had never met another person who cared more for her or tried harder to look out for her other than her parents and brother. Her life and its events were paramount to Jenny, as were Jenny's to her. She could not ask for a better friend.

As Eva drove, she thought about school and what she would do when she finished. Sometimes, she was unsure what the future held. Some days Eva seemed to know exactly where her life was heading and what she wanted out of it, and then there were days like today. She was going to school to get a better job and, as a result, hopefully, have a better life, at least as far as finances go. But that was the extent to which school could help her. Relationships and personal happiness were all on her. She had broken up with her boyfriend just before Christmas. They had dated for almost eight months, but it had not worked out and certainly was not a healthy relationship. There was a time when she was ready to try to make it work, but he was unwilling to make the changes she needed him to. She tried everything she could to make him happy, but the more she gave, the more he wanted. And the way he was controlling, combined with his hot temper, weighed on her a little more every day. The night he lost control and completely snapped was more than she could take. No matter how much love or commitment she felt for him, it was not enough. She always kept the details of that night from her parents and brother. They never knew how he really was. When she broke up with Kevin, her parents were disappointed. They liked him, or at least the Kevin they thought they knew. When her parents asked why she broke up with him, she told them that their lives were moving in different directions.

Eva loved Kevin, so whenever they would fight, she always felt like it was her fault, like she was doing something wrong. Even though he was mean to her, there were those rare moments when he would be so tender and act like the man she thought she had met. There was always that tiny flame in her that held some hope that he would stay that way, that maybe he had changed, but it never lasted. That kept her going and was why she stayed with him for as long as she had.

Eva wondered if she would ever be happy with someone if she found a man who would treat her the way they should. She wanted someone who would treat her with respect, the way someone who truly loved her would. She knew it was silly to think that, but right now, it just seemed that she would only find men like Kevin. Her relationship with him had caused her so much anxiety and bouts of depression. She knew that her family suspected that something was going on with her. Whenever her family asked, she would give an excuse and then change the subject. The only person she told was her roommate, Jenny.

She stopped herself before the thoughts ran away with her. She stared at the white road lit by her headlights and watched the snowflakes fall as she drove home, more than ready to be reunited with her bed.

She pulled in front of the house she shared with Jenny and two other girls. She wasn't as close with the other girls as she was to Jenny. They lived in a two-story brick structure, with a porch in the front with two white pillars on each side and an old brown wooden front door that was peeling its varnish. She turned the engine off but sat in the car and looked at the house to see if any lights were on, hoping she could slip inside unnoticed. She just wanted to take a shower and go to bed. There were no lights on, so she was sure that everyone had already gone to bed.

She got out of the car and carefully walked up to the front door, trying not to slip on the ice on the walkway. She searched in her purse for the key to unlock the door when suddenly it opened. She looked up to see Jenny standing in the doorway, staring at her. To Eva, Jenny looked like she should be in California, living a nomad life, surfing and tanning on the beach while drinking margaritas. Jenny had tan skin that made her blond hair appear even lighter, and she was fit like she imagined surfers to be.

"I was worried when you told me how bad the roads were, so I waited up until you got home."

"I'm fine, Jenny, but thanks for waiting up."

"You know that I always will," Jenny said as she reached out and hugged her.

Eva hugged her back, giving Jenny a warm smile when they moved away. "You can go to bed now that you know I am all right."

"I will. And you go to bed too and get a good night's sleep."

"I will." She was so thankful for Jenny and that they had met. The two of them had been through so much together.

Eva went up to her room, shut the door, and sat on her bed. She just wanted to go to bed but knew she should shower first. She showered quickly, then went back to her room and crawled into bed, falling asleep within minutes. Visiting family sometimes was tiring, and the concentration she had to do while driving didn't help.

Eva woke to the sun shining through her window. She blinked a few times, making out the branches of the pine tree in their backyard and the freshly fallen snow that covered them. It reminded her of something one would see in a painting. It was pretty but something she didn't enjoy experiencing. It had snowed all night, but now the sky was a clear blue, vibrant in the morning light. She realized that she had woken up on her own and not from her alarm; she did not know what time it was.

"Oh, crap."

Eva jumped out of bed and started changing out of her PJs. She was so tired the night before that setting her alarm had utterly escaped her. Eva looked at her clock and saw that it was already five-fifteen, and her class would start at eight. *I'm never going to make it on time,* Eva thought as she hurried into her clothes and ran downstairs, grabbing a banana on her way out to eat in the car.

"Eva, you're still here? I thought you were already gone?" Jenny said from the kitchen table.

"I did not set my alarm last night," Eva told her.

"Oh, no."

"Yeah, oh no, is right." She put on her coat, gloves, and shoes, grabbed her purse and backpack, and ran out the door. Then, she started her car and brushed the snow off the windows with her gloved hands. After clearing the windows, she brushed her hands together to remove the snow from her gloves and got in the car. She could not believe that she had forgotten to set her alarm.

As she turned on the road that faced the campus, she saw someone getting ready to pull out of a spot.

"Yes."

She stopped right before she got to the spot to wait for the car to leave, but just as the car pulled out, another car from the side street to her left pulled in front of her, stopped, and then started parallel parking into it.

"Seriously, you have got to be kidding me!" Eva shouted.

Eva honked her horn, but the car just kept backing in. The two guys got out and walked side by side, looking back at her while laughing.

"Sorry," one guy said with a smug smile and shrugged.

"I can't believe this," Eva said.

She drove on and, after several blocks, found a spot that was farther away on a different street. She parked her car, grabbed the backpack from the passenger's seat, and started running to school. She got to the building that her first class was in, opened the door, and ran up the stairs two steps at a time, stopping in front of the classroom door. Panting, she opened the door slowly, hoping that no one would notice her tardiness, then she slipped in and sat in the very back row. She looked at the clock and saw that it was already eight thirty-three. Unfortunately, the teacher noticed her coming in late and gave her an agitated, disapproving look as she took her seat. Eva looked down at the floor when the teacher looked up at her, trying to avoid his gaze.

Jenny's first class was not until eleven, and she had texted Eva right after arriving on campus to see if she had time to meet up for a coffee. After class, she waited for Jenny in the cafeteria. Jenny had something she wanted to talk to her about, and Eva could only imagine what that could be.

Eva sat at a table in the far right corner of the room, thinking about the rest of the things that she had to do today. After school, she had to go to work and the store, which sadly were going to be the day's highlights.

Eva looked up to see Jenny walking fast in her direction, then she sat in the chair across from her.

"So, how was class?"

"Well, I showed up half an hour late, and the teacher saw me come in and gave me an angry look."

"Oh no, Dr. Steves is the worst. He hates it when people are late."

"I know, but there was nothing I could do about it. And to make matters worse, this morning, when I got to school, I was waiting for a car to leave so I could take their spot. As soon as it left, these jerks pulled out from twelfth Street and backed into it, even though they knew I was waiting for it. I even honked at them, but they kept backing into it anyway," Eva said, dramatically gesturing her hand to the side.

"What assholes," Jenny said. "I would have run into the back of their car."

Eva laughed. "I don't doubt that. So, what did you want to talk about? Did you find some hot guy you're going to run away with?"

Jenny gave her a sarcastic smile. Eva didn't even know that was possible until she met Jenny, who bled sarcasm.

"I wish, but no. I found this paper on the bulletin board by the admissions office." She slid the piece of paper across the table towards Eva. "It's an internship at Cambridge University in England. I thought you could use some time away, you know, get away from this place and give your brain a rest and—"

"Wait a minute," Eva said, cutting her off. "You called me here to talk about an internship in another country. And my brain is just fine, Jenny! I know you're saying this because of Kevin, and you think I am emotionally broken, like shattered glass or something, but really, I'm fine. I don't need to go away and get better," Eva said, pushing the piece of paper back towards Jenny.

"Oh yeah, of course, I know that you're not, but… I thought you could use the money, that was all. Plus, you deserve it. Think how fun it would be to live in another country for a while?" Jenny said quickly. "Would you take it and just look at it for me, please? I admit I got it for myself when I first saw it, but then I thought about you and decided you needed it more than I did."

"Fine, just leave it on the table, and I will glance over it before I go to my next class."

Eva knew Jenny was only trying to be thoughtful. Jenny was always struggling with boys, which was constantly causing her anxiety. The anxiety caused her grades to drop in some classes, leading to more stress, which added to the pressure. It was a vicious cycle. Eva was always there for her, of course. Like the time she found Jenny drunk, crying in the bathroom at a frat party. A boy had taken her upstairs to a room and practically tried to rape her. When she poured her beer on his head and slapped him across the face, he called her a slut and said he knew she whored around with all the other boys in the dorm. That was only one of the times that Eva had been there for Jenny. Jenny had also been there for her more times than she could count. Jenny always talked about getting away, away from dumb boys, this school, this state, this country, and maybe even the planet if she could. So, it was no surprise that Jenny would be drawn to a flyer like that. It warmed her heart that Jenny thought she needed it more than herself. Maybe Jenny knew she couldn't go and wanted to live vicariously through her.

"Good, I'll leave it with you, and you can tell me what you think later," Jenny said, with a hint of excitement in her voice.

"You know nothing will probably come of this, don't you?" Eva said.

"I know. I have always thought it would be fun to do something like this and work abroad for a while. And you are definitely a better candidate than me. You adjust well and are such a quick learner."

"I will look at it. You better get going, Jenny, or you will be late for your class."

"OK, but you promise you will look at it, right?"

"Yes, yes, I will look at it. Now go," Eva said.

"Good."

Jenny got up from her chair, gave Eva a quick hug, and then left.

Eva reached across the table and picked up the paper after Jenny left. She held it in her hand for a minute while thinking about how silly all of this was. She had told Jenny that she would read it, and she would, but it would probably go in the garbage right after.

Eva had just started reading the paper when she heard someone call her name from across the room. She looked up to see Sam coming toward her. He was in her German class and also her math study group.

"Hey, Sam, what are you doing? Are you in-between classes, or are you done for the day?"

"I am just in between classes. What about you?"

"In between classes, too."

"What are you reading?"

"Oh, just a pamphlet that my roommate gave me about an internship in England."

"Oh yeah, I saw that too. I had thought about doing it myself, but I was unsure if I qualified for it. Are you going to do it?"

"I don't know. I haven't even read it yet. I just started to when I heard you call my name."

"Well, if you decide to do it, you will have to let me know how it goes."

"I will."

"Hey, I'll see you in class tomorrow," he said.

"OK."

When Sam walked away, Eva looked back down at the paper in her hand and sighed.

IF YOU WOULD LIKE TO HAVE A SUMMER ADVENTURE WHILE MAKING A LITTLE EXTRA MONEY ON THE SIDE, THEN GO TO WWW.CAMBRIDGE.HEALTHSCIENCE.UK: CLICK ON THE HS 2014 TESTING LINK AND FILL OUT THE

APPLICATION FOR THE 2014 INTERNSHIP. YOU WILL BE NOTIFIED BY EMAIL IF SELECTED FOR THE POSITION. IF YOU ARE CHOSEN, YOU WILL BE PAID 3,000.00 DOLLARS FOR THE DURATION OF THE INTERNSHIP. THE POSITION ALSO INCLUDES ROOM & BOARD AND YOUR FLIGHTS.

DR. TOLLY

When Eva finished reading the paper, she thought about what it said. She knew that being away from her family would cause her anxiety, but she could really use the money. She figured it couldn't hurt to apply. Even if she didn't get picked, she wasn't losing anything by doing it. *I don't even think they would consider me,* Eva thought. She looked at the clock and saw that she had to be in her next class in fifteen minutes. She folded the paper and stuck it in her backpack, zipped it up, slung the strap over her shoulder, and headed out of the cafeteria and to her next class.

Eva sat in her English class, hardly hearing what the teacher said, her thoughts occupying her attention. When class was over, she hurried to her car to go to work. When she threw her backpack in the passenger seat, she saw the paper that Jenny gave her poking through the open zipper. She pulled it out and stood by her car, looking at it.

"You know what, I'm going to do it."

She put it back in her backpack and then headed to the hospital.

Eva pulled into the parking lot right as the clock in her car turned three-fifty-seven, three minutes until her shift started. She grabbed her purse, ran into the building, and signed in on the computer behind the nurse's desk. It was four exactly when she hit the enter button. Eva breathed a sigh of relief; the last thing she needed was to be late for work. She wasn't sure she could handle anything else happening today. She put her purse under the counter, retrieved her scrubs, and went to the bathroom.

"Hey, Eva. You look tired, and you just got here," Tina said.

Tina was a trauma nurse who usually worked the night shift. She was a short, pudgy woman in her late forties with short hair dyed a bright red. She was one of Eva's favorite nurses to work with because she was always smiling, although she worked almost every night and saw horrible things in the ER. Working with Tina usually made the nights less stressful even if she had a bad day, probably because of her cheerful disposition and the fact that nothing ever seemed to get her down.

"Has it been a long day?"

"Yeah, you could say that," Eva said, resigned.

"I'm sorry to hear that. I'm going to get a hot chocolate. Would you like me to get you one too?"

"That would be great. Thank you so much, Tina."

After a few minutes, Tina returned with the chocolate. "Here you go, Hun," she said as she handed the cup to Eva. "Be careful. It's hot."

"I will. Thank you."

Eva sat in a chair behind the nurse's desk to drink her chocolate. Next to the computer, there was a folder with her name on it on the counter. "Are these my rooms for the night?"

"Yeah, there are only five right now. We got those patients all in the last few hours. You need to bring some water to the patient in room three, and the patient in room seven needs to be helped into a gown. You can check on the other three when you are done doing that, although I think they will be moved soon."

"All right."

After finishing the last of her chocolate, she threw her cup in the trash, picked up the folder, and headed to room three. It was an older man lying on the bed, gripping his blanket. They had monitors hooked up to him with the wires coming out from under his gown, and there was a nasal respirator on his pale face.

"How are you doing tonight? They tell me you need some water?"

"I could be better."

"I'm sorry to hear that, but they will take good care of you here. And I'll go get that water for you." She got one of the hospital cups with a lid and a bendable straw and filled it with ice water. She carried it back and sat it on his bedside table. "Here is your water. Is there anything else you need, maybe a pillow or an extra blanket?"

"No, but you can lay my bed down a little more if you don't mind."

"Of course." She pushed the recline button on the side of the bed, and the back moved down. She stopped before he was completely lying down. "Is this OK?"

"Yeah, that's better, thanks."

She helped the man in the other room into a gown, which proved to be more difficult than expected, but the rest of the night was surprisingly slow.

Tina looked at her watch. “It is pretty slow tonight, and you get off in twenty minutes. Do you want to just go home early?”

“Are you sure?”

“Yes, clock out and go home.”

“Thanks, Tina. I would love to just go to bed.”

“Good. You looked like you needed it when you first walked in.”

Eva gave her a weak laugh. “I’m sure I did.” She clocked out and grabbed her purse from under the desk. “Have a good night.”

“You too, drive safe!” Tina said.

“I will.”

Eva went back to her locker and grabbed her clothes. She would just change when she got home. It was 10:50, and she wanted nothing more than to go to bed and forget about today, but unfortunately, she had to do some homework, which included writing a brief talk that she had to give in her German class.

When she got home, she put her purse and backpack by the end of the couch and went to the kitchen. She opened the fridge to see what there was to eat; she was going to go to the store after work but was too tired, so she would have to go tomorrow. She saw that there was still part of the pizza she had with Jenny on movie night a week ago. *Well, this will have to do*, Eva thought. She pulled it out and checked to ensure it was still good. It didn’t have any mold on it, so she put it on a plate and placed it in the microwave; then went back to the fridge, got the pitcher of orange juice out, and poured herself a cup. When the microwave beeped, she took the pizza and her cup of orange juice and sat at the kitchen table. She noticed how quiet it was and wondered where everyone else was. As she started to take a bite of her pizza, the front door opened, and Carrie walked in.

Carrie looked at her sitting at the table. "Hey."

"Hey, Carrie, where is everyone else?"

Carrie was one of her roommates. Eva liked Carrie a lot, even though she was closer to Jenny. Carrie, unlike Jenny, was a serious person who worried a lot. She usually chose what needed to be done over the thing she wanted to do.

"Oh, they are all at the game."

"Oh, that's tonight. How did I forget about that? I really wanted to go. Why are you home then? Are we losing that bad?"

Carrie laughed. "No, my boyfriend is supposed to call in about fifteen minutes. This is the only time he can talk, and I haven't spoken to him in almost a week. He has been gone with his family for a while, and he was traveling around with the team."

Carrie's boyfriend had a football scholarship at the University of Tennessee, so she hardly got to see him.

"Well, I guess it is probably for the best that I forgot about the game. I have a lot of homework to do, and I need to start working on it."

"Me too," Carrie said. "But I really wanted to go to the game, so I chose the fun option, but I suspect I will suffer for it later."

"I'm afraid that is the choice I would have made if I had remembered that tonight was game night," Eva said.

"Well, I am going to go to my room and plug my phone in so it doesn't die while we are talking. Have fun with homework," Carrie jokingly said as she headed to her room.

Eva laughed. "Yes, I can't wait."

She finished eating and put her dishes in the dishwasher. She went to the couch and got her backpack to start on her homework. When she unzipped it, the flier that Jenny gave her fell out. She picked it up and looked at it. She then grabbed her backpack and purse and ran up to her room. Setting everything down on the floor except for the piece of paper, she got her computer off her desk and sat on her bed. When it booted up, she signed on and went to the website on the piece of paper. Eva just stared at the computer screen. Now that she was on the website, she started to feel unsure. Did she really want to go to England? *Just do it,* she told herself. She always overthought things, and this was something she didn't want to do because if she did, she would inevitably talk herself out of it.

She clicked on the application link on the website and began filling it out. After finishing, she paused for just a second, with the cursor hovering over the submit button, and then pushed it. When she did, a box popped up on her screen saying, *"Your application was submitted successfully. You will be notified if you are the selected candidate."*

Well, that is done, she thought. *Now, it's time for homework.* She stayed up past 1:00, studying and then writing her paper. When she looked at the clock and saw what time it was, she decided to take a shower and go to bed. She went to the bathroom, locked the door, removed her clothes, and turned on the shower knob. While she waited for the water to get hot, she stepped in front of the full-length mirror. She looked at her messy shoulder-length brown hair and the bluish rings around her hazel eyes from all the late nights spent doing homework and staring at a computer screen. She was not a big person but still stood above many of the girls in her classes with her five-foot-seven slender stature.

She slowly reached up and touched her stomach, and when she felt her hand contact the skin there, chills went up her body. She moved her hand and wondered what it would be like if a man touched her there softly. She never went all the way with Kevin. She had thought about it a few times, but it took little thinking to remember why that would have been a bad idea. She also was not ready to take that step in their relationship, which was one thing that angered Kevin. When he would kiss her, that was fine, but when he would try to touch her, it made her uncomfortable, so she would tell him to stop. That just seemed to make him want to even more. When she tried to push his hands away, he would resist, which never felt good. It never felt quite right when Kevin touched her. Eva cared about him, but something was missing. She always got a strange, tight feeling in the pit of her stomach, like something was wrong with their relationship. Eva knew she could never go all the way with Kevin, mainly because he seemed unwilling to wait until she was ready.

Eva saw the mirror was beginning to fog over. It snapped her out of her thoughts, and she stepped back from the mirror. *I'm being silly,* she thought. She got in the shower and let the warm water pour over her head as she stood with her hands on the shower wall, glad that this long day was finally over. Eva turned off the water and dressed quickly because the air was chilly, then returned to her room. She did not bother blow-drying her hair this time. She was simply too tired, so for tonight, she would go to bed with it wet. She crawled under the blankets but did not fall asleep quickly, although exhausted. She lay awake for a while thinking about the application she filled out and wondered if she would be the one to get picked. The thought of going excited her but scared her too. It would be such a huge change, and she would miss her family so much, but she really could use the money. She finally drifted off into a dreamless sleep, preparing to face another day.

Chapter Four

April 28th, 2014

When Eva's alarm went off, she jolted awake but didn't immediately get out of bed. She lay there for a second before realizing it was morning and another school day. She did not want to go to school today. She wished she could just stay in bed all day and binge-watch Netflix on her computer. She turned off her alarm and covered her head with her comforter, trying to find the motivation to get up. *OK, Eva, you have to do this*, she told herself. She threw the covers off her and stood up out of bed, trying to find the energy to move her feet. After she had changed and brushed her teeth, she went downstairs to the kitchen to eat before she had to leave. She ate a quick bowl of cereal, then got her backpack and coat and ran out the door. She got to her car and was happy that it had not snowed again during the night.

While driving to school, she thought about the application that she filled out weeks ago and wondered what it would be like to be the one selected. She had done a Skype interview last week and was told that after they were finished with all of them, they would notify the one who got the job via email. It had already been over three weeks, and she had heard nothing from them. *Well, I guess I should not be surprised. I'm not sure that I was a suitable candidate*, she thought. Eva liked science and was good at it, but it didn't always come naturally to her as it did to some people. She knew that there were more innovative, more educated people who must have applied. Students from schools like MIT were probably geniuses by nature and were far more qualified. More often than she would like, she struggled with self-confidence and belief in her ability to do things as well as others.

When she arrived on campus, she parked nearby and hurried to class. As usual, she found her economics class boring, so she played on her phone while she was there. After scrolling through Facebook and Instagram, she decided to check her email. She moved her fingers on the trackpad, finally reaching the bottom of the ones that hadn't been opened, and noticed an email from www.Cambridge.health science. She uncrossed her legs and sat up straight in her chair, staring at the email in disbelief. She hurried and opened it, not quite knowing what to expect. She impatiently waited for it to load. She was almost scared to read it, no matter what the news was.

Dear Miss Abrams,
We are pleased to inform you that we have selected you for the internship at The University of Cambridge in Cambridge, England.

You will receive another email with further information in a few days.

Sincerely, Dr. Tolly

She had to reread the email just to make sure that she had not read it wrong or that her eyes were not deceiving her. She kept staring at her phone in disbelief, unsure what to think. She had never been to England, or any other European country for that matter, and the thought of living in another country scared her a bit, but she considered herself extremely lucky to be the one they picked. She would not pass this opportunity up, not in a million years.

She saw out the corner of her eye that people around her were leaving; she raised her head and realized the class was over and had been for some time; the room was almost empty now. *When did class end, and how did I miss almost half of it?* Eva thought. *How long was I staring at my phone, and how many times did I read that email?*

She grabbed her things and left for the building that her German class was in; she wanted to talk to Sam before class started. She was hoping he was there and did not decide to play hooky today like he so frequently did. She wanted to let him know she got the intern job.

When Eva entered the classroom, she immediately started scanning the room for Sam and saw him standing towards the front of the class, talking to the teacher, so she hurried in their direction.

"Sam. Sam," Eva called from across the room as she moved towards him.

Sam turned around to see her walking quickly towards him. When she got close, she heard him saying thanks to the teacher as he turned to face her.

"Hey, Eva, what's up?"

"Can I talk to you for a minute, but over here?" she said as she pulled him by the arm to the corner of the room without waiting for him to answer. "You won't believe what happened today!"

"No, I probably won't. What happened?" Sam asked as he chuckled. "You seem excited about whatever you are going to say."

"I am," Eva said. "So, you know that flyer that was up about a month ago for an internship in England, and you said that I should apply?"

"Yeah."

"Well, I applied about a month ago. It has been almost four weeks, so I assumed I did not get selected. I was told they would notify you in an email if you were selected. When I was in my economics class today, I checked my email, and I saw I had an email from them. I opened it, and it said that they chose me for the internship. I must have been in shock or something because I don't even remember the rest of class after that, and before I knew it, the class was over."

"OMG… are you serious?" Sam asked, matching Eva's excitement. "And you are sure that you read it correctly?"

"Of course, I'm sure that I read it right." She slapped Sam on the arm.

"So, are you going to do it, go to England and everything, I mean?"

"I really want to. I just need to figure out how it will all fit in with school and both of my jobs. I think I will go, but there will be so much to do before I leave. They will send me an email with more information in a few days, probably what the next step is and what I should expect, so I don't even know when I will be leaving."

"Wow, I hope they give you enough time to get all your stuff in order."

"I do, too. I'm going to talk to my teachers tomorrow and both of my bosses. I cannot tell them exactly how long I will be gone just yet because I don't have the exact dates."

"Oh, class is starting," Sam said. "We better find some seats."

Sam and Eva hurried and found two seats together near the front.

When class was over, Eva waited in the hall near the door while Sam talked to the teacher. Once he was finished, she motioned for him to follow her to the side.

"I will let you know what I find out."

"That sounds good. I really want to know how all of this goes, and let me know what your teachers and bosses say about you going."

"I will. I'll talk to you later," she said and headed to her last class of the day. She was so excited that she wasn't sure if she could even focus on class.

After school, Eva went to the store like she did every fourth week. It was getting to where all they had left at the apartment was bread, overripe grapes, and melted butter. Each of them went to the store on their designated week; they figured it would be simpler instead of putting their names on the food they bought. On their week, each of them would spend fifty dollars on food that they would share.

As she shopped, her mind wandered to the significant changes her life was about to take. If her employers did not want to give her time off, she could always find another job when she got back. *I might just be able to make this work,* she thought. *I just need to find the right way to tell my parents so they don't freak out. No, that is asking for too much when it comes to my mom.*

Eva waited until Sunday to check her email again. She wanted to check it every day but resisted, not wanting to drive herself crazy. She figured waiting till the end of the weekend should be enough time. Sitting on top of her lavender comforter with tiny yellow flowers that matched her lavender curtains, she stared at the email icon. Finally, she opened the Gmail app and started scrolling through the unread emails. There it was, the one she had been waiting for, an email from the university. She clicked on it and impatiently waited for it to open.

Dear Miss Abrams,

Here is the information that you will need to proceed. We will fly you to Cambridge in the last week of May, as the internship is for the duration of the summer, June, July, and August. We have put you up in the Holiday Inn in Cambridge until we make the arrangements for you for an apartment. We will also cover all of your meals and transportation. You will receive your itinerary on Monday. Make sure that you bring your passport and any other appropriate documents. From all of us here at Cambridge, we wish you the best of luck and look forward to meeting you.

Dr. Tolly

May, she thought. *Well, I hope that will be enough time to tie up any loose ends.* She sat her computer down on her bed to get ready for the night. She knew that she would have to start getting things in order first thing tomorrow.

Eva got up earlier than usual the next morning so that she would have time to stop by one of her places of employment before her classes started. Eva decided to stop by the daycare where she worked first because it was closer to school. When she walked into the building, she could hear crying children. It was utter chaos. She was happy that she was not working today but felt bad for the people at work right now. She walked over to Pat, the manager of the daycare. She was usually in her office doing paperwork and making phone calls, but she was on the floor helping with the kids right now.

"Hey, Pat, looks like you have your hands full."

"This has been the craziest day I have seen in over a year. It's like all the kids are possessed or something," Pat said, flustered. Her face was red, and she had small beads of sweat on her forehead just below her hairline. Pat usually lacked color in her cheeks, but they were flushed a dark pink right now.

"Is there something I can do to help for a few minutes?" Eva asked, feeling a little guilty just standing there not doing anything, especially where she was going to take up more of Pat's time to ask her for a favor.

"Yes, there is something that you can do. Would you get Shawn and Allison a bottle? Hopefully, that will calm them down. Maybe if they are calm, they will fall asleep."

"Yes, of course, I can do that," Eva said.

She headed to the cabinet where the bottles were kept, got two down, put warm water in them, and added some formula, shaking one in each hand, then headed back to where the children were. She gave a bottle to the first crying child, then the second one. It immediately quieted them down. They sucked on their bottles, looking up at her with red, teary eyes.

"Oh my gosh, thank you, Eva, you are heaven-sent!" Pat said. Eva could hear the genuine gratitude in her voice. "I know you did not come here on your day off to help with the kids, so what can I do for you?"

"You are right," Eva said with a bit of a chuckle. "I came to discuss something that has come up. A few weeks ago, I signed up for a summer internship in England. It is a once-in-a-lifetime opportunity, and I could really use some extra cash right now to help pay for school. A few days ago, I got an email telling me I was selected for the position. I will fly to England in the last week of May to begin the internship. It is for three months, so I wondered if I could get a leave of absence for those three months. I know you are already shorthanded, but I feel that this is something I need to do."

There was a strained look on Pat's face as she focused on cleaning the toys. Eva was unsure if Pat would give her the three months off without a fight.

“I will let you have the summer months off if you work every other weekend from now until you leave and every weeknight for the next two weeks. Susan had surgery and won’t be in for two weeks. That is why we are down a person,” Pat said to Eva in a monotone voice.

Eva knew she would not get much better than that. So, she would agree to the terms.

“What days do you have school?” Pat asked.

“I have a class today at eleven and two classes tomorrow. One at eight and another at one.”

“OK, come in today at noon and work until five, and tomorrow at two until six. Is that doable?”

“I can do that. I will be here. Is it OK, though, if I bring some of my homework to do while the kids are napping? I don’t want to get behind.”

“That’s fine. Just do it close to where children are sleeping.”

“Oh, I will,” Eva told her.

She left the daycare wondering if working extra days, both weeks and the weekend, would cut too much into her study time, but it didn’t matter now because she had already agreed to it.

When Eva got home, she decided it was time to call her parents and tell them about it. She could not keep it from them forever. She was not sure how they would take the news of her going to another country for three months alone, but she had to tell them eventually. She spent a week in Egypt when she was in high school, but that was different.

Eva took her cell phone out of her purse, scrolled down to ‘Mom & Dad’ in her contacts, and hit send. It rang only twice before she heard her mom’s soft voice on the other end.

"Hello."

"Hi, mom."

"Hi, what are you doing?"

"Not a lot. What have you and Dad been up to lately?"

"Well, your father is tired of all of this snow and the icy roads. He says that if he has to buy one more bag of salt or shovel the driveway one more time, we are moving. So, we have not been getting out of the house much."

"I can understand that. I hate the snow too and wouldn't go out in it if I didn't have to," Eva said.

"Mostly these days we stay in and do a lot of reading and watching TV. I have started doing my craft stuff again, and your father still does his carpentry in the garage. Also, Fred and Marisa have invited us to come over tomorrow for dinner and to play Rage. We don't have any plans, so we told them yes. I'm excited to go. It will be a nice change from the day-to-day stuff. So, what have you been doing? I'm sure you have been very busy with work and school?"

Boy, that was a lot, but I asked, Eva thought. "Yeah, I don't have a lot of time for a social life these days."

"Hun, you should at least try to find a little time to do something you like. Have some fun, do something for yourself that you enjoy, that you want to do."

"I know, Mom, and I'm going to. Actually, I wanted to talk to you and Dad about something that has come up. I'm really excited about it, and I hope that you and dad will be happy for me, too."

Her mom was silent on the phone for a few seconds. "Oh, is everything OK?" her mom asked.

Eva's mom worried about absolutely everything, so it came as no surprise that as soon as she told her something had come up, and although she had said she was really excited about it, her mom immediately asked if everything was all right.

"Yes, mom, everything is fine. Why did you assume that something was wrong?"

"I don't know, just the way you said it, and that you said you hoped we would be happy too, like you are going to do something that we would disapprove of. My mind goes there sometimes, well, a lot, you know this."

"I do, but don't worry, Mom, nothing is wrong. What I have to tell you is exciting news."

"OK," her mom said in a curious voice. "Are you dating someone?"

"No, Mom, not that kind of exciting."

"OK, I'm all ears."

Eva laughed at her mom, the worrier. "Get Dad on the phone, and I will tell you guys about it."

"Joe, Eva is on the phone and wants to talk to us both," her mom yelled.

Eva heard a noise in the background.

"He will be right here. He was just watching the game in the living room," her mom said.

"I figured that is what he was doing."

There was a click on the other end. Then Eva heard her dad's voice.

"Hi, kiddo. Your mom says you wanted to talk to us about something."

"Yeah, I do." *Here goes nothing,* she thought. "So, at school about a month ago, on the bulletin board was a flyer about an internship in England, and it offered three thousand dollars. Jenny told me I should apply because of the money, so I did. A few days ago, I got an email saying that I was the one they chose for the internship."

"Wait, you want to go to England? For how long?" Eva's mom asked.

"Well, um… it's for three months." From her mom's silence, she could tell that she disapproved, just like she thought she would. "I'll be OK, mom. This is a great opportunity for me." It was still quiet on the other end of the phone as Eva waited for her mom or dad to respond.

"So why do you think they picked you?" her mom asked.

"I don't know. Maybe I was the best that the university could find. Obviously, none of those freakishly smart people applied."

"You are just as smart as any of them," her mom said.

"When do you leave?" her dad asked.

"The last week of May. They will pay for my plane ticket, my housing, and all of my food."

"And you have to go to England to do an internship? Couldn't you just have applied for one here in America? And won't all of this interfere with your schooling and work? Do you think it is a good idea for you to do this?" Her mom's voice was drenched with concern as she asked questions.

"Mom, I need to do this, and I would like to have some extra money to help with tuition, and it won't interfere with school because I'm only going for the summer."

"Oh honey, if you need more money for school, you could have just asked us."

"Mom, I don't want to keep getting financial help from you and Dad. I need to do as much of this on my own as I can." Eva hoped that this would be the worst of it and that her mom wouldn't become more worried and start to panic over the next couple of days.

"I know you will do what you are going to do, but I think that is a long time to be gone."

"Mom, I have already talked to both of my bosses. They are OK with it."

"I'm excited that you will get to go to England and get three thousand dollars for it, but are you sure there isn't something else you are not telling us? Are you having some emotional problem and are just afraid to tell your father and me about them?"

It finally happened. Her mom went there.

"No, it's nothing like that. I just need the money, and I would like to go to England."

Her mom sighed. "Well, I know you will go regardless of what I say, so I hope you have fun while you are over there and that you stay safe."

"I will, Mom, I promise. It will be such a good thing for me, and probably fun. I know I will never forget this trip, and whatever experiences I have will be with me for the rest of my life."

"I know," her mom said. "You know that I just worry about you."

"I will keep in touch with you; I will try to call as often as possible."

"Eva, I'm very proud that you got selected for this internship. They must have known you are a very bright young lady as I do," her dad said.

She could always count on her dad for support, even when her mom didn't offer it. He was her biggest fan and most enthusiastic cheerleader, and she loved him for it. Her mom's approach to love was very different. She showed it by worrying about her, even if that meant too much. And by not supporting her in the things she wanted to do if she thought there was the slightest chance she could get hurt, she always pointed out the flaws she saw in her choices.

"I think it sounds like a great opportunity," her dad continued.

There was a huff on the phone from her mom.

"Mom, Dad, I have to go to bed now. You can call tomorrow."

"Have a good night, Eva. You can tell us more about it when you get time," her dad said.

"Good night, mom, good night, dad."

Eva hit *End* on her phone and laid it on the bed beside her.

"Well, hopefully, the worst is over," she said aloud to herself, glad that she finally got this over with.

Chapter Five

May 23rd, 2014

Eva was trying to make everything fit into her suitcase, but she had over-packed like usual.

"Oh my God, why did I think that I needed so much stuff?" Eva said as she took the things out of her suitcase again, for the third time. "OK, I can do this. I will make it all fit into one suitcase," she said with determination.

She removed everything that she had packed, laid it all out on her bed, and sorted through it again. She still could not believe that this day was finally here. Time had gone by so fast. She was feeling nervous and excited, but mostly excited. She had gotten all her stuff in order, and the university had already sent her the e-ticket and the information for her hotel last week. Besides packing, everything was all done. Her mom and dad were even going to drive her to the airport in the morning.

"Eva," Jenny said from the doorway. "How is the packing going?"

"Not so well. This will now be the fourth time I have packed this stupid suitcase."

"You know, it would be easier if you didn't pack so much stuff," Jenny laughed.

"Really, I didn't know that," she said sarcastically. "OK, smarty-pants, why don't you come here and help me pack."

"I'm going to, and we will trim some of that down. That is a lot of stuff," she said, still laughing, peering at the many piles of folded clothes on the bed.

"I know. I have a problem and think I need way more stuff than I actually do."

Jenny came over to the bed and started sorting through the clothes. "You know that I will miss you while you are gone," she said, not looking at Eva.

Eva stopped putting clothes in a pile and looked up at her. "Of course, I know, Jenny, and I will miss you, too. I wish you could come with me. You and I would have so much fun together there. We would light up the town and go to a different country every weekend."

"That sounds amazing, but I could not live off of you while you were working." She hesitated for a moment. "I don't know, Eva. Something is off about this."

"What do you mean?"

"I just feel like if you go, something will happen; I don't know what, just something."

"Happen? If you mean me having the time of my life and coming back a more mature, independent woman, then yes, something will happen."

"No, that is not what I meant. I don't know how to explain it. It's only a feeling that I have."

"Have you talked to anyone else about this?" Eva asked, hoping she hadn't.

"No, no one. I wanted to tell you about it, though."

"So, you haven't told my parents anything?"

"No, really, I didn't, I promise. Why do you ask?"

"Because when I told my parents, my mom was worried, and she is still a little skeptical about it even now."

"Oh, I didn't know, but I promise I did not talk to them about it."

"I believe you, Jenny, I was just curious because you telling me now just seems a little strange, but my mom worries about everything, so I attribute it to that."

"I did not know that your mom was that worried. So yeah, I guess it does seem strange," Jenny said, picking up a pair of pants and moving it to one of the piles.

"Well, I'm still going to go. I don't have a bad feeling about anything, but it feels like this could somehow be life-changing in a big way."

"I trust your judgment, Eva. That's all I'm going to say on the matter."

"I understand, and I'm glad that you told me. I would have done the same thing." She wondered if she should be more worried than she was about going. She did not feel like she should not do this, but that could be her desire to go clouding her judgment.

They spent the next few hours packing Eva's suitcase and the rest of the stuff she would need.

"You should probably get some rest, Eva. You have an early flight tomorrow."

"I know, and I appreciate all of your help. Thanks for that."

"Any time, you know I will always be here for you," Jenny said and hugged Eva. "I will see you tomorrow, OK?"

"OK. Have a good night, Jenny, and thanks again for the help."

"I will get up early enough tomorrow to make sure I see you off."

"That sounds great."

Her alarm went off, and she jolted awake. She felt like she was still dreaming as she looked around the room in a fog, her heavy eyelids threatening to close. She looked at the end of her bed and saw her door opening, and then Jenny stuck her head around.

"Hey, you awake?"

"Yeah, my alarm just went off, and I was trying to decide if this was really the day I leave or if I was just dreaming it."

"Nope, today is actually the day. How do you feel?"

"Sleepy, a little nervous, but also excited and ready for this."

"That's good," Jenny said. "Well, I will let you get ready. I'll be waiting in the kitchen for you."

"OK, I'll be right down." She sat up and rubbed her eyes, then climbed out of bed and went into the bathroom to change. She looked at herself in the mirror. "Wow, I look tired; these dark circles are no joke. I look like I haven't slept at all." She changed and applied some concealer to try and hide the morning raccoon eyes. "This is as good as I'm going to look, I guess," she said, staring at her reflection in the mirror.

When she went downstairs, she saw Jenny making eggs and bacon, and there was some fresh fruit already cut and put into a bowl on the table.

"Boy, Jenny, you have outdone yourself. You did all of this for me?"

"Of course, it's the last time I will see you for a while, so I figure I need to do something nice for you. Making breakfast was the least that I could do. Besides, you cook for me all the time."

"I will be back, Jenny. It's not like I'm going to be gone forever."

"I know, but I still wanted to do this for you."

"Well, thanks."

"Oh hey, your parents are here," Jenny said, standing on her tiptoes to look out the kitchen window.

Eva's parents' black Toyota Corolla was sitting in front of the house. Eva went to the front window and peered out, then went to the door and opened it.

"Hey, mom, dad." She looked at her big brother Thomas as he got out of the car and gave him a half-smile before looking back to her parents. "Thanks for coming."

"Of course, we came," her mom said.

"How are you doing this morning?" her dad asked as he gave her a big hug.

"I'm great, Dad. I am so excited about this."

"I bet you are, and I am excited for you. On the other hand, your mother is still worried about you going, but I say good for you. If they gave me the opportunity they have given you, I would go too."

Her mom hit him softly on the shoulder. "Thanks for being supportive."

"I am, just not in the way you want. Eva is a grown woman. She can take care of herself."

"Thanks, Dad. I'm glad you are on my side."

"I do what I can," he said with a wry smile as he looked at her mother.

Still standing near the car was Thomas, who she was very close to. It had always just been the two of them growing up. He was always there for her, helping her through life's challenges and supporting her achievements. She tried to be there for him through his big moments, too, even when she was a child.

"Aren't you going to give me a hug, or do I have to chase you down for one?" Eva said to him, a challenge in her voice.

He smiled big and came up the stairs with his arms stretched. "Come here, silly. What are you getting yourself into this time? Am I going to have to bail you out like I did when you were seven and broke mom's glass rose?"

"No," she said, ruffling his brown hair.

"OK, so let's get on the road," her dad said. "We have a plane to catch."

"Wait, she has to eat first. I made her a nice breakfast," Jenny called from the kitchen.

"Oh, well, we can't let her miss the most important meal of the day," her dad said.

Eva loved her dad; he had a funny sense of humor and was one of the most caring people she had ever met. He did not let most things get to him or stress over much. However, life's unavoidable stresses showed on his face and in his gray hair which started changing in his mid-forties. He was now in his fifties and was still in pretty good shape, though he had put on a bit of weight in the midsection, and like so many men of his age, he had a receding hairline. Eva loved her mom just as much as her dad, but she had more in common with him, and her mom stressing all the time stressed her out. Her mom cared for her children so much that she loved them to a fault, but it made things difficult between them.

Eva hurried and ate her breakfast so that her parents didn't have to wait long.

"Oh, Eva, I'm going to miss you," Jenny said again as she held Eva in a tight embrace. "Who will help me do my laundry or let me keep them up late talking about all of my boy troubles."

"I'm only going to be gone three months, Jenny, and you know I can call you when I'm not busy, and we can also email."

Eva pulled away from the embrace. Jenny's eyes were watery. She was trying so hard not to go into full-blown crying. Eva got into the back of her parents' car with Thomas as her dad put the bags in the trunk. She looked through the car window at Jenny standing on the steps with her arms wrapped around her chest to protect herself from the cold. Her dad got in the front seat, and she waved at Jenny as the car pulled away from the curb. Jenny had such a sad look on her face, and Eva felt genuinely sorry for her. Even though she was coming back in three months, she knew it was still hard for Jenny.

Eva sat quietly in the back seat with her brother as her dad drove. She watched out the window as the other cars passed by on the interstate, and soon she could see downtown Salt Lake City. The snow-capped mountains off in the distance provided a perfect backdrop for the city. She had the feeling that she would not be seeing this again for a long time.

"Are you OK?" Thomas asked, concern evident in his voice.

"Yeah, it's just strange leaving everyone for so long and home."

"I still can't believe you are doing this! Little Eva, who was so afraid the people in the pictures would come out at night and get her while she slept that she had to crawl in bed with her big brother, is now going to live on her own in England. You know, they have a lot of paintings in England?"

"You realize I am not seven anymore, right?" she said, annoyed.

"I do. Just sometimes, when I look at you, I still see that version of you, the tender-hearted little girl who tried to save the skunk Dad ran over and who had a burial for the dead butterfly in the backyard."

Eva smiled. "I had almost forgotten about that. That was a lifetime ago, and we have all changed, Thomas."

"I know." He looked at her for a long moment before turning back to the window.

They pulled into the drop-off lane in front of the Delta terminal.

"OK, kiddo, are you ready?" her dad asked.

"I think so. I'm actually excited! It will be nice to finally get to see Europe and have some extra money to help with school. I'm going to spend all the free time that I have and explore as much as I can, and maybe I will even try to learn to speak with a British accent."

Her dad chuckled. "I would like to hear that."

"Don't worry, if I learn to do it, I will talk with my English accent on the phone when we speak."

"Well, I just want you to let me know how you are and if everything is OK, regardless of what accent you talk in," her mom added.

"I look forward to hearing it. Well, we better take your stuff out and get going before people start to get upset with us," her dad said as he opened his door to get out of the car.

Eva and her mom followed her dad and brother to the back of the Corolla to help her with her luggage. They sat the bags on the curb next to the car. Her mom turned to her, a look of defeat on her face.

"I'm going to be OK, Mom. Take a deep breath. I will call you as soon as I get to my hotel."

"I know, but as your mother, you know I still worry, and I always will."

"Well, I think you will be more cultured when you return home than when you left. Most Americans could use a little culture," her dad said in his usual calm, humorous voice.

"Very true, Dad." Eva looked at her watch. "I really should get going,"

Her dad looked at his watch, too. "Yes, you do, and we need to go before we get ticketed."

Eva hugged her dad.

"You will be just fine. I have faith in you. I know you are a smart girl and will make good decisions. Just listen to your gut," her dad said in her ear as he hugged her.

Eva looked up at him when he let go of her. She was not sure why her dad said that, but he never said anything he did not mean.

He must have had a good reason. For a brief moment, she and her dad locked eyes. They spoke a message that could not have been appropriately conveyed in words.

"What?" her mom asked.

"Nothing," her dad said. "Hurry and hug her. She has a flight to catch, and we have to get going."

Her mom leaned in and embraced her, but she held on longer than her dad had. When she let go of Eva, she had a sullen look. "OK. Well, call as soon as you get there."

"I will, mom."

She turned to her brother last. He was staring at her with his hands in his pockets, the breeze gently blowing his hair. The look he gave her was that of solidarity. She came and put her arms around him, and he did the same.

"I'm going to miss you." Her voice was slightly muffled as her face pressed into his chest.

"I will miss you, too. But hey, we will see each other in three months, right?"

"Of course we will." She smiled up at him. She loved his boyish face that always reminded her of when they were children.

"Better go now," he said, playfully pushing her towards the airport doors.

"If I fall, I'm coming after you." She returned in the same playful manner.

He smiled at her. Then she put her backpack on and reached for the handle of her suitcase. She smiled at her parents and brother, then started towards the doors. They waved at her as she walked away, and she waved back without stopping. She went through the sliding doors of the Delta International terminal. She looked at the line of people waiting to check in and felt a little panicked. Her heart was racing, and her palms were sweaty. She took a deep breath and released it slowly. It calmed her some, so she went to wait in line, getting in the one that looked to be the shortest, and then got out her passport and boarding pass. While waiting, she began making a mental list of what she wanted to see in her three months there. *I have to make time to sit in on a parliament session*, she thought. *I also need to eat some excellent fish and chips, drink at an authentic pub, and call from one of the red phone booths.* Eva had a smile on her face at all the cool things she would get to do while she was there. The line continued to move, and now she was next. She only had to wait a few minutes for the person in front of her to finish.

"Do you have your passport and flight reservation?" the man at the counter asked.

"I do." Eva handed the man her e-ticket paper and her passport and watched as he tapped on his keypad.

He typed for a while without looking up at her and spoke as he stared at the screen. "Do you have a seat preference?"

Eva did not even have to think about it. "I would like a window seat if you have any."

"I have a window seat towards the back of the plane, row 38D." He finally looked up at her, waiting for a response.

"Yes, that's fine."

He looked down at the monitor again and typed on the keyboard. Then she could hear her tickets printing. He put the boarding pass in her passport and handed it back to her.

"Down the hall to the left is security."

"Thank you," Eva said.

She grabbed ahold of her suitcase and got in one of the security lines. To her surprise, they were moving faster than the check-in lines. After Eva got through security, she went to find some food before she had to board. She had an hour and knew it would be enough time to eat.

She found a McDonald's in the food court and got herself a burger. She sat at the edge of the McDonald's lounge and watched the masses of people walking by. They all seemed so focused, busy, and in a hurry. These people had somewhere to go, a meeting early in the morning, family to visit, or perhaps a vacation to enjoy. They ranged from people in suits to people wearing flip-flops. She loved the atmosphere of airports; they were always so energetic.

She finished her food and began the walk down the long corridor towards her gate. She saw the *A-11* sign on the right at the end. She looked at her ticket to check that she had the right gate. 'A-11' was written on the glossy pass. Eva let out a sigh of relief; she saw it was already pretty full and wondered if she could find an empty seat. She might have to sit on the floor. She looked around and found a seat by the window at the far end. She rolled her suitcase over, took off her backpack, and sat it on the floor next to her chair. She sat down and looked around at all the people waiting to board. She wondered how many of them were English.

She heard them announce they were going to board first class and business. She looked at her ticket and saw that she was in zone three. *I guess that is because I am at the back of the plane.* When they finally got to zone three, she stood up and got in line.

She quickly made it to the booth and handed the woman standing behind it her ticket and passport. The woman opened up her passport and checked it with the ticket. When she was satisfied that it was her, she scanned her ticket and then returned her passport and boarding pass. Eva took it and headed down the corridor, still trying to comprehend that this was happening. She tried to find her seat as quickly as she could. Once there, Eva dropped her backpack onto it and looked up at the overhead compartments, wishing she had not brought so much stuff. She tried to leave as much as possible, but her carry-on bag still weighed considerably more than she thought. She reached down and grabbed it by the top and side handle, took a deep breath, and huffed, lifting it in the air. She got it part of the way up, but her arms gave out as she raised it over her head. "No," Eva said in a high-pitched voice as she flinched in anticipation of it hitting her in the head. Suddenly, it did not feel so heavy. She looked over to her left and saw the reason for it feeling lighter. A man was standing next to her, helping her hold it up.

"Are you all right? It looked like you were about to drop that," he said in a smooth English accent— similar to the ones she always heard in the movies.

"Oh my gosh, thank you so much! I'm sure that I would have dropped it on my head if you hadn't grabbed it when you did." She blushed a little as he stared down at her, feeling embarrassed that she had almost dropped the suitcase on her head and the fact that a nice-looking Englishman had helped her.

"Here, let me take it," he said. He put his other hand on it, lifted it into the overhead bin, and closed the door.

"Thank you again," Eva said to him.

"It's no problem," he said as he sat back down in his seat.

Eva picked up her backpack and sat down quickly in her seat because she was holding up the line. She pushed her bag under the seat in front of her and buckled up, taking a long breath. *Wow, I'm off to a great start,* she thought.

As they flew away from the sun, the sky turned a grayish-orange color, and she knew they would serve dinner in a few hours. She was not feeling tired, so she decided on an in-flight movie instead of looking out the window. She didn't want to overthink about tomorrow. It would only cause her more anxiety than she was already feeling. She scrolled through the menu on her little TV to see if any of the movies looked interesting. She had the choice between Paranormal Activity: The Marked Ones, The Legend of Hercules, Lone Survivor, Jack Ryan: Shadow Recruit, Vampire Academy, About Last Night, three Days to Kill, three: Rise of an Empire, Cesar Chavez, and Captain America Winter Soldier. What was up with all the guy movies? She decided on Vampire Academy; it wasn't as much of a guy movie as the others.

By the end of the movie, she felt tired and was ready to sleep. She got her neck pillow and eye mask out of her backpack and then slid it back under the seat in front of her. The older woman sitting in the aisle seat next to her looked at her and smiled before getting a book to read. She obviously was not planning on sleeping any time soon.

After the dinner trays were collected and the lights were dimmed, she covered herself up with the airline-issued blanket, put her eye mask on, placed her pillow around her neck, and was now ready to sleep. She thought about what the next three months of her life would be like as she tried to drift off, but it had the opposite effect. After moving in her chair for over an hour, she realized she would not fall asleep, so she decided to pass the time with another movie. This time, she would watch the manliest movie out of all of them, but it was hard to determine which one that was because they all screamed testosterone-fueled. She finally settled on Lone Survivor. She sat low in her seat with the blanket still over her, trying to get as comfortable as possible in the hard plane seat.

Eva jolted awake when the captain's voice came on the overhead speakers to tell them they were descending into London. It took a few seconds for her to register what he said in her groggy state. She had been in a deep sleep, drooling on herself, and she did not know where she was when she woke up.

"Is it morning already?" She pulled the eye mask off her forehead and blinked, looking around, trying to rationalize what was happening. After a few seconds, she looked at the TV screen and saw that it was displaying the main menu. "No, I actually liked that movie. Now I don't know how it ends." She had made it through most of the movie but must have fallen asleep near the end.

She could smell coffee and food, and when she looked around, she could see the sun shining through the windows. They were already serving breakfast towards the front of the plane, and the cart was coming down the aisle in her direction. Her legs were feeling cramped, and she needed to stand for a minute, so she asked the woman sitting in the aisle seat next to her if she would let her up. The woman stood in the aisle, waited for Eva to get out, and then sat back down. When Eva stepped into the aisle, her whole body felt stiff from sitting in the seat for so long, and it wasn't just her legs.

After using the bathroom, she stood in the small gallery between the aisles. There were a few other people standing there, too. Some were talking, but one woman was doing some stretches. Eva thought that was a pretty good idea, so she started doing a few. She wanted to loosen her tight muscles.

After a few minutes of stretching, she hurried back to her seat so that she did not miss out on breakfast. When the beverages and food finally reached her, she got a coffee to help her stay awake and a breakfast platter with eggs, a biscuit, a bowl of fruit, and some sausage.

She pushed up the shade in her window and saw a sea of gray clouds shielding the ground below. Once in a while, there would be a break in the clouds, and she could see the English countryside beneath them. There were fields and small towns below. It almost looked like it could be anywhere in the Midwest. Shortly, they would land, and she would officially be in England. She wondered what her internship would be like. Would she like it? Would she hate being there and want to go home? She doubted that would be the case, but she couldn't help but wonder.

The plane started its final descent into Heathrow Airport, and Eva was as emotionally ready as possible. She put her palms on the end of the armrest and her head against the headrest and closed her eyes; she tried to control her breathing and stay calm as the plane descended. She could feel the fear and anxiety coming to the surface. When the plane finally touched down and they turned off the *fasten seat belt* sign, she stood up and waited for her turn to get her luggage from the overhead compartment. When the line of people already standing in the aisle started to move, she put her backpack on and stepped into the aisle. She reached up to get her luggage when she heard a man's voice.

"I can get that for you."

She looked over to see the same man that helped her when she got on was now standing, ready to help her with her luggage again. "Oh, thank you," she told him as he got her bag down with ease and sat it on the floor in front of her.

"You are welcome. I didn't want you dropping it on your head trying to get it down. You made it this far unscathed; it would be a shame if you hurt yourself now that you are here."

She smiled at him again, her cheeks flushing. "I appreciate that."

She reached for her suitcase, pulled the handle up, and rolled it down the aisle in front of him. She stepped off the plane onto the jetway and immediately felt a chill in the air. At the end of the jet-way, she could feel the warmth coming from inside the airport. She rolled her suitcase over to a wall and looked around for the sign that pointed toward customs. Just over the main walkway was a sign that said *'Customs and passport control'* and an arrow pointing to the right.

Before Eva headed in the direction of customs, she looked around to take it all in. "Oh my God, I'm really in England. I'm here." She smiled. Even the nervousness that she felt could not drown her excitement. She was a little worried that she might not find the person who was there to pick her up. *Stop this, Eva; now you are being like your mother.*

After waiting in a long line, she made it to the window at the customs booth. Sitting in a chair was a tall, thin woman with brown hair pulled into a tight ponytail.

"Passport, please?" the woman behind the glass asked her without smiling.

Eva handed the woman her passport, and she opened it.

"What reason are you visiting England?"

"I'm here for an internship."

"And how long is the internship for?"

"It's for three months."

"I'm guessing you know you need a work permit to work here in England?"

"I am, yes, and I have one."

"I'll need to see that too."

Eva took her work permit out of her purse and handed it to the woman. She held it up beside the passport, then stamped the passport and handed it all back to Eva without so much as a smile or another word.

"Thank you." Eva took her papers back and grabbed the handle of her suitcase. *Wow, I hope they are not all like that,* Eva thought.

She headed in the direction of the luggage claim, where the person told her they would meet her and hoped that she would find them there. She had been in contact with them via email. It was there that they informed her they would wait by the luggage claim with a sign that had her name on it. As she neared the end of the last corridor, she could see the luggage conveyors. People were already getting their bags off of it. The luggage had come up quicker than she would have expected. Near the luggage claim were people holding signs with names on them. In the email, they told her that they would be of medium height, slim, with brown hair, and would be wearing a suit and black-rimmed glasses. She looked at all the people standing with signs. As she scanned down the line, she saw a man that matched the description she was given. She looked at the sign he was holding, and it read, *'Miss Abrams.'*

She walked over to the man. "Are you Jon?"

He looked at her and smiled. "Yes, I'm Jon. Are you Miss Abrams?"

"Yes, I am."

"It's nice to meet you." He held out his hand for her to shake.

She took his hand and gave it a quick but firm shake. "It's nice to meet you too, Jon."

Eva turned to look at the conveyor, searching for her other suitcase. When she saw her brown bag with the red strap come around, she pulled it off.

"Can I get that for you?" he asked, nodding to the bag.

"Sure."

He took the handle from her. "Follow me." He pulled her larger suitcase to the doors and then outside. He pointed to the parking garage. "My car is over here on the third level. You can wait here, and I will pick you up after I get the car?"

"That's OK. I don't mind walking."

He nodded his head. "So, how was your flight? Hopefully, everything went well."

"It was fine. A long time to be on a plane, though. I slept for most of it, and the food was actually not half bad. I didn't expect that."

"That's good. I'm glad that your trip went well. What do you think of England so far?"

“It seems all right, but the people at the airport I talked to have not been friendly.”

“Oh, well, the people at the airport don’t count. They are never very nice.”

She chuckled. “I will take your word on that. After all, you have been here a lot longer than me.”

“I’m serious, though; the people are very nice here. You will like them.”

“I believe they are. I think maybe people that work at airports are stressed all the time.”

“You are probably right.” Jon stopped next to a small blue Ford Escort. “This is my car.”

“I didn’t know that they drove Fords here.”

“Yes, they drive a lot of different kinds of cars here, kind of like they do in the States. Fords are actually really popular here.” He opened the hatch, put the suitcase he was pulling in the back, then took the one from her and put it in. “Do you want to put your backpack in here too, or keep it in the front with you?”

“I’ll put it in the front with me.”

He nodded, then shut the hatch and walked around to the right side of the car. Eva looked at him strangely for a second before she remembered they sat on the right side in England. She went to the left side of the car and got in, then put her backpack on the floor in between her feet.

“So, how long does it take to get to Cambridge?”

“It’s a little over an hour. I will take you straight to your hotel right now, and we will begin the briefing in the morning. I will be at your hotel around eight to pick you up. I hope that is not too early for you?”

“No, eight is fine. I will make sure that I am up and ready when you get there.”

They pulled out of the parking garage and headed towards the freeway. She noticed London looked different from American cities in a lot of ways. She liked it, although seeing the differences reminded her she was no longer in America and would now be away from home longer than she had ever been.

As they got out of the city and into the country, the grayness of the buildings gave way to green fields and budding trees—some of the first signs in May that spring was on its way. It was so green compared to Mays in Utah that it looked like it could be late June or even early July, yet still greener than Utah ever was.

“Is it always this green here?”

“Yes, the temperature is relatively moderate here, and it usually rains in the winter instead of snowing, which makes it green pretty much all year round.”

“That is crazy, I did not know that, but all of Europe is not like that, right?”

“No, not all of Europe is like this.”

Eva was quiet as she looked out the windows. Jon glanced in her direction. He knew she was admiring the scenery. For now, he would say nothing and let her enjoy it. Tomorrow was going to be stressful and confusing for her. He would let her have this moment to enjoy England, this England.

Eva was smitten with the city of Cambridge as they drove through it. It seemed different from what London did; it was not so industrialized, modernized, or commercialized. The city still retained its original authentic feeling because of the lack of destruction. It had not sustained the same level of damage that London did during the Second World War. Most of the buildings were the original ones, so there wasn't the mix of old and new that she had seen in London.

Jon pulled into a Holiday Inn parking lot and stopped at the front doors. It was an odd-looking Holiday Inn. To her, it looked like it should be in the country, not in a city. Wood paneling covered the outside, something one would have seen in the seventies or perhaps on a hotel in the mountains. She wondered if the inside matched the outside.

"Well, this is it," Jon said.

She gave him a half-smile before she reached for the door handle. Jon got out and went around to the back, opened the hatch, pulled her suitcases out, and sat them on the ground.

"I will go in with you while you check in to make sure that everything goes OK."

"I would appreciate that."

She put her backpack on, took the handle of her smaller suitcase, and walked into the hotel's lobby. To the left of the doors was the front desk, and to the right were various-sized tables, all of which had brown and white chairs around them. At the far end of the room was a fireplace with a mirror above it and a flower vase with fake flowers on the mantel.

"Can I help you?" the woman at the front desk asked with a friendly smile.

"Yes, I have a reservation."

"All right, what is your name?"

"Eva Abrams."

The woman typed on her keyboard for a second. "Eva Abrams, OK, and you will stay with us for seven nights, I see?" She looked up at Eva from her computer.

Eva looked at Jon to make sure that was correct. She knew they would get her an apartment soon, but she didn't know how long she would stay at the hotel. Jon nodded his head.

"Yes, I guess I will be here for seven nights."

"OK, I just need to see some ID?"

"It is all paid for, correct?" Eva asked.

"Yes, the bill has already been taken care of. Cambridge University has paid for it in advance," Jon said before the woman at the counter answered.

That's good, she thought. Eva got her passport out, handed it to the woman, and watched as she typed again on her computer.

"Do you have a room preference?" she asked.

"Oh, can I have a room on the top floor and non-smoking?"

"Let me see if we have one available." She typed on her keyboard. "Yes, I have two non-smoking rooms left on the top floor."

"Good," Eva said.

The woman booked the room and handed her a piece of paper to sign. Eva signed it and handed it back to the woman.

"OK, here is your room key." She laid it on the counter in front of Eva. "You are in room four-thirty, and your Wi-Fi password and breakfast time are on the back of the card envelope." She pointed to the hand-written information on the back. "When you get out of the lift, turn to the left, and it will be halfway down on your right."

"Thank you," Eva said as she took her room key.

She took the handle of her suitcase and walked beside Jon to the elevator. He got in with her, then followed her to the room after they stepped into the hall on the fourth floor.

"I will leave you here. If you should need anything, call me." He handed her a piece of paper. "This is my cell number. Anything at all, don't hesitate."

"Thank you, but I'm sure that I will be OK tonight. So, you will be here at eight in the morning to pick me up?"

"Yes, I will be here around eight, give or take a few minutes. You can just wait for me in the lobby. I will see you in the morning. Have a good night."

"You too."

She watched him walk back to the elevator, and then he disappeared inside.

"Well, hopefully, tomorrow will be exciting, and these nervous feelings and butterflies will have gone."

She put her keycard in the slot and pulled it out, and a green light lit up as the door made a beeping sound. She turned the handle, pushed the door open, and pulled her suitcases in, letting the door close behind her. She knew she needed to get a good night's sleep, so she decided to go to bed and not watch TV or play around on the internet.

As Jon drove home, he called Dr. Yug.

"Hello."

"Hi, Dr. Yug."

"So, how did it go?"

"It went well. She seems to be nice with a good head on her shoulders. I think she will do just fine. Have you figured out how we will tell her?" Jon asked.

"Yes, we have been discussing that today. We are all in agreement that you should be the one to do it. You have been the one communicating with her and the only one who has met her so far. We believe she will take it better coming from you."

"I agree with that, but I'm not sure what the best way to break it to her is," Jon said.

"I guess the best way is probably to start by informing her that what you are going to tell her is confidential and that she has to sign a non-disclosure agreement before you give her any information. I would tell her it is a different kind of internship than we led her to believe. Make sure that she knows it had to be done this way, and she will understand once she knows what it is. After she signs the paper, the best thing would be to tell her the truth. I will not be surprised if she needs time for it all to sink in. I would if I were in her shoes."

Jon listened as he drove, pondering what Dr. Yug said. "I agree. She will most likely freak out or think that we are crazy. Maybe it would be wise to show her the video of the puppy after I tell her about the time machine."

"I think that is a good idea," Dr. Yug agreed.

"We should show her the portal soon after the video so she realizes what we are telling her is true and has at least some idea of what she will be getting herself into," Jon said.

"I understand what you are saying, but if she knows about all of this and has seen the portal, she no longer has a choice; we cannot let her decide she does not want to do it and walk away after with that kind of information," Dr. Yug informed.

"I know," Jon said. "If it comes to that, we need to decide what our next move will be."

"Let's tell her tomorrow and see what happens and then decide how to proceed," Dr. Yug said.

Chapter Six

Eva opened her eyes when she heard the alarm going off. She reached over the nightstand, pushed the alarm button, then rolled back onto her back. She needed to get up but was so tired. It was hard enough for her to get up in the mornings without the jet lag. She wasn't a morning person.

"OK," she groaned. "Time to get moving."

She threw the blanket off and sat on the edge of the bed, staring at the window. The curtains were still closed, but she could tell it was dark outside because there was no light coming in around them. She got off the bed, grabbed some clothes from her suitcase and her toiletry bag, then went to the bathroom.

After changing and making herself presentable, she went down to the lobby and found the breakfast room. She figured she would try to eat a little something before Jon got there to pick her up. She walked around the food bar to see what looked good to her. She finally decided on a fruit bowl with some eggs and ham, monitoring the clock as she ate, ensuring she had enough time to finish before Jon arrived.

When Eva was done eating, she left the breakfast room and went to the lobby to wait. She sat in a chair facing the door so that Jon could see her easily when he entered the building and so that she could keep an eye out for him as well.

She had only been sitting for roughly ten minutes when she saw Jon walk through the double doors to the lobby. Standing up, she called his name so that he would know she was there. Jon nodded and headed in her direction. He had a strange look on his face, but she could not place it. He stopped a few feet in front of her.

"Good morning. How did you sleep?"

"I slept well. How about you?"

"Fine, thanks! Shall we go?" he said, a little short.

"Yes."

Eva slung her backpack over her shoulder and followed Jon out of the building to his car. He opened the door for her this time, then went around to the other side after she was in.

"So, can you tell me a little of what to expect today?" she asked, looking over at Jon. He was staring ahead as he drove, deep in thought. It took him a few seconds to process what she had asked.

"Oh… Well, we will start with some paperwork and a briefing of what you will be doing."

"OK, that sounds easy." She was wondering why Jon seemed so distracted today. He was acting differently than he had yesterday. Did something go wrong, or maybe something had changed about her job? Whatever the reason it was making her nervous.

Jon had put a lot of thought into how he would tell Eva, and he knew that telling her in the lab in front of strange people that she had never met might make the situation worse. He thought that the best way would be somewhere other than the lab. Plus, it made it where she did not see more than she needed to right now; before they knew if she would accept the things he told her, maybe they could allow her to walk away with just that information, maybe.

They did not drive far before Jon stopped the car and parallel-parked in a tight spot that Eva would never dream of trying to make the car fit into.

"Why are we stopping here? I thought we were going to the University?"

"We are, but I thought first we would walk around town. I figured you would like to see it before we start the boring things. Paperwork, the physical, the not-as-fun stuff."

"Thank you. Yes, I would like to see the city before getting into all of that. I'm sure you know where all the places worth seeing are."

"I do. Did you bring some gloves and a hat?" Jon asked.

"No, because I didn't know I would need them."

"I think I might have a hat in the glove box."

Jon leaned over her and opened it, taking Eva a little by surprise because of their close proximity. She sat still and watched Jon shuffle through the stuff in the glove box, trying to find a hat.

"Here it is." He pulled out a black beanie and handed it to her. "This should help keep you warm. Sorry, I don't have an extra pair of gloves."

"It's OK. Thank you for the hat. Won't your ears get cold?"

"No, I'm tough," Jon said with a slight chuckle.

The remark brought a small smile to Eva's face and made her feel a little less nervous.

Before they got out of the car, Jon grabbed a yellow catalog envelope from the back seat. When they got out, he put it under his arm. She looked at him curiously, wondering why it was so important that he felt the need to take it on the walk with them.

She put the hat on and followed Jon as he started down the street. She could feel the chill in the air, and there was a slight breeze, which made it feel even colder, causing her eyes to water and nose to run. She put her hands in the pockets of her coat to keep them warm.

"So, where are we going exactly?" she asked.

"Nowhere in particular, but the University is only about half a mile up the road."

"So close. Are we going to walk there, then?"

"No, we will drive when we are ready to go. There is a canal with a path that follows the campus. I thought we could stroll along there."

The walk seemed a precursor to something, but she didn't know what.

"How long have you been in Cambridge?"

"Not too long. I have only lived here a little over a year. Before I came here to work at Cambridge, I lived in New York and worked at NYU, but Cambridge offered me funding for my program. So, here I am." Jon took a deep breath and let it out deliberately loud.

She looked at him, and he still had that concentrated expression etched on his face. "Are you OK? You have seemed distracted all morning and a little out of sorts."

He hesitated for a second before speaking. "Eva, the reason for the walk is not just so you can see the city. We need to discuss something before we can proceed with your internship. And before we can discuss that, there is a paper that you have to sign."

Eva was concerned now. She had no idea what Jon was talking about and why he was acting so strange. "OK. What is it you need me to sign?"

"It's a non-disclosure form saying that you won't talk about any information that we discuss here today or henceforth or anything that we do or that you see."

She now gave Jon a confused look. What on earth could it be that they were going to talk about, and just what was it that they were going to be doing? Were they going to experiment on people, or something possibly even stranger? She could only imagine.

"I'm not sure that I want to sign anything, especially when I don't know what I'm agreeing to."

"The only thing you will agree to is that you won't discuss what we talk about today with anyone. And that you will discuss nothing that might happen beyond this conversation."

"This is sounding a little shady," she said, disliking the situation more and more.

"No, just sensitive," Jon said. "If you sign, I can tell you what you will be doing."

"You already have. I applied for an internship at the health science department, and there was the complete list of job duties you sent me via email, remember?"

"I remember, but what I said is not exactly what you will be doing. We did that as a front for the selection process. We needed people to fill out the applications to screen them as potential candidates. Then, get the person here for the next step, which is where you are now. This is the next step."

She stared at him, not knowing what to say or think. This was not what she expected. Everything she thought she knew about why she came to England was a lie. She was now unsure how to proceed. Did she sign and find out why she was really here and what this secret was that he would tell her only then, or did she walk away and go home back to her everyday life and pretend that none of this happened?

"Will you sign it?" Jon asked.

For a minute, she didn't even realize they had stopped walking. She could barely see their breaths as they stood looking at each other, Jon waiting for her response.

"So, if I sign and don't like what I hear, I don't have to go any further. I can walk away and return home with no resistance or pressure from you?"

"Yes, that is correct. You don't have to agree to it; you just can never talk about it to anyone, ever!"

Eva looked down at the sidewalk. "OK, I will sign. Out of sheer curiosity, I want to see what I will be agreeing to or walking away from instead of leaving without ever knowing." She felt like she had come too far now to go back and not even know the real reason why she was actually here.

Jon took the envelope from under his arm and pulled out a piece of paper with a pen clipped to it. "You can read it if you want to, but I told you what it says."

"I will just skim over it. Let me see it."

Jon handed the paper to her, and she stared at it, looking at all the words, yet she was not actually seeing them. Eva had a strange feeling in her stomach, not quite like butterflies but something unsettling, a twisting feeling, that if she signed these papers and heard what he had to say, she would give up the life she once knew for an uncertain one. She had to decide, and that decision boiled down to how badly she wanted to know the secrets hidden behind those lips.

Putting the paper against the building wall nearest her, she signed on the line, then handed the paper and pen back to Jon without saying a word. He looked at it. Satisfied with her signature, he put it back in the envelope.

"So, tell me, what is this thing you want me to do that is so secretive that I cannot tell a living soul?"

"Walk with me, and I will explain everything," he said, sounding a little uncertain himself, uncertain of what she didn't know. "I'm not even sure how to start. I need to say it in a way that you will understand and believe what I'm telling you," he said with a slight tremble in his voice.

"Believe you; why would I not believe you?"

"You will understand why I say that when you hear what it is."

"All right, you explain, and I will listen."

"Very well." He took a deep breath. "I will start from the beginning so it will be easier for you to grasp. About four years ago, I had this idea. Have you ever wondered what it would be like to see the great pyramids being built, to see what the Dark Ages were really like, or possibly see Emperor Augustus rise to power at the height of the Roman Empire?"

She started to answer, but before she could speak, he continued.

"Well, I have found a way, but the University I worked for in New York did not have faith in my idea or the belief that it was possible, so I started presenting my idea to other universities. After I submitted it to at least half a dozen or so universities, it caught the attention of Cambridge. They took a long, serious look at it, turned it over and then over again, and finally decided it was worth investing in, so they offered me funding to move forward with it, and now it has become a reality."

"You are saying you have found a way to travel in time?"

"Yes, but let me finish telling you before you ask any more questions. It will make more sense that way. Then, when I am done, you can ask all the questions you like."

"OK," she said, unsure what to think about what she had just heard and worried about how she fit into all of it. She had an idea but couldn't bring herself to accept it.

Jon continued. "I have worked on this for three years now. We finally sent something back to another time not long ago. We put a camera on a puppy and sent it back."

"What happened to the puppy? Did you get it back?"

"No, but not because we couldn't. We would have brought him back the same way we sent him, except that someone found him, and it would have been too risky to try. We decided it wasn't worth the risk of being seen just to retrieve a dog. But he was OK, happy, and healthy. I will show you the video so you can see for yourself."

"Aren't you afraid that they will see the camera that you put on the puppy?"

"It's not a real concern for us. Being seen is the bigger risk. The people of that time would not even know what it was."

"And how do I fit into all of this? Am I the puppy?" She could feel the cool breeze blowing across her face as she looked into Jon's honey-brown eyes.

He quickly broke eye contact and looked down at his feet. "This was the part that I was dreading telling you. You are not the puppy; the process will be different with you. We will be more cautious when sending you through, and there, of course, is a plan set in place before you ever set foot through it. The puppy was just a test to see if it would work, to see if we could safely send something alive through and have it survive."

"Oh, well, you are making me feel so much better about this. You sent one puppy through to see if it would survive, and now I will be the second thing you send through? I'm sorry, but I don't think so!"

"We will not just send you through. If you want, I will go with you. I can go through it first, and they can monitor me, and when we send you through, you will know that it is safe. There will be no reason for concern. You will be in the appropriate clothing, have the proper documentation, all of it."

He looked back up at Eva with anxious anticipation on his face. She was staring at him with a fixed gaze.

"Eva!" Jon took her arm just as she caught herself on the brick wall with her outreached hand. "Eva…."

"This can't be real!" She started laughing. "You just wanted to see how I would react. Very good, you almost had me there," she said as she waved her index finger in his face. She pushed away from the wall and pulled his hand off her arm. She put her left hand on her hip and her right hand on her forehead, trying to make sense of all of it.

"Eva, listen to me. Everything I told you is real; it's all the truth. You are not here for an internship; you are here to time travel. Eva, look at me."

She looked up at him. "You are crazy. No one can time travel, I don't know what you are playing at, but I don't want any part of it." She started walking back towards the car.

Jon took off after her and grabbed ahold of her arm. "Eva, wait."

"Let go of me!" she snapped.

He let go of her arm and held up both hands, letting her know he would not touch her again. "Can I show you something? I know you think I'm crazy right now, but maybe you won't if you see it. Besides, why would we pay to fly you to England and put you up in a hotel only to prank you?"

"Then perhaps you have some other agenda because time travel isn't real. It's something you watch in movies or read in books."

"I will show you all the equipment and explain how it works. We can even send something back in time for you. Maybe a puppy again, or perhaps a cat, whatever you want."

She was now more confused than ever; she didn't know if he had told her the truth or not. He seemed to believe what he said and didn't appear to be joking. But how could any of this be true? How was it possible to do the things that he said? She wanted to tell him no, that she was going to go home, but that did not seem like the right choice for her anymore.

"You keep saying we, who are we?"

“The other scientists I have been working with.”

“I will let you show me,” she said. “But you have to tell me why you want to send me back. What is it you think I will do, and I have to know everything.”

“Eva, I promise I will tell you everything, but not here. We can talk more in the car.”

She was willing to hear more because she was standing on the precipice of her life right now. How could she say no to something she didn’t even understand yet?

As Jon drove, she saw they were leaving the city.

“Aren’t we going to the university?”

“No, the equipment is not at the University. It is at a lab out of town, not really near anything.”

“Oh, so that part was not true either. This sounds an awful lot like a serial killer movie. Mysterious place out of town, not by anything, so no one can hear me if I scream.”

“Please understand that everything we did was out of necessity. We cannot just let the public know of our work. Keeping it a secret is of the utmost importance. We had to make sure that you agreed to keep it a secret before showing you the lab. Now, you can ask any questions that you like. And nothing is going to happen like in a serial killer movie, though I understand why you would say that.”

“Well, where will I… I guess we live?”

“We will go with enough money to live on for the first few months and other necessary things, then rent a hotel. After that, we will find an apartment.”

“And what will we do for a living?”

"We have already considered that now that we know what time you will be in. I mean, we will be in," Jon said, quickly correcting himself. "The time we have chosen is right before the Second World War. We thought that you, and I guess now me, should get a government job. We were hoping to keep track of the war. It is one thing we had planned for your visit, amongst other things. We wanted to see if we could find the answers to some of the clouded things surrounding the war. At the lab is all the paperwork to get the jobs. We need to have as much freedom as possible to observe the war but not alter things that would change the war's outcome. That is one thing we are uncertain about because no one has ever time traveled before, at least not to our knowledge. This is very important; we must not change big things like trying to murder Hitler. If we can help it, the less we alter, the better. We, at this point, don't know the repercussions of us even being there. We figured that helping people would not alter the war in any deleterious way. However, we can't exactly say what kind of impact it will have on the future."

"I see. So it could be like the story of the two men who went back in time to take pictures of the dinosaurs, and one tries to pick a flower. The other man tells him not to lest he change the future, then they get back to their own time, and they are the only people. The one man who said not to pick the flower looks at the bottom of his shoe and finds that he had stepped on a butterfly."

"I didn't know you knew that story. But no, it shouldn't be that extreme."

"And how long would we be there? Will it be the three months that was advertised?"

Jon looked out over the passing fields, taking a moment before speaking. "No, it will have to be longer. We will need to teach you things before you can go, and that will take some time."

She gave him a distrusting look. "The application said it was for the summer, and now you tell me it will be longer?"

"I understand it is a big decision, but we have to prepare you. When you get there, it could take longer to gather the information we need, and we want to monitor the effects of you being there might have on events."

His words kept playing over in her head. It felt like she was underwater, sinking to the bottom. She could not wrap her brain around it. There must still be some kind of mistake.

The naked trees set against the gray sky passed them as they drove in silence, but she hardly noticed as she stared at her reflection in the window.

"We are almost there," Jon said, noticing that she had stopped talking. He watched her from the corner of his eye. He was not sure how she was handling this. Was she going to snap and scream that she could not do it and was going home, or say yes out of fear? He wanted her to say yes because she truly wanted to, and he wanted her to be comfortable with it, but they could not wait forever for her to make that decision or until she was at ease with it.

It was already late into the afternoon when they arrived at the lab. Jon turned onto a dirt road that led them to a big metal building in a field with nothing around it but grass and a forest in the distance. The building looked as if it used to be a warehouse of sorts. It was tall enough to be two floors and was a brownish-gray color. He pulled next to the few other cars parked there and turned the engine off.

"Are you ready?"

"I'm not sure."

"I understand it's a lot to digest. Once you see this, it should help you decide. I believe it will be good for you to hear about it from some of the other scientists."

Jon opened his door and got out of the car, and Eva did the same. She followed him to the entrance of the building and watched as he slid a card in a slot next to the door and typed in a passcode. The door buzzed, and he opened it and motioned for her to enter. He followed behind her and put his hand on a glass screen next to the second door. A red light went up and down his hand twice, and then the door made a buzzing sound like the first. He turned the handle and held it open for her to enter.

She hesitated for a second, the distinct feeling that she would have to say yes and would no longer have a choice if she walked through the door pressed on her. If she were to follow Jon into that room, would she be giving up her right to choose? She wondered if she already knew too much or if seeing this sealed her fate. She contemplated not following Jon into the room for a brief second, but she didn't even know what her next step would be from there if she didn't. Would she refuse to step into the room, and if she did, then what? Eva understood that it made more sense to continue forward at this point. Was there really any turning back now?

She walked through the door, and Jon shut it behind them. Eva looked around the room that they were in. It was big and open, with long skinny windows towards the top and a few desks around the room. A small concrete room was in the middle of the building, just sitting there, looking out of place.

"So, I should introduce you to everyone," Jon said. "This over here is Dr. Yug."

The man came over to her. "Hi, Eva, it is so nice to meet you," he said as he shook her hand. "We are so happy to have you here."

The other people were standing around, anxiously awaiting to meet her, staring at her like she was the new animal at the zoo.

"I'm sorry, I am just so excited to meet you," Dr. Brandt said as he stepped forward and somewhat forcefully took Eva's hand. "I just can't wait to get started. I mean, there is so much out there to be explored, to be learned, to be seen and experienced! This is so incredible for all of us, but especially for you," he said with such conviction that it caught Eva off guard.

She looked into his eyes, and it was at this moment she realized that it all was true, everything Jon had told her. There was no way this many people could be confused or that serious about a joke.

"I'm sorry about that. Dr. Brandt is like that sometimes." Jon looked at Dr. Brandt and gave him a questioning look. "I'll make this quick. This here is Dr. Petterson."

"Welcome, Eva, it is a pleasure. I think you will be perfect for this job that we have chosen you for."

"Thank you, but I'm not entirely sure what I think of this job." She averted her gaze and looked down at the floor as she spoke.

"We will teach you, educate you, and make sure that we prepare you for whatever you encounter while you're there."

"But that's just it! We don't know what I will encounter, so how will you be able to prepare me for it?" she asked, looking back up at them.

"Eva, you will be OK. You will just need to trust us," Jon said.

Everyone waited for her response, but she didn't say anything. She understood she did not have enough information to know if she was in any kind of danger or not, but perhaps they did, and she should hear what they had to say.

"Hi, Eva, I'm Dr. Foster." A slender man with dark brown hair, narrow shoulders, and nineteen-eighties-style glasses sitting low on his nose held out his hand.

She took it, and he put his other hand over hers.

"Eva, I heard everything you said, and I will help ensure you stay safe. We will do everything in our power to prepare you and ourselves for whatever is to come! Our biggest concern is you." He squeezed her hand and patted it before letting it go.

"And last, this is Dr. Jensen," Jon said as he gestured with his hand in Jensen's direction.

"I understand that this must come as a terrible shock to you, Eva. We will give you time to adjust to all you will be doing."

Dr. Yug took her arm and led her to a chair at a desk. "Sit down, Ms. Abrams, and we will show and explain everything to you. Then, we will teach you about the culture and the era in which you will be living. We will show you how to act, talk, dress, and the things that are acceptable and not acceptable. We will teach you how to adapt to the culture because we want you to feel comfortable leaving your apartment and conversing with the people there."

"It sounds like that alone could take a long time," Eva said.

"We have already written a letter to your school informing them you will now be attending the University here; that way, you can stay. We are just waiting for the right time to send it. Then you will call your parents and tell them you have been offered a full-time internship and have accepted it and that you have decided to attend school here so you could take the job. We will eventually lead them to think that you are on an assignment where you don't have access to a phone but can still write," Dr. Yug said.

Eva looked around the room, angry at all of them for lying to her. "You should have been honest about the expected duration of the stay at least; that way, the people applying would know how long the job would be for and could have planned accordingly."

"We did not deceive you with malevolence. It was necessary," Jon said to her, his voice calm and even.

She listened to Jon intently, trying to take in what he just said and what Dr. Yug had told her. It all sounded very complicated, and she was sure it would cause confusion with everyone back home. Her dad would know that something wasn't right. She knew he would.

"I see. Wow, that is so much to think about! You guys probably put a lot of thought into an idea that will never work. The whole me deciding to stay in England will never fly with my parents. They will see right through it. And if they do somehow fall for that, they will insist on coming to visit me at some point. What will you tell them then? And a simple excuse will not work with my mother. She never falls for anything; that woman thinks everything is a conspiracy."

"Yes, we have put a lot of thought into this, Eva. We will tell her something that she cannot dispute," Jon said.

"I understand I can't expose anything that I see, hear, or do. But we are deceiving so many people, and I know that even if my parents believe all the lies we tell them, they will still be worried and wonder why, out of the blue, I took a full-time job and decided to go to school here or why they can no longer call me."

"They will wonder, yes," Jon said. "But there are few people out there who don't have someone who will miss them and wonder where they are. The trick is to develop a story so good that people will not question it. Ours might not be perfect yet, but we will work on it until it is. Don't worry, Eva; we will go over the things you should say and not say to them. Honestly, I think they will be proud of you and happy that you got this opportunity to live and work in another country. I know they will worry as parents do, but they will understand."

"How and when will I ever go home?"

"We will let you know an exact date, time, and place. We already know the place we will return to when it's time to go home. We will come back here," Jon said.

"How? What are we going to do? Bring a time machine back with us?"

"No, we will meet back here at this field on a certain date and time. They will open the portal from this time, and we will go through that way."

"And what if we can't make it back here on that day or are late? What then?"

"We will have several times on that day set and for the next few days in a row, too. That way, if we miss the first time or the first day, we have other windows."

Eva felt a little more comfortable with that.

"You should be perfectly safe, Eva," Dr. Yug said.

Chapter Seven

August 29th 2014

Eva had been in England for over three months, and so much of her life had changed in that short time, especially how she perceived her future. She thought her head might explode from all the information put in it over the last three months, and she missed her family and friends. Frankly, she was afraid of what was going to come next.

She had already packed the things she would take and was sitting on the bed dressed in the traditional 1940s attire they had made for her. A white flowery dress buttoned in the front, sheer silk stockings that were stitched down the back, and brown lace-up shoes. She was wearing a red felt wool fedora with her dress, as hats were the fashion in the forties. To finish her look, she had a small tan beaded purse with a long thin chain strap, the kind that was common in the late 1930s and early 1940s, and a pair of brown leather gloves.

She waited for Jon to come to her room and get her. She knew what time he said he would be at her door, but she was so nervous she couldn't sleep, so she got up early, put everything in the suitcase, and changed into her clothes. She had checked the room at least three times to make sure everything was packed; she did it more out of nervousness than worry that she had forgotten something. Then she tidied the room and checked it one more time. It was almost dinnertime now, but she had not left her apartment in fear that something would go wrong and she would miss Jon.

She stared at herself in the full-length mirror that stood in the corner across from the bed, but she no longer recognized the person looking back at her. The woman that she saw looked like one from a movie. Eva had one side of her hair pinned up, and curls framed her face. Her cheeks were rosy pink, and her lips a deep red. The person staring back at her was a person she did not know.

She had an easier time with the idea of leaving when it was still so far away. Now that the day was finally here, it was harder for her to deal with. Jon and the others had decided which year they would go to. They had settled on the year 1939, partly because she already knew some German and had known French since she was a little girl. Her grandmother had taught her because trying to teach her mom French had been a lost cause. Eva, however, loved learning it as a child. It was a novelty to her, and she had always romanticized France. She would spend three hours every Sunday with her grandmother, learning to speak, write, and read it. It had been years since she had taken lessons from her grandmother, but she still remembered most of what she had learned. Her knowledge of languages meant one less thing she needed to do to live in 1939 Europe. They decided on that era because it was not completely devoid of everything resembling the modern world, where her life would be at risk for simply being a woman with an education. Eva had pointed out that they were sending her to a time when the world was at war, but they assured her she would be relatively safe and away from the fighting or any real danger because France was still unoccupied in 1939. They had, however, informed her that just the nature of what she would do came with some amount of risk. While she was there, she wanted to do a job that was worthwhile. Most countries allowed travel passes to children, but she hoped she could help some adults, too.

She had written many letters to her parents and called as often as she could so they wouldn't worry, but now that she was actually leaving, she was not as confident as Jon and his colleagues that they could keep her mom and dad from worrying. They had told her family that she was going on a work trip in the Austrian Alps for a while and that there would be no cell signal up there. They told her parents that they would keep them informed about how she was doing and that she would continue to write them letters and have them mailed whenever she got a chance. They assured them they would always know how she was doing, even if it did not directly come from her.

There was a knock on the door, then it opened, and Jon's head peeked around.

"Are you ready?" he asked.

"I think so. I have all of my stuff packed, but emotionally, I'm not sure."

Jon quickly looked behind him before entering her room and shutting the door. He walked over to the bed and sat down next to her. He was also wearing his period clothing, a white shirt with brown pants and suspenders, and a pair of brown shoes that were a darker shade of brown. His shiny hair was combed to one side in a deep part. He wore his period attire well, and like her, he also looked like he walked off a movie set.

"I understand that this is a very emotional and confusing time for you and probably scary, but I really believe that everything will be OK and that this is going to be the most exciting and life-changing thing that will ever happen to us and possibly to the human race. The anticipation for something is almost always worse than the thing itself."

"I know, and I realize it is human nature to worry about the unknown. I'm ready now. I know I am. I just want to hurry up and get this journey, whatever it is going to be, started so I can stop worrying about it."

Jon stood up and reached his hand out to her. "OK, let's do it then."

She looked at his hand for a brief second, then put hers in his, and he pulled her up from the bed. They collected her belongings and left for the lab.

When they arrived, everyone else was already there, waiting. Dr. Yug and Dr. Brandt were standing near the concrete room, and the portal was already open inside of it.

"Hello, Ms. Abrams," Dr. Yug said. "Do you have everything you will need?"

"I believe I do."

Dr. Brandt reached his hand out for the luggage that she was holding. "Let me take them for you."

She held the suitcase and bag out to him. He took them from her and walked near the concrete room, sitting them on the floor by the door. Eva and Jon did not take much with them; they only brought what they could carry. They each had one suitcase, a small bag, and Eva a purse. Unfortunately, the suitcases did not have wheels like the modern ones did; they had to keep everything authentic so that they would blend in.

"Jon will go through first, then we will send the stuff through, then you will follow," Dr. Brandt said.

Eva nodded her head, acknowledging that she understood.

"We're all ready now," Dr. Yug said.

Jon knew that meant him, so he stepped up in front of the door.

Dr. Brandt came to stand beside him. "I can't believe we are doing this now. It is so fucking exciting!"

Jon looked at him with a smile at the corner of his mouth, but it didn't reach his eyes. "Hell yeah, it is, but I'm going to miss you, man!"

Dr. Brandt took Jon's hand, pulled him into a half-embrace, and patted him on the back. "Me too, Jon, me too!"

When he let go of Jon, Dr. Yug shook his hand. "Good luck in there. We will be waiting to hear from you as soon as you get to the other side. And we will be ready and waiting if or when you need anything."

"OK, let's do it," Jon said. He opened the door, walked in, and shut it behind him, then turned to face the black hole and whatever awaited him on the other side. He was going to stare fear in the face. Or death because he didn't quite know what was going to happen.

"On the count of three," Dr. Brandt said. "One... two... three... go!"

Jon took one last glance behind him through the glass at everyone but let his gaze linger the longest on Eva. He gave her a brief nod before turning around and stepping through the portal. In just a matter of seconds, he was gone.

Eva involuntarily gasped at the sight of Jon disappearing into the black mass. Everyone waited in anticipation, just watching for some sign that Jon was all right, or at the very least still alive. A few minutes later, the monitor flickered, and they could see a fuzzy image on the screen.

"Can you hear me?" Jon's voice echoed overhead from the speakers as the picture on the screen was coming into focus.

Everyone let out a breath of relief that Jon was alive.

"Jon, we hear you. What do you see? Are you all right?" Dr. Brandt said as he stared at the monitor.

"Yes, I'm fine."

"How was it? How do you feel?"

"It was OK. It seemed like just seconds for me to get here. I felt a slight tingle all over my body, but there was no pain. In the portal, it looked gray, like I was in a cloud, but with all the colors of the rainbow going through it, it was strange. I felt a little cool, and the sensation of electricity surging through my body while being pulled forward by some invisible force best describes it. I'm guessing that is why I felt the tingling sensation. I will say that when you get to the other side, it's kind of abrupt, though. You lose your balance because the pull is suddenly gone. Like if you were on a treadmill that abruptly stopped."

"What do you see around you?" Dr. Petterson asked.

"It's just a field with a bunch of trees." He looked up. "It's overcast and feels like a typical June evening in England."

"Does it look like the same place that you left from? Do you recognize the field that you are in?" Dr. Yug added.

"Yes, it looks the same. Not a lot seems to have changed except maybe more trees. I should be able to get us to the train stop without too much trouble."

"That is great, Jon, just great," Dr. Petterson said, excitement clear in her voice.

"We did it. I can't believe it," Dr. Jensen said.

Dr. Brandt tapped Dr. Yug on the back. "This is incredible!"

"It sure is," he said.

Eva was standing there in somewhat of a shocked state as everyone talked. Everything was more real than ever. She was up next, and what Jon had said about his experience made her less than comfortable. She also found it a little hard to believe that Jon made it through unscathed, based on how he described his experience. Her chest was tightening, and she knew what that meant. She was starting to have one of her anxiety attacks.

"OK, it's time to send the stuff through," Dr. Brandt said to the others. "Jon, we are going to send the luggage through now. We will do just one piece, and if you get it, we will send the rest."

"I'm ready. Go ahead," Jon answered back.

Dr. Brandt picked up Jon's small bag, carried it into the concrete room, and then pushed it into the black hole. When he could feel the pull on the bag, he let it go, and it disappeared into the blackness. Just seconds later, they heard Jon's voice again.

"It just hit the ground. I can see it."

"All right, good. We will send the others through then." Dr. Brandt took one bag at a time and pushed it through the hole.

Eva watched as her things got sucked into the strange blackness. Soon, it would be her. She thought she could do this, but now she wasn't so sure.

"It's all here, Sam."

"Good, we will prepare to send Eva through. Hang tight."

"All right, I'm ready for her. And Eva, if you can hear me, I want you to listen. It's nothing to be afraid of. It's over before you know it, and the tingling that I talked about really doesn't last more than a minute or two after."

Eva's mind raced with Jon's words. She could not believe that she was about to do this. She had no clue what the next few hours or days would be like, and that thought terrified her.

"Eva… Eva…" Dr. Brandt said.

His voice rang in her ears and snapped her out of her head.

"We're ready now," he said.

"Of course, yeah, I know." Her expression was of concern, and her complexion pale.

Dr. Brandt took her hand and led her near the room. "I think it's best to hurry and step in. Just let it pull you to the other side; thinking about it will only make it seem worse than it actually is," Dr. Brandt said.

"I agree with Dr. Brandt," Dr. Yug said.

"We will make sure you and Jon always have a connection to this time," Dr. Foster added.

"Is she ready?" Jon asked.

"Yes, she is getting ready to pass through now," Dr. Brandt said. He opened the door to the concrete room. "OK, Eva, I will count to three, and then you will step directly into the portal, just like Jon did. Understand?"

She nodded her head, swallowing hard as trepidation filled her. "Yes, I understand."

She stepped into the room, and he closed the door behind her.

He pushed the intercom next to the door. "OK, here we go, one… two… three… go now!" Dr. Brandt shouted.

The urgency in his voice startled her. She knew it was too late to change her mind now; she closed her eyes and stepped into the nothingness. She could feel the tingling electrical feeling that Jon had talked about. Eva opened her eyes and briefly saw the gray with the rainbow colors that Jon had described before it vanished. She could then feel grass beneath her feet as she watched the ground rushing towards her, falling to her knees and catching herself with her hands.

Jon rushed over to her. "Are you all right?"

"Yes, I'm fine."

He helped her off the ground and let go of her when he was sure that she was stable. She looked around and saw their stuff sitting close to where they were. The sun was setting, and she realized they probably needed to get to the train station soon.

"So, are we going to the train station now?"

"Yes, we need to get going. Let's grab our bags and start walking that way. Sam, we are leaving for the train station. We don't want to get there too late, so I'm going to put my earpiece and camera away now." Sam was Dr. Brandt's first name. Jon started referring to him by his given name after they had worked together for a few months and had become friends.

Eva watched Jon staring at the trees. She figured he was listening to Sam.

"OK, I'll try to reestablish contact when we get to the hotel." He stood still for another few seconds, then nodded his head. "OK, sounds great. Bye, Sam." Jon took his earpiece out, unclipped the camera from his shirt, put them in a small black bag, and zipped it up. He poked it in his shoulder bag and reached for his suitcase. "Get your stuff so we can go."

She put her purse in her small bag, draped it across her shoulder, and then reached for her suitcase.

They started walking in the direction of the road. Eva didn't know where the train station was, but she knew Jon did, so she was OK with following him. They had informed her earlier that her ticket was in her purse, so she knew that she could board the train and would not have to wait at the ticket counter when they got there.

They had walked for over half an hour, and the sun was almost gone. Just a dim orange glow low on the western horizon remained. Her arms were tired, and her hands were hurting from carrying her suitcase; she couldn't believe this was how people used to do it. It was exhausting. She had to keep switching the suitcase from one hand to the other and sometimes carrying it with both hands because one arm and hand would tire.

Eva had kept her feelings fairly well in check all day, but now that it was getting late and she was tired, she could feel the emotions coming to the surface, boiling over as they pulled her in different directions. She didn't know what she was doing or why she had agreed to come here and do this. Eva had not seen her family in months, her home, or even her country, for that matter. Now she wasn't just in a strange land, but in a time that wasn't her own, and with a person she had only known for three months. Right now, she wanted to crawl into bed, curl up in a ball, and cry, maybe scream, or perhaps just sleep.

"We are almost there, see," Jon said, pointing in front of them. "There are the lights to Cambridge just up ahead."

Eva looked past Jon and saw the lights from the city reflecting off the clouds. "Is the train station on this side of the city?"

"Yes, we should hopefully be there in ten or fifteen minutes."

"Good, my hands, arms, and legs are tired, and these shoes are rubbing my feet raw."

"Don't worry. Once we're there, we'll get on the train, and you can sit down. It's about a two-hour ride from Cambridge to London."

"So, does any of this make you nervous or scared?" she asked.

Jon thought about that for a moment before responding. "No. I mean, not really. I have dreamed about something like this since I was a little boy, so now that it has actually happened, I don't have time for those kinds of feelings. My colleagues and I have put a lot of thought into our safety, what we would need while we are here, and what we will be doing. I am focusing on the adrenaline, the excitement, the journey, and the achievement. I know that this is not your project and that you will probably never feel the same level of excitement as me, so if you are feeling anxious or scared, I understand."

Jon's confidence made her feel a little better, surprisingly.

They arrived at the train station a little after nine. As they walked into the central part of the station, Eva reached into her carry bag and retrieved her purse. She snapped it open and felt in it for her ticket. When her hand touched the piece of paper, she pulled it out.

Jon took the folded ticket out of his wallet. "We need platform nine and car three. It leaves in fifteen minutes, so we have to hurry," he said. "Help me look."

Eva started scanning the train station. Down at the far end from where they were, she saw the white sign with bold black writing on it that said 'Platform nine.' "Jon, it's at the end, on the left. We will have to cross over to get to it."

Jon picked up his suitcase and started walking fast along the train tracks towards the walkway that went over them. She picked up her suitcase too and followed, trying to keep up with his pace. It amazed her—the surrounding scenery with the steam trains, the clothing they were dressed in, the war posters that plastered the walls. It was unreal. It conjured the nostalgic glamour of a bygone era—bygone for her, that was. She was now glimpsing a time that was once lost to her.

When they got to 'Platform nine,' they walked along the train until they found car number three. Jon handed his ticket to the man at the door; he stamped it and handed it back to Jon. Jon then waited for Eva to give the man her ticket.

"Have a pleasant ride," the man said in a strong cockney accent as he handed her ticket back.

"Thanks," she said, taking her ticket from him.

They boarded the train and found an empty booth. The booth had two benches covered in red material and could seat four people. It also had a sliding door that offered some privacy from the people passing in the hall. Jon put his suitcase on the overhead rack along with Eva's, then he shut the sliding door and sat down. Eva took the seat across from him instead of sitting beside him.

Jon took a deep breath and let it out slowly. "Well, I think that the hardest part might be over. Now we just need to arrive at our hotel and get a good night's sleep."

"How did you find the hotel we will be staying in?"

"I don't have one in advance, but I'm sure we can find one that is not in the slums but is still fairly close to the train station."

"And you know where the bad parts of London were in the 1940s?"

"I did some research on the different parts of London in the 1940s before we left. I got the names of some hotels that were equivalent to a three-star. I wanted to make sure I had the names and addresses of several, just in case some of them are full. I also realized that many of the slums in 1940s London are still the slums of our time. It's funny how some things never change," he said with an amused half-smile.

"That was a good idea," she said. "What is on the agenda for tomorrow?"

Jon crossed one leg over the other and leaned back comfortably in his seat, leaning against the wall near the window. "The first thing we will need to do is find an apartment, one for each of us, then we will both go to the Friends Service Council and hopefully, we will get a job working there."

"What is that? I haven't heard of them. Is that an organization that works with the refugee effort?"

"Yes, it is. The Friends Service Council is actually the Quaker Peace and Service, and the Friends Service is a private advocacy group that works to help refugees. Working with them allows us a little more freedom because they do not affiliate with a government. We have already forged the paperwork that says you and I came from America to help with the refugee effort. It also says that I have a medical condition so that when the draft starts in America, I will not have to go back and enlist. I will stress again that we are mostly here to observe. And let's try to keep ourselves out of any unnecessary danger."

"I hadn't even thought of that, the medical condition thing, I mean," Eva said, wanting to say more about the observe part but held her tongue.

"I had to think of as much as I could; we don't want to have any setbacks or something to slip through our fingers. We are not here to make waves or change things that aren't already happening. We don't want to be noticed. We can't be recorded in history, and we certainly don't want to get stuck here. For now, we only planned this mission for a few months until we know more. I brought enough money for the time we will be here, and of course, there will also be the money we will make while working here."

For the rest of the trip, Jon and Eva were quiet. Jon closed his eyes to rest for a while, but Eva was too shaken to sleep. She looked out the window and wondered what tomorrow would bring. Unable to fathom her situation. She didn't know how well she would fit into this new life, even if for just a few months. She couldn't see anything out the window as the train moved except the occasional passing of a light that must have been from a house and her reflection staring back. She thought how different she looked in these strange clothes and the unfamiliar hairdo.

Time passed faster than she had expected. She looked up when the conductor announced they were arriving in London. She looked over at Jon and noticed that the voice on the overhead speaker did not wake him.

"Jon, we are here," Eva said as she lightly tapped his arm.

His head jerked up, his eyes droopy as he looked around their compartment.

Jon looked at her, obviously trying to process what was going on. He looked away from her out the window and saw that they were pulling into a train station. He blinked several times, fully trying to wake, then stood up. "I'll get our bags down." He grabbed Eva's bag from the rack, sitting it on the bench next to her, then reached for his own.

"So, do we get a taxi?" she asked.

"That's the plan; everything should go smoothly, and there is nothing to worry about as of now."

When Eva and Jon got off the train, she noticed how large the station was. When one exited the train, one would be on a platform that faced arched openings all along a wall with windows above it, and the facing wall on the other side was the same. A large arched ceiling made the train station very loud, every noise echoing off it.

"This way," Jon said as he walked towards the opening on the same side of the tracks they were on.

As they walked, she could feel a knot forming in her stomach. She wasn't sure if it was because she hadn't eaten in over eight hours or because of what was happening; she always got this way when she was nervous.

When they left the train station, they walked about a block before coming to a road that they turned on. The traffic on the street and the number of people walking on the sidewalks were quite heavy compared to Cambridge.

"This is a suitable spot. We will wait here and flag down a taxi," Jon said as he sat his suitcase beside his feet.

She also put her bag on the sidewalk next to her. She only then really noticed her hands and feet throbbing from all the walking and the carrying of her suitcase she had done today. She rubbed one hand with her other as she looked around at the nearby shops; it was just like something one would see in old movies, and it was the most amazing thing she had ever seen. One of the buildings on the street across from them was a pharmacy, and she could see all the little brown and clear bottles in the window, along with some chocolate and other items for sale. They had some glass candy jars on the counter that said 'five pence' along with various other goods. The same brown and clear bottles in the front window were also on the back wall, sitting on a large shelf that reached the ceiling. She could imagine that only the middle class and wealthy could afford to buy chocolate for their kids these days.

They made the pharmacy ceiling out of Celotex tiles that were popular in the 1930s and 1940s. The walls had it too, which made the pharmacy look fancier than the modern-day ones. It reminded her of an upscale restaurant in downtown Salt Lake City that she would sometimes go to with her family on special occasions.

"In the morning, we can meet up in one of our rooms and discuss how we will approach this," Jon said, pulling her out of her thoughts.

"I think that would be good because I am too tired to worry about any of it right now. I really just want to find a soft bed and go to sleep. Actually, I'm so tired that I could probably sleep on the ground here if it came to that."

Jon chuckled. "I couldn't agree more. That's about how I feel." He peered down the road. "I can see a taxi coming now. Taxi!" he yelled as he stepped partway out onto the street, waving his arm to hail the cab.

The cab pulled to the curb and stopped right in front of them. It was a small black car with foot railings at the bottom, running along the sides. The back doors opened opposite the front doors. Again, something that was common in the 1940s, especially in England.

Jon opened the trunk and put the luggage in, and Eva waited in the car for him.

"Can you take us to the Royal London Inn?" Jon said to the driver as he slid into the backseat.

"Sure can," the driver said.

The driver was in his mid-forties with a gimp leg and already graying hair which made Eva think that perhaps he had lived a hard, stressful life. His skin looked aged beyond his years, probably from all the sun exposure he got from driving a taxi day after day. *His leg must be why he was not in the military,* she thought.

They drove only ten minutes when the taxi pulled in front of a white stone four-story building with steps leading up to the front entrance. It had two tall wooden doors with twelve little windows in each one and gold metal plates along the edges of the doors where one could push to open them. At the bottom of the stairs were two square pillars with lamps adorning the tops of them. They were covered in gold plating, just like the metal on the doors.

"How much?" Jon asked the driver.

"Two quid," the man said.

Jon reached into his jacket pocket and pulled out two coins. Then, leaning over the front seat, he put them in the man's hand.

"We don't get too many yanks here now that there is a war," the man said. "What brings you?"

"Well, that's just it; the war brought us here."

"I take my hat off to you then, sir. For helping with a war that is not your own."

"Thank you," Jon said, with surprise in his voice.

"Good day to you," the man said.

"And you," Jon returned.

Jon opened the car door and stepped out onto the curb, holding it for Eva. Then he went to the trunk to retrieve their suitcases, and she met him around the back to help. He sat her things next to her, then got his and latched the trunk. The driver drove away as he waved to them through the back window without turning around.

She admired the building as she ascended the stairs, going through the two sets of doors into a lobby that was pleasant to look at. In the middle of the room was a circular red velvet chair that people could sit on while waiting. The ceiling was a drop-in ceiling with gold accents around the edges, and to the left of the doors was a tall front desk. The person at the counter was an older man who was just starting to bald at the top of his head. He wore a pair of glasses that sat low on his nose and a white shirt covered with a black vest. When Jon and Eva approached the counter, he looked up over the top of his glasses at them.

"How can I help you?"

"We would like two rooms, please. And near each other, if you can," Jon told him in a business-like tone.

"Let me see what I have." The man looked down at a large notepad lying on the counter in front of him. He stared at it for a few seconds before looking back up. "I have two rooms on the third floor that are relatively close. One is at the end of the hall, and the other room is two doors down from it; those are the closest ones that I have. Will that work?"

Jon looked at Eva to see if she was OK with that.

"Oh, that would be fine. I don't mind," she said, just wanting this day to be over.

"Yes, that works for me, as well. We'll take those two rooms."

"Very well, sir," the receptionist said. "And how many nights will you be staying?"

Jon looked at Eva before he glanced back at the man. "A week," he said, unsure of his own words.

"Both of you will need to sign," the receptionist said, laying a piece of paper in front of them with a pen. "And you have to pay for the entire week in advance."

"That will not be a problem," Jon said.

He signed the first line, sliding the paper over to Eva. She signed and then handed the form back to the man.

"That will be two hundred pounds and ten pence."

Jon got the money out of his shoulder bag, counted it, then handed it to the man. The receptionist re-counted it, then put the cash in a pullout drawer under the counter. He turned and retrieved two gold keys with long metal keychains attached to them from the wall behind him and laid them on the counter. The wall from which he took the keys had many more like them hanging on small hooks in neat rows up and down it.

"Take the lift on the right to the third floor. When you get off, you will turn to the right and go all the way down the hall to room 380. It will be the last room. That room is your room, miss," he said, looking at Eva, then he turned to Jon. "And your room will be on the right side just before you get to the end of the hall, room 377. Enjoy your stay."

"Thank you," Eva said.

Jon picked up the keys and handed Eva hers as they headed to the elevator. Jon pushed the two doors open when the elevator stopped on the third floor. "Well, we can finally get some sleep now."

"Yes, I can't wait." What Eva really couldn't wait for was to be alone in her room. She needed to make sense of all that had happened today. She was also worried that her emotions would unwantedly spill over in front of Jon if she did not release them soon. Nothing sounded more appealing right now than curling up under her blankets in a dark room while crying herself to sleep.

Chapter Eight

Eva woke to a knock on her door. She uncovered her head and squinted as her eyes adjusted to the bright morning light. For a few seconds, Eva thought she was back in her bed, in her apartment in Utah. But then she noticed the door looked different. She peered around the unfamiliar room, realizing where she was and that it must be Jon knocking.

"Just a second," she called. She crawled out of bed, grabbed her robe, and made her way to the door. She opened it and saw Jon standing in the hall, holding some coffee and muffins.

"I thought we could eat breakfast while we talked things over."

"Oh, that sounds amazing," she said with a sigh as she took a muffin and a cup of coffee from him and stepped aside so he could enter the room. "I need some coffee right now," she said, looking down at the steaming black liquid in the cup.

Jon sat in one of the chairs at the small wooden table near the window. He laid the rest of the muffins on the table as Eva joined him.

"You know more about all of this, so I will let you describe your plans, and then I will ask my questions," she said, then took a bite of her muffin.

Jon chuckled. "I suppose that is how it will go. After eating and doing whatever else we need to do to get ready, I thought we could head out and look for an apartment. I'm hoping that we can find a two-bedroom apartment. It will be cheaper than getting two separate ones like I had originally planned."

"Won't people talk? I mean, if we live together? People didn't usually accept that kind of thing in this time."

"I will tell people you are my cousin. That should stop tongues from wagging."

"Fair enough." Eva took another bite of her muffin.

"I'm hoping we can find an apartment today, but even if we don't, we can still go to the Friends Service Council and let them know we came here to help. Then we can look for an apartment again tomorrow."

"What if they tell us they don't need our help?" she asked.

"I doubt they would turn away help, but if they do, we could go to other organizations."

She sipped her coffee as she looked across the rim of her cup at Jon but said nothing. She knew that he probably had it all figured out without her input.

"I think that is all we'll have time for today. It will probably take up most of the day, anyway. How long do you think it might take for you to get ready?"

"I'm not sure. I would like to shower, and I need to figure out how to get my hair like this again," she said, pointing to her head. "You should have woken me earlier. You are ready, and I'm still in my pajamas. When did you get up? What time is it anyway?"

"I knocked on your door at around eight-thirty." Jon looked at his pocket watch. "And it is now nine minutes past nine. I have been up since seven. I couldn't sleep anymore. I was too excited about the day and wanted to get started."

"I probably would have slept the whole day if you hadn't woken me up," she said. "I shouldn't be more than an hour."

"I knew you were tired. That is why I let you sleep in. Well, I will go back to my room now and let you get ready."

She gave a forced half-smile as he got up and left.

She drank the last few gulps of coffee and set the cup down on the table, wishing she had another cup. "Let's see how the showers are in 1940," she said. She walked to the side of the bed, knelt next to her suitcase, and retrieved a fresh pair of clothes. She carried them to the bathroom and shut the door. She looked around for a second, noticing how dated everything seemed to her. She let out a long breath. "All right, how do I do this?" She turned the hot and cold knobs; they looked like white plus signs with an H and a C in the middle of them. She removed her clothes, stepped into the deep bathtub, pulled the white shower curtain around it, and let the warm, steaming water pour over her body. The warmth of it made her sleepy, so she decided to make it a quick shower.

When she was done, she sat at the vanity near the window and looked at her wet, messy hair. She did not know how to do it the way they had it the day before, but she knew that she had to hurry in any case. She picked up the brush and strange-looking hairdryer and dried her hair as she brushed through it. She then curled a few pieces of hair around her face with a curling iron to try and recreate the look they had done on her. She dumped the contents of her makeup bag out on the vanity and reached for the mascara, blush, and the classic red lipstick which was favored in this era. That was all she had time for. She applied them and looked at herself in the mirror, turning her head from side to side to inspect her work. This was as good as it was going to get right now, but she would have to practice more with it later. The mascara proved to be the most difficult to apply because of the applicator. It wasn't a wand like the modern ones; in the 1940s, they applied it with a little brush that reminded her of a toothbrush with long thin bristles.

She dabbed some perfume on her wrists, stood up, and put on her hat and gloves, then grabbed her purse off the floor near her luggage and the room key from the nightstand and dropped it in her bag. She went to Jon's room and knocked on the door.

He stared at her for a few seconds without saying anything when he opened the door. "Good job with the hair and makeup," he said, randomly gesturing in circular motions directed at her head. "And you did it relatively quickly, too. I had actually expected it to take you longer."

"Thanks! Are you trying to tell me I'm slow?"

His eyes widened. "No, not at all. I just meant that this was your first time trying to recreate the look. I thought it would have taken longer than it did, but you finished in less time than you said it would take." He seemed worried that he had offended her.

"I'm not upset, Jon. I was just teasing."

Jon gave a nervous chuckle. "Oh, OK. Well, should we go?"

“I’m as ready as I’ll ever be,” she said.

He shut his door, and they headed down the hall to the elevator.

They took the city tram to the housing department that was near the hotel instead of a taxi because it was cheaper. Jon had asked the clerk at the hotel for directions to the housing office and the Friends Service Council. He wrote it down on a piece of paper for them, and Jon had it in his pocket.

“This is our stop,” he said as the tram slowed.

She nodded, then looked out the window. There were a lot of multi-story brick buildings in this part of the city, and men in suits crowded the sidewalks. “This must be in the business center,” she said to Jon.

Jon bent down slightly to see out the window and looked around. “It makes sense that it is.”

When the tram stopped, Jon grabbed his briefcase from the seat, and they stepped off onto the street. Eva smelled the pollution in the air. The tall stacks of the factories that rose high over the city pumped out smoke that mixed with the gasoline fumes from the cars. It all settled in the streets as a hazy fog covered London. The honking and the dinging of the trams echoing off the buildings made the city a boisterous place. The car horns sounded strange and reminded her of the sounds you would hear at a circus.

“I think we are only a few blocks from the building we need. The clerk at the hotel said it is close to this stop.” He hurried in the direction of the address on the paper.

They made their way through the crowd of people and came to a single-story red brick building. A sign on the front of it read, ‘London Housing Department.’

“Shall we go in?” Jon said.

“I suppose we should unless we want to keep living in a hotel.”

“I have no desire to.”

They went through the revolving door that led to the lobby. It was already busy with people milling all around them, and the lines at the windows were almost to the door. People were waiting in three separate lines that led to glass sliding windows. Most of the people were men in trench coats and brimmed hats made of brown felt. There were only a few women among them.

“I guess we should get in one of those lines,” she said as she looked for the shortest one.

“Over here.”

Jon headed to the line farthest to the left, and Eva followed. The lines did not move quickly, especially the one they were in. The man at the window was having some kind of disagreement with the clerk. She could hear that it had something to do with money and that he had missed several months of rent. She felt bad for the man, but there was nothing she could do to help him. After more than forty minutes of waiting in line, they finally made it to the front, and it was now their turn to discuss housing.

“How can I help you?” the man at the window said in a tired, agitated voice, without even the slightest attempt at sounding cordial. His facial expression did not change from the stern look it seemed fixed in.

“Yes, I was wondering if you had an apartment with two bedrooms available?”

The man flipped through a stack of papers in a paper holder in front of him without saying a word. “I have a few. They are on different sides of the city and range in price. Do you have a preference as to where in the city you would like to live?"

"I prefer one near here," Jon said to him.

He ran his index finger down the paper almost to the middle and stopped on a line. "This one is the closest to the business district. It is, however, the most expensive one and is still a few miles away. You will probably have at least five or more stops on the tram."

"If that is the closest one with two rooms, then I guess it will have to do. How much is that one?"

The guy slowly looked back down at his paper, then back up with about as much enthusiasm. "It is £459 a month, and it requires a six-month lease."

"Six months…?" Jon said, taken aback.

"Yes," the man said, emphasizing the word.

"I have enough cash on me for three months. Is there any way that I can pay the first three months now and pay for the other three months in a week?"

The man stared at him like he didn't understand or didn't hear him correctly. "Let me check with my supervisor." He got out of his chair and went into the back.

Jon looked at Eva. "I had not expected that. I thought that I had covered everything. I guess I didn't."

"If they agree, will we go back for the money?"

"No, just me. We need someone here to continue working at the Friends Service Council and collecting data. If we were to both leave after just starting, I'm not sure they would look too kindly on that or even have us back at all."

"So how will you get your job back when you return, or will you just wait until you are back to get one?"

"I think that is probably the best option. Perhaps you can mention me to them and let them know I will come at a later date."

"Sure," she said. "I could do that." She was not keen on being there by herself. The thought made her extremely nervous.

The clerk returned from the back. "My supervisor said you can do that, as long as you have the money here in a week and not a day late."

"I will," Jon said.

"I'm guessing that the apartment is for the both of you?"

"Yes, that is correct."

"You both need to fill out an application then." He handed Jon two pieces of paper and two pens. "You need to fill them out over there, and when you are done, return them here at this window," he said, pointing toward some chairs to one side of the lobby.

"Do I just walk up to the window and hand them to you with the money, or do I need to wait in line again?" Jon asked him.

"You can come up to the side of the window and hand them to me from the other side of the rope," he said.

"Thanks," Jon said, taking the two applications from him.

They went to the chairs that he directed them to and sat down to fill out the applications.

Jon took the papers and the money back to the window when they finished. He reached over the rope and around the woman standing at the window and handed the clerk the documents and money. She gave him a side glance but said nothing. The clerk took the papers and money from Jon, then handed him a piece of paper, and nodded at him.

Eva watched Jon give the papers and money to the clerk and then head back in her direction. She stood up, knowing that they were going to leave now.

"He gave us the directions to the apartment, and it says that we are to meet the person with the keys there at five. They will let us in, explain the utilities, check our IDs, then surrender the keys."

"OK, and what about the other place? Are we still going to go there today?"

He looked at his watch. "We have time before we need to be at the apartment. We can go to the Friends Service Council and at least try to get you a position."

"I hope that goes a little better than this did," she said, flustered at the setback.

"No kidding, I was not expecting to sign a six-month lease."

"I wasn't either."

They made their way outside and headed in the direction the receptionist at the hotel told Jon the FSC would be. Only five blocks from the housing department was the tall, white stone building they were looking for. Eva thought it was fancier than many other buildings she had seen so far. When they entered the lobby, a directory was on the wall, with all the offices in the building, the floors they were on, and the room numbers.

"Here it is." She pointed to the bold letters on the sign that read, 'FRIENDS SERVICE COUNCIL, SECOND FLOOR. ROOM: 210.'

Jon turned to Eva. "I think it is best if I don't go in with you."

"Are you serious? Why?"

"Yes, because I don't want to have to explain all of this to them. It will be easier if they think I haven't arrived in London yet and you are the only one here right now."

She stared at him in disbelief. "I don't even know what I will say to them. Jon, I don't think this is a good idea."

"You have all the documents you will need already with you, and I have told you what to say. You'll do fine."

"But… what if they tell me they are not looking for help right now? What will I do while I wait for you to return?"

"I will leave you the names and addresses of the other organizations. If this one says that they aren't looking for help right now, you will go out on your own to check with the others." Jon pulled his pocket watch out and glanced at the time. "You better get going. They will close in an hour. I'll be right here waiting for you in the lobby. If something goes wrong or you need more information, just come down, and I will help." He put a hand on each of her shoulders. "You are going to be fine. I have faith that you can do this all on your own and won't need my help."

"You have more faith in me than I do and more than I deserve. When I go up there, something will not go as planned. I just know it."

Jon smiled at Eva and dropped his hands to his sides. She gave him a defeated smile in return; he would not say anymore on the matter. She turned and walked to the elevator, and pushed the button. Her hand was trembling slightly when she raised it. When the elevator doors opened, she turned and took one last glance at Jon before stepping inside and pushing the button with the two on it. As the doors closed, her breaths became more labored. *You can do this, Eva. Just like Jon said, you can do this without his help,* she told herself.

The elevator jolted to a stop, and the doors opened. But it wasn't a lobby like on the main floor, as she had thought it would be. In front of her was a room with desks running along both walls to the left and right. The people at them were on the phones, typing, smoking, and the ones not seated were milling around the room. It was a very chaotic scene. There was a lot of energy in the room, and it reminded her of a beehive. Some of the people stopped what they were doing and looked at her. She had been standing in the elevator staring into the room but made no attempt to leave the comfort of its confined space. She cleared her throat and unsteadily stepped out of the elevator into the busy room. The people staring at her went back to what they had been doing, except for an overweight middle-aged woman at the desk just to the right of the elevator doors. She had short brown curly hair and glasses with a chain connected to it that went around her neck.

"Can I help you with something?" she said to Eva in a soft, kind voice.

"Yes," Eva said, almost in a whisper. Realizing that she needed to speak louder, she cleared her throat again. "Yes," she said, louder this time. "I was wondering if you had any positions available?"

"We sure do," she said with a smile. "Have a seat."

Eva sat down in a chair on the other side of the desk from her.

"Now tell me, what kind of position are you looking for?"

"I'm not sure exactly. Just anything that I can do to help."

"All the positions here help people. Do you have any special qualifications?"

"Well, I can speak fluent French, and I'm fair in German. I'm not sure if that is what you mean by special qualifications?"

"Can you now," the woman said rhetorically, still in her kind voice as she gave an approving smile. "And can you type?"

"I can, but I haven't done it in a while." Eva told her that because she had never actually used an old-fashioned typewriter before and was unsure how proficient she would be with it.

"I think I have the perfect job for you," she said. "We need someone in France as a liaison. Your job would be to find locals who will take in people fleeing from other European countries and anyone else that might need our help. Right now, there are thousands who are homeless or in hiding, and there are still so many more who are trying to flee mainland Europe but lack the proper documentation. We are trying to help some of them with that, too."

Eva watched her in silence as she spoke, and when the woman stopped talking, she looked at Eva, waiting for her to say something.

"Let me make sure I understand this. You want me to work in France, which is currently at war with Germany and neighbors them?" Eva asked in disbelief.

The woman blinked several times. "Yes, you will live there most of the time and come to England only if you require assistance."

"And how long would I be in France?" Eva asked in a low, strained voice.

"As long as people need our help, or until you decide that you no longer want to do the job."

Eva did not know what to say. This was not what she expected. "And what about the other jobs you spoke of?"

"Two of them are receptionist positions and require fast typing, and the other one is a filing position."

"So, you think I fit this one best because I speak French?"

"That, and you also said you speak German, which would be a big help to us."

She was still unsure how to answer, so the woman continued.

"We don't get many people offering to help that can speak both languages, so when you walked in here and said that you could speak French and German, I knew you were exactly who we were looking for. What I didn't expect, however, was the person we needed happened to be an American. Is this something that you would be willing to do?"

"Um… well, can I have a few minutes to think about it? I need to process this and make sure that I understand what taking this job would mean?"

"Of course, you can wait at that empty desk if you like while you think," she said and gestured to the desk across from hers.

"Is it OK if I wait down in the lobby?"

"Sure—if that is what you prefer," the woman said to Eva, giving her a strange look, probably thinking she had asked that because she did not want the job but did not know how to turn it down and wanted to bow out quietly.

Eva got up to leave, then remembered that she needed to ask about a job for Jon, as well. "One more thing," she said. "My cousin will come to London from Cambridge in about a week, and he also wanted to help. Is there anything that he could do?"

"Does he have any special qualities like you?"

“Well, he is good at math, and I’m sure he can also type.”

“We don’t need someone good at math right now, but if he really is good with typing, as you say, and doesn’t mind doing secretarial work, we sure could use his help. Does he not speak any other language?”

“I don’t believe so, no.”

“Just tell him to come in when he gets here, and we will discuss the options with him.”

“Thank you,” Eva said and headed back to the elevator.

She pushed the button, and when the doors opened, she stepped inside and pressed the button for the lobby. The lady at the desk smiled at her as the doors closed.

“What the hell just happened?” she said. “Going to France is not what I was supposed to be doing.” She did not know how she would explain this to Jon or what his reaction would be.

When the elevator doors opened, she saw Jon stand up from the couch in the lobby and walk in her direction.

“How did it go?” he asked, the expression of worry evident on her face.

“I’m not sure.” She furrowed her brows and then put her hand on her forehead to think.

“What do you mean, ‘you are not sure’? Did they not offer you a job?”

“Oh, they did, but not anything that you or I expected.”

“Meaning…?”

“I mean, they offered me a job in France, not here.”

“Why would they do that?”

“To find local people who will house the escaped refugees, the ones fleeing from the German-occupied countries into France. I would also help with the documentation for some people who are having trouble getting theirs."

"Really?" Jon asked, looking away in thought.

"Yes. They said that I was perfect for the job because I spoke French and German."

"And what did you tell them?"

"I didn't tell them anything. I said that I needed to think about it first and asked if it was OK if I came to the lobby to think it over. What should I tell them, Jon?"

"And did you ask about me?"

"I did. They said they could probably use you for typing."

"I guess I'm fine with that for now."

"And what about the job they offered me?" she asked again. "What should my answer be?"

"Personally, if it were me, I would take it."

She huffed. "You would take it?" she said, disbelieving.

"Yes, I would."

"Why?"

"Because it would be an amazing experience!"

"Even though the Germans will soon occupy France?"

"I would leave before that happened. Remember, we know when that is."

"So, what you are telling me is I should take it?"

"I think you should do what you want. I said I would take it. I didn't say that you had to. If you turn it down, I completely understand, and you can probably take one of the other positions or try another organization altogether."

"I'm not sure what to do, but I know you are really telling me I should go."

"When do you need to give them an answer?"

"Soon, I suspect. I'm sure they thought I would be back already if I were going to take the job."

"Eva, it is a risk, but I believe only a small one. I think it would be an opportunity of a lifetime. You wanted to help people while you were here; well, here is your chance. And the things that you will get to do for those people will be greater than anything you could do sitting in an office. This will be the most effective way of doing it and far more rewarding."

"Oh my God, how did I find myself here faced with this kind of decision?" She plopped down on the couch, her purse falling to the floor. "Right now, I just want to go home to my simple life. I don't know if I can do this, Jon!"

He sat down beside her and gently put his hand on her shoulder. "You can, Eva. Look how far you have already come and what you have already done," he said calmly. "Just coming here was a brave thing. Here is a question for you. If you choose not to go and find yourself looking back at this moment when you are older, or not even then, maybe in a few years, do you think you will regret it or be happy that you made the decision not to go?"

"I think I would be torn between my choices now, even then. I would be happy that I was never that close to the war and never had to deal with the Germans. That being said, I think a part of me would always wonder what it would have been like and if I could have made a difference in even just one person's life. To have saved them from the horrors that awaited them if they had not gotten the documents they needed to flee their country."

"I think the answer is pretty clear," he said.

She knew Jon was right. If she could do something to help these people, she needed to do it, but wouldn't it fly in the face of the observe-only policy?

She picked up her purse and stood. "I will go back and tell them I have made a decision, that I have decided to take the job. However, I have to ask, won't this change history? You told me to alter nothing. That my job was only to observe."

He rose from the bench and stood in front of her. "I know that is what they told you, but the more I thought about it, the more I realized that just by us being here will change history. There are already people from this time doing exactly what you will do, so I don't see how it would change it, at least for the worse, by you helping. If anything, you would change it for the better. You can potentially help more people than anyone else because of your knowledge."

"And changing things more than we already are by being here doesn't worry you?"

"No, it doesn't. Maybe it should, but I can't help but feel that what we are doing is necessary."

"Necessary for what?"

"For science. Imagine the possibilities? Never before, as a race, have we come so far. We have finally found a lake of knowledge. Why just dip your toe in?"

"Because an unknown creature lurking in the depths could eat you if you just jump in."

He laughed. "I like your sarcasm, and funny enough, your lack of confidence in me."

"Not just you, but also myself." She laughed nervously.

“You will be fine, Eva. Whatever happens, I know you will find your way back.”

“Well, at least one of us is sure of that.”

He gently took her hand. “I will wait right here for you just like before.”

She smiled, but it didn’t reach her eyes. “I hope I don’t live to regret this,” she said.

She turned and walked to the elevator. She pressed the button, and the door opened, but her hand did not shake this time. She stepped in and again pushed the button for the second floor. As the doors were closing, Jon gave her a reassuring nod. Then he was gone.

The elevator jolted to a halt on the second floor, and the doors opened. Eva did not hesitate to get out this time. She stepped onto the light brown carpet and walked to the desk of the woman who had helped her last time, stopping only inches away.

“You came back?” the woman said, surprise mixed in her calm tone.

“I did. I gave your offer some thought, and I have decided to take the job. If this is how I can help, then this is what I will do.”

“I am pleased to hear that,” she said, looking at Eva, her warm smile returning. “Stay right here and have a seat. I need to get the paperwork for you and let my boss know because he will want to speak with you. He will go over all the fine details and the security involved.”

“Security?” Her stomach twisted in alarm.

“Yes, there is a risk. Being in France could be dangerous, as is what you will do while you are there. He will explain it all to you.”

you.”

The woman stood up from her chair and walked to a large office with windows that spanned all three walls. Eva could not see inside, though, because the blinds that covered them were closed. She wondered why that was. After a few minutes, the woman came out of the office with a man following behind her and stopped right in the doorway. He was an older gentleman with an enormous stomach, thinning hair, and a round face covered in tiny red veins. He had a thick grey mustache, bushy eyebrows that looked like they were taking over his face, and long sideburns connected to his five o'clock shadow. The man said something to the woman and pointed in Eva's direction. Then, the woman leaned in and said something to him before they started walking in her direction.

"I'm sorry, ma'am, but we never caught your name," the man said as he approached her.

"My name is Eva Abrams."

"Hi Eva, it's nice to meet you. I'm Peter," he said, reaching his hand out for her to take.

She took his large hand, and he squeezed her with a firm, strong grip, something she had not expected from someone his age.

"It's nice to meet you," she said.

"Why don't we come into my office where we can talk?"

"Of course."

She got up from her chair and followed him to the office. When they both were inside, he shut the door.

"Have a seat."

She sat in the chair across from him at a much larger desk than the one the woman sat at.

"So, Tina tells me you can speak French and German?"

"Yes, that is correct." Eva sat straight in the chair, not leaning against the back. Her hands were gripping the top of her purse tightly in her lap.

"And she says you have agreed to be our liaison in France?"

"I have."

"We are relieved that you are here. We have been looking for someone who can speak French and German for some time now, but until now, we have had little luck. We have had many people who can speak French, some who can speak German, but not both. A while back, a man was working for us who could speak both languages. We asked him if he would take the job in France, but he said no and later quit. He told us that he had a family, and the risk wasn't worth it. I think he believed that if he stayed here, we would pressure him to take it, and he didn't want that. But you came in wanting to be of use and can speak both languages, all the way from America, just to help the war effort. That is incredible."

"Thank you. Yes, I did. I know that my country doesn't want to be in the war, and I completely understand why, but I thought that just because they don't want to get involved doesn't mean that I can't help."

"Well, let's not waste any time. We need to do several things before you can work for us. I will first need to see your ID card, and you will need to fill out some papers. Then we will go over some things."

"Oh, yes, of course. The woman who helped me said I would need to do this." She reached into her purse, retrieved her ID card, and handed it to him.

"Can you fill this out as we talk, or do you need it to be quiet?"

"No, it doesn't bother me. We can do them at the same time."

"Great! OK, here are the papers that I need you to fill out. It's just basic stuff."

She took the papers he put in front of her and glanced at them. He was right about it being basic. It just asked for her name, address, sex, age, what languages she could speak, what country she was from, and a section at the bottom for her to sign. She put the paper back on the desk and picked up the pen.

"I have to ask; did Tina tell you that there are some risks involved with this job?"

"She did, but she didn't go into detail about what they were."

"OK. If you go to France and the Germans later invade like so many other countries, heaven forbid, which we think is likely, we cannot guarantee your safety. And if the Germans find out that you have been helping Jews or Polish, they will not look kindly on that. I'm not sure if they would arrest you because you would be going through the proper channels, but that isn't to say that they won't. At the very least, you will not be treated kindly by them, and it is a real possibility they will make you return to England."

"I expected that. The Germans don't have the best reputation in America either."

"I would imagine not. When you get there, we will communicate through letters and phone calls if possible, and you will get a paycheck sent to you once a month."

"How will I find these people I am supposed to help?"

"We will be the ones to find most of them for you. Often, they can't come to France because they have to have a job and a place to stay first, and if they don't have one or both of these things, they can't come. When we have some people ready, your job is to ensure that they have a place to stay and all the proper paperwork and employment, if possible. In situations where they don't have all the documents they need, you might have to hide them while we acquire it for them. It should only be for a short while, just somewhere they can keep their heads low until the papers arrive."

"That sounds risky."

"And that is part of the risk we talked about that you might be taking."

"What about lodging for me? Where am I going to stay while I'm there?"

"Ahh, good question. You will stay with one of the locals at their house, but we are going to need a few days to find someone."

"That makes sense, I guess. I figured I would be staying with someone."

"Yes, we thought it would make it easier for whoever we sent to adjust if they lived with a local."

"What part of France will I be going to exactly?"

"That we are unsure of as well. We have a few people around the country who have helped us in the past with refugees, so we will ask one of them. I don't know if any of them are still willing to help or if they even have the room or means to do so."

She nodded her head in understanding. "I have a few more questions."

"I would be surprised if you didn't," he said.

"Do you know when I will leave for France, and will I be allowed to visit home once in a while?"

"To answer your first question, you will leave as soon as we find someone for you to stay with, which should only be a few days and, hopefully, no more than a week. And for your other question, the answer is, I'm not sure yet, it depends on so many things. I would like to think that you would have opportunities to go home."

"I understand."

After finishing the paperwork, they told her to check back in a few days to see if they had found her a place to stay.

Jon was still sitting on the couch, waiting for her, when the elevator doors opened. He stood when he saw Eva and waited for her to reach him.

"So, how did it go?"

"It went fine. He said that I will probably leave in a few days."

"So soon?"

"I know. I didn't expect to leave that quick, but many unexpected things have happened today. I don't know what you will do with the apartment now, and I will need some money to hold me over for a while after I arrive in France. They said I will only get paid once a month, so it will be a while before I get my first paycheck."

"I can give you most of the money that is left. I will just keep enough to get back to Cambridge. As far as the apartment, I suppose I can ask and see if they will give me a smaller one, although I'm not holding out a lot of hope for that. It is getting late, and we still need to meet the guy at the apartment even if we won't be taking it."

She looked at the clock on the wall, and it read 4:47. "Oh wow, yeah, we better get going. I didn't realize that I had been up there for almost an hour."

Chapter Nine

September 17th, 1939

Eva's eyes were fixed on the widow as the French countryside passed by. The rolling hills were spotted with clusters of trees spaced far enough apart for the valley to be seen between them. White, yellow, and purple wildflowers littered the low spots, and white cows roamed the hills with their heads to the ground as they grazed.

Eva had been traveling for most of the day and felt its effects. She had left London at six that morning, taken a boat across the English Channel, and arrived in France at around nine. From there, she had been on the train since it left the Paris station at one in the afternoon and hadn't gotten off. The train had been moving for hours this time without making a stop. She had not minded sitting around the train station for hours; it allowed her some time to walk around and stretch her legs a bit before she had to sit again.

She had gotten a coffee at a café near the station and gazed at the people coming and going while she waited for her train. It was a fascinating thing to watch. No one seemed to talk to one another or smile, and they always had their heads down. In some way, it did not differ from watching people in a subway station in her time, except they looked down at their phones. These people perhaps did it because they were uneasy and on edge. They knew there was an impending invasion and that they again soon would find themselves in the throes of another war.

The sun was now low in the sky, and Eva hoped they were getting close to La Chapelle. She looked at her watch; it was now a quarter past five. It would not have taken as long to get to La Chapelle if they had not made so many stops at the beginning of the trip. When she had gotten on the train, she could hardly keep her eyes open. She had to get up at four-thirty to catch the boat from London to Paris. At their last stop, a woman and her small child had boarded and sat across from her while she was sleeping. The child started to cry, waking her after only twenty minutes of sleep. When Eva realized there would be no appeasing the child, no matter what the mother did, she decided to give up on sleeping. Eva offered the child a mirror that she kept in her purse and watched as she played with it in silence. The little girl would put it in her mouth and suck on it or sometimes chew on the edges, drooling on the glass as she did. Occasionally, she would look up from the mirror, out the window, or at Eva. When she did, Eva would play peek-a-boo with her, and the girl would smile, her cherub-like cheeks revealing two dimples and no teeth. Eva could not help it, but she always got a warm, happy feeling with children. She enjoyed them so much, but she was far from ready to be a mother.

She leaned closer to the window as the train pulled into the station at La Chapelle. It was considerably smaller than the one in London or Paris. This one only had a single platform and did not have a cover to protect you from the rain or sun.

The conductor announced in French that this was the last stop for this train. She stood up from her seat and got her bags down from the overhead compartment. She picked her purse up off the chair and put the strap over her shoulder. The woman handed her the mirror back and thanked her in French, then picked up a small bag beside her, put the child on her hip, and left the compartment they were in. The girl looked at Eva over her mom's shoulder as she walked away, and Eva waved at her. She wiped the mirror off with her handkerchief and stuck it back in her purse before leaving the compartment.

She stepped off the train and onto the platform; the air felt warm and smelled of flowers mixed with the fields' aroma. The scents assaulted her nostrils, almost making her sneeze. It certainly did not smell like London or Paris. There was no mistaking she was now in the country.

She walked along the train past the engine and turned towards the road. She looked around for the person who was supposed to be picking her up. Peter, her boss in London, had told her that the person they found was a widower that had two daughters. He said that the man was tall and muscular with black hair and a slight beard. He would be dressed in traditional farmer's clothing and drive a truck.

Eva looked across the other set of tracks and saw a man standing in front of a Model-T truck with his hands in the pockets of his overalls. She could not see his face well because the sun was setting behind him, shadowing his face, so she cupped her hand above her eyes to block the sun and squinted in the man's direction. He fit the profile and build of the man Peter said would come to get her. His shirt sleeves were rolled up, exposing tan, muscular arms, and the first three buttons of his shirt were undone, revealing a tan chest with black curly hair. He had broad shoulders to match his arms and stocky legs that finished his solid frame. It was evident that he was no stranger to hard labor and spent many hours in the sun.

The man saw her staring at him, took his hands from his pockets, and slowly made his way in her direction. She picked up her suitcase and walked across the tracks towards the man. They met about halfway, and he stopped in front of her.

"Bonjour," he said to her. "Are you Miss Eva Abrams?"

"Bonjour. Yes, I am Eva Abrams."

"It is nice to meet you, Miss Abrams. I am Fabien," he said as he put his sizable hand palm down on his chest. "Can I take your bags for you?"

"I did not know you spoke English. They did not mention that to me."

"Yes, I do, but not often. I rarely have the occasion to," he said with a thick French accent.

"Did they tell you I could speak French?"

"They did. It is good because my daughters cannot speak English or even understand it." He took the suitcase out of her hand. "Can I take that one, too?" he asked, referring to the bag across her shoulder.

She had almost forgotten it was there. "I can carry this one. It's not heavy."

He turned around. "My truck is this way." He started walking back in the direction he came from.

She followed him around to the back of his truck, and he put her suitcase in the bed. She took the bag off her shoulder, put it in the back with the other one, and then went to the passenger door to get in. She pulled on the handle, but the door didn't open. She furrowed her brows and pulled again, this time harder. The door groaned, and the hinges cried with resistance when she opened it wide enough to get in.

"Sorry about that. The door needs oiling. I would oil it if I had some, but with the war, everything is rationed, and things like oil are kept for the military now that we are at war with Germany. I knew it was only a matter of time, then when I heard Germany invaded Poland, there was no way France could stay out of it any longer," he said.

"I understand. There is no need for an apology."

She got in and closed the door, and they pulled away from the train station and headed through town. One of the first things that she noticed as they drove was the lack of men, at least not young ones. Most of the people on the street were women, a few older men, and children. She knew that the younger men and the older ones who were still in good health were now off training for the inevitable war with Germany. She also noticed the hills that surrounded the village and a decent-sized river running through it.

This was something she had not expected. To add to the beauty a castle sat atop a hill overlooking the town.

"How old are your daughters?"

"Sabina, my youngest, is nine, and Brigitte, my eldest, is seventeen. She has been a great help around the house since her mother passed."

"I'm sorry to hear that. How did—?"

"From the fever," he said before she could finish her question.

"And the younger one, does she help as well?"

"I try to have Sabina do the things that Brigitte doesn't have time for, but Sabina is a very free-spirited child. She spends most of her time in the fields with the cows or in the woods picking flowers and playing whatever game she has thought up that day."

Eva smiled. "Sounds like we should all be more like Sabina—picking flowers and playing with cows. It sure would be better than thinking about this war."

Fabien turned his head slightly to look at her. "I am glad that the war has not affected her. She is still yet free from it and can think of other things. Brigitte, however, is not. You can tell that the death of their mother and now this war is weighing heavily on her."

"It is hard to carry such burdens and be so young," Eva said.

"I know it bothers her, but she doesn't speak of it. And you, what of your life back home?"

"My life, well, it isn't so exciting. Things in America are pretty quiet, for now."

"What of your parents or siblings?"

"Well, both of my parents are still alive, and I only have one brother. He is five years older than me."

"And is he in the military?"

"No, but there is currently no draft in America. Because he is an only son, I'm not sure they could draft him."

Fabien didn't ask her any more questions, and they sat quietly as he drove. She was enjoying the wind in her hair from the open windows. It all seemed so peaceful here; it was hard to believe that there was a war so close to them. Fabien slowed down and turned onto a dirt road.

"How far out do you live from town?"

"About two kilometers on the main road and another half kilometer on this road."

He was referring to the dirt road they were now traveling down. Eva was unsure how far that was, and she knew Fabien would not know it in miles. So she still did not know how close they were to the house, but she kept it to herself.

At the end of the dirt road was a small house set in a green pasture with a barn off to its side, but there were no other buildings for as far as she could see. Near the back of the house were two clotheslines, one with white sheets blowing in the breeze. A girl was hanging pants, shirts, and dresses on the other one. When they got closer, the girl stopped and looked over in their direction. She turned her head to the house and yelled something. Soon, another girl ran outside to watch the truck approach. Fabien pulled in front of the house, and the little girl who came out ran to the driver's side.

"Papa, is that her?" she asked in a sweet little voice.

"It is, puppy," he said to her in French.

Eva opened her door and stepped out of the truck, and the girl ran around the front and stopped just on the other side of the door.

The girl's blue eyes pierced into Eva's, with her dark brown curls falling over her peachy cheeks that contrasted with her milky skin. Her face was sprinkled with freckles, mainly across her nose and the tops of her cheeks, making her look like one of those porcelain dolls. She wore a white shift dress with a blue belt tied into a bow at the back and long socks that had been pushed all the way down to her brown laced shoes. They were common for little girls at that time. Her entire outfit was.

She extended her hand. "My name is Sabina. What is yours?" she asked in her tiny voice.

"My name is Eva." She shook the girl's outreached hand.

The girl covered her mouth and chuckled. "Papa, she sounds funny."

"Be nice, Sabina," he said to her in a stern voice but smiled in spite of himself.

"Where do you come from?" she asked.

"I am from America. It is a country way across the ocean from here. Didn't your dad tell you that?"

"Nooo," she said, intentionally drawing the word out. "He didn't tell me anything but that a woman would come and live with us. And I know where America is. I go to school," she said in a matter-of-fact tone.

"Aren't you a smart little girl then," Eva said.

The girl stood still and looked up at her, focusing intently on her face. "You are very pretty. Papa didn't tell me that either."

Eva's face turned a light shade of pink.

"Off with you now, you little fox," her dad said, waving her away.

As Sabina ran to the house, the other girl had been watching the entire time and had a smile on her face. When Eva glanced in her direction, she stopped smiling and looked away, back to the laundry.

"I am so sorry about that. She speaks without thinking," he said as he retrieved her luggage from the bed of the truck.

"No, no, it's fine, really. I used to work with children. I know they speak their mind."

"Come, and I will show you your room."

She followed him in through the front door. When Eva entered, he could see just how small of a house it was. The room they were standing in was a tiny kitchen. It only had a stove, a counter, and a sink. To the left was a window just above the sink, and a table stood in the middle. The floor was made of untreated wood that had aged over time, especially where the sun would shine through the window. Behind the table was a fireplace and a narrow hallway leading to the back of the house. She thought the bedrooms must be down the hall because there was nowhere else they could be.

"This way," he said.

She followed him down the narrow hall. There were three doors on the right and one at the end of the hall.

"Are these all the bedrooms?"

Fabien nodded his head.

"It must be cramped for you guys as it is! I didn't know your home was this small. I would not have agreed to let you take me in if I'd known. I cannot take one of your bedrooms."

"It is not a problem. The girls will share a room."

"Share a room. I don't want to make them do that."

"Please, it is my pleasure."

"I really wouldn't mind staying in the barn."

"No, I won't put a lady in the barn."

She felt defeated. She did not want to impose or put any of them out, but she could tell that Fabien would not budge. He carried her bags to the first room and set them at the end of a twin bed. She looked around the room, and it, too, was small. It had a single window in the middle of the outer wall and a twin bed pushed up against both of the sidewalls. There were two dressers, one in each of the corners near the door, one for each bed. The beds were carved in a simple design and looked hand-carved, and the quilts on the beds were not done with a sewing machine. They were simple but pretty, with tiny white and purple flowers sown into them.

"If there are two beds in this room, I don't need it to myself. One of the girls can share it with me. Let Brigitte have a room to herself."

"I thought you should have your privacy."

"I don't need privacy to sleep. I would be happy to share it with one of them."

"Very well, I will speak with them."

She was unpacking her things and putting her clothes in the dresser when the scent of what smelled like stew flooded her nostrils. She peeked her head around the corner and saw Brigitte in the kitchen, standing over a pot on the stove.

She walked into the kitchen. "I can help you with that."

"It is almost done," Brigitte answered.

"I'm sorry I didn't introduce myself earlier. I'm Eva."

The girl stood holding a dishtowel but made no attempt to approach her. "I am Brigitte. It is nice to make your acquaintance."

She did not remind Eva at all of her younger sister. Sabina was so happy and full of life. She could now see what Fabien was talking about. Sabina had a sparkle in her eyes, a skip in her walk, and a smile like the sun. All Eva could see was sadness in Brigitte's eyes, and there was an ashy undertone to her complexion that added to her shallow features, not the rosy cheeks like her sister.

"What are you making?" Eva asked, not sure what else to say.

"It is potato and carrot stew with some rabbit that Father caught yesterday."

"It sounds delicious. And your father and sister, where are they?"

"Sabina is fetching milk from the barn, and father is washing up for dinner."

"I am imposing on your hospitality. The least I can do is set the table."

"If you like, the dishes are in there," Brigitte said. She nodded with her chin in the direction of a china cabinet in the corner just to the left of the front door.

Eva had somehow missed it when she came in. She took the simple white porcelain dishes from the cabinet and sat a placement on the table for four. She filled the bowls with stew as Brigitte went to tell Sabina and Fabien that dinner was ready.

Eva sat at the end of the table across from Fabien as everyone ate their dinner in silence. When she was serving the stew, she paid close attention to how much food she put in her bowl, knowing they were poor and could hardly afford to feed themselves.

"Papa, you said that one of us can share the room with Miss Abrams. Can I please?"

"It is up to Miss Abrams which one of you gets to share the room with her."

Sabina looked at Eva, her pleading eyes burning into hers.

"I suppose you can, on two conditions."

Sabina's eyes grew wide. "What conditions?"

"That you call me Eva, and we tell each other stories. I want to hear all about those fun places you go to every day; you cannot just share it with the cows."

Sabina smiled. "I will tell you all about them, promise. I go on treasure hunts in pirate ships, visit princesses in castles, and fight giant monsters in the sea."

"My goodness, your life sounds so much more exciting than mine." She laughed. She looked at Fabien. "Do you know where I can buy a bike? It will be so much faster than walking to town every time," Eva asked.

"I can take you in the morning. I am going to town anyway to sell some of the crops and hopefully buy a pig and a couple more chickens to help hold us over this winter."

"Did they tell you that I will give you some money each month?"

"They did." He took a bite of his stew without looking at her.

She was happy to pay. It was kind of them to take her in. She knew it must be a huge inconvenience and a burden on them.

The next morning, they left for town after the sun was up, with the truck's bed full of potatoes, carrots, and onions.

Fabien pulled in front of a shop. “This is the general store. They should have some bikes in the back. I will go sell my load; it rarely takes long, so I should be here to pick you up in half an hour.”

“I will just wait out front.”

She got out of the truck, and Fabien drove away. She entered the store, and a bell at the top of the door rang when she opened it. An older woman stood up from behind the counter and looked in her direction as she closed the door.

“Bonjour,” the woman said.

“Bonjour. Do you sell bikes here?”

The woman raised an eye when Eva spoke. She was probably not used to seeing foreigners in a town of this size, especially now that there was a war. “I have two in the back. You are welcome to go look at them.”

Eva thanked her and quickly headed to the back of the store, feeling a little uncomfortable by the way the woman was staring at her. When she reached the back of the store, she could see two bikes leaning against the wall. They were the same in shape, and both had a basket on the front, the only difference being the color. One was blue and the other one white. She decided she would take the blue bike, so she pushed it to the front of the store.

“I will take this one. How much do I owe you?”

“It is fifteen,” she said, still giving Eva the same piercing look she gave her when they first spoke.

Eva paid her the money and pushed the bike outside to wait for Fabien. She looked at her watch and still had almost twenty minutes. *I might as well ride the bike up the street and back to see how good it is. I don’t have anything else to do,* she thought. She pulled her dress up a little so that she could straddle the bike, but getting on was not as easy as she had hoped it would be. *Why do they think women need to wear dresses, especially when doing things like this? It's ridiculous.* Once she finally managed to mount the bike, she started peddling it slowly, ensuring that her dress did not get caught in the chain. A few people outside glanced in her direction as she rode by, their faces set in neutral expressions, but otherwise did not seem overly interested in her as she rode up and down the narrow, winding streets. She was glad of this after her exchange with the woman in the store.

The feeling of fall was heavy in the air as she rode, but the still-warm breeze caressed her face as the lazy sun hung low in the sky, though it was only midday. It was unusually hot for mid-September, but she knew it would not last. She would take advantage of the nice weather as often as she could and go for walks in the fields near the house. She wanted to pick some flowers that grew there for her and Sabina's room and the kitchen table before they were all but dead from the first frost. *I better turn around and go back to the store and wait for Fabien,* she thought, turning her bike around.

Chapter Ten

May 3rd, 1940

She sat on her bed writing the usual letters, one to her parents, her brother Thomas, and one to Jenny. By the time she finished the letter to Jenny, she was too tired to write anymore. She would just have to write Jon's in the morning. The holidays and winter were now behind them, and it was the loneliest Christmas and longest winter that Eva could remember. She had never spent Christmas away from her family before. The Dubois were kind people, and she got them all a gift and enjoyed spending the holidays with them, but it still wasn't the same. She missed her family so much! Christmas Eve was the first time she cried since arriving here at the farm. She didn't want to make anyone feel bad, so she tried her best to act happy while around them. It wasn't until the house was dark and silent and Sabina was asleep that she finally let the tears flow. Eva was alone that night with her thoughts and could no longer keep them back, nor did she want to. She was relieved when the holidays were over.

Eva got up to write Jon a letter before Sabina woke that morning.

Jon,
I was so happy when I received your letter; it has been so long since I had heard from you. I understand you needed to go back and take care of some things, and I got on just fine here without you, but it's always nice to hear from a familiar voice. I know they don't always tell you the details about my work at FSC, so I will fill you in on the latest news. There haven't been as many people that needed my help over the winter, probably because of the cold weather and the snow, making escapes more difficult. Since I have been here, I have helped five families and one individual. I know that doesn't sound like a lot, but sometimes it takes so long to get the paperwork needed for some of them that the number I quoted you is actually good progress.

The holidays were fun, and the children liked the gifts I got them. I was glad you sent some money along with your letter; the FSC does not pay much, as you are aware. I'm pleased that you got a different position with them than we initially thought. I know it is rewarding for you to help the refugees make it to the neutral European countries, America, Canada, and the UK. I have written letters to my family, though it was so hard writing them while trying to keep track of all the things I can't talk about. I know they must be concerned about me. I made sure to let them know I was OK and not to worry, that hopefully, soon, I would come home to visit. And I remember it is now the beginning of May, and the war will finally come to France and soon to my front door. Thanks all the same, though, for reminding me! I will leave here soon, hopefully in the next few days.

I have one more family that I need to help before I go. A single mother of two and her brother are stuck close to the Belgium border. They had to leave in such a hurry that they didn't have time to get their IDs from the house or any of their belongings before they fled. The woman was able to call and tell them she left with only her family. I received a letter from the FSC yesterday notifying me of the family and their situation. I am going to Belgium and retrieving some of their things, some clothing for them, and money they have hidden at the house, basically the essentials. It should be a fairly quick in-and-out job; they live on a farm just outside a village near the border. I will go to Belgium on foot through the forest to keep a low profile, enter the house after dark, and retrieve their things. I will keep the same low profile on the return trip and travel on foot. It will be sad to leave La Chapelle. I have made so many friends here, but it will be nice to see my family and home again. I should see you in less than a week. Take care, Jon, and I'll see you soon.

-Eva

She folded the letter and put it in the envelope with the other three, and then Fabien would mail it while she was in Belgium.

She had done extra work around the farm to help Fabien as much as possible before it was time for her to leave. They had all gotten so used to her being there and helping with the chores, and she understood it would be hard for them to adjust to her being gone for the first few weeks.

Eva grabbed her jacket, purse, and pillowcase to carry the people's belongings in and met Fabien in the kitchen. It was evening now, and the sun was setting. It was almost time for them to go. Fabien was going to drive her to the border of Belgium, which was not far, and she would then walk the rest of the way.

"I have a letter that needs to be mailed. Would you please drop it off for me tomorrow?" Eva had held onto the letter all day, waiting to give it to Fabien.

"I will do it first thing in the morning," he promised.

Eva turned to say bye to the girls and looked at Brigitte.

"Take care of yourself, Eva. I think you are so brave for doing this," Brigitte said.

"Thank you, Brigitte, but I don't feel brave right now." She held her hands out in front of her. "Look, my hands are shaking."

"I know you will be all right, and it is completely normal for you to be afraid. The fact that you are still going, even though it scares you, says a lot," Brigitte said with a slight smile, pulling Eva into a gentle embrace.

"Thank you for all of your kindness," Eva said after she released her.

"It has been our pleasure," Fabien said.

She turned to Sabina and opened her arms. Sabina ran into them, and Eva closed them tight around her.

"I will miss you so much. Please return to us, Eva!"

Eva leaned back to look at her face. Tears were streaming down her cheeks. She squatted to Sabina's height and put a hand on each side of her face. "I promise you, Sabina, I will return. I could never go long without seeing this sweet face and hearing about all of your adventures." She was having a hard time not crying herself. She could hear the quiver in her own voice when she spoke but hoped no one else could. She hugged Sabina again and held on tight before finally letting her go.

"We really have to go now," Fabien said.

She looked at him. "I know, and I will see you all in a few days."

She followed Fabien to the truck and handed him the letter after they were in; he laid it on the seat between them.

"I have never seen my girls take to anyone as they have with you. They have been happier since you have arrived, even Brigitte."

"You think so? I guess it's not as easy for me to see as it is for you."

"I see it, and I will be forever grateful to you."

"I'm glad that I made a difference in their lives."

Eva was touched. She had not known that her being there would have such a significant impact on them as well as herself. What she did know was that they had been such a blessing in her life, and them just being there made the long winter more bearable.

Fabien pulled off the road into an empty field and turned off the headlights as he drove. The truck bounced around so much that Eva had to put a hand on the dash to steady herself.

"I am sorry for the roughness, but this is the safest way. I don't want to be spotted on the road or seen letting you out."

"There is no need to apologize. I know you are taking a risk by bringing me here."

He stopped the truck when they reached the edge of the forest, where it met the field.

"Here." He held his hand out to her, and in his palm was a compass.

Eva took it out of his hand and looked at it. "I didn't even think to bring a compass."

"I know. That is why I brought mine. I knew you would need one. Here is a paper with directions back to the house. The letter you received said what side of the town the farm was on. I sat down last night and figured out the directions from where we are now to their farm and back. I doubt it is perfect, but it will be better than just wandering around in the dark."

"You read my letter?" she said, surprised and a little upset. No one had ever violated her privacy like that before.

"I'm sorry, but yes, I did. It was obvious to me that it was more complicated than just dropping you off at the forest's edge. I thought about how you would find the farm and then find your way back. That is never as simple as it sounds, so I looked at the letter to see what information and instructions they gave you if any at all."

"Thank you for doing that for me, but you could have just asked, and I would have let you read it."

"I wasn't sure. I didn't want you to think that I didn't think of you as capable."

"I don't think that at all. I'm glad that you saw what it said. You have thought of things I would not have until I was in the woods, like the compass."

"You never struck me as someone familiar with the outdoors or advanced beyond the normal survival skills."

"I've been camping…" she said, accusation in her voice.

"I believe you have. We better get to it. The longer we sit here, the higher our chances are of being seen."

"I know." She put the compass on the paper and folded it around it, sticking them in her pocket.

"Keep due east, and you should find it. It will most likely take you two hours on foot to get there, providing you don't run into any kind of trouble or stop often."

She nodded her head in response but wasn't sure he saw it in the dark. Her mouth was parched, and her palms were cold and sweaty.

They got out of the truck, and he walked with her to the forest's edge.

"Now remember, try not to use your flashlight if you can help it. It will only make you easier to spot. I know you will have to move slower without it, but it's best this way. Safer."

She swallowed hard. "Just use it in the house–I remember."

"Find due east on the compass," he said, nodding to her hand.

"Oh, I put it in my pocket." She pulled out the compass, unfolded the paper from around it, then turned to face the trees. "Due east is the same thing as true east, right?"

Uncertainty was apparent in her voice, causing him to crack a small smile at the corner of his mouth. "Yes, due east is the same thing as true east."

"Then due east from where I am standing would take me left at that angle into the forest." She held up her arm to line it up with where the compass was pointing.

"Good. OK, that is the way you want to go. And remember to keep checking the compass to make sure that you do not get off track."

The fear was creeping in. Her hands were shaking, and her legs felt weak like she had already run for miles.

He leaned down and gave her a hug. "You will be just fine. I know you feel scared, but you are braver than you think."

A tear ran down her cheek, and her throat felt like it was closing shut. Walking in the woods at night alone terrified her, but that wasn't even the scariest part. The dark woods were safer than what potentially lay on the other side; the woods offered her protection from the Germans.

"Go," he said. "It'll be fine."

She turned away from him and faced the woods. Slowly, her feet began to move and carried her to the perimeter of the forest. She looked back and could still see Fabien standing there. It somehow comforted her. She kept glancing back until she could no longer see him. When he finally disappeared into the night, she stopped walking. Her breathing increased, and she had the urge to run back to where she could see him, but of course, she knew that would be counterproductive. She took a deep breath. *OK, one foot in front of the other, I can do this. I knew I would be doing it alone.* She began walking again, feeling with each foot when she took a step so that she didn't trip. She couldn't see her feet as they moved and could hardly see her hands in front of her. *This isn't so bad. It was all in my head,* she told herself as she continued walking, still cautiously moving one foot in front of the other and holding her hands out to feel for trees or tall underbrush. Behind her, she heard rustling, which made her jump. She turned to look where she thought the sound came from and stared into the darkness. She stood still, not moving so much as a finger, but her breath came loudly. It was deafening in her ears. The bush rustled again, and she involuntarily took a step back, bumping into a tree, making her jump. Something emerged from a bush into the leaves, crunching them as it walked. The sound it made indicated it was something small, like a rabbit. *For heaven's sake, Eva, pull yourself together.* Although she knew she had overreacted, she continued to listen for more sounds as she moved through the trees, occasionally stopping to check her compass with her flashlight. She was not sure why being in the woods alone at night scared her so much, but the dark had for a long time, ever since she was little. Maybe it was the Blair Witch Project she watched at a friend's house while in middle school that started her fear of being in the woods at night, but being afraid of the dark scared her even as a young child. No matter the reason, she wished so badly that someone was with her right now.

She had walked for almost two hours when she heard sounds that were not coming from the forest behind her, so she stopped walking and listened. The sounds that were echoing through the trees were of people talking and the roar of engines. She hunched over a little, walking slower than she had been, and continued in the same direction. As she moved, the voices grew louder, although she could not see any movement. The trees were still blocking the headlights of the vehicles. She continued to move carefully forward until she could finally see headlights through the trees. She squatted down behind a single tree and tried to make out what was going on. There was more talking, and then someone shouted. This time, it was loud enough for her to hear that they were speaking in German. She gasped and leaned back too far, falling on her butt. *Oh my God, they are German. They are at the house. Why are they at the house? Are they searching it?* she thought. She did not get up but continued to sit in the same spot she had fallen, both hands on the ground supporting her. She was not sure what to do next. If the Germans had found the money and the IDs and taken them, the trip would have been for nothing. She knew that right now, there was nothing she could do but hide and wait for them to leave, hoping they did not find what she had come for.

She stood up, still hiding behind the tree, and brushed the dirt off her hands and the back of her pants. Then she knelt again to watch them. She could not quite make out what they were doing or saying because she was still too far away, but she was not about to move any closer.

They were going in and out of the house and the barn; the Germans made sure they did not miss anything. After twenty minutes of waiting, she saw them load up into two trucks and one car. They turned the vehicles around and headed down the only road that led to the farmhouse.

Even though the lights were no longer visible, Eva didn't move, still too afraid to step out of the trees. All the worst-case scenarios were running through her head, but she knew she could not sit there all night. The realization that the Germans had made it to this Belgian village meant they would be in France soon.

She needed to hurry, because there was no time to waste. She walked until she was out of the trees, then ran as fast as she could without tripping. She stopped when she reached the front door of the house, which had been left open by the Germans. She listened for any sounds from inside, but the only thing she could hear was the wind blowing through the trees. She reached in her bag and retrieved the flashlight, then switched it on. She knew where the IDs should be, in a dresser drawer in the master bedroom, and the money should be under the first-floor board to the right of the fireplace on the main floor. The Schullers had said where to find everything.

Eva stepped in through the open door, and the floorboards creaked beneath her feet. She shined the flashlight around to see which way she needed to go and noticed that none of the furniture was in its proper place. It was scattered around the living room, and the pictures that were once on the walls were now broken on the floor. She shined the flashlight around the room and saw a flight of stairs to the left of the living room. She first walked over to the fireplace and knelt on the floor, laying the flashlight beside her. She took ahold of the floorboard and pulled on it, but it didn't give.

"Crap."

She pulled on it again until her fingers slipped off, then picked up her flashlight and stood up, looking around for the kitchen.

On the other side of the living room was an open doorway that looked like it could lead to the kitchen, so she shined the light into the room. Chairs were lying on the floor there, too, along with broken dishes, pans, and a table turned on its side.

She walked up to the doorway and stuck her head through; they had trashed the entire kitchen, too, just like the other room. She pointed the light on the floor to see if she could find a knife because they had dumped all the silverware from the drawers onto the floor. Near the table was a butter knife.

"That will do."

She grabbed it and hurried back to the fireplace. She laid the flashlight back on the floor next to her and used the knife to pry at the board. After a few seconds of prying, she wondered if the blade was going to break because it was bending, and the board did not seem like it was going to give. She pried harder, and the board made a crack sound and then popped up, pieces of it splintering. She flinched, then let out a sigh of relief as she moved the board to the side and picked the flashlight up off the floor. She looked in the hole under the floor, and at the bottom was a brown bag sitting in the dirt, covered in dust. She reached down, pulled it up, untied the string, and peered inside. It was full of money and jewelry. She tied the bag up again and put it in the pillowcase before heading to the stairs.

This was taking more time than she liked. "OK, bedrooms, bedrooms…" she mouthed, looking around, but she didn't see any bedrooms on the main floor. She ran up the stairs and stopped at the top. All the doors were already opened, just like the front door. She walked down the hall, looking through the open doors as she passed. The first doorway she looked through was a walk-in linen closet with towels and sheets unfolded on the floor. She went to the next room and saw an overturned bed and dresser with the clothes from it strewn all over the room like they had been thrown. She could see that they were men's clothes and knew she had the correct room. She dropped the pillowcase that was over her shoulder and went to collect some clothes for the man. It was hard to find the things she needed because of the state of the room.

While she looked through the clothes for what she needed, she also looked for the IDs. After picking up what felt like everything on the floor, she found their IDs tied together, stuck in a roll of socks. She hurried and stuffed them in her purse and the clothes in the pillowcase, then went to the next two rooms and gathered some clothes for the woman and the two children.

Now that she had gotten everything she had come for, it was time to head back. She left the bedroom and went back the way she came. Just as she reached the stairs, the sound of engines echoed outside.

"Oh, no! No, no, no, no, no!"

She took two steps at a time down the stairs and jumped onto the floor when there were only three steps left. She almost fell when she hit the floor and had to grab onto the nearest wall. She had everything she came for and didn't want to wait around and see who was coming. As soon as she got her balance, she bolted out the front door, jumped off the porch, landed solidly on her feet, and ran for the trees. She was scared and so focused on running that she didn't even look in the direction of the lights and hardly noticed that they passed over her as she crossed the road. She wasn't about to stop. Getting to the woods as soon as possible was all she could think about right now.

Eva ran until she was in the forest, then stopped to catch her breath. She bent down and put her hands on her knees, panting. She couldn't remember the last time she had run that hard. She was still trying to catch her breath when she heard doors closing and distant voices. Quickly, she stood up and turned around. She could barely see the car and the people standing around it through the trees.

"Sie finden," a man shouted.

She panicked; they had seen her, there was no wondering anymore. She hoped they hadn't seen her running across the road, but now she knew they had. To run was all she could do now. She picked up the pillowcase and sprinted deeper into the woods, not knowing what direction she was running in. The only thing going through her mind was getting as far from the Germans as possible. Eventually, she would have to stop and look at her compass, but she did not know when that would be. She could hear other people's footsteps moving fast behind her, though somewhat far away.

Her heart was beating in her head, her lungs burned, and the air was hard to take in, even though her breathing was heavy and fast. She didn't stop running until she could no longer hear the people behind her. When everything was silent, and she realized she was finally alone, she plopped down on the dirt and cried as she gasped for air. When she regained her composure, she got the compass and flashlight out of her bag and tried to find due west. It didn't take long, though, before she realized it was not due west she had been running in all this time. She was looking in the direction she had been running, and the compass said it was almost straight north. She turned the light off and let her hand drop to her lap as she looked around the dark forest, only seeing the silhouette of trees from the little light the partially covered moon gave.

Eva had no idea now where she was or how far north she had run. She turned the flashlight back on and held the compass up again to find due west. "I can still go that direction; please be there, Fabien! I don't want to be lost out here." She could hardly see the compass between the tears and her shaking hand. She reached up, wiped her eyes and nose with the sleeves of her jacket, and sniffed as a child would. She put the flashlight and compass back in her bag and stood up. She started walking in the direction that should be west; she did not know where it would put her, only that it wouldn't be in the same field.

Eva was feeling disoriented by the forest and the darkness; they were the only things she had seen for hours. The sun was now coming up behind her, so she knew she was at least walking west, but she still didn't know where she was. Finally, she stopped and sat on a rock to rest; she hadn't taken a break since finding which direction was west. Eva knew that it only took her about two hours to reach the house, and she had now been walking the rest of the night, which would have to be over four hours because the sun was now rising. She didn't even know if she was still in Belgium anymore. Her stomach rumbled. She was suddenly aware of her hunger and thirst and how tired she was. She had to keep moving, but if she did not find someone or a town soon, she might die in these woods. She stood up, determined to keep moving, but her legs felt like Jell-O.

Eva had walked what felt like a hundred miles when she heard dogs barking in the distance. She smiled in relief, but it quickly faded when the thought occurred to her that the dogs might belong to German soldiers. She listened, but the sound of barking never got any closer. Eva was resolved now; she knew that she had to risk it, at least to see who it was. She had about a fifty-fifty chance of it being someone other than the Germans, which was better than her odds if she stayed in the woods. The sound came down the hill from where she was. Maybe if she made it to the base, she could see where the barking came from.

She started down the slope, stepping over rocks and fallen limbs, when she heard the barking again. She looked up in the direction the barking was coming from when the tip of her boot hit a rock that was covered by tall grass. She could see the ground rushing toward her and instinctively put her hands out to brace for the fall. There was a cracking sound as she hit the dirt, followed instantly by a sharp pain that ran from her left hand up to her left shoulder. She screamed in pain and immediately rolled onto her back and grabbed her left hand with her right. Her wrist was already swelling, and the skin was turning a bluish color. The pain was excruciating. Besides the pain radiating up her arm, the second thing she noticed was the succession of chills and waves of nausea. She had goosebumps even though she was sweating, most likely caused by the feeling that she was going to vomit.

The barking was getting closer. If they did not know she was here before, they did now. She tried to stand up, but the pain from the movement made her cry out again, and the nauseous feeling increased, followed by an onset of dizziness. She sat still, holding her wrist, hoping the feeling would pass. *Do I just let them find me, or do I try to run?* Her arm and hand hurt so badly she could hardly think. There was no way she would make it very far or very quickly.

A dog ran up to her out of the trees and started sniffing her legs. She could hear a person approaching just out of view from the same direction the dog had come from. She now knew that running wasn't even an option. That choice had now passed. She looked in the direction of the noise and saw an old man with a second dog by his side approaching. He had white hair and eyebrows that went with his wrinkly face and hands. It looked as though he had spent many years outside in the sun. He was wearing worn farmer's clothing and walked with a heavy limp. He looked at her cautiously as he got nearer.

"Who are you, and why are you on my land?" he asked with a raspy voice in French.

Eva had to be cautious and knew the importance of what she said; it was never clear who would rat to the Germans and who wouldn't. "I got lost. I don't even know where I am. I tripped on a rock, and I think I broke my wrist."

He tilted his head slightly. "You are not French?"

"No, I am not."

"Where do you come from?" he asked, still looking at her like she was a wild animal that might need to be put down at any moment.

"I'm American."

"Why is an American girl alone in the woods, in Belgium, in the middle of a war?"

"Please, sir. If you help me, I will tell you why I'm in the woods." Her eyes were tearing up now from the pain. Injured and frightened, she said what she thought he wanted to hear; she needed his help and had to do whatever it took to get it, or she would die out here, that she was sure of.

He pursed his lips. "Right, let's get you up." He limped to her side and bent down with an outreached hand to help pull her up. He took her by her good arm and pulled as she used her legs to help.

She flinched from the pain. "Ow, oh God, that hurts!" she said in English, not caring if he understood what she said. The tears spilled over and ran down her cheeks. The dogs were barking as the man helped her to her feet.

"Don't mind them. They won't bite. They are just curious who you are," he told her.

With great difficulty, they began making their way down the hill, but with her arm and his limp, they didn't move very quickly. When they reached the base of the hill, the trees started to clear, and she could see an enormous field. Near the edge of the trees, on the far side, was a small house and an even smaller barn.

Oh goodness, we have to cross over that? she thought. She wasn't sure if she would make it to the other side or not but doubted that the old man could carry her if she were to pass out or collapse. *I only need to make it to the house,* she told herself.

They made their way through the field, and when they got close to the house, the old man yelled to someone inside.

"Helen, I need your help. Come out here, please."

An older woman with a loose gray bun on the top of her head and a simple light blue dress with a white apron over it appeared behind a screen door. She was not as wrinkled as the man, but the years had not been kind to her either.

"Oh my," she said as she hurried out of the house to help them. She put her arm on the other side of Eva's waist, and they both helped her into the house. "Let's put her on the bed in the spare room," the woman said.

"Right," the man said in response.

They helped her to a room at the back of the house and laid her on a fluffy bed that looked like it was made of feathers.

"Is her hand broken?" the woman asked, looking at the man and not Eva.

"I believe so," he said.

The woman sat on the bed, facing Eva. "I need to look at your hand. You need to let go of it."

She reached out and lightly took hold of her arm. It scared Eva to have someone touch it. She was keeping it still but knew that the woman was going to move it. If it hurt this much already, she could only imagine what it would feel like when she did.

"It's OK," she said to Eva, still holding onto her arm, her voice a little softer this time.

Eva slowly let go of her wrist, and the woman supported her arm with one hand as she held Eva's hand in her other.

"Oh my, it is swollen. Can you move it?" She looked from Eva's hand to her face.

"I haven't tried."

When the woman heard Eva speak, she looked over at the man.

"She is American," he said. "At least that is what she told me. I said we can talk after her arm is fixed."

The woman looked back down at Eva's hand. "I'm going to try and move it now. I need to see how extensive the damage is."

"OK," Eva said, clenching her teeth together to brace for the pain.

The woman slowly started moving her hand upward.

"Oww, that hurts, it hurts, please stop!" Eva could feel the sweat beading on her forehead and neck.

The woman stopped, then reached for Eva's wrist and squeezed it lightly. Eva winced.

"It is broken, but I can't tell how badly yet. I won't know until the swelling goes down. We can put some splints on it for now, but you need to see a doctor."

"A doctor… I don't even know where I am." Eva's words were shaky as she spoke.

"The nearest town to us is Bouillon," the woman said.

"Is that in Belgium?"

The woman looked up at the man again, then back to Eva. "It is."

"I live in La Chapelle, in France. I need to get back there."

"France—oh, you cannot go back there right now, not with your arm the way it is. In any case, the Germans are already headed toward the area of La Chapelle. They will be there in a matter of days. They already came through Bouillon two days ago. You couldn't travel as fast as them with your arm the way it is and on foot, probably not even if it wasn't broken."

Panic from the possible future that awaited settled in her stomach. "You don't understand. I have to get back; I have to get there before the Germans do."

"You will never make it there before them. It's too late for that now. You would be on foot, they have a head start on you, and they are in vehicles," the man said, reiterating what the woman said.

The woman glanced at him. "Go get the stuff we need for her arm, and bring some of your laudanum."

He turned and disappeared through the doorway.

"We are going to put some splints on your wrist while we wait for the swelling to go down, and when it does, you will need a cast. Abraham and I will take you into town in a few days after the swelling has gone down to see a doctor."

"No, I told you, I can't stay here that long. Please, just put the splint on, and I will be on my way."

"You are going to walk all the way to La Chapelle and in your condition?" Helen asked, her tone disbelieving. "You look like you would fall over if you even tried to stand. Your face has lost its color and is pale, probably from dehydration, lack of food, and the shock of what happened."

"Do you have a car then?"

"I do, but we will not drive you to La Chapelle now, not with the Germans advancing in that direction."

Eva did not have enough energy to argue the point any farther with the woman, even though she wanted to. She felt like crying but knew that it wouldn't help the situation.

Abraham returned with two wooden splints, some long white strips of material, and a dark brown glass bottle. He set them on the nightstand next to Helen. She reached for the bottle and pulled out the cork.

"Here, drink some of this, about three large gulps."

"What is it?" Eva eyed the bottle suspiciously.

"It's medicine to help with the pain. It tastes like shit, but it's better than feeling everything," the man told her. "I used it when I hurt my leg in the field over the winter."

Eva took the bottle and held it up to her mouth for a second before taking one large gulp of it. She swallowed, and the liquid went down her throat, making her cough. "It's so bitter."

"Like I said, tastes like shit."

Eva took two more large gulps of it quickly and handed the bottle back to the woman. Helen took it, put the cork back in, and laid it on the bed.

Eva could still taste the bitterness in her mouth as it burned her throat. "Do you have some water?"

Abraham turned around and disappeared for a minute, then returned with a glass of water. He handed it to Eva, and she drank the water without stopping until it was almost gone, then took a breath before finishing the rest.

"I haven't had water in over a day."

Helen took the cup from her and set it on the nightstand by the bed. "I can tell. We will give you some more later after we have set your wrist, and when you feel better, I'll bring you some food."

She put Eva's arm on her leg, and the man came close to the bed, put a wooden splint on each side of Eva's wrist, and held them there. Helen picked up one of the long white pieces of cloth and slid it under Eva's arm towards her elbow. She wrapped it around several times and pulled until the wood was against Eva's arm.

She looked up at Eva. "I'm going to tie it now. This is where it's going to get painful."

Eva was starting to feel the effects of the medicine. Her head was swimming, and her eyelids felt like lead. It was becoming harder to process what was happening and what the woman was saying, and she was itching all over. She slowly nodded her head; it seemed like it took so much concentration and effort just to do that.

Helen pulled the string tight around the wooden splints and tied it. Eva was clenching her teeth together so hard that her jaw hurt, but she didn't scream. Helen then reached for the second string, slid it under her arm in the middle, and repeated the process. The second one hurt more than the first, and Eva let out a yelp. Helen reached for the last string and wrapped it around her wrist, paused for a second, then pulled it tight and tied it off. This time, it was more than Eva could take. She couldn't hold back by clamping her jaw any longer. She screamed loudly and started crying, then reached with her other hand and tried to untie the string around her wrist.

"Take it off. This one hurts too much," she said through the tears as she fumbled with the string.

Helen grabbed her hand. "No, don't take that off. Abraham, grab the laudanum. What we gave her obviously wasn't enough."

Abraham got the bottle from the bed, pulled the cork out, and then put it to Eva's mouth. "Take another swallow, and it will take the rest of that pain away."

With a brief hesitation, Eva opened her mouth, and he poured some in. It felt like more than she had taken the first time. She swallowed, then rubbed her tongue on the roof of her mouth, thinking how awful it tasted and how dry her mouth was.

"Lie down," Helen told her.

"But I can't. I don't know how." Her words were slurred, and Helen knew she didn't know what she was saying.

"Yes, you can. Lay down right here, and I'll help you."

Eva's eyes were closed, even though she was still sitting up.

"No, the man's there," she said weakly.

"Let's lie her down. She's out of it," Helen instructed.

Abraham pulled the blankets out from under her. Then they scooted Eva down on the bed, gently laid her on her back with her head on the pillow, and covered her up with the blankets.□

Chapter Eleven

Eva opened her eyes and looked around the room. *Where am I?* The memory of running from the Germans began to flood back. *Oh God, they must have caught me.* She turned her head to the right and could see different colors dancing on the wall like a disco ball, and standing just outside the window was Kevin, looking in at her. "Kevin, what are you doing here?" she whispered, lifting her head off the pillow. "Why did you follow me to Belgium? How did you even get here? Don't you know there is a war? Go back, Kevin. You have to go back to Utah."

He said nothing; he only continued staring at her through the window.

"Do you know what's happening? Do you know why I'm here? Kevin, say something. Why do you just stand there?" She looked away from the window to the bedroom door to her left. Her mom was standing in the doorway, looking at her. "Mom, why are you here? Tell Kevin to go home."

"You, stupid girl, what have you done? You should have never come here. Who is going to save you now?" Her voice rose in pitch with the word ‘now.’ “You should have listened to me. I told you this was a bad idea. I told you not to come!” Her mom started laughing. “You are going to die here, and no one is going to miss you.” Her voice was deep and sinister. She shook her head slowly from side to side as her eyes focused on Eva.

“Mom, no, why are you saying these things? Why are you being so mean?” She looked back to her right, and Kevin was now standing beside her bed. “Kevin, how did you get inside? Did you come in through the window? I told you already. You can’t be here.”

He looked down at her as he stood by the bed. His expression turned to anger, and he slapped her across the face with the back of his hand.

She screamed and put her hands in front of her face to shield it from another blow. “Kevin, no, you said you would never hit me again. You promised.”

Helen and Abraham came into the room to see what was happening.

“Oh my, she has been moving her arm.” Helen took Eva’s arms and laid them back at her side.

“I think she’s hallucinating, but I can’t tell because I don’t understand what the hell she is saying,” Abraham said.

They stayed in her room for a while to make sure she didn’t move. After half an hour of her laying still, they were convinced she would probably stay that way for the rest of the night, so they left her room and returned to their own.

Eva could see the light through her eyelids and slowly opened them. At first, everything was blurry, but after a minute, her eyes adjusted, and she was staring at the ceiling. She tried to remember where she was and what had happened, but nothing was coming to her. With her right arm, she reached over and touched her left arm; her hand slid over the wooden splints that were keeping her wrist from moving. The events of the day before slowly started coming back to her. She could remember everything up to the moment the woman put the splints on her arm, but not much past that, just a few fragments of memory. She continued to lie in bed, looking at the ceiling, trying to recall what happened after that, but still nothing. She decided to try and sit up. She pushed the covers down to her waist, but she immediately noticed the pain as soon as she started moving her arm.

"I thought I heard a movement in here," Helen said, standing in the doorway. "The swelling in your arm has gone down some. We were just waiting for you to wake up so we could take you to the doctor."

Eva looked past the woman and through the window behind her, and it occurred to her that the sun she saw was not the morning sun; It was high in the sky. "What day is it?"

"It's Wednesday. You have been asleep for over a day."

Eva was not sure she heard her right. "Over a day?"

"Yes, that's right. Honestly, we did not think you would sleep so long. You must have needed it."

Eva was shocked. She couldn't believe she had been here that long. If she had been here for over a day, the Germans were probably in La Chapelle by now, or at least close.

"Would you like to freshen up a little before we go into town?"

"I would, yes. Thank you."

Helen smiled at her. "I will put some water in the tub for you and set out a clean towel. I'm sorry that I don't have any clothes that will fit you, but if you take off the ones you have on, I will wash them."

"You have been so kind; I couldn't ask any more of you."

"It's no trouble; I will let you know when the bath is ready and help you out of your clothes. For now, you should eat. I put some food by your bed."

Eva hadn't noticed the plate with meat, cheese, a piece of bread, and some strawberries next to a cup of water on the nightstand. She had been too distracted with her arm and trying to figure out what had happened. When the woman disappeared from the doorway, Eva carefully pulled herself up and leaned against the headboard, then picked up the plate of food and sat it in her lap. She could not tell if she was hungry or not, but right now, she did not feel very hungry. She remembered how hungry she was in the woods, so she must be. First, the lack of sleep and food, then all the rest and medication she had taken on an empty stomach, probably caused her body to be out of whack. She reached for the cup of water and drank half of it before she set it back on the nightstand and started in on the food. She was close to finishing when Helen returned.

"The bath is ready. As soon as you are done, I'll help you up."

"We can go now," Eva said. She laid the plate back on the nightstand.

"Don't be silly. Finish your food."

Eva did not want to argue with her, so she picked up the plate and tried to finish the rest of her food. She ate the remaining strawberries and washed them down with the last of the water. There was still a little food on the plate, but Eva simply could not finish it all. She felt full faster than usual because she had not eaten for several days. Helen came to the side of her bed and reached down to help her.

"I think I can manage," Eva told her.

Helen stayed close to Eva, just in case she needed help. Eva swung her legs over the side of the bed and slowly stood up. She felt lightheaded and weak. For a minute, she thought she might fall back on the bed but studied herself by putting her hand on Helen's shoulder.

Helen took her arm, noticing that she looked a little unstable. "I've got you."

They carefully made their way to the bathroom. The woman helped Eva sit down on the toilet so they could remove her clothes. Just the trip to the bathroom was making her arm hurt, and somehow, she had exhausted all of her energy.

"How will I get my sleeve over the splints?"

"If it is not big enough to pull it over, I will have to remove the splints or cut the sleeve."

Eva looked at her arm, remembering how much it hurt the first time they put them on. She wasn't sure she could go through that again.

"We will give you some more medicine when you get out of the bath."

"The same medicine you gave me last time?"

"Yes, the same."

"I didn't like that medicine. It tasted terrible, and it made me unable to think straight, and I can't remember anything after I took it. The medicine made me see crazy things. I couldn't tell what was real and what wasn't."

“Yes, we know. Two nights ago, we heard you in your room talking.”

“Talking, what was I saying?”

“I don’t know. It was all in English. But then you screamed, so Abraham and I came into your room. You were holding both of your arms in front of your face like you were shielding yourself from something. Do you remember what you were dreaming?”

Eva shook her head. “No. When I woke up this morning, I couldn’t remember anything past the splint being put on.”

It was true that she couldn’t remember most of what happened, but she did remember the dreams, though they weren’t something she felt comfortable sharing with a stranger.

They got her shirt off without removing the splints and were now down to her undergarments.

“Take those off, too, and I will wash them with the others.”

“Oh, um, I don’t think—”

“I will step out. Just lay them on the floor. There is a robe hanging on the back of the door that you can use when you get out. You can wear it while your clothes dry,” Helen said, obviously not wanting to even hear Eva’s complaint about it.

Eva was not comfortable with the idea of someone else washing her underclothes, especially by hand. The woman turned and walked out of the bathroom, and closed the door. Eva stood up from the toilet and removed her underwear, but removing her bra was trickier. After she got it off, she put them on the floor with the rest of her clothes, stepped over the side of the tall white cast-iron tub, pulled the curtain around it closed, and carefully sat down. The warm water felt wonderful on her tired and sore body. She could see the steam rising off the surface of the water. She leaned back and closed her eyes, resting her head on the back of the tub.

When she heard the bathroom door creak, she opened her eyes and could see a figure through the curtain. It was Helen picking her clothes up off the floor.

"They should be dry in a few hours," Helen said from the other side of the curtain.

"Thank you."

"You are welcome. Holler if you need anything."

"I will."

Helen then turned and left the bathroom again and closed the door.

Eva kept her arm on the side of the tub so she didn't get it wet. As she stared at the blue sky through the bathroom window, the memory of her dreams kept playing in her head. She knew her mom would never say those things to her, but was there some truth to what her mom said in the dream? Was the dream trying to tell her something? And Kevin, she had not thought of him since leaving America. Why did he come back to haunt her now? She did not know the answers to her questions and probably never would.

There was little chance of her making it back to England now, that much she knew. The year she had spent here was enjoyable and rewarding but hard at times. Constantly feeling out of place was a challenge and often very lonely. What was even more challenging was not being able to talk to anyone about it, coupled with the secret she carried. No one could understand what she was going through, the loneliness and feeling of being trapped.

It was easier not being home with her friends and family when she knew she would be going back. Eva knew that she had the exact date and time all set and there shouldn't be anything to worry about, so getting trapped in France had not been an actual concern of hers. Of course, the possibility had crossed her mind, but becoming stuck there seemed so unlikely that she put it out of her thoughts and didn't worry about it.

After sitting in the tub for a while, she was tired of being in her head. She cleaned herself and sat up to get out; she gripped the side of the tub with her right hand and pushed up to help stabilize her legs. She stepped out of the tub, carefully onto the mat, and reached for the towel. It wasn't easy to dry herself one-handed, but it was even more challenging when she tried to put the robe on. After eventually getting it on, she cracked open the bathroom door and peeked out. She did not see anyone, so she opened the door and tiptoed back to her room as quietly as she could.

As she passed the window in the hall, she could see the woman outside hanging her clothes on a line. She felt guilty that they were doing so much for her, especially since she could not return the favor. She went to her bed and sat down. Her arm was hurting more now after moving it so much. She was trying to decide what to do. She wasn't about to go outside in just a robe, especially with nothing on underneath it. Though she had slept for over a day, she surprisingly still felt tired. *Maybe I overslept, and that is why I feel tired now? I guess it won't hurt to lie down for a few minutes and rest my eyes,* she thought. Finally being clean and having a nice, soft pillow under her head felt good. She pulled the blankets over her mid-section and closed her eyes. *I'll lie here for ten or fifteen minutes, then get up.*

She opened her eyes and looked around the room; it seemed darker than when she laid down. She bolted upright but quickly realized that was a bad idea. The pain shot up her arm, and clenching her jaw was all she could do not to scream out. She sat still and took deep breaths to help manage the pain. When she could think again, she looked through the window in her room. It was much later in the day, maybe four or five in the evening. *How long was I asleep for?* she wondered.

"Your clothes are dry," Helen said from the doorway.

Eva looked at her. "Why did you let me sleep for so long? I wasn't even going to sleep. I had just laid down to rest my eyes for a few minutes."

"I figured you could use it. I came to give you your clothes, and you were sleeping so soundly I didn't want to wake you. Your clothes are on the end of your bed. Would you like me to help you into them?"

Eva thought about telling her no, that she could manage, but she was not sure she could get her pants and socks on by herself, and maybe not her bra either. "Actually, yes. I think putting my clothes on might prove to be more troublesome than it was to take them off. I will put my underwear and bra on if you will latch it in the back?"

"Of course. I will turn around, and you let me know when you are ready." She turned her back to Eva in the doorway.

Eva picked up her underwear, put them on, and then reached for her bra. She slowly took the robe off and put one arm at a time through the straps, then turned her back to the woman. "I'm ready now." She could feel tugging on the straps, then it was secure, and she knew it had been latched.

Helen then reached for the rest of Eva's clothes and laid them next to her. She picked up the pants and helped Eva into them, put her socks on for her, and pulled the shirt over her arms.

"We have dinner ready on the table. We thought you would like to eat before leaving for the hospital."

"I would love some food, thank you."

"First, though, let's get you some medicine." Helen pulled the same brown bottle from her apron, took the cork out, and held it out to Eva.

"How much do I take?"

"Maybe not as much as you did last time. Just one or two should do for now."

Eva took one gulp and swallowed hard. It tasted worse than she remembered. She held it back out to the woman.

Helen put the cork back in while Eva was holding it. "No, you keep it," she said. "Lay it on the bed, and I will put it in your bag."

Eva laid the bottle on the bed and followed the woman into the kitchen, where she saw a pot of stew and a loaf of bread with butter next to it on the table. It looked and smelled so good that her mouth watered. She had not eaten since that morning.

"Have a seat," Helen said, pointing to a chair at the side of the table.

Eva sat down, and Abraham took a seat at the head of the table while Helen sat opposite her. Eva was beginning to feel the effects of the medicine now. She was getting dizzy, but her arm did not hurt as much.

Helen reached for the ladle in the pot of stew, filled up a brown wooden bowl, handed it to her husband, and then filled one for herself and Eva. She passed around some bread and filled their cups with water. She sat back in her seat, took her husband's hand, and then reached for Eva's.

Eva understood why he wanted her hand. She was familiar with saying grace at the dinner table because her grandparents always did it when she ate at their house. It was never something they did at home, so it felt a little foreign to her. She put her hand in the woman's anyway, and she gently closed it around Eva's.

"Lord, bless these gifts we are about to receive and the bounty in which they come. And Lord, bless all who are affected by this awful war, help this girl's arm heal, and help her along her journey. Amen."

"Amen," Eva said at the same time as Abraham. She let go of his hand and reached for her spoon.

"We will take you to the hospital after supper, but there are some things that we need to discuss before we do that," Abraham said. "First, we would like to know what you were doing in the woods in the first place, carrying IDs that weren't yours, along with a bag full of money and jewelry?"

Eva looked up at him from her bowl. She had forgotten all about the money and the IDs. "I…" she trailed off, then looked down at her bowl again, avoiding his gaze, not knowing if she could trust them with the truth.

"Don't be afraid. We are not supporters of the Nazi cause, but if you want us to help you further, you need to tell us the truth," Helen said.

Eva knew they were right, and she couldn't expect any more help if she wasn't going to be honest with them. "I help refugees flee from Nazi-occupied countries. A family I was assisting had to leave their IDs, clothes, and everything else they owned behind because they had to flee in such a hurry. It wasn't safe for them to return to Belgium to get any of it, so I agreed to come and get it for them. The money is theirs, too."

"And how did you end up lost in the woods?" Abraham asked.

"I went to their house to retrieve their things, but the Germans had gotten there first, so I waited for them to leave. They did, or so I thought. I went into the house and found what I needed, but I could hear a car approaching as I was about to leave, so I ran out of the house and into the woods. But they must have seen me. I stopped for a second to catch my breath when I heard voices not far off, speaking German. I understood they said in German to find me, so I started running again, but they followed. I don't know how far I ran before I lost them, but it felt like a long time. I have a compass, and I knew that I needed to go west, but I didn't have time to look when the Germans were chasing me. I just ran and didn't know what direction I was running in. When I realized that I had lost them, I stopped to check the compass. I found west and started walking in that direction, but I was already lost by that point. I wandered through the woods until I heard your dogs barking. I didn't know if you were the Germans or not, but I decided I had to risk it because I had already been lost all night and the better part of the day. I started walking towards the sound of the barking, and that is when I fell and broke my arm."

"Hmmm, that is some story."

Eva looked at Abraham. "But it's true. I'm not lying to you."

"We didn't say that you were. It's just not the kind of story you hear every day," Helen said.

"Is that why you were in such a hurry to get back to France?" Abraham asked.

"It is, but I think it is too late now. The Germans probably already have them."

"If they have evaded the Germans for this long, perhaps they still are." Helen's voice was soft and her voice hopeful.

"Do you know what will happen if the Germans are already there in La Chapelle? I mean, what will they do when I return?"

"I can't answer that. Who knows what the Germans will do. I think a lot of it depends on who the commander of the soldiers occupying your city is. Since they have been here in Belgium, some have not been very nice, and they allow their men to do lawless things, while others have been cordial and do a better job at keeping their men in line," Helen said.

"The best thing would be to enter the town unnoticed, if possible. No doubt it would raise suspicions if an American woman just walked out of the woods into the city," Abraham said.

"I live on a farm there, kind of like your farm. It is out of town on the east side."

"If we leave after dark, there is a chance we could get her there without being noticed," Helen said, looking at her husband for his opinion.

"OK. Then, let's eat and get you to the doctor. We can leave from there." He looked at Eva. "Make sure you have everything with you."

After supper, Helen helped Eva gather up her things, and they met Abraham outside by an old beat-up truck.

He took the bag from Eva and put it in the bed for her. "Let's get going."

It only took roughly thirty minutes to get to the town of Bouillon from the farm, but they wanted to make sure they had time to take Eva to the doctor and still get her back to France before it got too late.

"Oh, something we forgot to tell you at supper," Abraham said. "There will be Germans near town. We will have to show our IDs on the road in."

For some reason, the thought of stopping at a checkpoint never occurred to her. She couldn't believe that something like that had slipped her mind.

"Do you think there will be a problem because I'm American?"

"I'm not sure, but there could be. Let's hope not," Helen said.

"I have an idea," Abraham said. "What if I leave the two of you a little way back from the checkpoint, you guys could go through the woods, and I will pick you up on the other side after I am out of view? I know it is risky, but it might be even riskier if they check her ID and see she is American. Plus, they could find the money and other IDs, and then they would know something was off."

Eva looked at Helen.

She nodded her head. "I think he is right. It's better if we keep you out of sight."

Chapter Twelve

Abraham pulled off on the side of the road about a quarter of a mile from the checkpoint and let Eva and Helen out. Helen reached into the bed of the truck and got Eva's bag and the pillowcase with the money and IDs.

"I'll pick you up on the other side, about the same distance from the checkpoint."

Helen nodded her head in understanding.

When the truck pulled away, Helen and Eva headed into the woods. *Great, walking in the woods again,* Eva thought. They only went about ten or twelve feet into the trees, then started following the road. They walked in the woods for twenty minutes, then started back towards the road. As they got close, they could hear a car approaching.

"Get down. It might not be Abraham," Helen said.

They both knelt behind a tree and waited for the car to come into view.

Coming down the road, Eva could see a truck. "I think that is him," she whispered.

"Possibly, but we need to be sure. We can see it better when it gets closer, and then we'll know."

The truck slowed, and Eva could see Abraham sitting in the front when it got closer.

"That's him."

Helen squinted to see better. "It is. OK, let's go."

She picked up Eva's things, and they both ran for the edge of the road. Eva moved a little slower than Helen because of her arm. The jolting caused her a lot of pain. He pulled the truck on the side of the road next to them, and Helen put Eva's stuff in the bed, then hurried in the front after Eva.

The sun was almost set, just the top visible in the sky as they approached the town, and the last remaining light from it colored the sky. Once they got into town, Eva saw some German soldiers walking down the road in the opposite direction. This was the first time Eva had seen a German soldier up-close in the daylight. It was unnerving watching them walk down the sidewalk as if they belonged there.

"Don't forget about the curfew, Abraham," Helen said, interrupting Eva's thoughts.

"I remember. That's why we need to hurry."

He pulled in front of the hospital and parked. Helen grabbed Eva's purse and hid the laundry bag under some potato sacks in the back.

"Why do I need my purse?"

"They might ask to see your ID."

"Why?"

"If there are Germans keeping track of who goes in and out of the hospital, they will want to see it."

That thought was unsettling. They entered the hospital lobby and Eva looked around for Germans but didn't see any. Helen approached a nurse standing at a counter near the front of the building. She looked up at Helen when she got close.

"This girl has a broken wrist. Where do we take her?"

The nurse handed Helen a piece of paper on a clipboard. "Fill this out and give it to the doctor, along with her ID, when she sees him. What is your name?" She looked right at Eva, who was now standing beside Helen.

"My name is Eva… Abrams."

Eva cringed. She was sure that telling the nurse her name was going to get her into trouble.

The nurse looked at her strangely and handed her a piece of paper. "Write it down here."

Eva looked at Helen, who nodded, letting her know it was all right. Eva wrote her name while Helen filled out the paperwork.

"You can wait right over there." The nurse pointed in the direction of a small waiting area as she took the paper from Eva.

They sat in the empty waiting area for almost half an hour, and Eva's arm was hurting as the medicine began to wear off.

"Why do you think they wanted my name?"

"They need all patients' names," Abraham said. "It's standard procedure."

"Yes, but let's hope they had you spell it because they did not know how and not for other reasons," Helen cautioned.

"Miss Abrams," a nurse called from a set of double doors off to their side.

She did not immediately look up. She was not used to hearing her last name spoken by a native French speaker. Fabien and his daughters always called her by her first name. They only had called her Ms. Abrams when she first arrived. The way the nurse said it sounded different from when the French said it. Because of the unfamiliar accent, Eva wasn't sure it was her name being called. When the nurse called it again, Eva looked up.

"You are Miss Abrams and have come in for a broken wrist, yes?"

"Yes," Eva said.

"This way, please," she said, stepping to the side so Eva could enter through the open door.

Eva stood up and looked down at Helen. She knew it would be better if she came with her.

"Can she come back with me?" Eva asked and gestured toward Helen.

The nurse nodded her head. Helen got up and followed Eva through the doors behind the nurse.

"Have a seat on the table, please," the nurse told her.

Helen helped Eva up on the table.

"The doctor will be right in." The nurse then turned and left the room.

"So far, so good," Eva said.

"Yes, so far," Helen agreed.

Eva detected uncertainty in her voice, which made her nervous.

They were only in the room for a few minutes when the doctor entered with the same nurse helping them. He came up to Eva, took her hand, and started untying the strings holding on her stints.

She breathed heavily, and it was hard to keep her hand from shaking; she knew that this would be a painful experience because what he was doing already hurt.

"Hold still," he said.

Eva noticed that he never once asked her how she was doing or how much pain she was in; he said nothing to her except to hold still. She wasn't sure if it was a cultural thing or a different era thing. Perhaps it was both, but this doctor definitely lacked bedside manners.

After he untied the strings, he moved the stints away, and called for the nurse to come over. She came to stand beside him and waited for him to tell her what he needed.

"Take these." He handed her the stints and strings. "And bring me some morphine. Oh, and bring the cloth strips and the plaster for the cast as well."

"Yes, doctor." She then disappeared through the door.

"How long will this take?" Eva asked him.

"The entire process shouldn't take more than an hour. It would be best if you rest after, though."

"For how long?"

"You should take it easy for a few days, and the medicine I will give you will most likely make you feel nauseous. I would recommend taking it with food. It will take anywhere between six to eight weeks for the bone to heal fully, but as long as you are careful and don't move your arm too much, you can move around like normal in a few days. You just need to rest the broken wrist as much as possible in the first week."

"I can't—"

"Yes, doctor, I will take her straight home and make sure that she gets the rest she needs," Helen said, interrupting Eva.

Eva realized what Helen was trying to do. The less she said, the better. The nurse came back with the things the doctor had asked for.

"I'm going to need to move your arm. I have to see exactly how it's broken."

"Can't you X-ray it?" Eva asked.

"No, we don't have an X-ray at this hospital. It's too small. It's usually only the field hospitals that get them or the larger hospitals in the bigger cities. I'm going to move it now, all right?"

Eva nodded her head in response, but she wasn't looking forward to this.

The doctor picked up a needle full of liquid and squirted some in the air. "I'm going to inject the morphine into your arm."

She again nodded. He slowly pushed the needle into her wrist. She looked away and clenched her teeth. She always had to look away when she was getting a shot. She hated needles, especially if she was the one getting poked. Within a matter of seconds, the pain in her arm started to dull, and shortly after, she could hardly even feel it.

The doctor took her hand and started bending it at the wrist; he squeezed different parts of it with his thumb and middle finger. "Hmmm, it seems to be broken in two places, the trapezium and radium."

"What are those?" she asked.

"The trapezium is the bone in your palm near the thumb, and the radium is the larger of the two lower arm bones. Usually, it's the ulna, the smaller of the two bones in the lower arm, that people break, but it must have been the way you fell."

"How bad is it?"

"The radium is a transverse fracture, which means it is broken around the bone, not up the bone, and the trapezium probably just has a small crack in it."

He laid her arm on a small rolling table near the bed and began pushing hard on her arm. She thought he must be putting the bone back into place but wasn't sure. She could feel a lot of pressure while he was doing it, but not much pain. He then took one of the plaster-covered strips of cloth out of a pan filled with grayish goop and began wrapping it around her arm and hand. He worked meticulously until he had her arm wrapped firmly in the mold. When he put the last one on, he rubbed it all down with his hand to make the cast look smooth.

Eva kept looking at the clock while he was working, hoping that it wouldn't take him much longer. He started at six-ten, and it was now six-fifty-two, and that is not to mention all the time they had sat in the waiting room. She probably sat on the table for over twenty minutes before he even started wrapping her arm.

"That was the last piece, but you can't move your arm yet. We need to let it dry for thirty minutes before you do. After that, it will take about twenty-four to forty-eight hours for it to cure completely."

"Can I take her home after it has dried for the thirty minutes?"

"Yes, but don't let her move it around. Stay here while it dries, and I'll be back to check on it in a while."

The doctor then left the room with the nurse.

"We have to get out of here," Eva said.

"I know, but it would look strange if we just left. They would think we were trying to run. Plus the doctor is right; we can't move your arm yet."

"So, we just wait until he comes back?"

"Yes, that is exactly what we do."

"What if he comes back with the Germans?"

"Then there is nothing we can do, but I don't believe he will."

Fifteen minutes later, the doctor returned. He lifted Eva's arm and inspected the cast but said nothing. He just furrowed his brows as he focused on what he was doing.

"Is it dry enough to leave?" Helen asked.

"I know you are eager to leave because she is American. You know, I am supposed to report any non-Belgium patients I see," he said matter-of-factly.

Eva could feel a tight knot forming in her stomach. She looked at Helen to see her reaction. Her face was straight and calm; Eva could not read it.

"Why?" Helen asked the doctor.

"Because the Germans are looking for people fleeing or anyone that might be a spy. I don't believe you are, I have not said anything, but I recommend you leave town as soon as possible. Don't stop anywhere. Just go straight to your home."

"Thank you," Eva said.

He didn't answer or look at her. He just continued examining her arm. "Here is some medicine you can take. There is enough for two weeks."

He put a bottle of pills in her right hand. "That should be enough to help you through the worst part. The cast is dry enough now to leave; you should try and get out without being noticed."

Helen took the medicine from Eva's hand and helped her off the table. "Thank you again, doctor."

Even though the doctor never smiled, he had a kind face. Eva was thankful he was letting her leave.

Helen helped her back out to the lobby, where they met up with Abraham. "We need to go right now," Helen said to him.

"Right."

He assisted them out to the truck, and Helen helped Eva in, then got in beside her. Abraham came around to the other side and got in the driver's seat.

"We will need to do the same thing leaving the city as we did when we came in," Helen said.

"I know."

Abraham dropped them off at the edge of the woods, then picked them back up on the other side of the checkpoint just like before. "It will take two hours to get to La Chapelle," he told them.

"I think we are OK for now," Helen said.

They took the back roads as often as they could to avoid being seen or having to stop at roadblocks. After driving for almost two hours, they arrived at a Y in the road.

"Which way do we go?" he asked Eva. "Is it that way?" he said, pointing to the left.

"The one to the right is the one we need. It will take us to the farm."

He turned to the right. "How far down the road do we go?"

"I'm not sure; what I mean is that I don't know how far it is in kilometers, but it's roughly three miles, so it should only take us ten or fifteen minutes to get there."

The road was rough, and the bouncing made Eva feel sick; she wondered if it was the medicine they gave her; the drive seemed to take far longer than she thought it would, but finally, they could see a light in the distance.

"Is that the farm?" Helen asked.

"I believe it is," Eva said, squinting in the direction of the light, trying to see if it was the Dubois farm they were driving towards.

They went over a large bump, and Eva held her arm.

"Ouch."

"Is your arm hurting again?" Helen asked.

"Yeah, I think that shot he gave me is wearing off, and I feel like I might vomit."

"The doctor said it might make you feel sick. Unfortunately, you will have to take it for a while longer. Do you need us to pull over?"

"No," Eva shook her head. "I think I can keep it down. Trading one unpleasant feeling for another, that's life it seems," Eva told her.

Helen laid a hand on her arm and gave her a gentle squeeze in an attempt to comfort her.

As they got close to the farm, Eva could see it better now. "This is it."

Abraham pulled the truck around to the front of the house and parked, turning off the engine. A man was standing on the front porch, holding a rifle. Abraham got out of the truck and held his hands in the air to make sure the man could see them clearly and show that he was not there to cause trouble. Helen opened her door and stepped out, keeping an eye on her husband and the man with the gun the entire time.

"We believe we have a friend of yours," he said. "We brought her back from Belgium."

Fabien leaned down to look at the person still in the truck. "Eva?" he said, surprised.

Eva slid from the middle of the seat to the edge and hung her legs out of the truck.

"Oh my God, Eva, I thought we lost you." He leaned the rifle against the porch and came over to the side of the truck. He looked down at Eva sitting in the seat. "What happened to your arm?"

Eva touched her cast and gave Fabien a forced smile. "It's a long story. I'll tell you about it a little later. The Germans are heading towards La Chapelle, Fabien."

"I know," he said. "They are already here. A German soldier came by the house while we were eating dinner and said everyone in town and the surrounding farms had to be in the square by nine. When I went to town today to buy supplies at the store, Frank informed me that they will use the nicer homes to house the officers and that some farms might have to billet soldiers as well."

"What do we need to be in town for?"

"Not sure. They no doubt want to lay out the rules for us."

He took Eva's good arm and helped her from the truck and into the house. Helen and Abraham followed behind them.

"Eva!" Sabina squealed when she saw her enter through the door. She ran up to her, wrapped her arms around her waist, and pressed her head against her chest. "I thought you had died." She looked up at Eva while still holding onto her.

Eva saw tears glistening in her eyes. "It's all right, I'm fine."

"If you are fine, then what happened to your arm?"

"I will tell everyone what happened, but a little later. It's kind of a long story, and I'm exhausted."

"We need to be leaving now if we are going to be in the square by nine," Fabien said.

"I guess we will leave now, too," Helen said.

"I thank you for taking care of Eva!" Fabien told Helen.

"We were happy to help." She gave Eva a gentle embrace. "Take care of yourself and try harder to stay out of trouble."

"Thank you for all that you have done for me. I don't think that I would have made it out of that forest if it weren't for the two of you. I owe you guys so much. I owe you my life!"

"You owe us nothing. The only thing that I want from you is for you to stay safe. No more taking chances as you did, or all we have sacrificed for you will have been in vain."

"You guys should also be careful." Eva knew what Helen said was true, that they had taken so many risks for her. They helped her, kept her safe, and brought her home. She wanted to promise herself, Helen, and Abraham that she wouldn't take any more chances like that, but she couldn't.

"We will." Helen gave her a final, quick embrace.

"Bye now. Take care," Abraham said as he gave her a hug.

"Thank you again, really. For all you have done. I'll never forget it."

He kissed Eva on the cheek and squeezed her shoulder before letting her go.

Helen looked at Fabien. "She needs to take her medicine three times a day for the pain. I put it in her bag."

"I will make sure that she does. Thank you for taking care of her. It means a lot to me."

"We were happy to help."

Helen and Abraham shook Fabien's hand, then disappeared out the front door.

"The people you were supposed to help are here," Fabien said.

"Here…?"

"Yes, when you never came back, I got them. I hid them under the floor."

"Are they under the floor now?"

"They are. Did you get their IDs?"

"I did."

"Good, I'll get them out. We will need to bring the family with us. It's safer for them to be hiding out in the open, in plain sight, than it is for them to be hiding under a floor."

She watched as Fabien pushed his kitchen table to the side and pulled up the floorboards. He helped a woman up from under the floor, a small girl of about two, a boy around five, and then a man. They looked around the room, and soon, all eyes were on Eva.

"This is the woman that went to save you," Fabien said to them.

The man crossed the room and stopped in front of her, taking her right hand. "We are so grateful to you and thankful that you were willing to risk your life for us." He looked at his sister and her two kids, then back to Eva. "We are forever in your debt," he said to her in German but with a strange accent.

"You are welcome. I am so happy to see that you are all alive. I thought everything I went through was going to be for nothing, but I'm so glad to see that I was wrong. Oh, and your IDs, money, and the clothes I got are over there in that pillowcase." Eva nodded to the pillowcase by the door. "It's not much because I couldn't fit many clothes in the pillowcase, but It's enough to last a few days until you can get more."

The man went to the pillowcase and brought it over to the light to look at the things in it.

Finally, the woman came over to Eva. "As my brother has said, we can't thank you enough." She looked behind her at the kids. "My children are safe right now because of you, but I am sorry that you broke your arm trying to help us."

Eva looked down, not liking all the attention on her. She looked back up and smiled at her instead of responding to her praise. "Now, who do we have here?" she asked, looking at the children.

The woman waved the children to come over. "This is Esther. And this is Uri." The woman took the little girl in her arms.

Eva smiled at the children, and the boy forced a shy smile back at her.

"And what is your name?" Eva asked the woman. "I'm sorry, but I don't remember them from the letter."

"It's not a problem, I understand. My name is Rachel, and my brother is Ezra."

"You know you can't be referred to by your real names anymore? Whatever your new IDs say is what we will now call you until this war is over."

The woman looked at her son. "I know, and I need to make sure that he learns his new name."

"Does he know how to write his name already?"

"Yes, he likes to repeatedly write his name, Uri Schuller, on paper. He has just recently learned to spell them correctly."

The woman's brother came and stood next to her, handing the woman three IDs.

"Let's go," Fabien said. "We don't want to be late."

Eva sat in the front of the truck with Fabien and Brigitte, and Sabina rode in the back of the truck with the man, his sister, and her two children. Sabina wanted to ride in the front with Eva, but her dad told her no. Because of Eva's broken arm, he thought she might not leave her alone. Eva had remembered to take some of her medicine before they left. For the first time, she was going to have to interact with the Germans. She had only seen them at a distance but never conversed with them. The last thing she wanted was to be in pain while facing an unknown outcome.

As they arrived in the square, she could see what looked like most of the town gathered there. They were all standing in a circle around a large fountain that made a roundabout. Fabien parked near the fountain in the middle of the square so they didn't have far to walk to join the rest of the crowd.

As Eva climbed out of the cab, she could feel the air was cool, and despite the lights from the town, she could still see all the stars in the night sky. Looking up at the vastness of space calmed her. The fact that humans had been there and had now discovered time travel made all of this seem so stupid, vain, and uncivilized. She could not understand how people could stoop to this kind of behavior and treatment of their own kind. It was worse than animals. Who cared what country one came from, what religion one believed in, or what color one's skin was. They were all human, and the hate was so petty.

When they approached the crowd, Eva wanted to not be seen, so she hung back behind some of the other people but close enough to the front to see what was going on. Soon, a convoy came into view, heading into town; it was entering at the far end of the street. She could see row after row of soldiers marching in formation at the front as they entered. The sound of their boots on the paved road echoed through the town and off the hills, drowning out all other sounds. She watched as they passed by her. Was she really seeing this? It was more like she was in a dream. Behind the marching troops was a car with two low-ranking soldiers in the front and two German officers sitting in the back, and behind that car was another car, but unlike the first, it did not have its top down, and she could not see who was in it. Behind the two vehicles were four motorcycles; the two in the front had officers on them and the two in the back had enlisted men. The two motorcycles in the back had the usual German sidecars, and behind the motorcycles were four tanks and six half-tracks. Between the marching soldiers, the motorcycles, and all the tanks and half-tracks, the ground was rumbling under her feet. The convoy made its way around the fountain and came to a halt when they had encircled it, and the ground was still once again. Men started piling out of the tanks, the ones on the motorcycles dismounted, and the men in the cars got out.

One of the officers crawled on top of a tank and was handed a megaphone. "Mesdames et Messieurs," he said with a strong German accent. "The town of La Chapelle is now under the control of the German army. The Führer wishes for us to live harmoniously, but there will need to be rules for us to do that. Starting tomorrow night, a curfew will be instated. We will announce it at sundown on a loudspeaker every night after. Tomorrow morning, everyone will meet in city hall to register. You need to have your IDs with you, and IDs will need to be carried with you from now on. Everyone will also surrender their firearms; you will take them to city hall to be surrendered when you come to register. I am telling you this now so you will all be informed, and there can be no excuses tomorrow during registration. All firearms need to be turned in as of tomorrow morning. Despite what you all might think of us, we are fair and just. You will soon see this."

Sabina took Eva's hand and squeezed it tight. Eva looked down at her and saw the frightened look on Sabina's face. Eva didn't blame her; she also felt uneasy about the Germans' arrival and hoped that Sabina could not see it on her face. Eva wondered if she was trapped here; she did not know how she would get out of this town or even France. Eva was pretty sure that they weren't going to just let her leave whenever she felt like it. People needed a good reason for traveling.

"The people that are billeting officers will return to their homes and wait for their arrival. The rest of you will go back to your homes for the night. From now on, nine o'clock sharp will be lights out," the officer continued.

When he had finished speaking, he handed the megaphone back to the enlisted man standing rigidly next to the tank and climbed down. The crowd started thinning; some people were returning to their homes to wait for the Germans coming to live with them, and the ones not selected were just waiting for the dreaded morning. Several German soldiers headed in different directions around the square and began changing all the clocks to their time.

They drove back to the farm in silence. Eva stared out into the dark oblivion. The feeling of hopelessness and loneliness weighed heavily on her. She wanted to crawl into her bed and know that her loved ones were with her again. Why did she agree to do this? She was in this situation now because of her decision. She knew there was a risk when she decided to take the job in France, but she truly believed she would make it back to England in plenty of time. After all, she did know when the Germans would invade France. Jon, too, was confident that she would be in no real danger. A lot of good that did her. She could not have anticipated what happened in the woods. *I was so stupid to think that something wouldn't go wrong; something always goes wrong,* she thought. It was unthinkable that she would have to stay in this small village for the duration of the war. She just needed to get through tomorrow, and then she would find a way to leave. Tomorrow might be bad for her, but she could only imagine what it would be like for the Schullers. Nerve-racking, that was what. She would not think about it anymore. She was going to go to bed and pretend that she was back home, and all of this was just a terrible dream.

Chapter Thirteen

May 11th, 1940

Sleep did not come easy for Eva that night, and she struggled through exhaustion as they got in line just outside city hall for the registration. Her head was pounding, and she was having a hard time focusing, and the medicine was making it worse. She could probably lie down where she stood and go to sleep.

As they waited in line, she looked at the faces around her; some were scared, some angry, some unsure, and some defeated, but others had no expression on their faces at all. She knew that it wasn't because they weren't feeling anything; they were just good at masking it. She wondered what emotion she wore on her face. She hoped that it wasn't fear. She felt for all of these people, and like those who were not showing their emotions, she too had something she wanted to keep hidden, and some of them probably did as well.

It took them a while to get inside the building because most of the town was there, and it felt like they were behind all of them. They had left the farm later than Fabien had wanted, but it wasn't any one person's fault; everything just seemed to be running slow that morning. A few of the people made eye contact with Eva, and despite the expression on their faces, she could see the fear in their eyes. She could sympathize with them because the closer they got to the door, the more her fear increased. This was a kind of fear she had only felt once before—the night she came close to being caught when running from the Germans in the woods. She had no idea what they would do when they found out she was American; the thought of it was causing the tight feeling in her chest to return, and her fight or flight mode was on high alert.

They were finally close to the front of the line near the desk, with the German taking names and IDs. She tried listening to what he was saying to each of the people ahead of her as she waited. Most of them registered and turned in their guns without any trouble and were only there a few minutes. All they had to do was show their IDs, say where they lived, hand over their weapons, and then the German at the desk was on to the next person. But that wasn't the case for the man, just two people ahead of them.

He was a middle-aged man with a bad leg and used a cane to walk. She turned her head to try and hear their conversation better, but most of it was muffled. The soldier did not believe something the man was saying, but she couldn't quite hear what it was; they were whispering, and she was still too far back. The soldier at the desk turned and waved an officer over who had been standing next to the nearby window. Eva had not noticed him before now. She had been so preoccupied with watching the registrations and listening in that she had missed him.

He was a man of large stature, tall and formidable, with broad shoulders, and most likely towered over many people. He had striking blue eyes and dark blond hair that was buzzed around the sides and kept longer at the top, which he had combed in a deep part neatly to one side. There was a seriousness about him and an unreadable face like many of the people waiting in line. He epitomized the Aryan warrior. He looked exactly like what she thought a Nazi would look like. She had no idea what rank or branch he was in, but she hoped it wasn't the Gestapo.

He walked up to the desk and stood beside the soldier seated there. He took the ID the soldier was holding and peered at it, furrowed his eyebrows in concentration, then peered down at the soldier with a questioning look. The soldier said something to him then the officer handed the ID back to the soldier and said something to the man. Whatever it was that he said made the man quite upset.

The man spoke in a louder voice now. "Please, I am not a Jew, see." He pointed to something on his ID. "I am French, and I am Catholic."

The officer nodded to some soldiers standing guard not far off.

They walked up to the man, one standing on each side of him. "Come with us, please."

The man became more desperate. "Please, I beg you. I am not a Jew. Just ask anyone here, please, ask them. They know!"

The officer gave a second nod to the soldiers. They each took hold of one of his arms and pulled him from the line.

He jerked an arm free and held onto the desk. "Please, let me explain."

The officer gave the soldier that was not holding onto the man a look, then the soldier picked up his rifle and hit the man in the back with the butt of the gun. The man cried out and fell to the floor onto his knees. Eva gasped and put her hand over her mouth. She had never seen something like that in real life, only in movies. It was very different to see violence as opposed to watching it on a screen. The two soldiers reached for him a second time, and each took an arm again, then lifted him until his feet dragged on the floor and pulled him out of view.

Eva swallowed hard and held on tighter to Sabina's hand. She looked back at Fabien, fear flooding her eyes. What if that was soon going to be her? She looked past him at Rachel, Esther, Uri, and Ezra. She was concerned for them now, too. She wasn't sure if they could convince the Germans of their identity. She doubted the man who they carried away was a Jew, and if he could not convince them of that, how was the Schuller family going to do it?

Fabien reached up and squeezed her shoulder. "You'll be OK, and so will they. Don't worry."

The person in front of Eva took their ID from the soldier and walked away from the desk; it was now her turn. She let go of Sabina's hand and stepped up to the desk. Her heart was pounding so hard in her chest it hurt. She was sure they could hear it. Her hands were clammy and her mouth dry, so she licked her lips and rubbed her palms on her skirt to dry them.

"ID," the man said to her in French.

She slowly reached in her purse to retrieve it.

He looked up at her. "Quickly now, Madame, we are in a hurry. There are a lot of people to get through."

She pulled her ID out and handed it to him, trying to keep her hand from shaking.

He laid it on the desk and started to write the information on the clipboard in front of him when he stopped mid-writing. He raised his head and looked up at her slowly, his expression questioning. He then turned in his chair and looked at the officer that helped him last time.

"Hauptmann," he said.

The officer walked over to the desk again, and the soldier handed him her ID.

Oh shit! she thought.

He peered down at her ID, then at her. He focused on her for a long moment before speaking. He dropped his arm down to his side, still holding onto her ID.

"Come with me, Madame," he said to her in French. His voice was fluid and smooth when he spoke.

She looked behind her at the others, struggling to slow her breathing, yet she could hardly catch her breath. Was this going to be it for her? Was this how her life would end; in 1940 Nazi-occupied France? Were they going to drag her away like the old man, kicking and screaming? All these thoughts were racing through her head.

"Madame, I will not ask again," he said in a low, stern voice.

She turned back to face him, and he was looking right at her; his jaw was set, and she could see the tight muscles in his neck. Eva knew she had no other choice, or she would suffer the same fate as the man before her who resisted. She walked around the desk without saying a word and followed the officer down a short corridor to a door on the left. He opened it and gestured for her to enter. It was a small room with stacks of paper sitting along the back wall and a small desk with two chairs, one on each side. The desk sat in the middle of the room; there were no windows, just one small lamp on the desk for light. It looked as if it was once a storage room. He followed her into the room and closed the door, making it pitch black, then pulled the chain on the lamp.

"Have a seat," he said, pointing to the chair on the left side of the desk. He then sat in the chair across from her and crossed his legs. He picked up a notepad and pen off the desk without looking at her.

The small dark room reminded her of those rooms where people would be brought for torture, like in an old spy movie. *Stop that, Eva!* She really couldn't go there right now if she were going to retain some resemblance of being calm and make it through this.

"Why are you in France, Miss Abrams?" he asked her in perfectly spoken English but with a slight German accent. He never looked up from his notepad.

She was surprised that he could speak English. She had not expected that, and for him to do it so well. But she would not give him the satisfaction of responding in English. "I am here for work," she said to him in German. She thought that was the safest answer.

This time he looked up from the pad, there was a different expression on his face than the emotionless one he had, but he quickly tried to conceal it and cleared his throat. "And what kind of work do you do?" he asked but this time in French.

"I work with a humanitarian organization that helps refugees."

"And which refugees do you help?"

"Well, all of them," she said, a little perturbed that he cared who she helped. "I have the documentation for my work."

"You have it here with you now?"

"Yes."

"I will need to see those too, please."

She got the papers from her purse and held them out to him. He took them from her, glanced over them, then laid them on the desk next to her ID.

"How did you break your arm?"

"I tripped on a rock in the woods." She figured she couldn't go wrong by telling as much of the truth as she could in this situation.

"Why were you in the woods?"

"I was on a walk. I often go there for walks."

"Really?" he said incredulously.

"Yes, it's the only time I really have to be alone."

"And why do you need to be alone?"

"Because I live in a little farmhouse with three other people."

"Where is it that you live, Miss Abrams?" he asked while writing down everything she said.

"I live on the Dubois farm. It is about two kilometers east of town." She hoped she got the distance right.

"Are you aware that you can no longer work for the FSC here in France? The only organization with permission to work with refugees and POWs is the Red Cross. And if you are planning on returning home, that probably will not happen for some time. All travel has been restricted and stopped completely to England."

Eva was just getting ready to respond when he stood up from his chair and handed her papers back.

"You may go," he said in the same demeanor he had before.

She took the documents and stood as well. He went to the door and opened it for her, following her out. He walked behind her down the corridor back to the front of the building.

She made it a point to keep several paces ahead of him as she walked, but could still hear his heavy steps not far behind her. When they reached the desk, the footsteps behind her stopped, but she didn't look back. She scanned the people in the line but did not see any of the others, so she kept on walking toward the front door. *I wonder what happened to them. I hope none of them got taken to the back as I did.*

When she reached the front of the building, she could see them waiting for her just outside by the steps. She walked away from this unscathed, and they made it out, too. She felt a wave of relief wash over her, and the pain in her chest was receding.

"Eva," Sabina called and ran to her side, taking her hand.

"We were not sure what was happening in there. What did they want? Why did they take you to that room?" Fabian asked.

"He just wanted to know why I was here, where I lived, and he told me that I wouldn't be going home to America any time soon," she said as her voice cracked.

"He looked like a mean bastard," Ezra said. "Hopefully, we won't have to deal with them much."

"Let's get out of here," Fabian said.

"Gladly," she agreed.

They loaded up into Fabian's truck and headed back to the farm.

"Did you guys have any trouble?" she asked.

"No, it went fairly smoothly," Fabien said. "We just showed them our IDs and gave them the guns, and then it was over. The Schullers didn't have a problem either. They looked at their IDs and handed them back like they did mine. They didn't seem suspicious. When they took you away in the back, I had no idea what they were going to do to you. And to be honest, I wasn't sure that you were ever going to come back, at least not in the same condition you left in. But I wasn't going to leave until I knew what was happening to you."

"Thank you, Fabien. I'm glad that you guys didn't have any trouble. This is such a mess, the situation we are in."

"The only thing we can do is try not to dwell on it," he said.

"You are right, I know."

Eva was so tired that she felt like she might fall over from exhaustion if she stood. She knew how lucky she had been today to get off as easy as she did. It could be the fact that Germany was not yet at war with America. She was a little amazed that the Schullers were not suspected, at least not yet. She thought they looked Jewish, so it was probably only a matter of time before the Germans picked up on that.

"I am so glad you are back. It's been lonely since you have been gone," Sabina said.

"It's good to be back."

"I've put the Schullers in the barn for the night; we can start looking for them a place to stay in the morning," Fabian said.

"That's good. It could be dangerous if we continue to keep them in the barn."

They returned to the farm, and everyone turned in for the night, and Eva relished the silence. She took some medicine and went to bed, happy to be left alone with her thoughts. She was staring at the ceiling when reality hit her like a frying pan to the face. It finally had sunk in. She would not be going home like she thought when she came here and would not get to see her family and friends or return to her old life. This week had started off bad, first with having to go through the woods alone in the dark, almost getting caught by the Germans, and being chased through the woods, resulting in her getting lost. Then there was her breaking her wrist, which laid her up in Belgium. And to top off everything else, she was too late getting back to France, and now the Germans were here. What a week!

She wondered if she would even be allowed to write letters to Jon. *Oh, Jon,* she thought. *You don't even know what has happened. Are you going to try to find me? Will you wait in England until I come back, or will you just return to our time without me?* She needed to find a way to get a letter to England, but she wasn't sure how. She did remember that the Red Cross delivered letters for people; perhaps that was how she could do it, but how would she get the letters to the Red Cross? She didn't know where they were exactly. She didn't even want to think of the possibility of Jon not waiting for her or that she might not ever get back. She fought back the tears. Crying wasn't going to help her now. Even though she felt like bawling her eyes out, it seemed like she had already cried so much in the last few weeks she didn't want to cry anymore. Figuring out what she was going to do next was what would help her. She wanted so badly to tell someone, just to talk and unload all of the things that were burdening her. Her situation was precarious and frightening, and she could not speak about it to anyone. Her problem of being stuck in France was obvious; however, that was only part of the story. Jon was the only person she could talk to about this, and he was not here. She drifted off into a fitful sleep that lasted the rest of the night.

May 17th, 1940

Eva woke to the sound of banging. She reached for her robe that was hanging on the poster of her bed and went to find the cause of the noise. She saw Fabien laying some large wooden crates on the table as she entered the kitchen.

"Taking some of the crops into town today?" she asked.

"Yes, and I need to buy some supplies while I'm there, some food and seeds. I will look for a home for the family as well. The barn is no place to house people."

"Do you want me to come with you and help?"

He looked up from the crates. "Are you sure, with your broken arm and after what you went through last week?"

"I know that you would rather me be the one to go into town with you and help instead of your daughters now that the Germans are here." She was not upset with him for thinking that; she probably would too if she had children.

He didn't meet her gaze but instead stared at the crates on the table. "It is true that I want to limit my girls' exposure to the Germans as much as possible." Finally, he looked up at her. "But I want to make sure that you feel safe, too. I know that what happened shook you up. You don't need to see them again, especially so soon if you don't want to."

“You always look out for my well-being, and I appreciate it. But you need help, and there is something I need to do in town anyway.”

“Very well,” he said. “I leave in fifteen minutes. Do you think you can be ready in that time?”

“I believe so.”

She went back to her room to change and brush her hair. She decided to change in the bathroom so she wouldn’t wake Sabina. She changed as fast as she could with one arm. She didn’t want Fabien to have to wait for her. She put her hair in a bun as she walked back to the kitchen.

“I’m ready.”

“Grab the small crate, would you?” Halfway to the door, he stopped. “Did you bring your ID?”

“No, I forgot that I needed it.”

“Go get it. We have to keep it with us any time we leave now.”

Of course, she thought. *How could I have forgotten that?* She hurried back to the bedroom, tiptoed to her bed, and reached for her ID in her purse. *No, I’m just going to take the whole purse; I might need it today in town.* She grabbed her bag and the medicine bottle off her dresser on her way out. She had forgotten all about it as she tried to get ready in a hurry. She held up her purse as she entered the kitchen to let Fabien know she was ready. She picked up the small crate off the table and a piece of bread and followed him to the truck. She needed to eat something with the medicine. Fabien put his crates in the bed, took the one from her, and put it in with the others.

She took a swig of the medicine as they drove, wrinkled up her nose, then squeezed her eyes shut and coughed. “Oh gosh.” She decided to take the liquid today instead of the pills the doctor gave her. It was easier to take in the car because she didn't need water.

"Is it that bad?"

"It's that bad."

"Does it help?"

"Yes, it helps quite a bit." The liquid seemed to work faster than the pills, so she would use them when she ran out of this.

"That's good. Oh, I forgot to mention that while you were gone, Madame Blanc asked about you. She asked why you weren't there on Sunday for dinner."

"What did you tell her?"

"I told her you had to go to Belgium for work. When you didn't return, I told her that you had to stay longer than originally planned due to complications. If you had been gone longer than you were, I don't know how I would explain that to her. She was quite upset that you were gone at all."

"I will have to go see her and tell her how sorry I am for my absence."

Madame Blanc was an old widow who lived alone in the most prominent house in La Chapelle. She got to know Eva over the winter, and Eva would help her build her fires and shovel her walkway when it snowed. Eva would drink tea with her when she was finished and eventually started coming just for tea. Eva got into a routine of having Sunday dinners with her to give the old woman some company. Madame Blanc had a maid but preferred Eva's company to hers. She would tell Eva all about her late husband and how they came to live in that large house. She told her stories of the Great War and how she lost her only son to it.

They entered town and parked at the fountain again.

"I will bring the crates where the farmers are meeting. You don't need to come with me. Why don't you go to the store and get the food and seeds while I take care of this? We can visit Madame Blanc after if you want to."

"I can do that."

He handed her a piece of paper with the things they needed and some German Reichsmarks. Since the German occupation, they were no longer allowed to use French francs. They could only use the German currency.

"I say we meet back here in an hour?"

"That should be enough time for me to get everything on the list."

Eva headed in the direction of the store as Fabien drove to the other end of town. She unfolded the paper and read the list. As for the food, they only needed a few things, maybe a couple of bags worth, but he listed a lot of seeds. She did not know precisely how much each bag of seed weighed, but she remembered seeing Fabien carrying two of them at a time on each of his shoulders. They looked like the size of a bag of potting soil did her time but probably heavier. *I will have to carry those back one at a time*, she thought.

When she went into the shop, the same older woman who helped her with her bike almost a year ago was standing at the counter. She looked up at Eva and then back down to whatever she was doing. Not a lot had changed in the eight months she had been there. The woman still gave her the same cold glance she did then, the same look she gave her every time she entered her store. Eva put the things she needed on the counter as she found them. There were no baskets in the store to carry stuff in. She had brought some mesh bags with her that she had gotten out of the back of Fabien's truck to carry the food back to the fountain.

"I would like six bags of wheat seeds, three bags of corn seeds, and six bags of barley seeds, too, please," she told the woman as she rang up the items on the counter.

The woman wrote it down and gave her a total.

Eva paid her. "I will come back for the bags of grain later today."

"Very well," said the woman.

The woman helped Eva put the food in the bags because she could hardly do it with one hand. Eva picked both bags up with her right hand and left the store. She usually would carry one in each hand to balance out the weight, but with both in the same hand, the handles were cutting into her palm.

"Ouch," she said, looking up from the ground to see how far she had to go before she was back to the square.

She still had several blocks to walk, and the bags were really hurting her hand now. She stopped and put the bags on the ground to give her hand a break for a minute. Her hand was trembling, and creases from the handles were left on her palm, turning an angry red color. She rubbed her hand on her dress to try and make it feel a little better, then picked up the bags and started to walk again. As she took a step, one of the bags slipped from her hand, the food going all over when it hit the ground.

"Damn it," she sighed. She sat the other bag down so she could gather up the food that was now lying all over the road. She bent down, picked up the bag that had fallen, and began gathering up the things closest to her feet first.

"Can I help you with that?" a voice asked from behind.

She quickly lifted her head, turning to look behind her; she had not heard anyone approach. Standing over her was the officer who had questioned her the previous week. She wasn't sure how to answer. Why would he offer his help? Frankly, she did not want it from him whether she needed it or not. Part of her wanted to leave the food there and start walking back to the fountain just to get away from him, but that would be silly and make her look guilty of something.

He bent down next to her. "Let me help you."

He started picking up the apples that had rolled away. She didn't say anything or move; she just watched him pick the things up.

"I can pick it all up for you, but you need to hand me the bag."

Eva looked down and realized that she had been gripping tightly to the empty bag. She still didn't say anything; she just handed the bag to him. It was like a part of her mind wasn't responding. Eva knew that she should tell him she didn't need his help and pick it up herself, but instead, she stayed still, watching him do it for her. She got the last few remaining things that were by her feet and held them in her hand, waiting for him to finish picking the other stuff up. After he had put all the other food in the bag, he held it open for her to put the last remaining things in. She dropped them in the bag and reached to take it from him, but instead of giving it to her, he picked the other bag off the ground and stood, not giving her time to protest. She stood as well and faced him. For the first time, she really looked at him. When they spoke last week, he had his head down most of the time, and she tried to look at other things as often as she could, averting her gaze, thinking if they made eye contact, he would see that she was hiding something. Today, he did not have the same expression he did the last time. He seemed more relaxed, and the tone of his voice was softer.

Eva reached out to take the bags from him.

"I can carry them. Where are you heading?" he asked.

Eva's heart sped up, and she didn't want to spend another second with this man. He was making her uncomfortable. She was sure that not all Germans were bad people, but she did not want to spend enough time with any of them to find out which ones were and which ones weren't.

"It's OK. I don't need help."

He breathed loudly through his nose. "You know, instead of saying you don't need my help after I just helped you, you could have just said thank you."

She felt a little embarrassed. She looked down so he could not see it on her face. "Thank you for helping me."

She still did not want him to help her carry her bags to the truck, even if it hurt her hand. She did not want to accept help from the enemy—well, any more help. And she especially did not want to be seen walking with him. People would start talking. It was a small town, and it was not uncommon for tongues to wag and gossip to spread. The last thing she needed was to be seen as a collaborator or a Nazi sympathizer.

She reached for the bags again. "Thank you for your help, but I'll take them now."

He hesitated for a moment, then handed her the bags. She took them from him, turned in the fountain's direction, and started walking. The bags were really hurting her hand now; they almost seemed heavier than they had earlier, but she was not about to turn back and ask him for his help, especially since she had been ungrateful to him only a minute ago and told him no.

When she arrived at the fountain, the truck was there, so she put the bags in the back. It was such a relief not to have them digging into her hand anymore. It seemed like it took forever to reach the truck. The walk back felt like it was three times as far as when she walked to the store. She looked at her trembling hand; the lines across it were a darker shade of red now, angry lines visible across it. She wasn't going to go back for the seeds; she did not want to try and carry them to the truck, and she did not want to run into that German again. She would wait for Fabien, and then they would get the seeds.

After waiting fifteen minutes by the truck, she saw Fabien walking towards it.

"How did it go? Did you get what you needed?" she asked when he got closer.

"Fine. I got some strawberries from the Martins and some beans and peas from the Cassels. People in town are talking. They aren't happy about having to give up their food to feed the enemy. Those damn Germans! They take our land and our freedom, then our guns, and now they want our crops; what will they take next? I hate them, but one day I will get my revenge, as will a lot of us. Someday, they will get what's coming to them. They will get to see what it's like to have their land taken from them and everything they own, love, and hold dear gone," he said, swiping his hand in front of him, cutting the air.

"Fabien, don't talk like that. Not in town, the wrong person might hear you."

"Sometimes, I wish they would."

"No, you don't. Think of your girls," Eva insisted.

"They are the only reason I haven't done something already."

"No more talking like this! Now, we need to get the seeds from the store."

Fabien didn't respond but got in the truck and slammed the door, waiting for her to get in.

They drove to the store to pick up the seeds. Fabien didn't ask Eva to get out of the truck and help. Instead, he did it all himself. She knew that if she offered to help, he would just tell her he didn't need it.

"Shall we go visit Madame Blanc?" he said as he got back in the truck.

"We should. I would like to see her again."

"Didn't you say that there was something you had to take care of in town while we were here?" he asked.

She had all but forgotten about asking where she could mail a letter. She had been so taken off guard by the German helping her with the groceries that it had completely slipped her mind. The last thing she wanted now was to see more Germans.

"It's OK, I can take care of it next time we are in town, or I can make a special trip on my own later."

Chapter Fourteen

Madame Blanc lived in a Château just on the edge of town. It was set on six acres of land, and near the house was an acre and a half of gardens. Eva enjoyed spending time in the gardens whenever she visited Madame Blanc. It was her favorite thing to do there.

They parked in front of the house, and Eva got out and rang the doorbell. Fabien came to stand beside her, and they waited for the door to be answered.

Madame Blanc's housekeeper answered the door. "Miss Abrams, it is so good to see you again. The Madame has been asking when you would return." She looked at Eva's cast. "Oh my, what have you done to your arm?"

"I'm all right; I was clumsy and fell."

"Well, come in and have a seat in the parlor, and I will let the Madame know that you are here."

Eva and Fabien followed her inside to wait for Madame Blanc and sat in the parlor, but they didn't have to wait long. Just as they sat down, they heard her voice echoing in the hall.

“I am so happy that you have returned,” her voice boomed as she entered the room. “You were gone so long.”

Eva and Fabien stood up as she entered.

“I know, and I’m sorry. Things got a little complicated while I was away.”

“My dear, you have hurt yourself.”

“Yes,” Eva said with an embarrassed chuckle. “I fell. I wasn’t paying attention and tripped over a rock. I will have to be more careful in the future.”

Madame Blanc air-kissed both of Eva’s cheeks, then looked at Fabien. “It’s nice to see you again, Fabien.”

“And you, Madame.”

When Madame Blanc sat in her chair, Eva and Fabien sat down on the couch across from her. Eva always admired the antiquity of the furnishings and décor in the house, particularly in the parlor. The furniture was a light grayish purple with dark mahogany legs and armrests. It looked as if it was from the early 1900s, and a few pictures on the wall pre-dated the French Revolution. One particular painting hanging on the wall across from the couch always caught her attention, and she couldn’t help but stare at it. It was of a man with a sad face sitting alone on a chair in a dark room, and whenever Eva would visit and sit on the couch, it looked like the man was staring at her. She always wondered why he seemed so sad. Was that just how someone painted him, or did he have that sad expression while being painted? Was his life so bad that he felt like he had nothing to be happy about and, therefore, had no other look to give when they painted his portrait?

“So, have you heard?” Madame Blanc asked.

“Heard what?” Eva said, looking away from the picture to her.

“I have a German officer living in my house.”

Fabien pulled his brows together in confusion. “I thought you said they all had houses already and that your house was not picked?”

“That’s true. Mine was one of the few houses not chosen, but then there was a mix-up, and they had put two in the same house, so now I have one of them,” she said, disgusted.

“Have you met him?” Fabien asked.

“I have. He is not so bad for a German, I suppose. Hauptmann Gerhardt Von Schulz is his name. So far, he has been nice and polite and mostly keeps to his room. I have heard him up there playing the violin, but that is about it.”

Eva was less than pleased to know she was now under the same roof as one of them. It was like she couldn’t escape them.

“I know it is only Wednesday, but would you like to stay for dinner tonight? You could stay the rest of the week, and we can still have our normal dinner on Sunday, too, if you like?” Madame Blanc asked, looking at Eva with entreating eyes.

Eva looked to Fabien. She didn’t know if he needed her to come back.

“I have the girls to help. You can stay,” he said.

As if just being in the same house as one of them wasn’t bad enough, now I am to live in the same house with one for days and suffer their presence continuously, she lamented. It had been weeks since she had seen Madame Blanc, and if she told her no, she would moan about it until she finally got her way. She was a hard woman to say no to, plus she always gave Eva food for the girls when she would come to visit. She did not want to do anything that would change that.

She looked back at Madame Blanc. “Of course, I would love to stay.” She wondered how this would be, living in the same house with a German, even if just for a few days.

“Good, it’s settled then. Adele can drive you back.”

Fabien stood up. “I should go now. There are still things to be done. I’ll see you in a few days.”

“Thank you for the ride into town. If you need my help and want me to come back sooner, I will,” she said, almost hopefully.

“Thanks, Eva, but things will probably be pretty lowkey on the farm for a while. Just relax and enjoy yourself if you can.”

Eva knew what he meant by that. Relaxing in a house with a German might prove difficult.

“I will take good care of her,” Madame Blanc assured him.

“I do not doubt that,” Fabien told her. He left them in the parlor and disappeared into the hall.

“Adele,” Madame Blanc called.

Adele appeared in the entryway. “Yes, Madame?”

“Bring us some tea, please.”

“Right away.”

“Do you still enjoy living on a farm?” Madame Blanc asked when Adele left.

“I do. It can get a little repetitive at times, but for the most part, I enjoy it.”

“And how are those girls doing?”

“They are very well, and they are such a big help to their father.”

"That is good, I was so worried about them when their mother died, but sometimes I think they do better than their father."

"They are strong girls and so brave, given all they have been through," Eva said.

There was a thud on the floor above them. Eva and Madame Blanc looked up at the ceiling.

"Is the officer home?" Eva asked.

"I didn't think he was. He left this morning, and I have not seen him return."

Adele came in with the tea tray and set it on the table in front of them.

"Adele, has that officer come back?"

"Yes, Madame, he is in his room."

"How did we not see him come in when he returned?" Madame Blanc asked her.

"He came in the back through the gardens."

"Thank you, Adele."

Adele nodded her head and left the room again.

"It is good for you that he keeps to himself," Eva said.

"Yes, but I, too, stay out of his way. It's better that way."

Madame Blanc poured them each a cup of tea and put one lump in Eva's, remembering that she did not like hers very sweet.

"Renée, do you know where the Red Cross stations are here in France?"

Eva knew Madame Blanc well, and their relationship had moved past the point of formalities. She rarely referred to her by Madame and usually called her by her first name, Renée.

"I'm not sure. Why do you ask?"

"Because I need to get a letter to England."

"England! Who do you know in England? Is it a man?" Her smile was suggestive.

Eva smiled back. "Yes, but not like you think. He is just a friend. We work together—well, we did until Germany invaded France."

"I don't know where the nearest Red Cross post is, but I'm sure the officer here could find out for you. They would probably be the ones with access to that kind of information."

Eva hated to admit it, but she was probably right.

There was a knock on the front door.

"Are you expecting someone?" asked Eva.

"No."

They listened to Adele answer the door, and then a man's voice echoed down the hall. The talking stopped, and Adele came into the parlor.

"Madame, there is a German office—"

"Sorry for the intrusion, Madame," the man said as he stepped into the parlor entryway, putting his hat under his arm, not waiting for Adele to invite him in or for her to explain why he was there. "I am here to see Hauptmann von Schulz. He is expecting me," he said with a courteous smile.

"Of course," Madame Blanc said, sounding a little agitated. "Adele, would you go tell Hauptmann von Schulz that…" she looked at him, waiting for him to tell her his name.

"Obersturmbannführer Bauer," he said.

"That Obersturmbannführer Bauer is here to see him."

Adele nodded, then quickly left the room and headed up the stairs.

This officer was not like the other one she had seen earlier. Unlike the other officer, this one had brown hair but a similar stature, except for the shoulders. His was slightly narrower than the German she saw today, and his complexion was darker. Something about him made her more uncomfortable than when she was around the other one if that was even possible.

"Do you mind if I sit while I wait?" he asked politely.

"Of course, please, have a seat," said Madame Blanc.

As they waited, he sat still and ridged in the chair across from Eva and stared at her. The intensity of it was making her even more uncomfortable than she already was. She focused on her cup of tea instead of looking at him, but she could still feel his eyes on her.

"And who are you?" he asked in French, finally breaking the silence.

"My... um, name is Eva," her voice cracked on her name.

His eyes widened. "You are the American; I have heard about you. I think your country is wise to stay out of the war. No need to get their hands dirty."

You would know all about getting your hands dirty, she thought, but knew it would be unwise to say it aloud. "It is not our war, though we feel for the countries involved."

"I'm sure they do," he said condescendingly. "You know what, we are aware they help England yet still claim that they are neutral. But you see, they are helping the wrong side."

Eva did not want to be having this conversation with him; she could see it going south fast. She needed to think of a neutral response, one that did not come off as confrontational. As she was preparing her response, someone appeared in the doorway, and she could see them out of the corner of her eye. She turned her head and saw the officer who helped her with her groceries standing just on the threshold.

He seemed surprised to see her there. “Madame Blanc,” he said, nodding his head to her. He looked at Eva. “Miss Abrams.”

She slightly dipped her head to acknowledge him.

He looked at Obersturmbannführer Bauer. “I’m ready to go,” he said in German.

Obersturmbannführer Bauer stood up and nodded to Madame Blanc, then turned to Eva. “Perhaps we can finish this conversation some other time, Miss Abrams.” He nodded his head one last time. “Ladies.”

Oh, gosh, I hope not, she thought.

That evening, Eva and Madame Blanc had a small dinner with just the two of them. It was a simple meal of just soup, bread, and wine. Eva didn’t mind, though. She at least had food. Few people these days do. Eva went to take another bite of her soup when she heard the front door open and close. Then, there were heavy footsteps on the marble floor. She heard them getting closer, and then they stopped at the edge of the dining room.

“It will be curfew soon. I recommend you leave before then.”

Eva turned in her chair to look at him, the German she met in the street.

“Unless you are staying here, then, by all means, take your time.”

“No, I was not planning on staying the night.”

She didn’t want to tell him she actually had been planning on staying the night.

"Then I would hurry." He turned and headed up the stairs without saying another word.

Eva turned back towards the table, fuming at his impertinence. "I thought you said he was nice?"

"He has been so far. I have not seen him so stern with anyone before, but then again, he hasn't been here that long. You had agreed to spend the weekend with me?"

"I was, but there really are things I need to take care of back at the farm, and right now, I don't think I can put up with one of them. How about I come another time?"

"I suppose that would be fine." Madame Blanc did not try to hide her disappointment.

After dinner, Madame Blanc had Adele drive Eva home. Eva stared out the car window and watched the sun setting in the west. She could no longer see it in the sky, just the little light left that merged with the ground. The clouds looked orange and pink, and the silhouette of birds could be seen against the magenta sky as the trees and fields were now blanketed in the darkness. *He is probably less than nice to me because of what he learned of me during the interrogation, possibly because I am American, or maybe he feels somehow that I am a threat to the Nazi cause,* she thought. *Perhaps it's because of how I treated him when he tried to help. He has to know why people are standoffish with him, and he shouldn't take it personally.* It puzzled her, his seemingly up and down moods.

Adele pulled in front of the house and stopped. "Take care, Eva. I'm sure I'll be seeing you again soon."

"Thanks, Adele, you are probably right about that. Maybe I will spend the weekend with her after all, but I'm not sure yet."

“She would like that,” Adele said.

“I know she would.”

Eva got out of the car and waved to Adele as she drove away. Eva just wanted to take her medicine and go to bed. She walked in the front door as Fabien and the girls were sitting down for their dinner.

“I thought you were staying for the rest of the week?” Fabien held his cup in his hand as he stared at her in the doorway.

“I was,” Eva said, not wanting to tell him about her encounter with the Germans. “But then I realized I didn’t have any of my stuff there, not even a change of clothes.”

“I had thought about that. I was going to have Brigitte gather up some of your things, and I would bring them to you in the morning.”

“Thank you for remembering that. I told Madame Blanc I might stay with her this weekend.”

“Now that you are here, would you be OK with taking the family in the barn some food?” Fabien asked.

“You could not find them a place to stay today?”

“I didn’t have time to look. I will tomorrow.”

Eva felt bad now for staying at Madame Blanc’s. “I can come with you and help look.”

“No, that’s all right. The girls need some company, and I can manage. You can check on the people in the barn tomorrow and see if they need anything. They are probably tired of being here by now.”

Eva took a plate of bread over to the barn and had Rachel and Ezra come back with her to help carry the bowls of soup. When they returned to the barn, Eva sat down on a stack of hay and watched the children play.

"Do you know what you will do now that you are in France?"

"I have asked Fabien if I could help him in the fields, and he said yes for the time being, and Rachel will work as a seamstress if she can."

"And what about the children?"

"I will send Uri to school and keep Esther with me," Rachel said.

"Will you try to leave France soon?"

"Maybe in a month or so. We don't know for sure yet. It depends on how safe it is here and how big of a risk it would be to try and leave, but as soon as we find a safe way, we will," Ezra said. "What about you? It must be hard being stuck in a foreign country because of a war that isn't even your own?"

"It is really hard, and I miss my family a lot. I want to go back to my old life."

"I'm sure you do," said Rachel sympathetically.

"Do you think they will question you more because you are American?" Ezra asked.

"I don't think so. The German I talked to in the room seemed satisfied with my answers. After only answering a few, he told me I could go."

"Let's hope it did," he said.

"I think I'm going to turn in for the night. You guys can bring the dishes to the house in the morning. Have a good night." She stood up, brushed the hay from her dress, and walked back to the house.

Eva spent the following day helping Brigitte with the chores. Fabien was in the field and always told her no when she asked to help. She knew he thought she couldn't with her arm in a cast but was too polite to say it, so he always came up with things that needed to be done around the house. He had chopped some wood that morning before leaving for the field, so she stacked it beside the house for him as something to do. She would carry one piece at a time in her right hand and lay it on the pile beside the house.

"That looks challenging," Ezra said. Ezra was standing on the other side of the woodpile with a sickle over his shoulder.

"What are you doing with that?"

"I was cutting in the east field and came back for some water. Would you like me to help you with that?"

She looked at all the wood. Doing it one-handed would take hours. "Sure, if you have time. Will Fabien mind you not being in the field?"

"He won't care that I took a few minutes to help you with the wood."

He laid the sickle in the grass and started picking up pieces of wood with his right hand, stacking them in his left arm. Then he carried it to the side of the house, and she carried her one piece, feeling somewhat inadequate.

He laughed. "Don't worry about it, Eva. I will carry all the wood over."

"What, and I am to just sit and watch you? No, I don't think so. I will continue and help even if it is just one piece at a time."

"It won't make much difference, so why wear yourself out with all of that walking back and forth."

"If I don't stack this wood, I don't know what else to do."

"You don't always have to be doing something. You can relax once in a while, and no one will think you are lazy."

"Well, I would feel lazy." She picked up another piece of wood and carried it to the side of the house.

After all the wood was stacked, Eva brought them out some water. Ezra was sitting on the porch, looking out at the trees.

"What made you decide to help people in Europe? You must have known it would be dangerous?" He lifted the glass to his lips and took a sip.

"I did, but I did not think I would get stuck here, and I never thought I would miss my home so much. When I was there, I always hated how boring it was. Nothing really ever happens, and there isn't that much to do unless you like the outdoors. It is the same thing day in and day out."

"You make that sound like a bad thing."

"It's not, but I thought it was at the time. Now I see how fortunate I was to live in a place like that. Nothing happened, and that was the good thing about it. I just couldn't see it at the time."

"What part of America are you from?"

"I lived on the west side in a state called Utah."

"Is that by California?"

"Umm, no, not real close. You could get to the east side of California in a day and to the coast in a day and a half."

"That sounds so far."

"Not to an American, it's not. We are like Russia in that way; distance is relative because our country is so big."

"I see. Your state sounds lovely."

"Why do you think it sounds lovely?"

"You had said people who live there would have to like the outdoors, which makes me think it has many beautiful lands and lots of things to do outdoors."

"Yeah, I guess. One of the things people like to do there is ski because there are a lot of mountains around. People who enjoy hiking go there, too, but the southern part of the state is a desert, so you get the extremes. The part I live in is the north of the state and has mountains, so it can get very cold and snow a lot. I hate the snow, so I guess I'm living in the wrong place."

"I guess so. But it sounds like a place I would like to go to someday."

"Well, when this awful war is over, maybe you can go there."

He held up his glass of water. "To Utah."

She smiled and clinked her glass with his. "To Utah." She put it up to her lips when the sound of a car engine echoed in the trees. She lowered her glass and looked at Ezra. "Did Fabien take the truck to the field?"

"No, I have it down in the east field."

"Do you think Fabien would have gotten it and driven it back?"

"I don't think so. I'm pretty sure that is not Fabien."

She set her water down. "We need to get you out of here. Where is Rachel and the kids?"

"In the barn."

"Get them to the field and hurry. I will be right there to help."

He handed her his glass of water and ran to the barn. She took the cups inside, sat them in the sink, and then hurried to the barn. Ezra was hiding their stuff under the hay when she got there.

"Where is Rachel?"

“She took the kids to the field already, and I am hiding things in case they came in the barn.”

“Go, I will do this.”

“Thank you, Eva.”

“Go.”

He ran past her out of the barn, and she finished hiding their stuff in the hay. She could hear the car engine right outside the barn now. Then it stopped. There was the sound of doors being opened and closed but no voices. She had no idea who it could be; they were not expecting anyone. She brushed the hay from her dress and walked out of the barn, trying to keep calm, when she saw the black car with the Nazi flags; it stopped her in her tracks. She squinted to see the car better and noticed that there was no one in it, so she looked around but did not see anyone. She started walking again slowly towards the house, looking around the property for the Germans who obviously came with the car. She peeked on each side of the house but still could not see anyone. But when she started walking back to the other side, she noticed that the front door was ajar. She tiptoed up the steps, opened the door, and peered in; the kitchen was empty. She walked into the house and made her way to the back. As she passed her room, the movement of something to her right caught in the corner of her eye. She jumped, startled, and turned to face her open bedroom door. A man in a black leather trench coat and an officer’s hat was standing in her room with his back to her.

“Can I help you?” she asked him, annoyance clear in her tone. Who was this man in her bedroom?

“It has been most interesting looking at your things, Miss Abrams.” He turned around to face her.

Her breath caught in her throat. Obersturmbannführer Bauer was standing near her bed, holding the yellow flowery dress that she had laid there that morning after taking it off the clothesline.

"You have been going through my things?" she asked, eyeing the dress.

"Of course. People's belongings tell a lot about them, oftentimes more than they will say." He had a severe look on his face. He was not joking with her, and she knew it.

"And why do you need to know more about me?"

The anger was gone from her voice, replaced with a tone of compliance. She knew he had won. There was nothing she could do to make him leave her room.

"Follow me, Miss Abrams."

He laid her dress back on the bed and walked past her, out of the room and down the hall, heading to the front door; she studied her breathing and then followed him. Heaven knew what he wanted with her.

When she got outside, she saw his orderly standing by the car. Where the devil had he been? She had not seen him this whole time. As they neared the vehicle, the orderly opened the back door.

She stopped when only a few feet away. "Why do you want me to go with you? I haven't done anything."

"Get your ass in the car!" he ordered.

She walked to the open door, and he tapped her on the back to hurry her up so she would get in faster. She climbed in the back seat, and he motioned for her to scoot over, so she slid to the other side, and he got in the back with her. The orderly shut the door, then got in the front, started the engine, and pulled away. She was panicking now. The thought of jumping out of the car crossed her mind, but that would only make things worse. Besides, where could she run to? She did not know the reason for him taking her. Although it did not appear to be on friendly terms, maybe he just wanted to re-question her. Whatever happened, she had to do her best to remain calm. If he could tell that she was scared, it worked in his favor, not hers.

She was squeezing her fingers that were sticking out of the cast with her other hand to have something to focus on; she wanted so desperately to ask him why he was bringing her into town, but she doubted he would answer, and it could agitate him further.

The car pulled in front of the city hall, where the townspeople had to register and where she was interrogated the first time. The orderly got out, came around to the back door, and opened it. Bauer got out first, then she slid across the seat and stepped out.

Chapter Fifteen

"This way."

He put his hand on the center of Eva's back to push her along. When they got inside, he guided her to the back and down the same hall she had followed Hauptmann Von Schulz down, but they did not stop at the same room. They walked past the door to that room and stopped at one at the end of the hall. He opened it, and she walked in. He followed her and shut the door, then pulled out a chair at the desk for her to sit in.

"Have a seat, Miss Abrams."

She sat down, and he poured her a glass of water, then poured himself one. It struck her as odd that he gave her water after forcing her to come here.

He sat in the chair across from her, folding his hands together on the desk. "We need to ask you some more questions. You said that you help refugees. Who do you help exactly?"

She was afraid she would start crying if she talked. She took a deep breath as she squeezed her hand under the table. "I help any refugee that needs my assistance. That is how the organization works."

"Even the Jews?"

She had to tread lightly here; how did she answer that and not incriminate herself? "I suppose. I don't ask their religious preference."

She looked him in the face as she talked and spoke slowly, trying to appear calm and unafraid. For the first time, she noticed his uniform. It was gray but not the same gray as Hauptmann Von Schulz. Bauer's cap on the table had the death head skull in the middle that was worn by the SS and Gestapo, and on the right side of his collar were the double SS ruins and an SD patch on his left arm sleeve. She did not know that he was SS; she had missed it when he was in her room and had not noticed it at Madame Blanc's either. She had been so distracted by the fact that he was there and in her room, going through her things. This definitely made the situation worse. She knew the things the SS and Gestapo did.

"But you had to have known that some of them were Jews. You can tell just by looking at them?"

"I believe some of them were, but that was not my focus or concern."

"So, you think it is good to help the Jews, and probably the Polish and the communists too?" He unfolded his hands and leaned back in his chair.

"I just help people."

"When you help them, you are helping people as low as parasites. They are no better than the rodents that infest your house, living off the filth and making you sick."

"That is not how I see it."

"You Americans, you can't see the problems in your own backyard, nor do you believe there is a problem here in Europe."

There is a problem. It is you and your kind, she thought but didn't say. Instead, she chose to only look at him.

"I hate all that you stand for," he said.

She stayed still, fearful of saying anything.

"Are you helping any Jews now?"

She had an unpleasant awareness of her heartbeat as it spiked. "No, I haven't helped anyone since the invasion of France." She could not believe she could lie about that so easily.

"You are lying, and I will find out the reasons."

Well, she thought she lied about it convincingly, but maybe not. "I'm not lying. How could I help someone now? I don't have access to resources like I did."

"Are you spying for the British?"

That caught her off guard. "What… no. No, I am not spying for anyone."

He slammed a letter from Jon down on the table in front of her. "Explain this, then? Why do you have a letter from England?"

Her eyes grew wide as she looked at the envelope in horror. Oh God, he had found the letter from Jon in her room. She had destroyed all the others, but that one she got right before she went to Belgium and forgot to get rid of it when she returned. There was so much going on and so much that had happened. She was racking her brain, trying to remember exactly what that specific letter said. She did not know if he could read it or not; she was not sure if he spoke English.

"He is a co-worker I had when I was in England."

He took the letter out of the envelope and laid it on the table before her. "Read it," he said with venom.

To her surprise, his question confused her. Did he want her to read it in English or translate it into German? "In German…?" she asked.

"No, I have already read it. Read it to me like it is written."

So, he could at least read English and must understand it if he wanted her to read it to him in English. She reached for the paper on the table and picked it up with a shaky hand. She held it in front of her and started reading slowly, worried about what information it might reveal.

Dear Eva,
I went back home and took care of the things that needed to be done. I got the extra money and found a new apartment when I returned; they were very understanding about it. I have a new position at work now; it is better than the secretarial job they had initially offered. I now help find placements for children. They don't tell me much about what you have been doing, but I get to see some of the work you have accomplished while you are there. You are amazing; keep doing what you are doing. Please write to me and tell me more about it, and your experiences.

She paused and glanced up at him, gauging his mood.

"Keep reading," he instructed.

I called your parents while I was home and told them you were OK and keeping busy, and that's why you have not written them more than you have. They were worried and asked a lot about why you had not called. I assured them again that you were fine but were not in a place where you had access to a phone. It will get more challenging as time goes on to assure them. It is good that you will go home soon. And remember, don't forget to leave France any later than the 5th.

I was tempted to look and see what impact we had made by being there when I was home, but I decided against it. It would only put stress on both of us while we are here. I figured it was best not to. We can look when we are both home again. Please be careful and take whatever precautions you have to. You are almost done. You can't slip up now; your time window will soon be up.

-Jon

She laid the letter back on the table and looked up at him as he now sat on the edge of it.

"Well, Miss Abrams, there are many strange things in that letter. Do you care to explain what he was talking about?" he asked her in perfect English but with a strong German accent.

"Which parts did you find strange?"

He picked up the letter. "Well, for starters, the part where he said that he went home to take care of some things and got some more money. What did he need extra money for?"

"I don't know. As you can see, he didn't say what things he had to take care of. I would imagine the money he got from his bank account in America because he needed more to live on."

"But he says, 'the things that needed to be done,' as if you already knew what they were."

"I'm sorry, I don't know what he is talking about. Maybe he is just referring to the money."

"He also says your parents are worried. Do they not know that you are over here?"

"No."

"Now, why would you keep that from them?"

"Because they know there is a war in Europe. Would you want your child going to a place where there was a war?"

"Why did he say that you needed to be home by the 5th? And he said your window of time will soon be up. What does that mean?"

She noticed his blatant avoidance of her question. "I'm guessing because he told my parents that I would be home by then."

"You have a convenient answer for everything. What you are saying could be the truth, or everything he said has a different meaning to you, and you are lying about it. The fact that he told you to be careful and take whatever precautions necessary sounds a lot like what a spy's contact would tell them. 'You are almost done; you can't slip up now.' You are no more an aid worker than I am a Jew." He tossed the letter back on the table. "Why don't we start from the beginning again? Tell me why you are really here?"

"I am an aid worker. I gave that other officer all of my documentation on registration day. I would show it to you now, but I don't have my papers with me. You did not give me time to get them."

"I don't doubt that you have documents. I doubt their authenticity. I'm sure that the family you live with knows something. If you don't tell me, maybe they will."

She looked up at him. "They only know what I told you because that is all there is to tell."

He smacked the table and leaned down, placing his face next to hers, and spoke in her ear with a slow and deepened voice. "You will tell me the truth. You will give it to me the easy way, or I will get it from you the hard way."

He slid the letter in front of her. "What does he mean?"

Her hands were shaking, and the bile rose in her throat. She could feel his breath on the side of her face. All the other things that she had experienced up to this point were nothing compared to this. The fear was mounting, making her sweaty and dizzy. She was beginning to wonder if she would make it out of this.

"I told you what it meant," she couldn't stop her voice from trembling. "It's nothing more than a letter from a friend."

Tears wailed in her eyes that she could no longer hold back.

He straightened. "All right, let's do it my way then."

She knew something terrible was about to happen. The tears spilled over, running down her face. She honestly didn't know what to do next. She felt defeated but would never let him see the struggle she was going through now and how emotionally taxing it was for her to try and appear calm.

He opened the door and called in some of the soldiers who were at the front of the building. Two low-ranking soldiers came into the room and waited for their instructions. He leaned towards them and spoke in a hushed voice; she could not make out any of what he said. He then left the room with one of the men. The other stayed behind and stood guard at the door. After a few minutes, the other man came back but without Bauer.

He came to stand behind her. “Stand up.”

When she stood from her chair, she felt weak, like her legs could hardly support her weight. The man took both of her hands and tied them behind her back. Then everything went black. They put a bag over her head and pulled it snugly around her neck. When she would breathe, it sucked the bag into her mouth.

She was now being pulled from the room. “No… noooo, noooo. I’m telling the truth. Please, I’m telling you the truth.” That was all she could manage to say as they dragged her from the room and down the hall to another room.

They dropped her on the floor, and she fell onto her side, her head hitting the hard surface. She could hear a squeaking sound, like a knob being turned, then the sound of water running. She knew what was going to come next. She started screaming. Talking did not seem like enough. She felt like screaming was all she could do now. She would stop only long enough to catch her breath as she sobbed, the tears running down her face, making the bag stick to her cheeks.

The door opened, and a man spoke in German to the other men in the room. She then heard multiple footsteps on the floor, and then the door shut. The only sound in the room now was the running water and her heavy breathing. The door opened again, and the footsteps clicked on the floor as the person made their way across the room. The sound of the running water stopped, and then the footsteps approached her. Someone began untying the bag from her neck and pulled it off her head. She blinked a few times as her vision adjusted and looked around the room. The source of the water sound had come from a large metal sink directly in front of her, but she could not see anything else in the room.

"You are lucky today, Miss Abrams. Something has come up that requires our immediate attention more than you," Bauer said.

She could feel him loosening the ties around her wrist, and then her hands were free.

"You will be taken back to the farm, but know this, after a while, everyone breaks, and I always get the truth. Why don't you save yourself some pain and just admit that you are a spy?"

Through the tears, she could get a few words out. "I am not a spy…."

"We will see."

He went to the door and called out to someone in German. A soldier came into the room, and she heard Bauer telling him to take her home.

"Until we meet again, Miss Abrams."

He walked out of the room, and the soldier helped her off the floor. He held onto her arm and led her through the building and out to a car. He opened the back door for her, then shut it once she was in; he got in the front seat, started the engine, and headed out of town.

Eva sat in the back seat and cried as she rubbed the rope burn on her wrist, her other wrist now hurting under the cast from being squeezed and pulled on. The side of her head also throbbed from hitting the floor. She reached up with her good hand and touched the spot where it hit. She could feel something warm and sticky in her hair. She looked at her hand, and there was blood on her fingertips. She could not believe this had happened. And was it going to happen again? The thought of it scared her so much. She was not sure she could endure it again if it did.

The car pulled in front of the house, and the driver got out and opened the door for her but did not speak. She got out and hurried to the house, then stopped when she reached the front door; she was not sure she wanted anyone else to know about this. She turned around and watched the car pull away and then disappear down the hill. She looked back at the door but decided it would be better to check and see if anyone was inside before she opened it. She went to the window and peeked in but saw no one in the kitchen, so she opened the door slowly and tiptoed inside, going to her room and shutting the door. She looked around, and her yellow flowery dress was still on the bed where Bauer had laid it. She walked over to the dress and picked it up, squeezing her fingers tightly around it. Just seeing it made her think of him. She angrily threw it across the room and sat on her bed, hiding her face in her hands as she sobbed. She laid down on the bed, curling into a ball, and cried herself to sleep.

Chapter Sixteen

May 24th, 1940

It had been almost two weeks now, and Fabien still had not found the Schullers a home. Finding them a more permanent place to live was more challenging than he thought. No one else wanted to take the risk of housing someone who was hiding from the Germans. He told Eva that he would keep looking and still insisted that he didn't need her help. She wondered why he seemed opposed to letting her but thought she might have an idea. She knew he worried about her being in town after what had happened during the registration. He, however, did not know about her being taken in by the Gestapo. Bauer had not come back for her since that day, but he had alluded to the fact that he would be back for her at some point. She waited every day in fear that he would show up again and take her. The image of the German car coming up the road had played over in her mind. Ezra had seen the German car bringing her back and had asked why they had taken her, so she told him it was just for questioning. She left out the other parts, though, and asked him not to tell anyone else about it, not even to mention that they had been there. It was apparent he did not wholly believe her story, that all they did was ask questions, but he still agreed not to mention it to the others and never asked her about it again.

She did not want to go into town, anyway. Just the sight of a German uniform made her jump. Now that she spent most of her time at the farm, she helped Brigitte the best she could with the use of her one arm. The rest of the morning chores had already been done, and Brigitte was currently washing laundry. Eva would not be much help with laundry, only having the use of her one arm, so she sat on the porch listening to the birds sing and watching as the breeze gently blew the newly blossomed leaves on the trees.

"Can we go on a walk?" Sabina asked.

"Of course, let's go," Eva said, smiling, happy to do something other than sit on the porch feeling useless. It would have been better if she'd gone with Fabien. At least then, she would be doing something worthwhile.

She stood up and reached for Sabina's hand. Sabina took it, and they walked up the hill towards the trees.

"Do you still like it in France now that the Germans are here?" Sabina asked.

"I do. France will always be France; it is still lovely even with the Germans."

Sabina smiled at her. "I'm glad you like it here. I hope you stay."

Eva looked down at her. "Sabina, you know I will have to return home someday?"

"I do, but I can still hope." A twinge of sadness was in her voice.

On their way to the woods, they picked flowers until they reached the edge of the trees.

Sabina laid her flowers down, picked up a stick, and pointed it at Eva. "I am here to take your plunder," she said, trying to sound like what she thought a pirate would sound like.

Eva laughed, laid her flowers down, and picked up a small, twisted branch near her feet. "Not if I can help it, argh. I will make ye walk the plank and spend eternity in Davy Jones' locker."

They began hitting the sticks together.

"You hornswoggle other pirates. You are a disgrace to the jolly roger," Eva said, squinting one eye and talking out of half her mouth.

Sabina lunged at Eva, and she jumped back.

"That's it; there will be no quarter given, savvy." Eva was using all the pirate words she could remember from the movies. She knocked the stick out of Sabina's hand and pointed hers at Sabina's chest. "Me hearty will help, then maroon ye winch on an island, and there will be no invoking the rights of Parley for ye. Arrrggghhh."

Sabina giggled. "Where did you learn to talk like that?"

"You know, pirate school."

Sabina ducked down and ran across the grass to her stick. She picked it up and started swinging it at Eva, knocking her stick out of her hand. "Surrender. You are my prisoner now."

Eva feigned a swoon and put the back of her right hand on her forehead. "Someone save me…."

"Ahem," Eva heard from behind.

She whirled around to see Gerhardt von Schulz leaning against a tree not far off, with his arms crossed over his chest. He had an amused smile on his face.

"Go back to the house, Sabina. I will be there shortly. Help your sister and wash up for supper. Go."

Sabina turned and ran towards the house.

Gerhardt walked past her and picked up the flowers that she had laid down. He held them out to her. "I do believe these are yours."

She took them from his outreached hand. "I picked them with the girl."

"And play pirates with her, too. I haven't seen something so amusing in a long time."

Eva's cheeks flushed. "You saw that?"

"The whole thing," he said.

He sat in the grass on the side of the hill and leaned back, supporting himself on his elbows. He looked more casual and relaxed than Eva had seen him. The jacket he wore was unbuttoned down the front, and she could see his white shirt and suspenders underneath.

"There are some beautiful flowers here in France. Which ones are your favorite?" he asked.

He is trying to have a conversation with me, she thought. *But why?* "I like the blue ones that have purple bulbs in the middle and yellow things sticking up from them. I believe they are called

Blue-Pimpernels," she said. "But I have not seen any for a while. I guess they don't bloom this early in the year."

"I have seen those, but I didn't know what they are called. When we were going through the Alps a year ago, a few of us decided that we would climb to the top of the mountain above the tree line."

"Why?"

"We climbed to the top because it was hard. It's just a thing guys do. We feel like we always have to prove ourselves. Anyway, when we got to the top, I saw this pretty white flower peeking through the snow. In Germany, we call it Edelweiss. It is a small flower with thin white petals that grows high in the mountains. It's supposed to be the mark of a true soldier, so I picked one and kept it in my pocket until it died. As we started back down, there were fewer and fewer of them the closer to the tree line we got, and by the time we reached the forest, they were all gone." Noticing her silence, he stopped talking and looked up at her from where he was sitting.

"I would like to have seen one," she said, not knowing what else to say.

"Is this where you go walking?" he asked, looking around.

"This is one place, yes."

He peered into the trees. "Is this the forest you broke your arm in?"

"Ummm, I don't remember exactly where I was when I broke it, but it was somewhere in here." *Liar,* she thought to herself. She sat down in the grass a reasonable distance from him. "Madame Blanc says that she hears you playing the violin in your room."

"Yes, I have had it with me since I left for the war. It breaks the monotony and gives me something else to think about and do."

"How long have you played the violin?"

"I learned to play when I was six. My brothers and I all had to learn an instrument, so I chose the violin."

"Brothers, how many do you have?"

"I have two."

"And where do you fit on the age scale?"

"I'm the middle child. I have an older brother, Hans, and the younger one is Fredrick."

"Are they in the military like you?"

"Yes, Hans went to Poland, and Fredrick is in Greece."

"And are they officers, too?"

"Hans is, but Fredrick is only twenty. He is just a sergeant."

"Do you hear from them often?"

"I heard from Fredrick a few weeks ago, but no one has heard from Hans in over three months."

"I am sorry. That must be awful. You think something happened to him?"

"I try not to think about it. If I do, it makes my job harder. I have to focus on winning the war, so if Hans has died, at least it won't be in vain."

"And you want to fight in this war?"

"I want to see a unity in Europe as there has never been before, where we all want the same things, work towards the same goals, and share the same dreams. I think that would be a better world."

He is delusional, she thought.

"And what about you, do you have any siblings?" he asked.

"I have one brother who is older than me."

"And what is his name?"

"His name is Thomas." She played with a blade of grass, not looking at him.

He nodded his head, then looked back out at the trees. "Why do you never speak in English?"

"I guess because I am not in an English-speaking country."

"When I spoke to you in English the first day we met, you responded in German. Why?"

"I don't know. I just didn't want to say it in my language." Eva was curious why he wanted her to speak in English.

"How do you come to know German?"

"I took it in high school and college. I could ask you the same question, why do you know English?"

"My brothers and I had a privileged upbringing, and because of it, an excellent education growing up. We went to the finest schools, and they expected a lot of us. I studied for a while at a university in England, which helped my English a lot. Then I did a semester in Paris, where I picked up my French."

She was somewhat impressed; he was more intelligent than she had considered. "You are lucky to have had all of that and be where you are now. I mean your education and with so many talents."

"Luck has nothing to with it. It's all about hard work and dedication."

"But you would not have had those opportunities available to you if your family wasn't wealthy."

"My father never gave us anything that we didn't work for. We had to earn it first. We never got a handout. That was just the kind of man he was. Going to school in France and England happened because I worked hard and got good grades, and I can play instruments because I spent countless hours practicing them, same as the languages I speak."

"I'm sorry. I didn't mean that you got handouts. What I was trying to say was that you might not have gone to those same schools if you didn't have a wealthy family to pay for it."

"They didn't. I paid for it."

"Oh… I didn't know that. I should not have assumed."

"Don't worry about it. I know why you came to that conclusion."

"So, what did you study in school?" she asked, changing the subject to take the attention off the ignorant comment she made.

"I majored in international relations with a minor in economics. What about you? You said you also attended university?" he said to her in English.

Eva smiled at his choice of words; it was apparent that he had learned British English. "I was taking science classes. I was planning on being a nurse."

"I see. And can you or your brother play any instruments?"

"My brother can play the guitar, and I can sort of play the piano."

"I also can play the piano, but it is not my instrument of choice. I started playing around with the one in our sitting room when I was a boy and continued with it until I was a teenager."

Of course you can, she thought. *So, he has a college degree, can speak three languages, and play at least two instruments. Is there anything he doesn't do? None of that matters. It doesn't matter how educated he is. He is still part of this terrible regime and idolizes its values. If I were to put one foot out of line, he would probably have me shot without a second thought,* she told herself.

He looked over at her because she suddenly was quiet. She lifted her head to him, and they made eye contact for the first time since they had been talking. She saw kindness in his eyes that was not there the other times they had met, at least not that she had noticed. She also saw something else that she had not seen before. There was a scar about an inch in length, just under his left eye. She wondered how he got it but was not sure it was appropriate to ask him about it.

"How well do you know SS Obersturmbannführer Bauer?" He seemed taken off guard by her question.

"I know him fairly well. Why are you asking?"

"Because you don't seem like him. He is so… mean."

"Mean," he repeated, sounding surprised by her description of him. "You think he is mean?"

"No, I know he is mean."

"How do you know this? I don't understand the basis behind your statement?"

"A few weeks ago, he took me into city hall and questioned me for a while. When he was not satisfied that I was telling the truth, he had me bound, put a hood over my head and dragged to a room with a sink they were filling with water. Would you like to guess what they were planning on doing next?"

"He did that to you only a few weeks ago?"

"Yes. He never got to put my head under the water, though. He came into the room and said something came up that needed his attention more than I did. He made it very clear, though, that he would be back for me." She wondered if he even believed her.

"I knew nothing of this. Eva, I am so sorry that it happened. I will talk with him and get to the bottom of it. Do you know why he brought you in?"

"Sort of. He came to the farm, and I found him in my room. He had been going through my things and found a letter I had received from a friend of mine in London, and of course, to him, that means I am a spy."

"SS Obersturmbannführer Bauer is very dedicated to his work and his men, as well as the idea of a thousand years of the German Reich. He loves his country and would do anything to see it return to its former glory, and he has zero tolerance for anyone who gets in the way of that or he thinks is in the way."

"But he goes too far."

"Not in his mind. Don't worry about it. I will try to find out what I can do. But you have to remember that he is my superior officer even though we are not in the same branch. My inquiries about it cannot sound like I am questioning his authority."

"I know that."

"Eva!"

Her name came loudly from behind them, making Eva jump. She looked up to where the voice had come from. Sabina was standing at the top of the hill, peering down at them.

"Where have you been? You said you would be right behind me?"

Eva looked at her watch and realized that they had been talking for almost fifteen minutes. "I am so sorry, Sabina, I lost track of time."

Gerhardt stood up and held his hand out to help her. She stood up, ignoring his hand, and brushed off the back of her dress. She gave him a quick side-glance and headed up the hill towards Sabina.

"What kept you? Why did you not come when you said you would?"

"We had to discuss some things, but don't worry. It won't happen again."

"I would not tell Papa that you were talking to that German man. Papa doesn't like them."

"I know he doesn't. Don't worry, Sabina. I won't." Eva saw Fabien's truck parked in front of the house when it came into view. "How long has your dad been back?"

"I saw him coming down the road. That is why I came to get you."

Eva was relieved that Sabina was paying more attention than she was. She was so stupid to lose track of time like that.

Fabien was washing his face and hands in a bucket of water under the hand pump as they approached.

"Did you have any luck?" she asked.

"Not yet, but I will look again tomorrow. Also, the Germans are here to look at the fields. They say they will take half of everyone's crops from now on."

"Really?"

"Yes. Like I told you before, they take anything they want without consideration for the people they are stealing from."

Now I know why he was here, she thought.

"You don't have to stay out here if you don't want to. You can go in the house."

"It's OK. I think I'll just sit on the porch. At some point, I will have to get used to seeing Germans."

She looked in the direction where she had been and saw Gerhardt coming over the hill towards them. When he reached the house, he walked right past her without even a glance in her direction. He went up to Fabien, and they started talking about something she couldn't make out. She saw that there were three other soldiers there. They must have come with him. Gerhardt and Fabien headed towards the fields, along with one of the soldiers. The other two stayed behind near the car.

Gerhardt could be a hard man to read. Sometimes, he was stern with her; other times, he was nice to her, then he was indifferent to her, then nice, then back to being uninterested. Men were so confusing, especially this one. She wasn't sure why, but it annoyed her more than it should that he treated her that way, maybe because she had been treated that way before.

She watched the two soldiers pace back and forth near the car, occasionally glancing in her direction as they smoked for what must have been twenty minutes when Gerhardt and Fabien could finally be seen coming back out of the fields. Gerhardt nodded to Fabien and got in the back of the car, still not looking in her direction. The soldier that was with Gerhardt in the field sat in the back with him, and the other two got in the front. She watched them drive away, thinking what an odd encounter it had been.

That night, Eva lay in bed staring at the wooden ceiling, contemplating the conversation she had with Gerhardt. For some reason, she couldn't get it out of her mind.

"What did you talk about with that man?" Sabina asked from her bed.

"Just adult stuff, things about the war."

"Will you have to talk to him again?"

"I don't believe so. Why do you ask?"

"I was just wondering."

Eva knew she was asking for a reason but was not saying. "Go to sleep, Sabina. We have to help lay seeds in the fields tomorrow, so it will be a long day."

Chapter Seventeen

June 17th, 1940

"So, will you do it?"

"Renée, I don't know…."

"Oh please, it would be so nice to have some more company in the house besides just Adele, me, and the German officer, who we rarely see. Besides, you owe me for the weekend you didn't stay. I don't blame you. I know it is hard for you to be around them, but staying here a couple of days in the same house as one won't be that bad. You won't even see him. I thought it would be terrible to live with one, but it has not been that bad, not as it is now."

Madame Blanc had been trying to get Eva to spend a few nights with her for a while. Eva knew she got lonely, and even though she had Adele, she didn't socialize all that much with her. Renée had this thing where she did not think servants and employers should mingle casually.

“Fine, but just for a few nights.” Eva finally conceded.

“Eva, you have made a lonely woman very happy.”

Eva knew it would. That was the only reason she agreed to it.

“So, did you ever find out how to get that letter to England?” Madame Blanc asked.

“No, not yet. I need to do it soon, though. I really need to get a letter to him.” Eva finished her cup of tea, got her purse off the sofa beside her, and stood up to leave. “I need to go back to the farm and get some of my things if I’m going to stay.”

“Adele can drive you.”

Renée rang the little bell on the table next to her chair, and Adele appeared in the doorway to the parlor.

“Adele, will you take Eva to the farm so she can get some of her things?”

“Of course.”

Eva followed Adele to the car.

“You know that you have made the Madame happy?”

“I do. If spending a few nights here makes her that happy, then I am happy to do it.”

When the car pulled in front of the house, Eva got out and then leaned in through the open door. “I will be right back. This won’t take very long.”

“No worries, take your time.”

Eva ran into the house and down the hall to her room. She pulled her small carry bag from under the bed and sat it on the mattress. She went to the dresser and got three dresses, three pairs of undergarments, and three pairs of socks. Then she grabbed her toiletry bag off the top of the dresser. She poked it all in her bag and headed for the door, realizing that no one else was in the house. *Where is everyone?* she wondered. She thought that Fabien and the girls might be down in the fields. She turned around and went back to her room, got a piece of paper off the top of the nightstand, wrote that she would be staying at Madame Blanc's for the weekend, and then laid it on the kitchen table. She picked the bag up off the floor where she had set it near the front door, went to the car, and tossed her bag in the back seat. "Adele, I will be right back. I need to go check on something in the barn."

"All right."

Eva went to the barn and knocked on the door, but no one answered. *Are they off somewhere, too,* she wondered.

She knocked again. "Hello."

Still, there was no answer, so she opened the barn door and peered inside but could see no one. She walked in and started looking in all the stalls. As she got to the back of the barn, something moving in the corner caught her attention. Just as she turned in its direction to see what it was, she got hit with some flying hay. She fell to the ground and quickly started pulling the hay off her head so she could see.

"Oh my gosh, I am so sorry!"

She looked up to see Ezra standing over her. He was shirtless, and his skin was damp with sweat. She had not noticed before how tan his skin was, but now that he was standing over her, glistening with sweat, it was very noticeable. She stared at him without blinking, taken a little off guard by his appearance. He reached his hand down to help her up, and she reluctantly took it, then he pulled her to her feet.

"I am truly sorry about that."

"It's OK, Ezra. I was just trying to figure out where everyone was. I am leaving to spend a few days with Madame Blanc and wanted to let someone know."

"Fabian is in the fields, and I think the girls went on a walk. I will let him know when he returns."

"I figured that was where he was but didn't know about the girls. And thank you, Ezra. I left a note on the kitchen table, too. OK, bye."

She hurried out of the barn without saying anything else before he could continue the conversation. It was too distracting talking to him when he didn't have a shirt on.

She reached the car and climbed in. "Let's go," she said, a little out of breath, without looking at Adele.

Adele looked over at her. "Are you Ok? You looked a little flushed?"

"Yep, I'm fine. Let's just go." She motioned forward with her hand.

Adele started the engine, put it in gear, and turned the car around to head back to the road. Eva rolled down her window, feeling the breeze on her face. The situation with Ezra made her more uncomfortable than she had expected. Not because she had feelings for Ezra; he was friendly, but those kinds of feelings were not there for him. Eva liked Ezra, but not in that way. She just wasn't used to being that close to a shirtless man.

When they arrived back at the Château, she saw Gerhardt's motorcycle parked in front of the house. She was so hoping he would not be home. Eva got out of the car, grabbed her bag from the back seat and followed Adele inside.

"I will show you your room," Adele told her.

They went up the stairs and stopped at the door just to the right at the top.

"This will be your room. All the other rooms are filled with stuff right now. Madame doesn't get rid of anything these days." She opened the door and let Eva go in first.

It was a small room with a single twin bed, a white vanity with a small stool, and a chair in the corner of the room. The room was covered in brown and white striped wallpaper with a small chandelier hanging from the middle of the ceiling, and a fireplace set into the wall to the left of the bed near the door. A dresser was against the wall at the foot of the bed, and a window behind the headboard looked out over the gardens.

"When you are ready, the Madame would like a word with you."

"I am ready. Let me just put my bag down." She set it on the bed and followed Adele to the parlor.

"She is in there. I'll be in the kitchen if you need anything."

Eva thanked her before going into the parlor and sitting down across from Renée. "Adele said that you wanted to see me?"

"Oh yes, I do." Renée looked around the room like she was making sure they were alone. She got out of her chair, came around the coffee table, and sat on the couch next to Eva, which was strange. "After you left today to get some things from the farm, I went up to talk to the officer and see if he knew how you could get a letter to England. I knocked on his door, but he didn't answer, so I went into his room to see if he just hadn't heard me. I then realized that he wasn't in his room at the moment. As I was leaving, I happened to walk past his desk and saw some papers sitting on top, and something caught my eye. The name of someone I knew was on one of the papers. Then I noticed I knew the names on all the papers. I picked up a couple of them to read to see why he had their names. While I was reading the papers, I heard footsteps coming up the stairs, and as I was trying to put them back on the table the way I found them, I knocked some to the floor. I panicked. I knew I would not have time to put them back in their place with the others, so I picked them off the floor, put them in my pocket, and hurried into the joining room. I don't know if he has noticed them missing yet, but eventually, he will realize it, and it will be very bad when he does."

"Oh my God! Renée, what have you done? Why did you have to touch those papers in the first place?"

"I know, I should have just left well enough alone, but I was curious what he does up there when he is not playing his violin and why he had the names of people from the town."

"Renée, do you know what would happen if they caught you with those papers? For all we know, he has noticed them missing already."

"I know. The papers need to be put back before he does if he hasn't already. I hate to ask this of you, but you are faster than I am in my old age and quieter on the stairs than I would be. I think you could get in and out much quicker than I could without being noticed."

Eva couldn't believe what she wanted her to do. "You are asking me to return them for you? I think that is a bad idea. Besides, he is here; I saw his bike parked next to the house when we arrived. Maybe we should just burn them so he doesn't find you with them."

"His motorcycle is here, yes, but he left on foot right before you got here."

"To go where?"

"I don't know, but I think you will have time to return them. It should only take you a few minutes."

"Renée, he knows you. If he caught you, I think he would go easy on you, but if he caught me, I'm sure that I would not get off so easy."

"But if you were the one caught, you could lie to him about why you were in his room, and he would probably believe you." Renée insisted.

Eva huffed. "No, I don't think that is true at all. I think he would be just as lenient on you as he would on me. He doesn't like me; besides, he knows you, and you could lie to him just as easily as I could."

"Please, Eva, you could do it in a fraction of the time it would take me. Please!"

Renée was pleading; she seemed so desperate. Eva had never seen Renée like this before. "All right, fine, I'll do it. Where are the letters?"

Renée reached into her pocket, pulled out two pieces of paper, and handed them to her. "Please hurry!"

Eva took them from her. "On the desk, you said?"

"Yes."

"Which room?"

"It's the door just at the top of the stairs to the left."

Eva wasted no time. As soon as Renée told her what room he was in, she stood up and jogged up the stairs, turned to the left, and stopped just outside the door that should be his room. Eva took a deep breath, held it, and then let it out slowly. She turned the doorknob, pushed the door open, and peeked her head in to check. To the left of the door was a twin bed against the wall and a dark brown wooden desk covered in papers in the middle of the room. There was a fireplace on the right wall next to another entrance and two windows on the back wall. There was also a small bookshelf with a glass door covering it to the right of the windows.

She pulled her head back out of the room and looked to her right, realizing that the door just to the right of his room was her room. That was where the other door in his room led. That was what Renée meant when she said she went through the joint door. She sighed at the prospect of being neighbors with him for the weekend but knew that she would have to fret about that later.

She opened the door wider and slipped into the room, closing it behind her, then went to the desk. There was a pile of papers stacked on the right side of the desk and a lamp sitting just to the left on the corner. She went to the desk and laid the two papers on top of the stack, figuring that was probably where Renée got them from, and then looked at the door to the right. She walked over to it and tried to turn the knob; it turned with ease, and the door opened inward to the other room. She peered inside and saw her room and the bed with her bag still sitting on it. She closed the door quietly and turned to take a quick look at the rest of his room. His bed was neatly made, and there was a suitcase sitting in the corner and a violin case next to it leaning against the wall. At the foot of the bed, lying on the edge, was a folded white shirt. Against her better judgment, she walked to the edge of the bed and picked up the shirt. It felt crisp like it had just been starched. She put the shirt to her nose and lightly sniffed; it smelled of soap, starch, and the faint scent of cologne. Footsteps echoed in the hall at the top of the stairs. She laid the shirt down and backed away from the bed just as Gerhardt entered the room.

He stopped in the doorway when he saw her. "What are you doing in here?" he snapped.

Eva felt paralyzed. She couldn't move or speak. Her mouth opened, but no sound came out.

"Answer me!" he said again, losing his patience.

From the expression on his face, she knew he was angry.

"I… I needed to get a book." Her voice sounded small as she spoke, looking over in the bookshelf's direction.

"And you couldn't have gotten one from the library downstairs. Instead, you come into my room without permission?"

"I'm sorry."

"Have you touched anything?"

"No!"

"Are you sure?"

"Yes, I promise. I did not look at anything."

"Then why are there papers on the floor?"

Eva looked on the floor by the desk and saw four or five papers lying beside it. *I must have bumped it without noticing when I was backing away from the bed,* she thought. "I didn't touch them. I bumped into the desk," she told him.

"Pick them up!" he said in a stern voice.

She hurried and picked the papers off the floor with shaky hands and laid them back on the desk, stepping back again. She put her hands behind her back and turned to face him so he couldn't see that they were trembling.

"Now get out!"

She hurried past him to leave the room and shut the door behind her. There was no way she was going to be able to hold back the tears. She quickly went into her room and shut the door behind her. She leaned her back against the door and slid down until she was sitting on the floor, then started crying in her hands. The fact that she almost got caught and he was so mean made it that much worse.

There was a knock on her door; she wiped her eyes and nose on the back of her hand. "Yes."

"Eva." She heard Renée on the other side of the door. "Can I come in?"

Eva got up and opened the door for her, then sat on the bed. Renée came into the room and shut the door. Eva couldn't hide that she had been crying. Renée walked over to the bed and sat on the edge beside her.

"What happened?" Her asking what happened made the tears well in her eyes again. "Oh, it's OK, honey." She took Eva in her arms and hugged her tightly. She didn't say anything. She just held Eva and let her cry into her shoulder.

Eva looked up at her. "He came in before I got out, and I bumped the desk, knocking a bunch of the papers off. He thought I had been looking at them."

"But he let you go without doing anything."

"Yeah, after he yelled at me, and who is to say he won't punish me for it later."

"Do you want to come down for some supper? If you don't, I understand."

"No, I'm not hungry."

"It will make you feel better."

Eva thought about it for a minute. Her stomach was upset, and she couldn't tell if it was from hunger or the ordeal she had just gone through.

"All right, just a little, then I'm going to go to bed."

Renée kept her arm around Eva as they headed downstairs to try and comfort her as much as she could.

Eva ate a little of the leftover chicken, and some bread Renée had for dinner earlier and drank a glass of wine to help calm her nerves. She was feeling exhausted now after the stressful situation and then the wine.

"I am going to turn in now. Goodnight, Renée."

Renée had sat at the dinner table with her even though she had already eaten; she wanted to make sure she was OK. She hoped that Eva would want to talk about what happened some more; she was afraid that Eva was mad at her and wanted to feel assured that she wasn't.

"I am truly sorry for what happened, Eva. I didn't think he was going to come back so soon."

Eva sighed. "It's OK. I just want to go to bed."

She got up from the table and walked up the stairs, not looking at his room as she reached the top and entered hers. She took her dress off and crawled into bed. She was too tired to brush her teeth, shower, or find her PJs, for that matter. Almost instantly, she was asleep.

The birds chirped outside, so she opened her eyes. She turned her head to look out the window; the sun was shining, and the sky was a light blue with a few fluffy white clouds scattered across it.

She sat up and could feel her heart beating in her head. She went to the bathroom and got a drink out of the sink, then got her bag and took some clean clothes out. She took the clothes into the bathroom, shut the door, laid them on the counter, pinned her hair up, and started filling the tub. She stepped into it and sat down, leaning her head back against the wall. The warm water felt so nice. She wished she could stay there all day and not leave or see him.

Eva turned the water off when the tub was half full. That was when the sound of violin music came from the other side of the wall. She sat still in the water and listened. She did not know what tune he was playing, but it was beautiful, and he played it so well. It seemed sad to her, though she didn't know why. It was one of those melancholy tunes, the sound made by a violin weeping.

She listened until the water was cold, then got out, pulled the plug and stepped onto the mat. She took a towel from a rack over the toilet and dried herself. She dressed, returned to her room, and put the clothes she took off on the floor next to her bag. She went to the door that divided their rooms and opened it a crack; she knew it did not squeak from when she had opened it yesterday. When she peered inside, she saw he was sitting on the edge of his bed, playing. His eyes were closed, and there was no sheet music in front of him. He looked utterly consumed by it, and she could see that he enjoyed playing a lot. She slowly closed the door back and tiptoed to her bed. She wanted to eat without him noticing; she figured doing it while he was playing would be the best time.

She went down to the kitchen to get some food. It was Sunday, and she knew that Renée and Adele would be at church. She got a piece of bread and put butter and jam on it, then put some fruit in a bowl and filled up a cup with water. She put the bread on top of the fruit bowl so that she could carry both in one trip and went to sit at the little table in the kitchen instead of the one in the dining room.

She put a grape in her mouth and pulled the stems off her strawberries when she heard a knock; she looked up, and Gerhardt was standing in the entryway holding a book in his hand. He walked to the kitchen table and laid it next to her bowl.

She looked down at the book. *The Wizard of Oz* was embossed in gold across the front of the blue-hardback cover. She picked it up and held it in her hand, surprised to see it. She wondered where he got it and why he kept it. And why was he showing it to her now? She looked up from the book and stared at him.

"I thought you would like to have that. I got it off an English POW."

Eva looked back at the book; it was strange for her to see something other than Jon's letters written in English after all this time. "Have you read it?" she asked.

"I did. I know it is a children's book, but sometimes our posts can get very boring," he said with a faint smile at the corner of his mouth.

She looked back up at him. He was standing at the end of the table with his hands in his pockets, staring at her.

"It wasn't real," he said.

She gave him a questioning look. "What wasn't?"

"What happened, I mean. Dorothy just dreamed it all. In the end, she never really left Kansas."

It was funny to hear a German speaking of Kansas; she was sure he didn't even know where that was.

"I always liked the scarecrow best," she said. "He was my favorite. My mom used to read this book to me when I was a child."

"Eva?" he said softly.

She looked up to meet his gaze.

"I am sorry for yelling at you yesterday. I did not mean to lose my temper and upset you. You were not supposed to be in there. I didn't even know that you were here. So, you can imagine my surprise when I saw you standing in my room. I didn't know why you were there, and I saw the papers on the floor. Again, I'm sorry!"

She nodded. She was feeling emotional right now. Seeing that book made her miss her family and home. He reminded her of what happened yesterday, a memory she wished to forget, and then he apologized. It was all a little much.

"Do you mind if I sit down?"

Eva shook her head.

He got some fruit off the counter and sat down in the chair across from her. Just as he put his plate on the table, the front door opened. Renée and Adele's voices could be heard in the entryway, echoing down the hall. Eva took the book from the table and stood. She turned to leave when she heard him call her name. She stopped and turned back towards him.

"Would you take a walk with me later?" he asked.

That was something she did not expect him to say. She didn't know why he wanted to go on a walk with her, but she was pretty sure it would be taking a step backward if she said no. Their encounters hadn't been the most pleasant, at least for her. And she hadn't been the warmest towards him either. Perhaps it could be beneficial for her to make peace with him. So, if she said yes, no one would see them as long as they kept to the gardens. What harm could it do? Aside from being an unpleasant situation for her, it was better to keep on his good side than continuously upset him and have a potential enemy in the future. So she softly nodded her head yes.

"I have to do some work in town after I eat. Meet me in the gardens at 9:30 tonight."

She turned from him, walked out of the kitchen, and met Renée and Adele in the hall. "How was church today?" she asked, trying not to give it away that she was just in the kitchen with Gerhardt.

"It was nice. Father Lambert gave a wonderful sermon about acceptance. You would have enjoyed it, but I understand why you didn't want to come."

"I just didn't feel up to it today."

"It's no matter, dear." She walked close to Eva, put her hand on her shoulder, and leaned her head next to hers. "Again, I am sorry that you went through that yesterday. I hope you can forgive me someday! They are devils, and I hate them all. The one living here does not seem as bad as the others, but I don't believe any of them are good. They are not human; they lack common decency and compassion. You don't have to suffer him while you are here. If he speaks to you, just turn and walk away." She pulled back and cleared her throat. "So, what would you like to do today?" she asked as if nothing ever happened.

Eva was a little surprised by what Renée said. She hadn't realized Renée hated them that much. It was of the utmost importance that they did not see her in the garden with him, especially now that she knew what Renée thought of them. Renée probably believed that she would avoid him at all costs and not that she had just agreed to meet him in the gardens later tonight, so she would have to be furtive when leaving the house. Eva would have told him no if she had not thought it would make things worse for her.

She looked at her watch; it was a quarter past eleven. "I am happy to do whatever you want."

"You know what, why don't we go shopping in Paris."

"Paris? How would we even get there? You need a pass to travel anywhere now?"

"I know. I have a pass because of my property near there. I could try to get one for you, too."

"How far are we from Paris?" Eva asked her.

"It's about three and a half hours."

"Three and a half hours each way, seven hours of driving total?"

"I know. We would spend the night and have a nice day to ourselves there."

Eva had to admit, that sounded nice, but if she went, she could not meet Gerhardt in the garden. "I am still feeling worn out and a little tired today, Renée. Why don't we try to go tomorrow or maybe next weekend?"

"That would be fine, I guess. It would give us time to get you a pass."

"And how exactly will we get me a pass?"

Renée stared down at the floor, obviously thinking hard about it.

“Don’t stress it, Renée. I will try to get one tomorrow morning.”

“That would probably be easier, anyway. They might not give me one for you. Now that I think about it, they might not give you one at all. You don’t need a pass. You would be going to Paris just for leisure.”

Eva was going to ask Gerhardt for one when she met him tonight. “I will still ask. We don’t know for certain that they won’t give me one. We could always tell them I’m going because you need my help.”

“I suppose that is true. That is a good idea,” Renée said.

It was eight forty-nine, and Eva was in her room to kill some time while she waited to meet Gerhardt in the garden. She sat on her bed and wrote in the journal Jon gave her when the front door opened, and voices echoed in the hall downstairs. Then, there were multiple footsteps coming up the stairs. She hopped off the bed and turned off her light, strangely feeling the need to hide, not knowing who it was coming up the stairs. The door next to hers opened, and the voices were now in Gerhardt’s room. She walked carefully on her tiptoes to the joint door and put her ear to it.

“France fell in just over ten days. It shouldn’t be too hard to take England.”

“True, we were lucky to take France so quickly because we had the element of surprise, but we don’t have that with England.”

Eva pulled away from the door; she recognized both voices on the other side. One was Gerhardt’s, and the other was SS Obersturmbannführer Bauer’s. What was he doing here? She knew that they probably saw each other every day and wondered if he had told Gerhardt about what he did to her, but somehow, she doubted that. She was sure that Gerhardt never brought up that Bauer tried to torture her. He probably did not want to get into trouble with him. She put her ear back to the door; she wanted to hear more of their conversation.

"The British are giving us a lot of Hell. They just don't realize that they've already lost the war," Bauer said.

"That is something that is hard for people to accept. I don't blame them. They have so much at stake. There is very little in this world that compares to losing your country. I'm sure America will come to their rescue soon," Gerhardt said.

"Of course, they will. There is no doubt of that. America already helps them and still tries to say that they are not in this war. They are, I believe, a large part of the problem. England would have fallen already if it wasn't for their aid. They are only prolonging the inevitable."

"This battle with England will take a lot of German lives."

"Indeed, it will, and all will be worth it. But their deaths won't be in vain," Bauer told him.

"You say that because you are not the one on the battlefield risking your life," Gerhardt accused.

"You couldn't be more wrong. This war is not just about conquest, not for me at least. I would gladly give my life for my country if it was required. To me, this war is about protecting what we hold most dear."

"It's not about protecting your family?" Gerhardt pointed out.

"Of course it is. It's making sure that our country doesn't fall to that same fate. It's about ideals, values, our way of life, our culture, and preserving it. So in a way, it is about protecting my family," said Bauer.

"Those are all crucial things worth fighting for, of course, but it doesn't make the loss any less tragic."

"No, I never said it did. What are your thoughts on Miss Abrams?" Bauer asked, changing the subject.

"My thoughts in what regard to Miss Abrams?"

"Do you think she is a spy or maybe harboring Jews?"

"A spy, no. And I don't believe she is harboring Jews. And her views, perhaps she has them because of her circumstance."

"I don't trust her. She is hiding something," Bauer said accusingly.

"Hiding something. What do you suspect her of hiding?"

"I don't know what exactly, but I will find out. She has ties to England, and I want to know in what way."

"We all hide things, but I doubt hers are as grievous as you think. I believe she is just a scared girl stuck in a foreign country in the middle of a situation she is not equipped to deal with." She heard Gerhardt say to Bauer.

"You always think too kindly of people, Gerhardt. They are rarely as they seem. You just have to get them in a stressful situation or scared enough, and they will show you what they are really made of."

"I really don't think she is an enemy to Germany. We have nothing to worry about with her."

"That is where you are wrong. Her opinions and beliefs fly in the face of ours. Just her being here is an insult to German values. She thinks this war is an atrocity and that we are the bad ones."

"Can you blame her?"

"Yes, I can. Think about those prisoners we had in Wroclaw. If we had let them live, they would have caused great harm to Germany. What we did was for the greater good of the fatherland. In the end, the good outweighs the bad that had been done that day."

"What is it you are suggesting?" Gerhardt asked.

"I am not suggesting that we do anything with her, for now. Look, I have some paperwork that needs to be done tonight. Then I thought I would get a drink. Do you want to join me?"

"Thanks for the offer. Another night, perhaps. I'm going to stay here. Today was long."

"See you tomorrow then."

She could hear footsteps in the room, then the bedroom door opened and closed. The footsteps traveled down the hall and the stairs, then the front door closed. She walked back to her bed and sat down. He despised her. She had never done anything to him, but that didn't matter. He hated her simply because she was American and believed differently than he did.

It was seven minutes until nine-thirty, so she peeked out her door but saw no one in the hall, nor could she hear anyone awake in the house. Renée usually read in the lounge by the fire, then went to bed around this time, and she wasn't sure what Adele did at this hour, probably preparing things for the next day. Eva had told them she was going to turn in early tonight, and they didn't ask questions or seem the slightest bit suspicious. Eva slipped out of her room and tiptoed down the stairs barefooted to the back door that led into the garden, holding her shoes in her hand. She bit her lower lip in concentration and turned the doorknob, hoping that it didn't make a noise. She opened the door just enough to fit through and shut it quietly behind her. She put her shoes on, then turned to scan the gardens for him, but she didn't see him anywhere.

"Eva."

She heard the whisper of her name come from somewhere in the darkness. She turned toward the sound of his voice and looked around but still couldn't find him.

"I'm over here."

She scanned the garden and finally saw him standing under one of the trees, so she walked over and stopped in front of him.

"I come here when I want to be alone to think," he said.

"So, you don't need to be alone to think tonight?"

"No, this time I wanted to be with someone to think."

Eva couldn't help the trace of a smile that broke across her lips. Gerhardt put his hands in his pocket and nodded towards the rest of the gardens. As they walked, he took a pack of cigarettes from his jacket.

"Do you care if I smoke?"

"No, that's fine." She didn't know that he smoked, but it made sense because most people in this era smoked, especially men.

He took one out, put it in his mouth, and lit it, inhaling deeply as the cigarette's tip glowed. He put the pack back in his pocket. "What do you do in America besides going to school?" he asked after blowing out the smoke.

"I worked at a daycare on the weekends and at a hospital during the week."

"What did you do at the hospital?"

“I helped them with things like going to the bathroom, changing their gowns, that kind of stuff mostly. And what did you do in Germany before the war?”

“I worked at the Ministry of Defense. Then, when I got engaged, I went to work for my fiancée’s father at his law firm. I worked for him until the war started, then I enlisted.”

For some reason, this completely took her off guard. The thought that he had someone back home never crossed her mind, but then again, why wouldn’t he?

“I’m sure she is eager for your return.”

He threw the cigarette butt on the ground and smashed it with his foot. “I’m not sure anymore. Her letters have become less frequent over the last year. And when she writes, it is vague, and the letters are short like she has things she would rather be doing with her time than writing to me. She doesn’t say much about what’s going on in her life and rarely asks me about mine. I don’t know if she will still be waiting for me when I return home.”

Eva strangely felt sorry for him.

“And what about you? Do you have someone back home waiting for you?”

Her mind went to Kevin. “No, there is no one waiting for me. I was dating someone, but that ended a while ago.”

“I’m sorry to hear that.”

“It’s OK. It was for the best. We were not compatible.” She rubbed her right arm with her fingers that stuck out of the cast.

“Are you cold?”

“I’m all right, I—”

"No, you look cold," he said before she could finish. He unbuttoned his jacket, took it off, and draped it over her shoulders. "There, is that better?"

"Yes, thank you!"

Eva noticed the jacket smelled of the same cologne that was on his shirt, but instead of it mixed with the scent of soap, it smelled like him. He sat down on the grass and patted the spot next to him. She sat down beside him but a little farther than where he had patted.

"Do you like swimming, Eva?"

"I do."

"We will have to go when you get your cast off. There is a pond near here. I have been swimming there a couple of times."

"I haven't been swimming in years, actually," she said.

"Really? That is a long time."

"I know, it's sad. So, tell me, Gerhardt, what has being a soldier in the war been like for you?"

His expression changed from relaxed to severe. "You don't want to hear about the war."

"And why do I not?"

"Because war is not pleasant, it is violent and cruel. You see terrible things and do terrible things. The kind of things you wish you could undo or forget about, but the images are there every time you close your eyes."

Eva swallowed hard. She was not sure she wanted to know what the terrible things that he was referring to were, plus it was evident that he didn't want to talk about it, so she would not press him. She remembered she needed to ask about a pass. "So, I have a favor to ask."

He raised a brow.

"I want to go to Paris with Renée and help her. She has property there that she needs to check on and has asked me to accompany her."

Gerhardt didn't say anything. He just looked at her.

"I know it is not a need, but I would like to go. I haven't been out of La Chapelle in almost a year."

"Let me think about it. Ask me again tomorrow," he said.

"OK. There is also something else…" Eva felt uncomfortable asking him for one favor; two seemed like she was pushing it. "I need to get a letter to England."

"England?"

"Yes. I told you about the letter Obersturmbannführer Bauer found in my room from my friend in England. Well, they don't know what has happened to me. I was supposed to leave and go back to England about a week before France was invaded, but then I broke my arm which complicated things, and now I'm stuck here."

"And this friend, what do they do?"

"They are not in the military if that is what you are asking. We work together at the same organization."

"And you want my help getting the letter to England how?"

"Well, I don't know how to get a letter there now that France is under German occupation." She stopped for a second to see if he was going to respond, but he didn't. "I'm sorry to ask you for so many favors. But it's crucial that I get this letter to him."

"I will help you with the letter, but you have to do something for me."

Her breath caught in her throat.

“I would like to play you something on the violin.”

Eva relaxed a little. What he was asking wasn’t unreasonable and not something scary like she had initially thought it might be. “Yes, you can play me something.”

“So, your family is not big into music?” he asked.

“Some of them like it. About three years ago, my grandfather passed away. He really liked music and could play the violin too, like you. I grew up with him always around. He was my best friend. We would always say that we were partners. He would call me Frank, and I called him Jessy as a nickname because we were always doing naughty things together. Grandma would buy treats, and he would wake me up in the middle of the night and say, ‘Hey, let’s go downstairs and get some of that ice cream.’ The next morning, my Grandma would see the empty carton in the trash, and she would say, ‘You guys were up stealing my sweets again.’” Eva smiled at the memory.

“Why did you call him Jessy, and why did he call you Frank?”

“Oh, because of the outlaws, Jessy and Frank James. Haven’t you heard of them?”

“The names sound familiar.”

“They were notorious bank robbers. The law finally caught up to them, though.”

“Oh, I see. So, you two stealing the ice cream was like them stealing the money?”

“Yeah, kind of. We did a lot of things, like stealing ice cream. He was my best friend in the whole world. We were really close. He was my number one supporter, like my dad is, but even more so. When we had company over, he would say, ‘Eva, I’ll play the violin, and you sing.’ And I would laugh because this was something he would do all the time. It was like our thing. I was always shy at first, and he would tell me not to be. 'The Lord has blessed you with that voice. Let the world hear it,' he would always say. Six months after I started college, they diagnosed him with cancer, and it hit me hard. At the time, I was going to a university away from home, in another city, and I had to choose whether or not I would finish school there or be with him. I decided I would take those last moments with him and cherish them. So, I got in my car and drove home, and two weeks later, he passed away. I was with him when he died. I remember holding his hand. I was crying. He looked at me with a smile and said, 'Don't be sad. I can see Jesus, my brother, and Mom and Dad. They are all here in the room with me.' That was the first time I had lost a loved one. His passing was the most real thing I have ever experienced, but it was also the most peaceful thing. I believe he saw Jesus and his family that day. At that moment, I was grieving but also happy because I knew where he was going when he passed. I could just imagine him walking through the gates of heaven. I could have chosen to go to a dark place filled with depression and sadness, or I could be thankful for the years I had him in my life. I miss him every day, but I am so happy that there is no more pain for him. I truly believe there is a purpose for everything, and I know that he watches over me from up there."

She looked up at the starry sky.

"I know I suffered a loss, but I am no longer afraid of death after being with him through all of that. I don't think of it and say, 'I don't want to do this. I don't want to die.' It will be a beautiful thing when it comes, no pain, no sorrow. I get to see my loved ones again. How could you not want that? I truly believe I experienced a brief glimpse of heaven that day while he was dying. Not many people can say that." She chuckled. "I'm sorry, I don't know why I told you that story."

"I didn't mind. It was the most touching story I have ever heard, and I am sorry for your loss. But Eva, there is so much to live for."

"I know. I'm not saying that I want to die. What I'm trying to say is if I died tomorrow, there would probably be happiness and peace in even that."

He stood up and held his hand out to her. It reminded her of when they were in the field near the farm, and he offered her his hand, the hand she never took. She hesitated for a second, then put her hand in his. He closed it around hers, and she felt like her hand got lost in his large, warm one. He had a firm grip, and with little effort, he pulled her to her feet. Then he released her.

"I will go in first. Wait a few minutes, then come in. Go to your room, then come in mine through the joint door."

"OK."

He reached out and touched her arm, and it made her jump. Her reaction made his hand freeze there on her arm.

"I need this back," he said as he then slowly pulled the jacket off her shoulders.

She suddenly felt stupid for reacting the way she did. He wasn't trying to do anything except get his jacket. "Of course, yes," she said.

He took the jacket and walked out of view towards the house.

"Oh, my gosh, I'm such an idiot!" she said, covering her face with her hand.

After waiting a few minutes, she walked to the house and opened the door quietly. She removed her shoes again and tiptoed back to the stairs, then up to her room. She went in and shut the door as quietly as she could. The others weren't asleep, and she didn't want them to know that she had been out in the garden. She laid her shoes by the bed, went to the door that joined the two rooms, and knocked lightly on it.

He opened the door. "You didn't need to knock. You could have just come in."

"I didn't want to walk in."

He stepped aside for her to enter, then shut the door and gestured for her to sit on the bed. She sat on the very edge, unsure why it felt strange for her to do so. He picked the violin up off the desk, put it up to his chin, brought the bow to the strings, and began to play. He was so focused; it was like he didn't even know she was in the room anymore. He had his eyes closed, just like the last time she saw him play. She wondered how he could just tune everything out; she wished it was that easy for her. When the song ended, he opened his eyes and looked at her. She could tell by the look on his face that he was trying to gauge if she enjoyed the song. She more than liked it; it was the prettiest melody she had ever heard. She would not tell him that, though. He laid the violin back on the desk and then turned to her.

"That was beautiful. I have not heard that song before, but it was lovely all the same, especially the way you played it."

"It is an old German song," he said. He turned and walked to a little table in the corner with a gramophone sitting on it. He cranked it, then put the stylus on the turntable, and French music played. He walked back over to her and held out his hand. "Dance with me? Let's forget all of this for one dance?"

She realized she was not totally opposed to dancing with him and had no compelling reason to say no, so she reached up, put her hand in his, and stood. He lightly closed his fingers around hers this time and gently pulled on her hand, trying to get her to come a little closer to him so that he could put his other hand on her back and lead. He had his hand reached out, waiting for her, so she took a step closer. He put his hand on the middle of her back, and she put her hand in the cast on his shoulder, and they started moving. She looked down at his feet so she would know what he was doing and how she should move. She was not very good at dancing but could tell that he was. That, of course, didn't surprise her either.

"You don't dance with your eyes. It's all about feeling," he said.

She looked up at him, and he leaned in closer to her, touching his cheek to her hair, and his chest was now touching hers. It was closer than she had been to a man in a very long time; it felt nice and weird. He moved his head back and smiled down at her. His gaze was so intense. He seemed different in this moment than he had before in any of their other encounters. There was tenderness in his deep blue eyes, compassion, warmth, and something she did not recognize. When they were talking in the field, it was like she had made it over his moat, but now she was on the other side of the wall. All she had to do was penetrate the castle, the last line of his defense, and maybe she could finally see who he really was. She had never noticed these things in his eyes before; they were always like an empty ocean. But she still couldn't see to his soul in those eyes of his, only a glimpse of the few emotions she saw now. But beyond that was like a turbulent sea, nothing but the murky waves.

When the song ended, he did not let go of her immediately but stood there holding her. They could hear a knock on her door in the other room. He let go of her and stepped back.

"I need to go," she whispered. She turned and quickly went through the joint door into her room, closed it, and then went to the bedroom door and opened it.

"Madam just wanted to let you know that she is turning in for the night, and if you need anything, ask me."

"Thank you, Adele. I think I will go to bed now, too."

"I thought you already turned in for the night?"

"I was tired, so I came to my room early, but I was not sleepy, so I wrote in my journal."

Adele leaned her head to the side, peering into her room, then turned and went back down the stairs.

Eva sighed and closed her door. Then she heard a light knock on the joint door. She went to the door and stopped. "Yes?"

Gerhart cracked it open and peeked his head through. "I just wanted to thank you. Tonight was the first time that something felt normal. And I can't remember the last time I just sat and talked to someone like that, casually and not about war. Thank you. Goodnight." He closed the door, and she could hear him walk away.

She went and sat on her bed. *What just happened? I thought he hated me, but I am not so sure anymore. I don't know which one is worse, him not liking me or him liking me.*

She got off the bed and grabbed her PJs. It was getting late, and she needed to go to bed and get her mind off what had happened tonight.

Chapter Eighteen

The sound of footsteps in the downstairs hall and the front door shutting woke Eva. She looked at the clock on her nightstand. It was ten minutes past seven in the morning. *It must be Gerhardt. No one else would be leaving the house at this hour,* she thought. She sat up in bed and leaned against the headboard, knowing she would not be able to fall back asleep. She threw the blankets off, slid out of bed, and went into the bathroom to do her usual morning routine. She started to open her door to head down to the kitchen for breakfast when she saw a piece of paper on the floor near the bottom of the door. Someone must have pushed it under her door while she was sleeping. She bent down and picked it up, turning it over to look at both sides, but it had no name on it. She unfurled the piece of paper and saw that there were only a few lines written on it.

Eva,

Meet me in the square by the fountain today at noon, and I will have the information you need to get your letter to England.

-Gerhardt

She folded the letter back up and held it in her hand. Even though he had told her last night that he would help her with her letter, she had her doubts that he actually would. Meeting him today would also allow her to ask again about a travel pass to Paris.

I will meet him, she thought. She put the letter in her bag so that no one would find it, then went downstairs. Renée was already in the dining room, eating her breakfast. Eva took the seat next to her, and Renée eyed her as she sat down. Adele brought her a plate and a cup of coffee, then poured some in it before she left, returning to the kitchen. When Adele was out of the room, Renée finally spoke.

"How did you sleep?"

"I slept well, surprisingly."

"Hopefully, you will not have to interact with that German anymore while you are here. You can merely see him pass in the halls. I can also ask today for you to get a pass so that you don't have to."

"Actually, I am going to the German headquarters in town today to see if there is a way to get my letter sent, and I can ask for a pass while I'm there."

"Are you sure? Wouldn't it be better if I went instead?"

"No, I need to do this, Renée. I'm going to ride the bike there later, probably around lunchtime."

"Don't be silly; Adele will drive you."

Eva didn't want Adele to drive her and see them together. She didn't want Adele to get the wrong idea about what was going on between them, but Renée would not take no for an answer. "Thank you, Renée. I guess that's fine. There is no reason for her to wait around, though, because I don't know how long it will take. Then I'm going to go to the bookstore after."

"Are you sure? How will you get back?"

"I will walk."

"But that is such a long way."

"It is not that long of a walk, Renée. I have walked farther. Besides, I like to walk."

"Very well," she said, knowing that Eva would not budge. Renée was like a mother hen, always trying to look out for her. She meant well, but sometimes it bothered her.

After they finished their breakfast, Eva returned to her room to wait until it was time to go. She did not want to get interrogated by Renée right now. She pulled the letter from her bag that she had written to Jon.

Jon,

I hope you get this letter, because you need to know what has happened. And you need to get me out of France. I can't stay here any longer. I do not know what will happen if I don't leave.

-Eva

There was a knock on her door.

"Yes." The door opened, and Adele walked in.

"If you are ready, we can go?"

"Yes, let me grab my purse." She put the letter to Jon in her bag and followed Adele to the car.

"Are you OK doing this, especially by yourself?" Adele asked.

"I think so. I mean, I don't know what will happen today, but I have to hope that it will go well."

"You couldn't hope for anymore, I suppose. I have to ask, though, what is going on between you and Hauptmann von Schulz?"

Eva froze. "What do you mean?"

"I mean that I saw the two of you in the garden last night. You guys did not look to be fighting. Actually, you two looked pretty comfortable together."

Eva could not believe that they had been seen. How could she be so careless? Would Adele tell Renée, or worse, Fabien? "We were discussing me getting a letter to England and a pass for Paris so I can go with Madame Blanc, that is all." She was not going to mention that they talked about more or that she had gone to his room after.

"I believe you, and I am not judging you. I just want to make sure that you know what you are doing. Getting close to a German in an occupied country is dangerous, even if you are just friends."

Eva knew Adele was right, and she knew all too well what happened to women who were friends with the Germans in occupied countries. "I know. I need these two things from him, that is all, and we are not friends. I ask you to please keep this to yourself and not tell Madame Blanc or anyone else. I don't want people thinking that I am fraternizing with the enemy."

"I will keep this to myself, but I want you to promise that you won't do what you did last night again. Stay far away from the Germans, and this war will be easier for you. You need to be careful. You are in a unique enough situation where nothing you do anymore goes unnoticed, not by the Germans or the locals."

"Thank you, Adele, for keeping my secret. I won't get in over my head. And I promise I will do my utmost to avoid him."

Adele looked at her with disbelief before turning her gaze back to the road.

They pulled in front of the fountain, and Eva opened her door to get out. Then stopped and turned to look at Adele. "Adele, how did you see me in the garden last night with him?"

"I went to your room to check on you, to make sure that you were OK. I knocked on your door several times, but there was no answer, so I went in and saw that you were not in your room, then I heard voices coming from outside your window. I looked out, and that is when I saw you and him sitting on the grass, and you had his jacket over your shoulders."

"I did. But Adele, I promise you, nothing is going on between us. I barely even know him, and I don't want to get to know him. I just want us to be civil with one another. I'm sure that he suspects me of something. After all, I'm American. That is probably the only reason he is even talking to me. I know that SS Obersturmbannführer Bauer suspects me of something. He has told me as much."

"He is meeting you here then, I'm guessing?"

"Yes, I am meeting him here. He told me to meet him today at the fountain, and he would give me the information that I needed to get my letter sent to England."

"Let him do that for you and nothing more. You don't want to be indebted to him in any way."

"Understood," Eva said, letting Adele know her message was heard loud and clear.

She got out of the car, and Adele gave her one more warning glance before driving away.

Eva checked her watch. It was ten till noon. She sat on the edge of the fountain to wait for Gerhardt. She replayed the things Adele said over and over in her mind. Adele was worried that something was beginning to form between her and Gerhardt, but as far as Eva was concerned, it wasn't. Or was it? What did it mean when he helped her with the groceries? Or when he gave her the book? And what about the dance, or when they walked in the garden, and he loaned her his jacket? What did it all mean? Or did none of it mean anything, and was he just being polite? Did he feel bad for how he had treated her and was trying to make up for it? Perhaps what she told Adele was true and that he suspected her of something. God knew she had plenty to hide. If feelings were starting to bud on his part, they needed to be squashed. She had to prevent it from going any farther. She could not allow it to blossom.

The sound of her name jolted her out of her thoughts. She jumped, putting her hand on her chest.

"Oh my gosh, you startled me," she said to Gerhardt, who was standing beside her.

"I imagine I did. You looked like you were deep in thought. I called you from across the street, but you didn't seem to hear me. Is everything OK?"

"It's fine. I was just thinking about what I have to do when I get back to the farm today. Your letter said that you had the information I needed?"

"Yes, I do have it."

He handed her a piece of paper with an address written on it. It was the address of the Red Cross in Paris.

She looked at him. "But I don't have a pass to go to Paris."

"Yes, you do. Look on the other side of the paper."

She turned it over and saw there was a travel pass clipped to the other side. "But you said I had to ask you again today about the pass."

"True, I did. But while lying awake in bed last night, I thought about it and decided what harm could it do to let you go to Paris? I instructed my orderly to issue the pass this morning. I'm not sure if they can help you with the letter, but if you want, I can put it in with the stack of our mail that is going out tomorrow. Or you can ask the Red Cross if they handle that kind of thing. I think they do, but you should check just to make sure. If they do, then you will know how to mail letters in the future."

She flashed him a smile. She was so surprised he would do that for her, and she was grateful. He did not do one but both of the things she asked and he didn't have to. "Thank you, Gerhardt. Truly. I wasn't sure if you would give me the pass, but you did without us even discussing it further." The thought of what Adele said to her about not being in debt to him popped into her head. She had to let this be the last time she allowed him to do anything for her, and after today, they could spend no more time together, and she could not ask him for any more favors.

"This is why I came. I guess I need to go back and pack now. Thank you again."

"You are leaving now, so soon? You just got here," he said, disappointed. "Have you had lunch?"

"No, I was going to eat at the château."

"Let me buy you lunch; it's on me. We can go to the café by the train station because that is the only one in town."

"Oh, no, you don't have to buy me lunch. You have done enough."

"What, the pass and an address to the Red Cross? That took all of five minutes. I don't mind paying for your lunch, but if you do, then you can pay for your own. Is that doable?"

"I suppose that is doable."

"Good, it's settled then."

Eva could not believe she had just agreed to this. Didn't she just tell herself that they could not spend any more time together after she got the address and pass? *OK, after today, then,* she thought.

They walked together along the main street towards the train station. The sun was high in the sky, and Eva could feel its warmth on her face. There weren't many people on the street, which made her feel better about walking with him. The fewer people that saw them together, the better it was for her.

"Does it hurt?" Gerhardt asked. "Your arm, I mean."

"No, not so much anymore. It hurt a lot right after I broke it, but with each passing week, it gets better. I should get the cast off in a few weeks. That will be a welcomed day."

"When you get the cast removed, we should go swimming. The pond truly is amazing."

"Yeah… maybe we can do that." Eva knew she shouldn't agree to do more things with him, but she didn't want to say no, either. "So, are all of your brothers educated like you?"

"My older brother has a degree from a university like me, and my younger brother was only a year into his studies when the war started. My father is a stringent man. He had an idea of how things should be, and you do not disappoint him. He wanted all of us to be cultured, educated men. Choosing not to go to school wasn't an option. We always had to do exceptional in school as well, not just in university but throughout our lives. If we ever got less than a hundred percent, that was simply unacceptable, and he would let us know, and not always in the nicest way. Don't get me wrong, I love my father, and I would not be the man I am today without him, but I think he lacked compassion in how he dealt with his children."

"And what about your mom?"

"My mother," he said with affection. "She is the most caring, giving, selfless person I have ever met. Every memory I have of her is warm. She never yelled at us, and when Father would scold us for something we did, she was always right there to comfort us after. I remember that on Christmas mornings, she would always wake each of us up with a cup of hot cocoa, and the night before, she would put a hand-written note and candy in the socks that hung from the end of our beds. After we opened our gifts, she would read us stories by the fire. Those are some of my fondest memories. I love both of my parents, but they are very different people."

That was a tender story he told, and Eva loved it and hated it. She loved hearing how kind his mother was and how his dad being strict shaped him into the person he was today, but she hated the fact that it made him seem more human, and she wanted to dislike him.

"What about your family?"

"Well, neither of my parents sounds quite like yours. My mother is a very caring person, almost to a fault. Sometimes, she cares so much to where it is annoying. When I was eight, we got some new neighbors, and they had a little boy who3 was nine. My mom would not let me go out to play anytime he was outside playing, nor would she let me introduce myself to him. All because she had heard him say a swear word on the second day of them being there. The boy also wore a shirt without sleeves, and she saw that as being a bad thing. She did these things because she loved me, but sometimes it was too much. She worries about everything, and I mean everything."

Gerhardt chuckled. "She sounds like a force of nature."

"Oh, you have no idea."

"And your dad, is he like your mom?"

"No, not at all. He is kind of quiet and keeps most of his opinions to himself. Unless he thinks it is important and needs to be said, then he will mention it. I think my mom sees the world as bad, but my dad looks for the good in everything and everyone, like me."

"So, you are close to your dad?"

"I am. I mean, I'm close to my mom, too, but not in the same way I am with my dad. My mom didn't want me to come here, but my dad thought it was a great opportunity."

He chuckled again. "Your dad might have been supportive, but look at the situation you are in now. Wouldn't you be better off if you had listened to her?"

Eva couldn't help but smile at his honesty and also the fact that he was completely right. If she had listened to her mom, she would still be in her time, her country, and in no danger. "Good point," she said. "My dad was supportive of something that did not turn out well for me, but how could he have known? How could I have known?"

"True, we can't tell what the future holds, but perhaps you didn't weigh the risks against the gains well enough. To be honest, I'm surprised that they let you come at all. I mean to let their daughter travel halfway across the world by herself, without someone coming with her."

Eva looked at him with her mouth ajar. She could not believe that he said that. They weren't in the sixteenth century.

He saw the look on her face. "I don't mean that to be offensive. I'm just saying it is a little strange, that's all. It's not conventional for women to do that kind of thing."

"I'm not a child, you know. I can take care of myself. I have been for years now. And I don't need my parents' permission to work in another country."

"I'm sorry if I have offended you. I was pointing out something that appeared obvious to me. It seems that you are having a hard time and have been struggling. I also get the impression that more or less you feel alone here, and your feelings are not far off from what I think."

"Well… you are wrong. I don't feel alone, and I certainly am not alone. I have friends here, as you can see with Madame Blanc, and she is just one of many." Eva was not about to admit that he was right about almost everything.

Gerhardt stopped walking. "I think you know that is not what I meant."

"Well then, what did you mean?"

"We are here. Shall we go in?" he said, deliberately not answering her question.

"I guess." She looked at the front of the café set near the edge of town.

He held the door open for her and then followed her in. He walked towards the back of the café, found a table in the corner, and sat down. It was a small café with windows only on one side that faced the road and train station. All the tables were covered in white tablecloths and had little candles in the middle. It was not busy, and only a few other tables had people seated at them. There was a group of old men sitting together, puffing on their cigars and pipes, which made the inside of the café smoky. Eva didn't enjoy breathing in all the smoke, but there wasn't much she could do about it. The table that Gerhardt had chosen was the farthest from everyone else, so the smoke was not as thick where they were.

A man wearing black pants, a white button-up shirt, and an apron came to their table. "Bonjour, what can I get for you?"

"I will have a coffee and your ham and cheese croissant." He looked at Eva, letting her know he had finished ordering.

"I will have the same, please. Oh, can I get a glass of water, too?"

"Of course," the waiter said as he wrote their orders on a notepad. He then turned and disappeared back behind the counter.

"You told me you have a brother. Are you close with him?"

"I am. We used to do everything together, but then he met this girl, and we started spending less time together after that. She is his girlfriend now. They are still together, the last I heard. And you and your brothers, what is your relationship like with them?"

"It's good. My older brother and I were always very close. I think a lot of that is because we are closer in age. My little brother is nine years younger than me, but Hans and I are only two years apart. When the war started, Hans and I signed up on the same day, so I guess you could say we were pretty close."

"Is your brother married or have any children?"

"No children, but yes, he is married. He has been married for a year and a half now. They got married when he came home on leave for a week, but they have been separated the rest of the time they have been married. That is why they have no children, I suppose. Emma and I have not seen each other since the war started, either. Like I had told you before, I don't know what will come of our relationship when I return home to Germany."

"What do you hope happens?"

"Well… I would like to say that I hope she will be waiting for me when I return and will be happy to see me. But just like I am not sure of her feelings, I am also not sure of my feelings anymore."

Eva thought it was sad that he wasn't sure he wanted to be with his fiancée anymore, but she understood in a way. His fiancée might have fallen out of love with him from what he had told her.

"So why did you and your boyfriend break up?"

"We were just... I guess you could say we just wanted different things in life. And we definitely had different opinions about what a relationship should be." Eva figured that should satisfy him without her needing to say more.

"I see. That is unfortunate."

The waiter brought their drinks and sat them on the table. "Your food is almost ready. I will have it right out." He turned and left again.

Eva picked up her cup and took a sip of the black, steaming liquid. It was strong, but it wasn't coffee. No one but the German military or individuals buying off the black market could get real coffee these days.

The waiter returned after just a few minutes with their food. He sat one plate in front of Eva and one in front of Gerhardt. "Bon appetite," he said before leaving.

"It looks good," Gerhardt said.

"Yes, it does."

Eva hoped they would eat fast and with little conversation. She should get back soon and needed to wrap up her time with him. As much as she hated to admit it, she was enjoying their time together. He was an excellent conversationalist, and though he did not seem friendly when they first met, he had been exceptionally kind to her the last few times she had interacted with him.

Though they ate in relative silence, Eva could feel Gerhardt's gaze on her. She wasn't sure why he kept staring at her, but it made her uncomfortable.

"Do you like your food?" he asked.

"Yes, it is delicious. Do you like it?"

"It is good. I rarely go out and eat. Typically, I scrounge up whatever food is left in the kitchen after Madame Blanc is done with her dinner."

"You don't have Adele make you anything?"

"No, I don't want to bother her. There is no need to make two dinners. Sometimes, I will eat with the other officers, but only once a week or so."

As they were finishing their food, the waiter brought their checks.

"We are paying separately," Eva told him as soon as he laid the paper down on the table.

"Of course, I will bring two separate checks." He picked up the check and left again.

"Are you sure? I don't mind paying for your lunch."

"No, I couldn't ask you to do that. You have no obligation to pay for my food."

The waiter returned with two checks and put one in front of each of them. Eva looked at the amount on the check, then got the money out of her purse and laid it on the table. Gerhardt handed him the money along with his bill, and then the waiter picked Eva's off the table and smiled before he left.

"I guess we should go," he said, looking at the clock on the far wall.

"Yes, I do need to get back."

"Is Adele picking you up?"

"No, I was going to walk back."

"All that way, that is a long walk. Please, let me accompany you?"

"Won't you be missed?"

"I am done with my work for the moment. I was going to go that way, anyway."

"All right."

Gerhardt was making it hard for her to escape him. She wondered if it was on purpose or if he didn't realize he was doing it. Maybe she was too subtle in the way she was going about getting rid of him.

They walked out of the café into the warm summer air. It was so refreshing after being in the stuffy, smoke-filled café. Eva closed her eyes, took a deep breath, and then let it out. When she opened her eyes, she saw Gerhardt watching her.

"Yes, it was a little stuffy in there," he said. "Shall we?" He gestured with his hand in front of them.

"Yes."

He started walking back down the main street, and she walked beside him, although she made it a point not to walk too close. More people were out on the street now than when they went to the café, which worried her. She knew these people and had to interact with some of them. She could only imagine what they must think of her now. If she had her way, they would walk around the town back to the house. She could feel people's eyes on her, but she didn't dare look at them. No doubt they were all looking at her in disgust. After witnessing this, they would probably view her as a traitor, a collaborator.

Gerhardt didn't speak until they were out of the village. "Walking back through town made you nervous. I know everyone was staring. I'm sorry, I didn't think it would be that bad."

Of course, you didn't. You're a German, the people who invaded, she thought. "True, it made me uncomfortable, so we should not do this again. We can't make it a habit of being together, especially seen together."

He took a while to respond, and Eva took note of it.

"You are right, of course. It would be better for you if we only saw each other in passing and said pleasantries to one another."

She was glad that they had finally established the fact that it was a bad idea for them to be seen together, and the truth was it was a bad idea for them to be together, even if no one saw them. She could not get any closer to him than she already was, and she did not want feelings for him to develop. But the truth was, she had already started to develop feelings for him. She wasn't exactly sure what these feelings were yet, but she knew where they could lead. Right now, it felt like the beginning of a friendship. Whenever she was with him, she felt content, calm, and happy. Something about him, though, verged on fear when she was with him, but she did not know why. She thought maybe because he was simply German. After her experience with Bauer, she could never look at any of them the same. Every time she saw a uniform, she saw Bauer, and it scared her. Her nervousness when she was around Gerhardt could also be because his emotions were not always consistent. She did not know for sure what his feelings for her were, but she suspected she was correct in her assumption of what it could be.

He noticed how silent she had been after they agreed not to see each other anymore. He looked to the side at her; she was staring off into space, not even noticing the road in front of them. He wondered what she could be thinking about that would take that much attention. The thought of what it would be like for the rest of his time in France, knowing that she was close but not being able to see her. The whole time he had been fighting in the war, he had never met a kinder, more interesting person than her. He considered her a friend, and so far, she had been a ray of light in these dark days. That thought hurt. He did not expect to feel sad because of her inevitable absence. He realized he had stronger feelings for her than he thought, and before now, he was not sure what his feelings for her were. This confirmation was a little unsettling and yet exhilarating. He was unfamiliar with the feelings he had felt for her over the last few weeks. He had known his fiancée for years, and his father expected him and his brothers to marry well. Emma came from a wealthy Aryan family, and because they had known each other for so long, it made sense for them to marry. He loved Emma in his way, and he knew she felt the same way about him, except maybe not in the year and a half the war had separated them. What love he felt for her had waned, and he knew hers had too. In the past, he had very little interest in committing to one woman. He had been with many women and dated some of them, but he eventually tired of them and moved on. He did his best not to lead them on and made his intentions clear at the beginning that he wanted nothing more than just a physical connection. He had never felt a deeper connection with them than raw desire, which was OK at the time. It was all he had wanted. His dad got frustrated with the flings he had and his lack of commitment. When he reached his mid-twenties, that was when his dad decided that he needed to settle down and have a family. He realized his dad was right. At some point in his life, he had to take his relationships more seriously and figured his mid-twenties was an excellent time to start. So, as his dad wanted, he conformed and got engaged to Emma.

Eva could not have asked for a better day to walk back. The air was warm with no wind, and the sun was shining high in the sky with not a cloud in sight. The fields touched the horizon for as far as the eye could see under the pale June skies, and the only break was the country road they were walking on. The smell of the flowers and grass was a pleasant scent, but there was an underlining smell in the air that came from the fields. It was the scent of manure. Its smell seemed to add to the country feel, and all the scents made Eva feel at home. She loved being in the country and enjoyed the quiet solitude. And being here right now with just him and no one else felt like serenity. It was the happiest she had been since leaving home, but she knew all too well that it had to come to an end and that the end would come sooner rather than later because she could see the top of Madame Blanc's house just over the trees.

Eva noticed that Gerhardt slowed his pace when he saw the house. She wanted to ask him if he would like to sit by one of the trees along the road but resisted. It would not have been a good idea. She knew he was trying to make the walk last as long as possible. She glanced at him, trying not to be obvious; he was looking down at the road with a straight face. Maybe he slowed down because he wasn't paying attention. She wasn't sure.

She could see the entire house on the left side of the road. It would only take minutes to get there now. When they arrived at the house, Gerhardt walked her to the front door and stopped, then turned to face her.

"This is where I leave you. I have to go back to town now. Thank you for the walk and lunch. It was a pleasure."

He took her hand and kissed it, his lips lingering for longer than she expected before he released her. His kiss reminded her of one someone would have given if they were more than just a friend, more like a lover would. He started walking down the road towards town without looking back at her.

She took a deep breath, smoothed over her dress, and opened the front door. As she stepped into the foyer, she could hear Madame Blanc calling her name from the lounge.

"Eva, is that you?"

"Yes, it's just me."

"Come in here and tell me how it went. I want to know everything."

Eva walked to the lounge and saw Renée sitting in her usual chair, drinking her afternoon tea. "Well, don't just stand there; sit down and have some tea with me."

Eva sat in the chair across from her and poured herself a cup of tea.

"So, how did it go? Is he going to help you?"

"Yes, he had his orderly issue me a pass this morning, and he gave it to me today when we met."

"Good, we should leave for Paris right after tea, then. And what about the letter?"

The letter, oh shit, she thought.

"I forgot to give it to him. I will give it to him later," she said.

"Yes, that would probably be the best." Renée looked at her cup of tea, then took a sip.

"I was actually going to ask if it's OK if we leave for Paris over the weekend and not today?"

"Oh, I guess I don't see why not. But why would you want to wait?"

"Well, I need to get some extra things from the farm, and I should let Fabian know that I will be in Paris. I just need some downtime before I travel again."

"If you feel that is what you need. Is Friday too soon?"

"No, Friday would be fine. I will come back Thursday night, and then we can leave in the morning."

Chapter Nineteen

June 24th, 1940

"Adele is coming with us and will drive. She is going to be a big help while we're there," Renée said as she sipped her tea.

"I'm sure she will be glad to get away too."

"I suppose so. I don't usually ask her what kind of things she enjoys. No matter, we will all have fun in Paris, I'm sure."

Renée sipped her tea again, and Eva knew that was her chance to leave. "I'm going to go to my room and make sure that everything is ready."

"All right, but try to be quick. We need to get on the road soon."

"I will be fast, I promise."

She left the parlor and took the letter from her purse in the hall, ran up the stairs, and stopped in front of Gerhardt's room. She could not believe she forgot to give it to him earlier this week when she was here.

She hesitated for a second before opening the door and entering his room. She closed the door behind her and looked around. It looked mostly the same as it did the last few times she was in it. She kind of wanted to look around but remembered what happened last time and decided against it. She went to his bed and laid the letter on his pillow. She hoped that he would remember telling her that he would mail it. She wondered if she should put a note on it reminding him what it was for.

She went to his desk and got a piece of paper and a pen.

Gerhardt,
I had forgotten to give you this letter when we met at the fountain so you could mail it. I am leaving with Madame Blanc soon and will be gone before you get back, so I decided to leave it here. I hope it is all right? Thank you again for doing this for me and giving me the travel pass so that I could go to Paris.

-Eva

She laid the note on top of the letter and then put the pen back on his desk. She went through the door that joined the rooms, shutting it behind her. She pulled her suitcase from under the bed and laid it on top. She gathered up her clothes when she remembered that she didn't even ask how many days they would be gone. She wondered if maybe she should just take all the clothes she brought here from the farm. She grabbed the whole pile and put them on the bed next to her suitcase. It would be enough to last her for a week if need be. She then went to the bathroom and gathered up all her toiletries and makeup. She quickly folded her clothes, put them in her suitcase, and then snapped the lid closed. She put her suitcase and the toiletry case on the floor by the door and sat on her bed. She looked at her watch and checked the time; It was one thirty-five. She got off the bed and walked back over to the dividing door. She opened it again, peered in, and felt the warm air coming in through his open window. It was blowing the white curtains, rippling them in the gentle breeze. She was so confused by the feelings she was having right now and did not know why she had them for this man. At first, she was convinced she would dislike all of them and use the stereotypes about the Germans in the 1940s to base her opinions. To be honest, she didn't think she would see any Germans because if things had gone the way they were supposed to, she never would have. She would have gone to France for a few months, then returned to England, and then home. She could not have guessed that she would have to live among them, much less in such close proximity. She liked Gerhardt now as a friend, as a person, and something else besides those two things was stirring deep inside of her, and she wanted it to stay that way, deep inside. She closed the joining door, went to her door, and picked up her luggage. She carried it downstairs and sat the bags in the hall near the front door beside her purse. She peeked in the lounge and saw that Renée and Adele were having tea.

"I'm ready if you guys are," Eva called to them.

They both looked up at her.

"Oh yes, we are quite ready. Did you get everything you needed?" Renée asked.

"Well, I'm not sure. You never said how long we would be gone, so I packed for a week."

"Oh, I guess it slipped my mind. I was planning on only being gone for this weekend, so three days. We should be coming home on Monday."

"OK, well, I haven't overpacked too much then. You never know when you will need an extra outfit anyway."

"Quite right," Renée said. "Well, shall we go, ladies?"

Renée and Adele stood, and Adele put the teacups and pot on the tray and carried them to the kitchen.

"Would you help me with my bags, dear?" Renée asked Eva.

"Of course."

Eva took Renée's bags to the car first, sat them on the ground behind it, and then went back for her own. While getting her bags, Adele came down the stairs carrying hers. She walked past Eva and gave her a look that she did not understand. Eva followed her to the car and helped her put the bags in the trunk while Renée waited in the front passenger seat.

While they were leaning down in the trunk to put the bags in, Adele said in a hushed voice. "How did it go with Hauptmann von Schulz?"

"It went well. He gave me the pass and said that he would mail the letter for me. Then we had lunch at the café, and he walked me home, nothing more. I have not seen him since."

"Good. Now you have no further reason to have contact with him except to say hi if you happen to run into each other."

"You are right. I don't. And I don't see us having any real interactions after today unless I stay here again while he is still living with you so you can stop worrying."

"I'm glad to hear it. Now let's go and enjoy all Paris has to offer."

She closed the trunk and went to the driver's side, and Eva followed. Eva crawled in behind the driver's seat, and Adele got in behind the wheel and started the engine, put the car in gear, and pulled out onto the road. Eva was hoping that this trip to Paris would lend hope and opportunities for her, that maybe the answers to the solution she needed for a way out would be there, anything to help her get back to England.

Chapter Twenty

June 25th, 1940

Paris indeed was the city of lights. It held a certain glamour and allure beyond most other cities. She could see now why people romanticize it. Even Woody Allen was smitten with it, saying it had Gallic charm. It had style and culture, which made it an artist's dream.

She walked the streets in the finest clothes she brought, although they were not fine enough for Madame Blanc, who that morning took her shopping and bought her four new outfits with matching gloves and hats so she would look like a true Parishioner. Finding fashionable clothing in wartime-occupied France was difficult due to the Germans closing most of the fashion houses. They accused some of selling clothing to the Jews and were considering moving most of the French haute couture to Berlin or Vienna. There were, however, a few of the newer remaining shops still open in Paris, and Madame Blanc took her shopping at two of them, Marcel Rochas and Nina Ricci's. Even in the high fashion shops that were still open, the selection was limited because they sent most materials to the front for the soldiers. During the occupation, the only proper way for a woman to flaunt herself and add color and style to a drab outfit was to wear a hat. They often made hats in this period from scraps of material that would have otherwise been thrown away, but surprisingly it made some of the prettiest hats.

They had been in Paris for a day and a half now and managed to see the Eiffel Tower, The Arc de Triomphe, and walk along the famous Champs Elysées Avenue. Tomorrow, they were planning on having lunch in the Latin Quarter and visiting Notre Dame Cathedral, but they wanted it to be a more relaxed day, so when they were done with the Cathedral and lunch, they hoped to look at some of the gardens Paris had to offer.

They collected the money for the rent and the sale of the crops from Madame Blanc's land the first day they arrived, which left the rest of the time for having fun. Eva could not believe how much she had been enjoying her time in Paris. Aside from seeing German soldiers everywhere, it seemed normal and untouched by the war. She loved everything about it and couldn't figure out why she had waited so long to visit.

"Should we go back to the hotel? It is getting late, and the sun will set soon, which means curfew," Madame Blanc said.

Eva looked at Adele, who nodded in agreement. "That is probably a good idea."

"We will have room service tonight; my feet are killing me. I'm not young and spry anymore like the two of you. I'm an old woman, and I need to sit down."

"For a woman of your age, you have done well these last few days," Adele complimented.

"Maybe so, but today has been a particularly long day, and I'm tired. Let's get a cab."

Eva waved down a cab for them, and after they were all in, she told the driver to take them to 19 Avenue Kléber to the Peninsula Paris. Eva loved the hotel they were staying in. It was in the traditional Paris style architecture, with the tan-colored stone and domed roof covered with blue shingles. At the top was a balcony that went all the way around the building, and all the windows had green awnings over the top of them that blocked the sun. The inside of the hotel looked like the inside of a palace to her. She had never stayed in a place so elegant.

The car pulled in front of the hotel and let them out, and Renée paid the driver. They walked up the covered steps between the two white stone lions guarding the entryway.

When they got to the top floor, Renée stepped out of the elevator first.

"I will see you two in the morning. Goodnight."

She turned and walked down the hall to her room. Each of them had their own room, which Renée had paid for. She said they all deserved their privacy.

Eva headed for the door that led to the roof of the hotel. It was at the end of the short hall in front of them.

"Are you not going to your room right now?"

Eva turned and looked at Adele. "No, I'm not tired yet. I thought I would sit on the roof and look at the city for a while. It is so pretty at night."

"Do you mind if I join you?"

"Not at all."

Eva was not being completely honest with her. She wanted to be alone for the rest of the night because it had been so long since she had time to herself. For the last couple of weeks, she had constantly been with someone and wanted to take this opportunity to be alone with her thoughts. When she was on the farm, she could go on walks by herself when Sabina had chores to do, and in the evenings, when everyone was in bed, she could write her letters or just think, but she had not had that time to herself since staying with Madame Blanc so much.

Eva and Adele climbed the stairs to the hotel's roof and sat at a table near the edge. That way, they would have a better view of the city.

"Beautiful, isn't it?" Adele asked.

"Yes, very. I see now why people always talk about Paris the way they do. It even looks romantic. Have you been here before?"

"A few times since I have been working for Madame Blanc. We were always too poor to travel when I was a child, plus my dad hated coming here. He did not like cities."

"At least you finally got a chance to come," Eva told her.

"Yes, I'm very grateful." She turned in her chair to face Eva. "You know that Hauptmann von Schulz likes you, right?"

Well, that was a sudden change of topic. "Ummm… I don't know if he does or not."

"I'm telling you he does. You don't have to look hard to see it. He's in love with you. I watch how he acts when you are around, even when you are not together. You just being in the house seems to lift his spirits."

"I promise you he is not."

"Can't you tell by the way he looks at you and acts around you?"

"No, that was never the impression I got from him."

"I don't know how you feel about him, but I know he loves you. I believe that you could get him to do just about anything for you, like asking him for that pass and having him mail your letter. He did it for you the very next day. You pull the strings, and he does whatever you ask like a marionette doll."

Eva's cheeks were flushed, and she hoped it was too dark for Adele to see. "I guess he might, but if that's true, why does it matter? Nothing will come of it?"

"Because I think you like him too, and if you do, that is a dangerous road you are going down!"

"Why do you think I like him?"

"Because you don't seem to have a problem spending time with him, and when I see the two of you together, you act like a woman who is in love or, at the very least, infatuated by him."

She was going to have a hard time arguing with that, and the thing was, she was not entirely sure why she agreed to spend time with him. But deep down, she knew she was in denial about anything that concerned him.

"And you think because he gave me a travel pass, that it means he likes me?"

Adele released a loud breath through her mouth and smiled. “Not just that, but for the fact that he seems to go out of his way to do things with you constantly. No man spends that much time with a woman unless he likes her. He makes time and creates opportunities just so he can be with you.”

“OK, let’s say that you are right. Why do you say that it is a dangerous road?”

“Because he is German, Eva. People here will look at you in disgust and not trust you anymore. They won’t like you. Actually, no one in any country will, except those fighting with Germany. Think about what that will be like for you. And what if Germany loses the war? What then? Who knows what people would do to you? You would most likely be branded as a traitor, put in prison, or killed. There are so many reasons to stay away from him. You are a nice girl, and I would hate to see you get mixed up in something you can’t get yourself out of. Sometimes there are things that happen, and there is no coming back from them, and this could be one of them.”

Eva knew exactly what Adele was talking about, and one or all of those things could happen to her if she got involved with a German; even being friends with one was risky. Why did she sometimes think that the risk she took by being friends with him was worth it? They, however, would not continue to be friends. After their last conversation, she was sure that she would not be seeing much of him anymore.

“Adele, I understand your concern, but I have already told him we should not spend any more time together or be seen together. He agreed with me, so you can put your worries to rest.”

Adele raised an eyebrow. “And you think he will stay away?”

"Yeah, I do."

"I hope you are right, but I believe you will find that you are wrong."

"Adele, why do you hate the Germans? You know they are not all bad people, right? Not all of them want to be here. They would rather do something else and not be soldiers, just like men who fight for other countries. They would rather be home with their families. You can't blame them for what their leaders do. Besides, he is not a Nazi or in the SS."

"I know he isn't, but that doesn't make him good either, just because they are worse. Let me tell you a story," Adele said. "I used to have a brother named Claude. He was the sweetest, kindest soul you would ever meet. He had the biggest and brightest blue eyes, always filled with wonder, and a heart so full of love. He adored the world and everything in it, and he enjoyed learning about everything he could. There wasn't anything or anyone he did not see beauty in. He was such a joy to be around because he had such a gentle disposition. When this war started, he joined like all the other dutiful boys did. Because of his age, they stationed him on a base close to home, but when the Germans were pushing west towards the English Channel, and the bulk of our troops, along with the British, were still fighting in Belgium, they had no choice but to send him and his company to Normandy. His company was made up of mostly boys who were too young to be fighting on the frontlines. When they arrived in Normandy, though, it was too late. There was little to stop the Germans from advancing as they sliced their way through what little supply lines we had between here and Belgium. Claude and his company reached the English Channel on May 20th, but unfortunately, so did the Germans. Within a matter of hours, they were surrounded, most of them had been slaughtered, and the ones that weren't were taken prisoner. As you might or might not know, the Germans are not known for treating their prisoners well, even though they are supposed to under the Geneva Convention. They sent Claude to a POW camp. I'm not sure exactly where, but I think it's in Germany. The guards at this camp were not nice to the prisoners and did not follow the rules set by the Geneva Convention. They were supposed to give them two meals a day and all the packages that arrived from the Red Cross. Well, they didn't. They took all the things that arrived from the Red Cross and would only give the prisoners one meal a day, a bowl of broth, and a slice of bread. One day, I guess Claude had had enough. When the Germans took the Red Cross packages again that had arrived one morning, he stood up and told them they could not do that. The packages were for the POWs, and they had no right to take them. That did not go over well with the guards. They dragged him away from the lineup to a room with only a sink and a table with a single chair. They put a bag over his head and began dunking it in a sink filled with water. Both men would take turns punching him in the stomach while his head was under the water. They kept doing this over and over. Putting his head under the water, then hit him in the stomach so that he would suck water in, then pull his head up. Just as he was catching his breath, they would do it again, but they did it one too many times. When they pulled his head up from the sink the last time, he was not breathing. They left him on the floor and went about their day; it wasn't until that evening that they had two other POWs retrieve his body. They sent a letter telling us he got sick and died from complications. A month after we got the letter from the Germans, we got a visit from a family that lived in our town. They, too, had a son who was in the POW camp. He wrote to them and told them what had happened to Claude; he said it had happened before to other prisoners. If the prisoner did something wrong, they would take them to that room, and sometimes, they would do it even if they had done nothing wrong. I have not heard of any more deaths like his; perhaps Claude died because he wasn't the most robust person. I don't think his body could handle that kind of stress like some of the others. So, you see, the Germans are lying, heartless sons of bitches. They stole the light out of that beautiful boy's eyes, and for what? Telling them not to take packages filled with letters and chocolates? He died for nothing." Adele put her face in her hands and wept softly.

Eva could not contain the sadness she felt for Adele. She did not know that she had gone through so much at the hands of the Germans. And to think that what happened to him came close to happening to her. She got out of her chair, walked over to Adele, and gently wrapped her arm around her shoulder. Tears spilled from Eva's eyes and ran down her cheeks. She could not understand how someone could be so cruel, but at the same time, she still knew in her heart that not all Germans were like the ones at the camps. Not all of them were cruel and heartless. But she understood why Adele felt that way. If it were her brother they killed and her country they had taken, she probably would feel the same way about the Germans as Adele. Eva let her cry but said nothing. She didn't even know what she would say.

Adele raised her head from her hands and began wiping the tears off her cheeks and from her eyes. "I'm sorry that you had to see me like that. I didn't mean to cry."

"It's OK. I would cry, too. He was your brother, and you loved him. Did you ever get to have his funeral?"

"No, they buried him in Germany. We never even saw his body."

"Oh…."

"I did not tell you that story to make you sad or to feel sorry for me. I told you because I don't want to see another young life get snuffed out because of the Germans. Your situation might differ from Claude's, but it could still end the same. Even if you make it out of this war alive, there would only be a lot of heartache in the end. For your sake, don't do this."

Eva realized at that moment that she could not talk about the Germans to Adele or be seen with any.

"It's getting late, Adele. Why don't we turn in for the night?"

"Yes, I suddenly feel exhausted. Let's go to our rooms and get some sleep. Tomorrow will be a fun day." She gave Eva a forced smile.

That morning, Eva sat on her balcony eating her breakfast, thinking about the conversation she had with Adele the night before. It had gone in a direction she did not expect; it was not a surprise when Adele told her to stay away from Gerhardt, but she did not think it would get so personal.

After eating breakfast, she met Madame Blanc and Adele in the lobby.

"How did you sleep?" Madame Blanc asked.

"I slept well. Thanks for asking! How did you sleep?"

"Like a baby, all this walking is wearing me out."

Eva looked at Adele. "How about you?"

"It took me a while to fall asleep, but once I fell asleep, I slept well."

"That's good." Eva could tell that Adele was tired by looking at the bags under her eyes and the dark circles around them. She wondered if Adele was lying about sleeping well but figured it was better not to ask.

"Let's get going. The day is fading fast," Madame Blanc said.

It was such a nice day that they decided to walk to Notre Dame Cathedral instead of taking the tram or a taxi to Sainte Chapelle. After seeing Notre Dame Cathedral and Sainte Chapelle, they walked the streets, admiring the beauty of the city and enjoying its atmosphere.

"I don't know about you guys, but I'm starving," Madame Blanc said. "Should we walk to the Latin Quarter now and get lunch?"

"Yeah, I'm getting a little hungry, too. What about you, Adele?"

"I could eat, sure."

They made their way to the Latin Quarter and looked for a café to eat at. They chose one that was not as busy, and Eva noticed that it also did not have any German soldiers there as the others did. They each took a seat at a small black metal table outside, under the awning. She looked around at all the soldiers that were at the cafés. Some were enlisted, and some were officers. Because of the proximity of the buildings, they were sitting close to the soldiers at the café next to them. While they waited to be helped, Eva listened to the conversation between the two German soldiers behind her. They talked about what they were going to do with their money when they got paid. One said that he was going to get so drunk he wouldn't remember the night before. The other said he planned to get himself a whore or maybe two. They started laughing and continued talking about the whores when one asked the other if he would share them with him.

A waitress came to the table. "Bonjour." She laid three menus on the table, one in front of each of them. "Can I get you something to drink?"

"Yes, I will have a glass of wine, whatever your sweetest red is," Madame Blanc said.

The waitress looked at Eva.

"I will have the same," she said. "Oh, and a glass of water, too, please."

"Our sweetest red wine is a Sauvignon Blanc," the waitress said.

"That is what I will have then," Eva said.

"Of course." The waitress smiled, her red lipstick making her teeth seem extra white. She looked at Adele. "And you?"

"No wine, I will just have water."

"I will have those right out." She turned and left.

"I'm sorry that we could not find a table farther away from the Germans," Madame Blanc said. "It's terrible that we have to sit so close to them. I can even smell their cologne and cigarettes from here."

"It's no matter," Adele said.

"Adele is right," Eva agreed. "Let's just eat and not think about them." She opened her menu and looked at the lunch options. She decided on a simple soup with a side of steamed vegetables and bread.

When the waitress came back with their drinks, they ordered their food. Eva sat back in her chair to wait for the food while sipping her wine. The wine was really on the sweet side, and she liked that. Renée chose an excellent one. They both obviously had the same taste.

Madame Blanc and Adele were discussing one of her tenants, so Eva decided she would people-watch. While she was scanning the people at the other tables, she noticed a man sitting in the shadows at the café across the street from them; he seemed to be staring at her. He appeared to be alone; she didn't see another cup or plate on his table. He looked furtively from his chair in her direction with a piercing stare and did not change his gaze from her; he didn't seem to notice the people walking by or anyone at the other tables. She looked around her to see if maybe there was something or someone he was looking at behind her, but she did not see anyone standing near her or anything out of the ordinary. She looked back at the man; he was still sitting in his chair, staring in her direction. It was making her uncomfortable.

Why is he staring at me? she wondered. *Maybe he is looking at something else, and it just looks like he is staring at me. I guess he could be lost in thought and doesn't realize he is doing it.* She looked around again to make sure she hadn't missed something, but nothing had changed from the last time she checked. There was no doubt in her mind now. It was her he was staring at. The man appeared to be in his late thirties, was tall and lanky, and not at all the muscular type. He had brown hair that was starting to thin at the top, a very chiseled jaw for such a slender man, which added to his already brooding face, and a thin black mustache. Even when she looked away from him, she could still feel his stare. It was as a shape amid the shadows, like in horror movies, when something lurked behind a bush in the night, and one didn't see it but could feel its eyes on them. That was how she felt now.

The waitress came back to the table with two plates; she sat Eva's in front of her and Madame Blanc's in front of her. "I will bring yours right out," she said to Adele. The woman returned with her food and left as quickly as she came, circling to the other tables.

Eva occasionally glanced at the man across from her as she ate, hoping that he would be gone, but unfortunately, he was still there and still staring at her as he now smoked a cigarette. She finished her food, looked at Madame Blanc and Adele's plates, and saw they had only eaten half of their food. She forgot how slowly Europeans could eat sometimes.

She looked at her watch; it was a quarter to one. "Do you mind if I take off? I need to go to the Red Cross and ask about mailing letters."

"I suppose so. Can't it wait until later?"

"I'm sorry. I really need to get it done. I'm afraid if I wait and keep putting it off, I will miss my chance. Besides, I think they might close soon. You guys enjoy the rest of your lunch. I will meet up with you back at the hotel."

Adele drank from her water glass and stared at Eva over the rim but kept her thoughts to herself.

"OK, go then if you must," Renée said.

Eva could tell that Renée was disappointed, but she needed to do this. She got up from her chair and retrieved her purse from the ground. "I'll catch you later."

She looked one more time in the direction of the mysterious man sitting across from them, but to her surprise, he was no longer there. Eva instantly looked around to see if she could find him amongst the people, but he was nowhere to be found.

"What are you looking for?" Renée asked.

"I… I'm not looking for anything. OK, I'll see you back at the hotel." She didn't tell them about the strange man that was staring at her, not wanting to alarm them.

She walked past them and left the Latin Quarter before turning onto the main street. She had the address of the Red Cross and knew roughly where it was. It should be within walking distance from the Latin Quarter. As she turned from street to street and weaved amongst the other people, she got a distinct feeling that she was still being watched, which meant that she was being followed. Eva wished she could lose this person, but it was hard when she didn't even know where he was. When she looked behind, she only saw unfamiliar faces, none of them the man who had been watching her from across the street.

She had only walked for twenty minutes when she saw the white canvas sign hanging above the door of a brick building that read 'Red Cross' in bold red letters and the traditional red cross symbol next to it. *Oh, thank goodness,* she thought, hurrying inside and closing the door. She peeked out the window and looked for the man from the café, but she didn't see him. She hoped, for now, she was safe and turned to look at her surroundings to see where she needed to go. In front of her was a long hall with doors on both sides and at the end was an open door. To her left was a sign that read, 'Red Cross' in French, like on the front of the building, and an arrow pointing down the hall to the open door. She followed the arrow and heard people talking as she neared. When she entered the room, she saw a desk close to the front and some hospital beds lining one wall. Women were wearing white nurses' uniforms with white hats that had the Red Cross on the front of them. They were assisting the few patients that were there. No one was sitting at the desk, so Eva approached the woman nearest the door.

"Excuse me, Madame."

The woman turned from what she was doing and looked at Eva; she was an elderly lady with a lot of wrinkles on her face and a very stern expression.

"Yes," she said in a deep, raspy, monotone voice.

"I'm here to inquire about a position and ask if you knew of ways to mail letters to England and possibly travel there?"

"Have a seat over here." She gestured to the chair at the desk.

Eva went to the side with the visitor chair and sat down, and the woman sat across from her.

"To answer your first question, we never turn down help. But I believe your assistance would be more beneficial elsewhere."

"Why do you think it would be better somewhere else?"

"Because, as you can see, we don't have that many wounded now that France has surrendered to Germany. The Red Crosses in other occupied countries, I'm sure, need the help much more than we do. The Red Cross in Germany is not helping certain groups of people, like the Jews, the Polish, and the Russians. They have started turning away the people that the Third Reich has deemed unfit."

"That's awful. How are they getting away with that?"

"Because the Nazis control everything now, but there are still members of the German Red Cross that are doing what they can.

As an American, I'm sure you don't conform to the Nazi ideology and would be willing to help the people they turn away."

Is she asking me to go to Germany? she wondered. "Of course, I would help them, but I don't know if I want to go to Germany. Is that what you are asking?"

"Yes, if that is something you would be willing to do. Would you feel comfortable going there? I'm sure that they could also use you as a Red Cross nurse in their hospitals since they get far more patients there than we do here. All of their wounded from the front eventually go back to Germany."

"Um… I'm not sure. I would have to think about it."

"That's fine. Now, to answer your second question. Yes, we can send letters to other countries. It takes a long time, though. And to your last question. No, we cannot let people go from country to country without a good reason and a pass. England is not an occupied country, so you could not go there."

It was as she feared. She would go back to La Chapelle, no closer to going home than when she arrived.

"Oh, OK, that's good and bad news, I guess. I will have to think hard about the offer to go to Germany. I will let you know next time I'm in Paris. I don't know when I will be back, but I'm hoping it will be soon."

Eva already knew the answer. It was no, but she didn't want to tell her outright. She thanked the nurse for her time and left the Red Cross building, temporarily forgetting about the man who had been watching her.

When she stepped through the door onto the sidewalk, it all came flooding back, and chills ran down her spine. She looked up and down the street before stepping away from the door to make sure he was not there. She did not see him, or anyone for that matter; the street was empty. It made her feel relieved and concerned at the same time. If she did not see anyone, then perhaps he was not there, but if no one else was there and he was hiding, there would be no one to help her. She turned to the left to go back the way she came. Eva hoped to meet Renée and Adele in the Latin Quarter, but if they weren't there, she would just head back to the hotel.

She made it to the end of the street without the feeling of being followed this time or seeing the strange man. She turned onto the next street feeling relieved, but the feeling was fleeting when she saw the man who was watching her at the café step out of an alley in front of her. She stopped dead in her tracks, and they stood there staring at one another for some time. She didn't look away; their eyes were locked like that. Her hands turned clammy, and her mouth was dry as she tried to focus on her breathing. Her body tingled from the sudden rush of adrenaline, but she tried to look calm. She wasn't sure how long she stood there before deciding what to do. She turned and started running down the street in the opposite direction when he called after her.

"Are you English?"

She stopped, turning on her heels to face him. When she spoke, her breath was labored. "Why, what do you want?" she asked him in French. "Why are you following me?"

"Because if you are, I think we can help one another."

"What could you possibly help me with?"

"Walk with me, and I will explain."

"I'm not going anywhere with you. I don't even know you."

"Very well, that was a little vague. Would you be willing to go to the café with me, where you were earlier?"

Eva thought about it for a second. She did not know what this man was playing at or what he wanted with her. They had never met, so how could he help her, and how could she help him? Maybe his true intent was to rob her. Everything he had done up to this point had been creepy. Why was he being so mysterious?

"I will meet you at the same café. You walk first, and I will follow behind you at a distance," she told him.

"Fair enough," he said, then turned and walked in the direction she was headed when he cut her off.

She cautiously followed him at a distance, making sure not to get close. When they reached the café, he sat at a table with two chairs and gestured for her to sit across from him. She slowly pulled back the chair and sat down, keeping her focus on him. The café was still quite busy, making her feel a little better about the situation.

"I'm listening," she said.

"I'm guessing that you are stuck here and wish that you weren't. And because of that, I think that you are not too fond of the Germans, who are the cause of the circumstances you are in. Now that they have my country, they are going after yours, bombing it every day, killing your countrymen, destroying your cities. I'm sorry for that, and I'm sorry that I can't help you get home, but I can help you get back at the people responsible for what is happening to you and your country."

Eva didn't trust him enough to tell him that she wasn't British. She didn't know what harm it could do, so she kept quiet.

"I'm asking if you would like to join us and help fight the Germans?"

"I don't live in Paris. I live in the country. I don't know how I could help you if I'm not here."

"It doesn't matter where you are. You can still help and be one of us. There are resistance pockets all over Europe, not just in France or Paris. It doesn't matter if you are in the country or a city, France or Poland."

"You are asking me to take an enormous risk."

"Yes, I am because there is a lot at stake."

She pondered what he asked; she knew she couldn't answer him now. "I will be in Paris for another two days. I need some time to think about it. I will let you know on my last day. Meet me here at noon on Monday."

He stood up from his chair. "I will see you at noon." He then disappeared around a corner as if he was never there.

Chapter Twenty-One

She let out a deep breath. *What a day,* she thought. She was asked to go to Germany to help unwanted refugees or work in a German hospital, and now she was asked to conspire against the Germans, all in one day. *I'm just going to go back to the hotel. I have had enough excitement.*

She got up from her chair and was putting the strap of her purse over her shoulder when she heard a familiar voice call her name. She would know that voice anywhere. Her head snapped up to look at where the voice had come from. Gerhardt was standing across the street, smiling at her. He, of course, was in his pressed gray uniform and cap, and the sun was reflecting in his eyes, making them the deepest ocean blue. There were three other officers with him; one of whom she recognized as the man she met at Madame Blanc's, the man who tried to torture her, SS Obersturmbannführer Bauer. Her heart rate spiked at the sight of him. The memory of the room with the sink flashed in her mind. *You have got to be kidding me.*

Gerhardt waved her over from across the street, and she glanced around subconsciously. Eva feared that someone she knew would see them together. Actually, she did not want anyone to see them together. Being seen with a German in La Chapelle was one thing, but being caught in Paris with one was quite another. She stepped off the curb and headed their way, feeling self-conscious about even speaking to them. She thought they had agreed not to talk to one another in public except to say hi if passing in the street. And why on earth was he in Paris? Also, what were the chances of them running into one another here? It was such a large city; their meeting was one in how many million? It almost seemed staged, fate, or something other than random.

She stopped in front of him. "What are you doing here?"

"I am on leave for the weekend, and they gave the officers passes to come to Paris." Gerhardt turned to the other officers. "Go ahead without me. I'll catch up later."

"It's nice to see you again," Bauer said with derision.

She did not respond; she did not think it was nice seeing him again.

Bauer gave her a once-over with just his eyes, pursed his lips, then turned and walked down the sidewalk. As the other men followed and walked past Eva and Gerhardt, one gave him a strange look which Gerhardt understood, but she didn't. Gerhardt furrowed his brows at him, and the other man smirked. Eva observed the exchange and felt it was somehow about her.

"They gave you a pass to come to Paris and nowhere else?"

"I didn't say that. I just said they gave us one to Paris. We had the option of going to Paris or Normandy, so I chose Paris. The only one who isn't here on a pass is SS Obersturmbannführer

Bauer. He is in Paris a lot because this is where the Gestapo headquarters is for France, but he goes to La Chapelle and other towns on business."

"Hmmm, so why didn't you want to go to Normandy?"

He chuckled. "Eva, you have a knack for always coming to the wrong conclusion. It's not that I didn't want to go to Normandy. It's that I would rather come here."

"Can I ask then why you would rather be in Paris than Normandy?"

"Of course, you can ask me anything you want, but it doesn't mean I will always answer. But I will answer the question you asked. The answer is you. Eva, you are the reason I would rather spend my time in Paris than in Normandy."

She was taken aback by his honesty, and it was like a punch to the gut to have him finally say that she was the reason that he did something. Adele was right; he liked her, and he went out of his way to see her.

"Me… I'm the reason that you came to Paris?"

"Yes, you seem surprised. When I first met you, Eva, well, to put it nicely, I thought you were an ignorant American who got stuck in Europe during a war because of your lack of understanding of how the world works. To me, it seemed even stranger because our countries are not at war. So that made me wonder why you were here in the first place. Maybe you were for reasons that you shouldn't be."

Not yet, she thought.

"Which made me even more curious about your situation," he continued. "But when you told me your reason for being here, I realized I was wrong in my assumption and my first impression of you. Even though you had told me why you were here, and I believed what you said, you still remained a mystery to me. You intrigued me. So, when you dropped the bag of food, I decided to help and perhaps get to know you and find out why you intrigued me so much. Of course, I would have helped you anyway, but I wanted to get to know you better. The more I got to know you, the more I wanted to know about you. From what I have seen, you are a kind person and have a soft heart, something I think is rare, especially in times of war."

She was having a hard time comprehending what he said. After what Adele told her and what she experienced, she knew he probably liked her, but she never thought it was this intense.

Gerhardt noticed her blank stare. "There is an Italian opera playing tonight called Madame Butterfly. I'm sure you have heard of it. Would you go with me?"

The present started coming back to her, flooding in like a raging river more than a trickling stream. It was overwhelming.

"Ummm… an opera? You want me to go to an opera with you tonight?"

"Yes, that is what I said."

"What would I tell Madame Blanc and Adele? I don't even have a dress to wear to an opera. I don't think it's a good idea."

"I know what you are afraid of, and I don't blame you. But please, take a chance. It will be in the evening, and there won't be many people out because of the curfew. I can't tell you what to say to Madame Blanc and Adele, but I know you will think of something."

She was torn; she wanted to go but knew that she shouldn't. What she told him about it being a bad idea was the truth. She thought of all the things Adele had told her and could only imagine what she would think or say if she saw them together now. Or heaven forbid she agreed to go to the opera with him, to be found out later. She honestly didn't know what to say to him.

"Eva…?"

She had to give him an answer, but how could she if she didn't even know what the answer was.

"What about the dress? I don't even have one to wear."

"It won't be a problem. We can get you a dress before you go back to the hotel."

"Really, you think it's a good idea to take a fancy dress to my room where someone could see? They would ask why I have it."

"I will keep it with me. We can meet somewhere close to the hotel, and you can change at the opera house."

He was trying to think of a solution for everything. "If we can be stealthy and keep a low profile, I will go with you," she finally ceded.

Gerhardt smiled. "Thank you, Eva."

"For what?"

"I know you wanted to say no, but instead, you said yes."

"You are only partly right. It's true that I wanted to say no, but I also wanted to say yes. I didn't answer right away because I was conflicted about what to do. Part of me knew that I should do the sensible thing and tell you no, and the other part of me wanted to do the non-sensible thing and tell you yes. The logical and emotional parts of my brain were feuding with one another, but the emotional part won out."

"You're right. You probably should have said no, but I'm glad you didn't. There is a dress shop close to here. We can go there now if you want?"

"It doesn't matter to me. I'm not familiar with any of the shops here so that one is as good as any."

"We should head that way. It might take a while to pick out a dress, and you still have to go back to the hotel and tell Madame Blanc and Adele something. You could tell them you want to keep to your room tonight."

"I guess that's true. I could do that."

As they walked, she admired all the shops they passed and could smell the scent of freshly baked bread and pastries waft out from the cafés of the Latin Quarter.

When they reached the other side of the Latin Quarter and turned down the adjacent street, Gerhardt stopped walking.

"We're here."

She looked at the storefront that they were standing next to. It was a narrow building with two floors. It read, 'Chloe's Dress Shop' in black on the window. He opened the door and held it for her. She walked in and noticed all the dresses in different designs and colors hanging from racks around the store.

"Bonjour," a woman sitting at a small counter near the back of the store said. She had black hair that was cut short and a pair of glasses with a gold chain connected to both earpieces sitting low on the bridge of her nose. She wore a long, sleek black dress that hugged her slim figure. "How can I help you?"

"I'm looking for a dress that is appropriate to wear to an opera," Eva told the woman.

She slid her glasses up on her nose and looked at Eva; she was studying her with a questioning look. Eva knew she picked up right away that she wasn't French, and it must have looked funny, her being there with a German. She got off her stool, walked to one of the racks in the middle, and started sliding the dresses around, pulling different ones off and draping them over her arm. After removing three dresses from the rack, she handed them to Eva.

"Try these on. I think they should fit you. They all should look good on you, but I don't know what your taste is. The changing rooms are over here." She walked Eva to a row of three rooms with sliding curtains and pulled one back. "You can change in here. I will be at the counter if you need me." She weaved through the racks of dresses back to the counter.

Gerhardt sat in a chair that faced the dressing rooms. "I'll wait right here."

Their eyes locked right before she pulled the curtain closed. She hung the dresses on a hook on the wall. She had a realization. How on earth was she going to accomplish changing into all the dresses with her cast on? *Crap,* she thought. She went through the usual slow process of getting her clothes off and then took the first dress off the hanger. It was a lilac-colored dress with a full skirt that came to her ankles and a high neck. It was sleeveless except for a small piece of lace that covered the shoulders, like what was on the skirt, but the part that covered the chest looked like it was made of silk with embroidery on it. There was a thin silk strip with a small bow attached to it in the front, and in the back were laces that tied only at the small of the back. A lace string connected the high neck, and most of her back was left bare. Eva did not have too much difficulty tying the one at the neck, but she did not know how she was going to lace the one in the back. On the other side of the curtain, she listened to the muffled voices of Gerhardt and the woman, but she couldn't make out what they were saying. She then heard his voice clearly just on the other side.

"Eva, the lady gave me a pair of shoes for you to try on with the dresses and some things for your hair."

She pulled the curtain back to look at him, and he seemed to be surprised by it. He turned to the side and held out the shoes, some flowers, and a flowery headband.

She took them from him. "You don't have to look away. The dress is on, but I can't tie the stays in the back. Would you mind?"

She laid the shoes, flowers, and headband on the cushioned chair in the changing room and turned her back towards him.

He came behind her and began pulling the laces tight. When he got to the end of the lace, she could feel the tips of his fingers brushing against her back as he tied it. It sent chills down her spine and goosebumps on her skin, causing the hair on her arms and the back of her neck to stand on end.

He tied it in a bow, then his hands left the back of her dress. The touch of his warm fingers was no longer there. She turned to face him, and he looked her up and down.

"Well, what do you think?" she asked.

"I will give my answer on which one I like the best after you try them all on. What do you think of the dress? It is, of course, your decision which one you choose," he told her.

She stared into his deep blue eyes. They really did remind her of an ocean because she could drown in them.

"You decide. You are taking me to the opera, so you can choose the dress."

He seemed to like this idea. The suggestion of a smile crossed his face as she looked at him inquiringly.

She turned her back to him again. "Would you untie it now?"

She could feel him untie the bow and loosen the silk strings, and again, his fingers brushed across her back, giving her chills. She walked back into the changing room and pulled the curtain closed as she looked at him once again. The next dress she tried on was a long silk red dress covered in lace. It had see-through lace pieces covering the shoulders and a V-neck in the front and back. The dress was long and dragged on the floor, but the most noticeable thing to her was that it hugged her body all the way down until it got to her knees, where it flared out. This dress was easier to get in than the other one. All she had to do was pull it over her head. Getting it off could be a real problem, though. She slipped the shoes on so the dress would not drag on the floor so much, opened the curtain, and walked out.

He looked up at her; he had been staring off into space, but the sight of her in that dress definitely caught his attention. He stared at her longer with this dress than the other one. He didn't say anything but took a deep breath and put his hand over his chin and mouth, obviously in thought. He moved his hand. "Let me see the back?"

She turned around for him and stood still.

"All right, you can try the other one on now."

She gave him a quizzical look, then went back into the changing room and closed the curtain again. He really wasn't going to tell her what he thought until the very end. It took her a while to get this dress off, and it almost got stuck on her cast. Her hair was messed up and sticking in the air from the static when she looked in the mirror. *Oh, my.* She straightened it and reached for the last dress. It was green and had a straight neckline from shoulder to shoulder like the nineteen-fifties dresses did. It, too, touched the floor but did not drag as much as the other one. The way the other one hugged her body reminded her of the dress in the 1980s movie Elvira. This one, on the other hand, was flowery at the bottom, kind of like the first one, and was covered in mesh material with flowers embroidered on the skirt and jewels around the sleeves. She smoothed her hair over once more, then pulled the curtain open and walked out again, waiting for his response.

He stood up from the chair and walked around her, obviously taking the dress in. "They all are beautiful dresses, but the second one you tried on is better suited for the opera. The other two would be good for a ball. So that is the one I choose."

Somehow, she figured that would be the one, although she agreed she couldn't exactly dance in a dress like the second one, so it was better suited for sitting. But she still wasn't surprised that he picked the body-hugging one.

"I will change and pay for the dress."

"Do the shoes fit?" he asked.

She looked down at her feet. "They do, actually," she said, a little surprised.

"That's good. You change, and I'll wait by the counter."

"All right."

She went back into the changing room and pulled the curtain shut. She realized she had not even bothered to check the price of any of the dresses or the shoes. When she got the dress off, she put it back on the hanger and looked for the tag in the red dress; she found it hanging inside the dress near the arm sleeve. She pulled it out and read it. It was two thousand francs. *Holy shit, I can't afford that.* She figured it up in her head; it would be equivalent to one hundred Reichsmark. That was a lot of money, probably comparable to four hundred US dollars in her time. She looked at the piece of paper she took out of the shoes before she tried them on. They were three hundred francs. That would be twenty five Reichsmark, so roughly seventy US dollars. She couldn't get them. How was she going to tell him?

After she changed, she gathered up the other two dresses, put them back on the hangers, got the shoes, headband, and flowers, pulled the curtain back, and walked to the counter. Gerhardt and the woman turned to look at her as she approached.

The woman reached out her hands. "Let me have the red dress and the shoes so I can put them in some boxes for you."

"I'm sorry, but I can't afford them, so I won't be buying anything today. I didn't realize they were so expensive."

"They have already been paid for," she said.

Eva looked at Gerhardt. "You paid for them? I can't accept these." She felt strange about the fact that he paid for them. She didn't want to feel like a charity case, and she didn't want him spending his money on her and buying her things, especially such expensive things.

"I told you earlier it wasn't a problem getting you a dress."

"Yeah, I thought you meant just finding a place to buy one, not that you would buy me one."

"I meant both."

"But you didn't say that."

The woman at the desk watched them as they discussed who paid for the dress. "Should I put them in boxes or not?"

"Yes."

He took the red dress and the shoes from Eva and handed them to the woman, who then disappeared to the back of the store to box them up.

"I will pay you back, no matter how long it takes."

"Eva, there is no need. They are a gift. If I wanted you to pay me back, I would have let you pay for them now."

She knew he had no expectations of her paying him back, but she did not want to be in his debt again. And this time, it was real debt, not just returning a favor. It always made her feel strange when people did nice things for her. She wasn't entirely sure why. It just did.

The woman returned from the back with the dress folded up and wrapped in brown paper tied with a black silk bow and a small shoe-sized box sitting on top of it. She put them on the counter. "You are all set. If you have any issues with the dress, just bring it back in, and I can alter it."

"Thank you," Eva said with a smile.

Gerhardt picked up the dress and shoebox and put them under his arm. "Let's go. We don't have a lot of time before the opera starts. What hotel are you staying at?"

"We're staying at The Peninsula Paris. It's not far from here."

"Good. Look, I'm sorry if I made you uncomfortable by buying you the dress and the shoes. It made more sense that I bought them than you because I asked you to go to the opera, not the other way around. And I know you don't make much money and don't have access to your money back home."

"I understand you were doing something nice for me. It's just that sometimes, when people do nice things for me, I freak out a little. I'm not used to it. I mean from people other than my parents and close friends. I appreciate you buying me the dress and the shoes, I do, but I also don't want you to feel sorry for me and think that I need help if that is why you bought them for me. I have some money put away, a place to stay, and food to eat. That is enough for me. I'm just in an unfortunate situation right now, but the war won't last forever, and eventually, I'll go home."

"You are looking forward to that day, I'm sure. I would be, too, if I were in your shoes. Do you miss home a lot?"

"It doesn't matter now. I would rather not talk about going home. It only makes it harder."

"All right." He wanted to press the question but understood that would not get him the desired results. He had to let her come to him and tell him in her own time when she felt comfortable enough to. "I see the hotel just up there. You go do what you need to, and I'll be waiting right here."

As she walked away, he called after her.

"Eva, bring a jacket or a shawl. It can get cool at night."

She nodded in response. She hoped that Madame Blanc and Adele were already back at the hotel because if they weren't, she wasn't sure how she would explain her absence. She could leave a note under their doors, but one of them might come to her room and check on her anyway. This was becoming more complicated by the minute. Why did she ever agree to go with him?

She entered the lobby and looked around to make sure that Madame Blanc and Adele weren't there. She approached the front desk. "Can I get my key? It's room 303."

The man pulled the key off a hook on the back wall. The wall was made of wood, and a sizable portion was covered with tiny hooks and keys.

"Here you are, Madame," he said, holding it out to her.

"Merci."

She rode the elevator to the third floor, got off, and then went straight to Madame Blanc's room. She knocked softly on the door. "Renée."

She could hear someone walking inside the room. *Thank goodness, she's here,* Eva thought.

Madame Blanc opened her door. "Well, come on in, don't just loiter in the hall."

Eva liked Renée's straightforwardness; she had difficulty not saying precisely what she thought.

Eva stepped around her into the room, and Madame Blanc closed the door.

"Have a seat, dear," she said, pointing to a chair in the corner near a small table.

Eva sat down, and Madame Blanc sat across from her.

"So, how did it go?"

"It was interesting. The Red Cross said they could help with mailing letters to England, but they could not help me with getting home."

"Oh, I'm so sorry, my dear. Although I must say, I was not expecting them to help you with that, so your news doesn't surprise me. People need travel passes with this crazy war and how strict the Germans are with movement."

Eva stared down at her hands folded in her lap, not wanting to tell her that she wanted to keep to her room tonight. "I'm feeling tired. I think I will just stay in my room for the rest of the evening. Relax, maybe go to bed early."

"Sure, if you are tired, it's best not to push yourself."

"Are you and Adele going back out before curfew starts?"

"No, I think we will stay in too."

Eva was glad to hear it. That way, it lowered the chance of them noticing her absence. She felt relieved. "OK, I was just wondering. I'm going to go back to my room now and maybe take a bath, so if you guys decide to go out, there is no need to knock on my door in case I'm sleeping or in the tub."

"I understand. I have days where I don't want to go anywhere and just want to stay in. Like our first day here."

Eva stood up from the chair. "I'll see you tomorrow, probably down in the café for breakfast."

"Get some rest. I'll see you in the morning," Renée said.

Eva went back to her room and quickly began freshening up her makeup, then pinned her hair in a loose French bun. Last, she applied some perfume on her wrist, rubbed them together, and put some in her hair and décolletage. She went to her door and opened it slowly, peeking her head out into the hall. She looked both ways, but there was no one there. She stepped out into the hall, turned the handle to keep the latch closed, pulled the door shut as softly as she could, and then tiptoed down the corridor to the elevator. She looked behind her again while waiting for the doors to open; she wanted to ensure no one was coming. When she heard the ding and the doors opened, she slipped in and pushed the ground floor button. She fidgeted as she waited for the doors to shut; she was so worried that Adele or Madame Blanc would come out of their room and see her, even though that was very unlikely. Her heart was beating fast, and her hands were sweaty. *Get it together, Eva,* she said to herself. *Am I nervous because I'm afraid of being seen by Adele or Madame Blanc, or am I nervous because I'm spending the evening with him?* she wondered. The answer was probably both, and she knew it.

The elevator dinged again, and the door opened to the lobby. She stepped out and hurried across the room to the front counter, returning her key; then, without bringing too much attention to herself, she went through the revolving door and stopped as soon as she was outside. She looked in the direction Gerhardt said he would be waiting, and just as he said, he was there leaning against the wall of a building, smoking a cigarette. Seeing him standing in the dark, leaning up against the wall in his uniform while smoking a cigarette, was like a scene in an old movie. It wasn't something one would see in her time unless it was on TV. Seeing it now in real time gave her chills, so she rubbed her arms to make them disappear. As she rubbed her arms, she noticed how the air had cooled; it was verging on jacket weather, and at the moment, she was happy she listened to him and brought a shawl. She crossed the street and walked towards him.

He looked up from the sidewalk, took a deep inhale of his cigarette, then turned his head and blew it out in the other direction. He flicked the cigarette butt off to the side. "Your hair looks nice."

"Thank you. Was I fast enough?"

He looked at his watch. "You were fast enough. We have time. We will need to hurry, though."

To her surprise, he took her hand and began walking at a brisk pace, pulling her along. She didn't move her hand away but instead closed her hand around his. It was large and warm, which felt good in the cool night air. She had to stop being in self-denial about him liking her. After tonight, how could she be? But now, she faces a different dilemma. What was she going to do with this knowledge and this new affirmation? Her leaving France became more complicated, and being around the people she knew became more difficult. If she wasn't mistaken, everything about her life just got more complicated. But one step at a time; tonight, she would go to the opera with him and enjoy his company and figure the rest out tomorrow—more like she would start trying to figure it out tomorrow, and in three months, still wouldn't be any closer to having it figured out.

"How far are we from the opera house?"

"It won't take too long to get there if we take the subway."

Eva hadn't even realized that he was leading her to the subway station near her hotel. She had been lost in thought as she tried to figure out what this was.

He led her down a flight of concrete steps leading under the ground. When they reached the bottom, she could see the walls were covered with tiny white tiles, and there were a few posters with German propaganda on them. She did not bother to read them. She just noticed that some had a German soldier on them. No telling what lies they were spewing. It wasn't even worth her time. Now that they were underground, he led her up a flight of stairs to a walkway that went over the tracks, then down the other side. Once they were on the other side and standing on the platform, he let go of her hand and looked at his watch.

"Good, we are right on time."

It was obvious that he knew this subway well. After all, he had gone to school in Paris for a while. Her hands felt strange; her left hand was cool and dry, and her right hand was hot and clammy. She rubbed her right hand over the fingers sticking out of the cast of her left hand to try and balance the feeling. She then wondered if he would take her hand again. She looked up at him and watched as he looked down the tracks, waiting for the train. He must have seen her looking at him from the corner of his eye because he turned his head and looked at her.

"Are you all right?"

"I'm fine. I was just wondering why we are taking the train when you must have a car and a driver at your disposal."

"Well, that's because you wanted to keep a low profile. I didn't think you wanted to be seen pulling up in front of the opera house in a German car with Nazi flags flying from it. So, I figured it was best this way since you wanted to be as inconspicuous as possible."

"Good point. I guess I'm silly for not thinking of that."

"You're not. I understand why you were confused about taking the train. That is how we would go to the opera if it didn't bother you so much being seen with a German."

"I'm sorry, Gerhardt, you have to understand where I'm coming from."

"I do. It doesn't make it any easier, but I understand."

She could detect a hint of bitterness in his voice. She felt awful that it had to be this way. The truth was, she shouldn't be with him at all, so he was lucky she was going to the opera with him now.

The sound of the train echoed out of the tunnel.

"This is our train," he said.

When the train stopped, he got in the last car without taking her hand. He stood near the door, waiting for her. She stepped in and took the seat by the window, and he sat in the chair beside her.

When the train started to move, she decided to attempt an apology. She couldn't just leave it like this, not after he had been so nice to her. Plus, the truth was, under any other circumstance, it would thrill her to be seen with him. She had to try to make him understand that it wasn't personal.

"Gerhardt, I'm sorry that it has to be this way. If there weren't a war now, things would be different. But these people view you as the enemy, and I have to live among them. I can't tell you how it will be when the war is over. I mean, let's be honest with ourselves, no matter how this war ends, how could we possibly remain friends? I won't stay here forever; I will go back to America as soon as I get the chance. You wouldn't want to move there. Besides, depending on how the war ends, it could be horrible for one of us. Just distance alone is enough for it to be nearly impossible, so there is no need to even go into any of the other reasons."

He sat staring at the floor in silence, not acknowledging what she had said, not even looking at her.

She leaned down so she could see his face. "Gerhardt?" she asked, hoping that he would say something, anything.

"Eva, you don't think I already know this, that I haven't already thought of all the impossible reasons why this wouldn't work? But can we try to be friends, even for just this one night? Can we not pretend that there isn't all of this craziness around us, that life is simple, and that we are just two people going to the opera together? And pretend that no one cares that I'm German or you're American, and so there is no shame in being seen out in public together?"

She wished it was that simple, that they could spend time together carefree, but the reality wasn't that simple. People would look at her if they saw them together, and they would judge her. Germans were disliked and thought of as all being the same, and whenever she was with him, she noticed how people looked at her. They thought of her as the same kind of person they believed him to be. She knew Adele felt that way, that they were all cut from the same dirty cloth, were ruthless, cold-hearted killers. Right now, she believed that wasn't true, but she had never had one wrong her the way Adele did.

She cautiously reached out and touched his hand, not knowing if he wanted her touching him now. When she rested her hand on his, he looked up at her. The eyes that looked back at her were full of mixed emotions. He took her hand in his and closed his fingers around it, squeezing gently.

"As I have said before, I am thankful that you are going with me tonight, and I know this must be difficult for you. I am glad you can see that I'm not the person people think I am and that just because I'm German doesn't mean I'm like all the others. I know you and most people don't have a good impression of us right now, but I'm relieved that you can look past the stigma and prejudice. You will find, Eva, that I don't have a lot in common with most of them. They are my people, and I have a duty to them and my country, but that doesn't mean I have to act as they do, think like them, or be like them in any way."

She knew he was sincere in everything he said, but it was still hard not to look at him as just a German soldier, someone who invaded a country and oppressed the people there, a pawn in this war. Especially when he was wearing his uniform, it was hard to see anything but that, even though she knew it was superficial. Part of her wanted to hate him, but she couldn't. In her heart, she knew Gerhardt wasn't a bad person. Everyone had a dark side, but he didn't seem to act on his like so many of the other Germans.

The train slowed, and they announced the stop on a speaker overhead.

"This is our stop."

He stood and pulled her from her seat. They waited by the doors, and when the train came to a complete stop, he held her hand to help her as she stepped off.

"The opera house is just up at the top across the street. Do you think you can change quickly?"

"Yes, I think so."

"Good, we should be on time, then. I will wait somewhere close by, and if you need any help, let me know."

"Thanks."

When they emerged from the subway station, she took in all the lights of the city reflecting on the clouds. She hadn't even considered that it might rain.

"There it is," he said

She turned to look in the direction he was pointing. There was the Paris opera house in all its beauty. It looked much smaller than it did in The Phantom of The Opera; it seemed so massive in the movie when she watched it, but it was still pretty even though it was smaller in real life. It was made of the same white stone as most buildings in Paris, and it had a dome made of green-colored glass, and at the top stood three statues. There were two large gold statues at the front on each corner, and gold also ran along the roof's edge. It was an amazing building, and she couldn't believe she would get to see an opera there.

For the first time, Eva realized Gerhardt was not carrying her shoes or the dress. "Where is the dress and the shoes?"

"I had my orderly bring them here already and drop them off ,so I didn't have to carry them around for an hour."

"When did you have time to do that?"

He smiled. "While you were in your room getting ready, I called him."

"You called him…?"

He chuckled. "Yes, from the shop across from your hotel. You have the funniest expression on your face right now. Why is this so strange a concept to you that I had them delivered here ahead of time?"

"I don't know. You just seem to be full of surprises, that's all."

"I have done well then in surprising you, seeing as how I surprise you even when I'm not trying."

"I just don't expect you to do some of the things you do, more like most of the things you do. I agree that you are not like the other Germans because you have not been what I expected since that day you helped me pick up my groceries. The first time we met, however, I did think you were like I expected you to be. You acted just like people said the Germans would."

"I'm sorry I treated you that way. I did not know who you were then, Eva."

"I know."

"We better go in, or we are going to be late."

"Oh, yes, we better."

She followed him across the street; it wasn't hard to cross because there wasn't much traffic now that it was past curfew. As they entered the main lobby, there was a single staircase that ended at a landing, which then turned onto two different sets of stairs, one leading to the left and one leading to the right. There were entryways on the main floor to the left and right of the first set of stairs and balconies on each side at the top. The banisters were made of the same dark marble as the floor, and chandlers were everywhere.

"Where do we go?" she asked.

"This way."

He took her hand again and led her through the entryway at their left. They entered the most beautiful hallway she had ever seen. Everything was covered in gold, including the pillars lining both sides of the hall, and from the ceiling were more chandeliers, one in front of each pillar and one hanging from the middle of the ceiling about every thirty feet. On the wall with the windows was a marble bust of a woman's head and shoulders, and at the end of the hall was a fireplace with a large mirror above it and a vase set on its mantel. They painted the ceiling in typical Greek style with a flurry of people, some on thrones, some sitting on clouds holding spears, and some half-naked.

When they got to the end of the hall, there was another opening that led to the right. It was a drastically smaller and less elegant hallway. He led her down to the end, where there were two doors.

"It's in here," he said, pointing to the door to the left.

"How do you know it is in here?"

“Because I called the opera house first before I had my orderly bring them to make sure that it was OK if we left them here. They told me it was fine and where to leave them.”

There was no point in even responding. What would she say to this? He seemed to accomplish so much in such a small amount of time; she wasn’t even in her hotel room that long.

He opened the door for her. “You might want to change now. We don’t have long before it starts.”

She stepped into the little room and switched on the light. It looked like a changing room; it had a vanity with a mirror, but nothing else was in the room except her dress hanging from a hook on the wall and her shoes on the floor. She turned when she heard the door close behind her. All of this entranced her; it was so much to take in; it felt like she was dreaming. She went to the dress, took it off the hanger and, laid it on the dressing table, then pulled out the chair. When she sat down to undress, she saw a clutch bag that matched the dress hanging on the hook, which must have been hidden behind it because she hadn’t noticed it when she came in. She stood up and removed it from the hook; it was beautiful and elegant. She had never owned something so exquisite before. There was a white piece of paper partially sticking out from under the flap. She pulled it out and unfolded it.

Look inside.

She opened the flap on the bag and peered inside. A necklace wrapped around a pair of silk gloves laid at the bottom of the bag. She reached in, pulled out the gloves with the necklace, and unwrapped it from around the gloves. It felt heavy and looked authentic, and she was sure it was made of real silver and diamonds. She plopped down on the chair. This was too much.

Tears ran down her cheeks. She quickly began dabbing at them with the back of her hand so that the tears didn't mess up her makeup. Why was he being so nice to her? What did she ever do to deserve these kinds of gifts and this kind of attention? There was a knock on the door, which made her jump, dropping the necklace.

"Have you changed yet?"

She sniffed and took a deep breath, then let it out. "I'm changing now. I'll be done soon."

"OK, we need to hurry, though. Do you need any help?"

"No, I've got it."

She picked the necklace off the floor and laid it on the table. She pulled her blouse out from her skirt and unbuttoned it. She laid it on the table and stood to take off her skirt; she let it fall to the floor and stepped out of her shoes. She picked the dress up off the table and pulled it over her head, trying not to catch it on her cast or drag on her hair. Once she had it on, she sat back down, slipped the shoes on, then turned and looked at the necklace. It made her feel like a gold digger. She knew that his family had money, but that wasn't why she was spending time with him, and she hoped he didn't feel like he had to buy her friendship.

She had to hurry, so she picked the necklace up and unclasped it when she had a thought. Maybe she would let him put it on. *Eva, I hope you know what you are doing. This is all a lot,* she thought. *I don't understand why he is doing this.* So many thoughts about Gerhardt's actions ran through her head, and none of them gave her a warm, fuzzy feeling. She put the gloves on, transferred the contents from her purse into the clutch, and stood up. She walked to the door with the necklace in hand, closed her gloved hand tightly around it, and then opened the door.

He turned when he heard the door opening and smiled at her. He came to stand in front of her. He was a formidable man, towering over her, and she felt small, even more so than usual.

"Very nice. You are a beautiful woman, Eva." He stopped smiling and furrowed his brows. "Where is the necklace?"

She held her hand out to him and unfolded her fingers. He looked down at the necklace, then looked back up at her, not sure if she was giving it back or not.

"Would you put it on?"

There was an unsure smile that broke at the corner of his mouth. "Of course."

He took it from her hand, and she turned around. He reached his hands in front of her and brought the necklace around her neck. Then she could feel him clasping it. When he let go, she felt its full weight.

She turned back around. "Thank you."

"You are welcome."

"Why did you give me all of these things?"

"We can talk about it after the show. Right now, we have to go because we are already late."

He held his hand out to her, and she looked at it, him waiting for her to take it. This would be the first time she would take his hand. All the other times tonight, he took hers. This somehow seemed to mean something different. When he would take her hand, it was him making the decision, making the moves. Now, it was like he was asking her to do the same. He wanted her to make a move; he was asking for it to be her decision; he was asking for her permission. But to her, it felt like when someone told another person they loved them. Then stood there staring at them, waiting for them to say it back. They had made the first move and taken the first risk. Now they were waiting for her, the other person to jump too. It felt like that to her, just not as intense as if someone told her they loved her. But, of course, this still felt like a commitment. Holding someone's hand was always the first step to bigger things. One rarely held someone's hand that they were just friends with; it signified that feelings had crossed over from friendship to something else, to something more. She figured there was no escape now, like when someone decided to bungee jump, but after they jumped off the bridge, they started to wonder if it was a good idea, only at that point, it was too late to turn back. They just had to see it through. She had allowed something to start that she was sure she could not just walk away from, especially now, not after he had tried so hard and done so much.

She reached out and took his hand; he closed his fingers around hers and smiled warmly at her. The look on his face said it all, that it pleased him that she took his hand and did not just walk past. She understood that the action spoke volumes.

They went through a door that led to a flight of stairs, which took them to a small private box with only two chairs. He pulled the curtain shut behind them and held the back of a chair for her. She picked the glasses off the seat and then sat down. He then turned to his chair and sat next to her. Their box had a perfect view of the stage. Although they didn't look at the actors directly, they viewed them from the side. It was the second box to the left of the stage.

"When you said we were going to see an opera, I assumed we would sit down there," she said, pointing to the main seating of the opera house.

He chuckled. "Why would we sit down there when the view is better from up here?"

"Because it is considerably cheaper to sit down there than up here."

"True. All right, let me rephrase it. Why would we sit down there when the view is better from up here, and I can afford it?"

"OK, I see your point."

The lights dimmed, and a man came out from behind the curtains and made an introduction about the opera they were about to see. After telling everyone to enjoy the show at the end of his announcement, he disappeared behind the curtains. Gerhardt had told her they were already late, but the show was just starting. Germans must think that being on time was late.

There were a few seconds of silence, then the curtains went up, and she could see a makeshift building that looked oriental in design. The opera began with a Caucasian man coming out of the building and singing to a Japanese man. Eva skimmed the story from the pamphlet that was in her seat. Though the opera was all in Italian, she still knew what was going on for the most part. She knew it was about an American naval officer stationed in Japan who married a Japanese woman at the suggestion of his friend. He returned home, and while still married to the Japanese woman, he married an American woman like he said he was going to do all along. He later returned to Japan with his American wife only to find that Cio-Cio-San had been pregnant when he left, and they now had a son. He couldn't bring himself to tell Cio-Cio-San that he was married, so he had his new wife and his friend tell her. The new wife wanted the child, and Cio-Cio-San told her they could take him if the father came and told her himself. When he arrived, she blindfolded the child and put an American flag in his hand, then killed herself before the father could save her.

Eva knew the story would be sad, but when the scene at the end finally came, and the woman placed the flag in the child's hand, it tugged at her heart and brought tears to her eyes for more than one reason. She hadn't seen an American flag in over a year, and it was strange and wonderful to see one now. She wanted to run down and take it from the boy and keep it for herself. And then there was the fact that she knew Cio-Cio-San was going to die because she was heartbroken. She waited all that time just to be rejected in the end.

Eva was so consumed by the story that she didn't realize Gerhardt had been watching her most of the time and not the opera. He had seen her tear up, noticing which part she started to cry. Finally, the lights dimmed, the curtains dropped, then the lights brightened once again, and the curtain rose with all the actors and actresses holding hands and bowing to the audience. The crowd began to clap, and Eva joined in. She clapped her hands hard and could feel the tears escape her eyes and run down her cheeks. It was just an act, yet she felt sorry for Cio-Cio-San and the boy. She looked over at Gerhardt, but instead of watching the actors on stage, he was looking at her. He wasn't smiling but had a look of contemplation on his face, like he was trying to figure out what she was thinking. The curtain fell again, and the clapping ceased.

Gerhardt leaned in close to Eva so she could hear him speak over the noise of the crowd. "So, did you like it?"

"Oh yes, I loved it. I only wish that it had ended a little happier. And… well, I liked the part where Cio-Cio-San gave her son the flag. It was nice to see that."

"I thought you would like that part."

"You have seen the play before?"

"Yes, a couple of times."

"So, do you watch a lot of opera?"

"Yes, and plays. My family and I have always enjoyed going to the theater. It is entertaining and refined, unlike some other forms of entertainment."

"True, I think a certain kind of people go to the opera."

"You mean more sophisticated people?" he asked.

"I guess you could say that."

"I know some well-refined people who don't like the opera, but most of them do. Anyway, we should go."

"Yes, we should. It's getting late, and I better get back. I need to get some sleep. I don't want to look too haggard tomorrow."

They went down to the main entryway, and as they neared the doors, she could see it was raining.

"Oh no, I guess we will have to walk in the rain." She paused. "I almost forgot. I still need to get my clothes from the other room."

"Let's go get them, and perhaps the rain will have subsided a bit by the time you are done."

They went back to the small changing room to collect her belongings.

"Gerhardt, after I change, I will return the dress, shoes, bag, gloves, and necklace. I can't take them back to my room, anyway.

Madame Blanc and Adele will see them, and there will be questions."

"How about this, why don't I take them with me? I'll take them back to La Chapelle and give them to you when the time is right?" he said.

"I think that would be good, but just the dress and shoes. That is what we had agreed on at the shop. The necklace, gloves, and clutch are extra things that I did not agree to accept. You can't just buy me things, Gerhardt."

"I can, but if you think the necklace is too expensive, then I will keep it. But please, keep the gloves and the bag. I have no idea what I would do with them, anyway."

She wondered why he didn't mention giving them to his fiancée, but it didn't feel right to broach the subject. They probably weren't more expensive than the dress and shoes, except probably the necklace. She could only imagine how much it must've cost.

"OK, I'll keep those two. But I couldn't possibly accept something as expensive as the necklace. How much did it cost anyway, if you don't mind me asking?"

He gave her a smug smile. "Wouldn't you like to know? Besides, it's not yours, remember? So, no, you don't get to know how much it cost."

"So, you are saying that you would tell me how much it cost if I had agreed to accept it?"

"No."

He was just toying with her now. She could tell he was getting some strange pleasure from not telling her what she wanted to know. She shook her head at him, then went into the changing room. She took the dress off and put it back on the hanger. After she had her clothes back on, she took the necklace off, put it in a napkin from her purse, and wrapped it up. She removed the stuff from the clutch and put it back in her bag, then placed the gloves in the clutch and hung it back around the hanger. She took the dress off the wall, picked up the shoes, and then came out of the changing room.

"We should see if it has stopped raining."

"It hasn't. I checked the windows while you were changing, and it is coming down harder now than it was before."

Eva started to worry about getting back to the hotel at a decent time. "How are we going to get back?"

"Let's go up the front, and I will make a call. I'll have my orderly come and pick us up. I would walk in the rain, but there is no need for you to get all wet. Plus, the dress should not get wet. It would probably ruin it."

Her first instinct was to tell him no, but then she thought that if they took a car, she would get back much faster and could get more sleep. "All right," she agreed.

He took the dress from her and carried it with him as they walked to the front. She watched him speak to the man at the desk about using the phone. The man sat the phone in front of him, and Gerhardt turned the rotor several times and leaned on the counter to wait. He stood up straight when someone came on the other end and spoke in German. After a few seconds, he hung the phone up and thanked the man at the desk.

"My driver is on his way. He should be here in five to ten minutes. Let's wait by the door."

They both sat on the staircase steps that faced the door, and he laid the dress on the steps beside him.

"What now?" he asked.

She looked at him, confused. "What do you mean?"

"I mean, what are we going to do when we return to La Chapelle? Do we go back to acting the way we did? Do we actively avoid one another as we talked about? What?"

Eva sighed. "To be honest, I'm not sure. Maybe we can see each other but only in secret. I can't afford for anyone to know. But what is this, really? What is it that we are doing, Gerhardt?"

"Who cares? Does it really matter what this is? Why don't we just enjoy it for now? Like you told me on the train, it wasn't possible for us during the war and most likely won't after the war either. So, for however long this lasts, I want to enjoy it and not worry about what comes after."

She wanted that, too, because it felt good no matter how wrong it was for her to be with him. "Deal. Let us see each other in secret and keep it simple."

He gave her a slight smile. "In secret, then."

"When I get back, I have to go to the farm. They are all probably wondering by this point if I'm ever coming back."

"They are probably missing you, I'm sure. We can meet in the forest when you go for walks if Sabina is not with you."

"I go on walks on my own a lot, too. I think it will work."

"Good, and perhaps when you get your cast off, we can go for that swim."

"That would be fun."

It was almost July now, and it was getting hotter with each passing day.

"He is here," Gerhardt said and picked up her dress and shoes.

Eva looked up to see a car parked out front with the engine running and the headlights reflecting off the rain.

She followed him out to the car, and his orderly was holding the door open for them; she got in, and he put the dress and shoes on her lap, then climbed in the back next to her.

"It sure is coming down tonight, Hauptmann."

"It is, Sergeant."

They traveled in relative silence to the hotel. The rain was so heavy that it made it hard to see, which extended the car ride to twice as long as it normally would have taken.

Finally, they arrived at the hotel.

"I will walk you to the front with the umbrella," he said.

He took the dress and shoes off her lap and laid them in the front seat. The Sergeant handed an umbrella to Gerhardt, who stepped out of the car as he opened it, then went around to Eva's side and opened her door. She stepped out of the car and tried to stay under the umbrella as he walked her to the covered walkway. He stopped when they were under it.

"Goodnight, Eva."

He leaned in and kissed her on the cheek. Her face flushed at his touch and the rhythm of her heart increased. He turned to walk back to the car when she remembered that she still had the necklace wrapped up in a napkin in her pocket.

"Wait," she called.

He turned around, looking at her as the rain poured off the umbrella.

"I still have the necklace." She reached in her pocket, pulled out the napkin, and held it out to him.

He walked back to her and looked at the napkin in her palm. "You could just keep it, Eva."

"You know I can't, not a gift this expensive."

He took the napkin from her hand and put it in his pocket. "Goodnight," he said curtly, then walked back to the car, closed the umbrella, and got in the back.

The car pulled away from the curb and disappeared into the rain. She stood there staring out into the darkness for a minute before turning and walking through the doors into the hotel lobby.

When she got to her room, she took a quick bath and crawled into bed, pulling the blankets up around her neck. She couldn't believe that she got away with this night, as far as she knew at least. As she thought about the night, she realized how many risks she had taken and how careless it was for her to go out in the city with him. From now on, all of their encounters had to be lowkey and less conspicuous. She was going to have to take being discrete more seriously.

Chapter Twenty-Two

Eva woke to a knock on her door.

"Eva?" Adele said from the other side.

She bolted up in bed, thinking something was wrong. "Yes?"

"We have already eaten. Are you not going to eat?"

She looked at the clock on the nightstand. *Eight-forty-seven, that's the time?* She thought she was waking up in the middle of the night, not late morning. "Yes, I'm going to eat. Let me just put some clothes on."

"Are you feeling OK?"

"I'm fine. I was just more tired than I thought. I'll be right out. I'll knock on your door when I'm ready."

"All right, I'll wait there."

She could hear Adele's footsteps in the hall. She jumped out of bed, opened the blinds to let in the morning sun, and grabbed some clean clothes from her suitcase. She went to the bathroom and looked in the mirror to see how bad the damage was from staying out late last night. Her eyes were a little puffy and bloodshot. *Crap.*

She splashed her face with cold water, then reached for her makeup bag. She quickly applied some lotion, powder, mascara, and red lipstick, and then she pinched her cheeks to make her look more awake. She changed into her clean dress and quickly brushed through her hair, and pinned it up on one side. She went back to her bed and put on her stockings and shoes, then got her purse off the floor and headed for the door. She had tossed it there last night because she was so tired that all she could think about was going to bed. She was definitely going to need some caffeine this morning.

When she got to Adele's door, she knocked and waited for her to open it. The door opened, and Adele looked at her quizzically.

"Are you all ready?" Adele asked.

"I am. I hope I didn't make you wait too long."

"Not at all. We were just surprised that we didn't see you down for breakfast this morning."

"I couldn't fall asleep. It was probably around one before I dosed off."

"I'm sorry. Any particular reason why?"

"No, sometimes I just have a hard time falling asleep."

"Madame Blanc and I can sit with you while you eat if you like?"

"You don't have to do that. I'll be fine. Oh, and I need to go back to the Red Cross today at noon. I have a letter they are going to mail for me. I'll meet you guys back at the hotel when I'm done, and then we can leave."

She did not want to tell her where she was actually going. The Red Cross seemed like a believable enough story. She hated lying, but some things were just better left unsaid and unknown, like her and Gerhardt.

"Sure. I'll let Madame Blanc know. That's nice that they can mail your letters." She gave Eva a warm smile.

"Yes, it is. Well, I'm going to eat now. I'll hurry so I can pack my stuff before I leave for the Red Cross."

"Come to my room when you get back from the Red Cross so we know it's time to leave."

"I will."

She went to the café on the main floor, filled a plate with bread, grapes, cheese, and cold-cut meat, poured a glass with room-temperature orange juice, found an empty table, and sat down. She looked at all the food on her plate and thought of the starving people, especially the ones with children who could only get the bare minimum, and it made her feel guilty that she was in a position where she had access to what was now luxury items, like orange juice. She looked around the room. Over half of the people there were German soldiers. That was probably why the hotel could get orange juice and fresh fruit because they catered to the Germans.

She made sure to eat all the food she put on her plate and drink all the orange juice so that she wasted nothing. She took the napkin from her lap, laid it on the table, and then stood up to leave when she saw a familiar face a few tables away. She squinted to make sure she wasn't mistaken, and she wasn't. Two tables from her was SS Obersturmbannführer Bauer, seated with three other officers, but none of them were Gerhardt.

About the same time she saw him, he looked up and made eye contact with her. She panicked and started walking briskly to the doors.

He stood from his chair. “Miss Abrams,” he called across the room to her.

There was no way she could pretend that she didn’t hear him. She froze. *Shit.* She looked around, feeling like she needed an exit, but it was too late. He was already approaching her. There was going to be no escaping him. She slowly turned around to face him.

“Miss Abrams, I thought that was you. You seem in a rush. Where are you going in such a hurry?”

“I have somewhere to be at noon. That is why I need to go now.”

“Oh, where is it you are going?” His voice was not casually enquiring but more demanding.

Why did it feel like this man was interrogating her again? She knew he did not trust her, even though she never gave him a reason not to.

“I am mailing a letter from the Red Cross, and it is far from here.”

“There is no need to be in a hurry, then. I can take you. Come, have a seat with us.”

She felt like a lamb being put in a lion’s den for the slaughter; the lamb knew what would happen, but there was no point in resisting; it was futile.

She took one last glance longingly at the door. “Sure, I can sit for a minute, but there is no need to drive me. I enjoy walking. I can see the city best that way.”

"Let's have a cup of tea together, and I will walk with you. Come." He nodded with his head towards the table.

She reluctantly followed him back to where he was sitting. While they were talking, the other guys at the table watched them, along with a few other people in the lounge. When they got close, one of the other guys stood up, pulled a chair from an empty table, and put it at their table next to where Bauer was sitting. She went to sit down, and he pushed it to the back of her knees to make it easier, then sat back in his chair.

"Thank you," she said to him.

"So, Miss Abrams, is this the hotel you are staying at?" Bauer asked.

"Yes, it is. But you guys aren't staying at this hotel. Why are you here?"

He quietly chuckled. "Not to worry, Miss Abrams. We are just here for the food. They have one of the best restaurants in this part of the city."

She forced a nervous smile. "So, where is Hauptmann von Schulz?"

"He returned to La Chapelle already."

He would have had to leave early in the morning if he had already gone. She felt bad now that they stayed up so late. There was no way he got much sleep. She could only imagine how tired he must be. He hadn't said anything to her about having to leave early this morning.

"Why did he have to leave today and so early?" she asked.

"He had a meeting with the commandant."

"Just him?"

"Yes—just him."

Bauer seemed to be less patient now. Just by the way he was looking at her, it was apparent she had already asked too many questions about Gerhardt. Either he suspected something was going on between them, or he thought she was trying to get information about him because she was a spy. Either one was not good.

He waved a waiter over to the table. "Que puis-Je vous faire?" he asked them.

Bauer asked for a black tea, asked the other men what they wanted in German, and then relayed it back to the waiter in French. His French was as good as Gerhardt's, which was better than most other Germans, although they both spoke it with a German accent.

He looked at her. "What would you like, Miss Abrams?"

She looked at the waiter. "I'll just have a green tea with one teaspoon of honey, please."

"Je vais l'avoir tout de suite," the waiter said, then turned and left.

"You speak very good French, Miss Abrams. Where did you learn it?"

"My grandmother taught me, but I have picked up a lot by being here, and it's helped with my accent, too. It's not great, but a lot better than when I first arrived." She realized that the other men at the table must not speak French or very little. She wasn't sure if Bauer knew she could speak German; Gerhardt must not have told him. She looked around the table at the other three men; they seemed bored now that she and Bauer were speaking French.

"Grandmother, really? Is she French?"

"Yes, she is."

"How interesting. Is that why you came to France?"

"No. I mean, that is not the only reason. But it helped in my decision."

"Well, Miss Abrams, you certainly look French, with dark hair, hazel eyes, and a fair complexion."

"I imagine I do. No one has ever mistaken me for a German," she said patronizingly. She looked at the other officers again. "Do you guys live in La Chapelle, too?" she asked them in German.

They exchanged glances with one another, including Bauer.

"No, we are in Sedan. We came here on a weekend pass."

The officer who answered was so large that he could probably lift the front end of a small car. Of course, he was blond, unlike Bauer, who had brown hair and hazel eyes like her. The other two men at the table looked very stereotypical German as well, with blue eyes and a medium build. One was blond like the larger man, and the other had light brown hair. The large one had kind eyes and was soft-spoken. His voice did not seem to match his body.

The waiter returned with their tea and placed a cup in front of each one of them. "Merci," Bauer said.

"Where is it that you are from?" asked the one with light brown hair.

Eva took a deep breath. "I'm American."

"American, I have never met an American before. Is it true that you guys only use cars to get around?"

"That's kind of true. We do have buses and trains in the big cities, and buses and trains that take you across the country, but not many. We usually use cars as the primary form of transportation. There is just so much land, and a lot of the country is very unpopulated, so there isn't a compelling reason to put public transportation there."

“Are you a good representation of what most Americans look like?” the other one with blond hair asked.

“I’m sorry, I don’t know what you mean.”

“Like your hair color, eye color, and size?”

“Oh, no. I think there is a good mix of about everything. People in America have red hair, brown, black, blond, and skin of all different colors, and the same goes for the eyes. As far as my size, I am rather small, a lot of women are bigger than me and of course the men. I would say our size is comparable with German people.”

Bauer took a pack of cigarettes from his pocket, pulled one out, put it between his lips, and then stuffed the pack back into his pocket. He lit it, inhaling deeply, then slowly blew the smoke out.

“Miss Abrams is staying for a while with the lady that is housing Hauptmann von Schulz. They met the other day on the street, so I left them and went back to the hotel. Did you two have a nice visit?” Bauer asked her suggestively.

Eva was a little surprised that he mentioned it, embarrassed, and somewhat annoyed with him for saying it in front of the others. “I guess… we didn’t talk for very long, then we said our goodbyes.”

The other guys looked at Bauer, then at her.

“So, you and the Hauptmann know each other?” the larger one asked.

“We are acquainted, that is all.” This conversation had taken a turn she was not comfortable with.

“Have you ever been to Germany?” the larger one asked again.

"No, I have not. I would like to go someday, but not until the war is over and has been over for a long time. But where I would really like to go is home."

Everyone at the table grew quiet. The larger officer no longer looked at her but down at his hands. She understood the change in him because he knew she couldn't go home. *How does it feel to be the one put on the spot and uncomfortable?* she thought.

She stood up from her chair. "I really must go. I don't want to be late. Thank you for the tea."

All four of them stood.

"But you haven't finished your tea, Miss Abrams," Bauer said.

"It's OK. I really have to go."

He leaned in and said something to the other officers. But it was too fast and quiet for her to catch.

"I will accompany you," he said.

She had forgotten about him offering that earlier. The officer with light brown hair shook her hand to say goodbye, as did the other one, but the larger man took her hand and kissed it.

"It was so nice to meet you, Miss Abrams. My name is Helmut. That might be easier for you to remember."

His farewell surprised her. "My name is Eva. You can call me that."

He smiled. "I will if we ever meet again."

Bauer got his hat and brown leather gloves off the table and followed her to the door. She took a deep breath when they got outside. The lobby of the hotel had become stuffier by the minute, and not just because of the cigarette smoke.

"The Red Cross is far from here. Are you sure you want to walk?" she asked, hoping he would change his mind.

"I'm sure."

She needed to get rid of him when they left the Red Cross. Because now that she had to go there for real, it would chew up a big chunk of her morning. As it was, she was probably already going to be late. She began walking fast, hoping that it would discourage him from talking to her, plus she would get there quicker, but he didn't seem to have any trouble keeping up with her. *Damn his longer legs.*

"Do you always walk this fast?"

"Yes, when I'm in a hurry. The people I came here with are waiting for me back at the hotel. We are going home today, and I don't want to hold them up."

"Then perhaps you should have let me drive you."

She wanted to ask why he was truly walking with her, but the truth was, she already knew.

When they reached the Red Cross, she stopped at the door. "Would you wait here? I'll be right back?"

"Of course, Miss Abrams," he said mockingly polite.

She went inside, closed the door behind her, and leaned against it. She took a deep breath and closed her eyes, wishing that this would all just go away, but she wished that he would go away more than anything else. There was no way he was going to leave her until they were back at the hotel. So there was no way she would be able to meet the guy at the café on time.

She paced up and down the hall for a minute to take up time so her story would appear believable. After ten minutes, she opened the door and went back out.

"That was fast," he said.

"I told you it wouldn't take me long." She wondered now if it was too fast. Maybe she should have given it another five or ten minutes.

"We can go back to the hotel then," he said.

"Actually, I would like to walk around for a bit. I want to have a few minutes by myself."

His gaze was burning a hole in her. "Nonsense, I'll walk you back. A woman alone in a strange city is a terrible combination. You never know what will happen. And as much as I hate to say this, some of our soldiers aren't as obedient as they should be."

He just would not leave her alone. It was as if he knew she was trying to do something she didn't want him to know about. But she also wondered about the last thing that he said. She didn't doubt that he was right about it, though. She looked at him with the same piercing stare. She did not like this man; his eyes and demeanor alone made her uneasy. She knew he watched her every move anytime he was near her and that he assessed every word that came out of her mouth, filing them away for some future use. No doubt he was just waiting for her to slip up and make a mistake. God only knew what he would do if she did.

"Do you mind if we walk fast again? I need to hurry," she asked.

"By all means, Miss Abrams." He gestured with his hand for her to take the lead.

She settled into a brisk walk back to the hotel, with him following beside her.

"You said that you came here with some people. Who might they be?" he asked.

"I came with Madame Blanc and her maid, Adele."

"And what was her business in Paris?"

Was this how the entire walk was going to be—him incessantly asking questions?

"Madame Blanc has property here that she rents out. She came to collect the rent money."

"And she needed you for that?"

"No, I think she just wanted me to come with her for the company."

"I must say, I'm surprised that you got a travel pass when there was no actual need for you to be here."

"You think people should not travel unless it is absolutely essential?"

"It would make things easier."

"So then, why are you here?" she asked, even though she already knew because Gerhardt had told her.

"For work, but I stayed over the weekend, seeing how I was already here. I work in Paris most of the time."

"But you are staying the weekend even though it is not essential."

"I beg to differ. If the men are not given a break from the everyday grind, they will get burned out, and their performance will suffer, and that includes me, which means the war will suffer."

"War is already suffering," she spat at him.

"I meant Germany's victory will suffer. I don't mean that people don't suffer in the war. That is inevitable."

"I think wars are awful and pointless. People lose their lives for their leader's gain. Hundreds of men and boys go to their deaths every day, and what did they get out of it? Nothing," she said, her voice becoming more impassioned.

"That's because you know nothing of war or how the world works."

"How dare you…!" She stopped walking and looked at him, anger boiling inside her.

"I say it as I see it. You come over here from your charmed life in America with the audacity to think you understand this war. You couldn't comprehend why Germany needed it or why its people needed it. You can't know what it was like to live in Germany after the Great War, and you sure as hell can't begin to understand the struggles of the German people. So, don't tell me wars are pointless."

She walked past him, but he caught up and stayed at her pace.

"I do understand what it might have been like, but it always seems to be the innocent that suffers the most in war."

"You should be careful, Miss Abrams. Some might think that you are part of the opposition."

Was he threatening her? "I'm just saying how I see it," she responded in kind.

"That's because you have a very skewed perspective. And many of those people you call innocent are not so innocent. They have made life harder for other people for their own gain."

"Children made life harder?"

"No, not per se, but their parents did, and they will someday, too, when they become adults. You share the sentiments of the people you view as the victims, and you align yourself with them. You see them as the victims because you've never been in my shoes. You have never seen the world through my eyes."

And this is how all of this started. Because people felt like they were victims. The Germans were only the victims of their own demise, she thought.

"Then what did I ever do to you? I'm not even European?"

"You side with those people you see as innocent. That is what you have done."

Tears welled up in her eyes, not from sadness but from her anger and frustration towards him for what he had done to her and what he was saying.

"You were going to torture me because I don't share your views and because I don't see things the same as you do?" her voice rising with every word.

"No, Miss Abrams, I was going to torture you because I wanted you to tell me the truth. I grow tired of dealing with people like you, who stand behind the true enemies in this world. People who murder women and children, steal the hard-earned money of men, and loot and pillage, showing no remorse. Taking all the food while a child dies on the street in front of them from hunger. People who turn a blind eye to your struggles and hardships simply because it is not their own, leaving you to be crushed by the injustice of the world. They don't care because it's not them."

Her anger began to subside, and she almost pitied him. She had never met anyone so angry at the world, so quick to believe everyone was against him and to judge so harshly. He had hardened his heart and was blinded by his hatred for what he deemed injustice. For him, everything was black and white.

"I am sorry, that is how you see the world and me. But it is not like that, and war is not the answer. It won't make it better; it will only make it worse."

"And you wonder why I don't trust you." They stopped when they reached the hotel steps. "I bid you adieu, Miss Abrams."

"And you."

She watched him walk to a car and get into the back seat before it drove away. What a tormented mind he must have. No one could have those views and be willing to do the things to people he did if they weren't.

She walked in the opposite direction at a brisk pace and breathed easier once she was far from him. She would have to be careful around him. He was a dangerous man.

The café wasn't crowded; only a few tables had people. She checked her watch, seeing that it was already fifteen minutes past noon. She looked at all the tables again, but he was not among the people there. Maybe if she had a seat and waited, he would come out and meet her, if he was even still here. She sat at a table near the street, and when the waitress came, she ordered a glass of wine, hoping it would help calm her nerves. She had thought a lot about his offer, but ultimately, her answer would have to be no. She had responsibilities in La Chapelle, friends, and Gerhardt. Even if she didn't have any of those, she should not be taking any more risks than was necessary. What she really needed to focus on was getting home.

She kept an eye on her surroundings while she sipped her wine, but there was no sign of him. *Where could he be? Hopefully, he did not decide to leave because I was late.* After waiting for over half an hour, she decided it didn't make sense to wait any longer. He wasn't coming, and the longer she sat there, the more uncomfortable she felt. Just like the first time she was at this café, she again had the distinct feeling of being watched, but no matter how many times she looked, he was nowhere to be found. If he was watching her, she could not figure out why he would not come out and meet her as they agreed. She laid some money on the table by the empty glass of wine and walked away. She had far to go and didn't want to keep Madame Blanc and Adele waiting any longer.

Chapter Twenty-Three

July 29th, 1940

Eva enjoyed the cool earth on her back as she lay in the grass. This July had been unbearably hot, and the sweltering heat didn't look like it would subside anytime soon. It was almost August now, and the temperature was only getting hotter. She had enjoyed spending the 4th with the Dubois'. They even tried to sing the national anthem with her, which was funny to witness. Sabina especially enjoyed it. They sat outside and looked for shooting stars, and when they would see one, they pretended it was fireworks. After that night, Sabina insisted on looking for shooting stars almost every night.

"What are shooting stars, Eva?"

"Well, it is a meteor moving fast, and when it enters the earth's atmosphere, it catches fire. That is why it looks like there is a streak of light behind it."

“What makes meteors?”

“It’s a piece of space debris that collides with earth; usually, it’s just rock.”

“How do you know that?”

“In school. I think we have stayed up late enough. Let’s go to bed.”

“Do I have to?”

“Yes, you have to. Besides, how will we do fun things tomorrow if we are both tired?”

“I guess,” she said with a pout.

Eva tucked the blankets around Sabina and then crawled into her bed. “Do you want to go with me tomorrow to get my cast off?”

“I can go?” she asked excitedly.

“Of course, as long as it’s OK with your dad.”

“Would you ask him, please?”

“Of course, don’t you worry. Now go to sleep.”

As the room grew quiet, she found her thoughts drifting to Gerhardt. She wondered how he was. She had not seen or heard from him in a month. He had business in Berlin, which she found out by asking around, and had been there ever since. She often found herself missing him, which surprised her a little. She knew that she had become fond of him and was used to his company, but she didn’t realize just how much until he left. She thought of him more often than she would like to admit. Was their time in Paris the last time she would see him? Did they have their one night, and that was it? Perhaps it should be that way. He had a fiancée, and even though he did not think it would last between them, it still wasn’t right; he wasn’t free, and she knew it.

The chirping from a flock of birds woke her early in the morning. She looked over at Sabina, who was still sound asleep in her bed. The house, too, was silent. She got out of bed as quietly as she could and wrapped her blanket around her. She tiptoed to the front door and slipped out, shutting it behind her, then sat on the porch to watch the sunrise. It looked like the sun was peeking up from the top of the earth, making the sky the most beautiful colors of orange and purple. She liked to watch the sunrise but didn't enjoy getting up early enough to see it, especially in the summer when the sun came up so early. But she couldn't sleep this morning, so she figured why not.

Back home, everyone is still asleep in their beds. I guess they are not because they aren't even here, she thought, strangely considering this.

Most of the time, she could keep herself from thinking about her family or missing them too much, but for some reason, some days were more challenging than others, like today. Maybe her missing Gerhardt made her miss them more. She wasn't sure, but right now, she felt like crying and wished that someone would hug her and tell her it was OK, even if that wasn't the truth. She missed the embrace of a loved one; outside of Sabina, she hardly had any real physical contact with anyone, and with every passing day, the feeling of being trapped was more pressing. It was almost suffocating, like it was closing in on her. It was as if the world continued to turn except where she was. That time stood still like being in a snow globe, constant and unchanging. She knew the date the war would end, but at times, it didn't feel like it was ever going to. She could only imagine what it must be like for everyone else. They didn't know when or how the war would end. It must make it that much worse for them. She would not want to be in their shoes.

She could hear banging outside the barn. She stood up and looked to see what the noise was but couldn't see anything. She stepped off the porch and walked barefoot towards the barn, looking around for the source of the noise; she heard it again, and it sounded like it was coming from the opposite side of the barn, away from the house. She peeked around the side of the barn and saw Ezra collecting some metal buckets.

"Good morning," she said.

He stood up quickly, not expecting anyone else to be up this early. "Eva, what are you doing up?"

"I couldn't sleep in any longer, so I got up to watch the sunrise. I didn't know you were up as well."

"Yes, I get up every morning around this time to milk the cows. Do you want to help?"

"Milk cows? Oh, I don't think that is a good idea. I don't know how, I've never done it before. I don't think I would be much help to you; maybe I will just watch." Eva realized she had been talking fast and rambling, which she did a lot when she was nervous.

"There's not a lot to it, really. Here." He held out a bucket to her. "I'll teach you."

She took the bucket. "Are you sure you want to take this on?"

"Absolutely. You'll do great."

She followed him into the barn, and just to the right of the door were two white cows tied to wooden posts. "Which one do you want me to milk?"

"Here, let's have you do this one. She is a gentle girl and just stands there while you are milking her," he said, nodding to the one closest to them.

He pulled up a small wooden stool and sat it towards the back of the cow.

"Sit there and put the bucket directly under the utter."

Eva draped her blanket over the rail, sat on the stool, and placed the bucket under the cow's utter.

"Now what?"

He took hold of one teat, gently pulled it down, and milk sprayed into the bucket. "Just like this, squeeze as you pull down and then repeat the process." He stood and crossed his arms over his chest, waiting for her to try.

She took the teat in her right hand, squeezed, and pulled it down. Milk sprayed out in a stream into the bucket. She looked up at Ezra. "Look, I'm doing it."

"See, I told you there is nothing to it. If you had the use of both of your hands, I would have you take one in each hand and alternate between the two."

She kept working with the one and looked back up and smiled, quite pleased that she got the hang of it so fast.

"Eva…" he said, raising the pitch of his voice.

She turned her head back to the bucket just as the cow stepped to the side. The teat turned, and milk sprayed all over her nightgown and the ends of her hair. She let go, almost falling off the stool.

Ezra put his hands out to catch her. "Are you OK?"

"I'm fine," she said, no longer feeling pleased with herself but rather embarrassed.

“I saw her getting ready to take a step and tried to warn you, but it was too late.”

“I thought you said she just stands there?”

“She usually does, but once in a while, she will move.” He helped her up from the stool and chuckled. “It’s all over you. She got you good.”

Eva glared at him. “Well, it wouldn’t have happened if she hadn’t moved.”

“Let me help you get some water for the bath. It’s the least I can do.”

She wasn’t going to argue with that. “All right.”

She followed him to the well, and he filled two wooden pails with water and carried them to the house, sitting them on the porch.

“I will bring you guys some breakfast after I take a bath,” she told him.

“That would be great, thank you! Do you want me to carry them in for you? I can sit them by the tub. I don’t mind.”

“Sure.”

She opened the door for him, and he carried the pails of water into the house.

“You know what, just leave them in the kitchen because I’m going to have to heat the water.”

“All right.” He sat the pails on the floor in the kitchen near the stove.

“Thank you, Ezra.”

“You are very welcome.”

“Well, I don’t think I will be helping you milk the cows anytime soon.”

"Nonsense, you did great. You will be out milking those cows again in no time."

She gave him a half-smile. "We'll see."

He returned her smile and nodded his head as he turned and left.

She poured the pails into two large pans, sat them on the stove, and then lit a fire underneath. She could hear the floorboards creaking near the back of the house, most likely from Fabien's room. She sat at the kitchen table to wait for the water to heat up.

"You are up early. Couldn't you sleep?" Fabien asked as he entered the kitchen, pulling his suspender over his shoulders.

"I did, but I woke up early and couldn't fall back asleep, so I got up."

"What's that on your nightgown?"

"Oh…" she chuckled. "Milk. I tried to help Ezra milk the cows, and this is what happened."

"It happens sometimes. Is that what the water is for?"

"It is. Oh, I was going to ask you. Today, I will get my cast off, and Sabina wanted to know if she could come with me. Is that OK?"

"I don't see why not. That girl would do anything with you. I think she has adopted you as her second mother."

That concept gave Eva a warm feeling but also made her feel a little strange. It was going to be so hard to leave Sabina when the time came to return home to her own time and country.

"Sometimes, I think you are right," she told him.

The water in the pans began to steam, so she got up and grabbed a towel to pick up the pot.

"Let me get those for you. You can't carry them with your arm like that." He took the towel from her, picked one up by the handle, carried it to the bathroom, and poured it into the small French galvanized bathtub, then returned to the kitchen for the other one. He took it to the bathroom, poured it into the tub, returned the pot to the kitchen, and sat it on the stovetop next to the other one.

"Thank you."

"It was no problem."

She quietly entered her room so she didn't wake Sabina. She got a light flowery dress to wear. No doubt it was going to be another unbearably hot day. The dress was made of a thin yellow material covered with blue flowers and lace around the sleeves; she loved this dress, and it made her feel good when she wore it. Seeing how she was going to get her cast off today, she thought, *why not wear it?* She grabbed the rest of the things she would need and tiptoed out of the bedroom and down the hall to the bathroom. She removed her milk-soaked nightgown and slipped into the warm water. She slid down in the tub, submerging her head in the water so she could wash the milk from her hair, but kept her left arm on the side, out of the water. As she lay on the bottom of the tub, she could see the sun shining through the small bathroom window, reflecting off the water, making it look like tiny diamonds. She finally sat up and leaned on the back of the tub. With nothing else to do but sit, her mind wandered to Gerhardt and what he might be doing right now. Was he with his fiancée, doing fun things together? Was he having military meetings? Or maybe he got transferred somewhere other than France, which is why he hasn't come back. At the same time, she wasn't surprised that she hadn't heard from Gerhardt. He had no obligation to her, and it was not like they were in a relationship, so why would he bother to let her know where he was and what was going on in his life? She was pretty sure at this point that Adele was mistaken in her opinion that he loved her. Maybe this was really a blessing in disguise because Adele was probably right about one thing. If something had developed between them, there was a good chance it would have ended badly for her and for more reasons than Adele could even fathom. She just needed to get him out of her head, but it was proving to be harder than she thought. There wasn't a day that went by that the thought of him didn't pop into her mind. She had to constantly find things to keep the thoughts of him away.

She could hear Sabina talking to Fabien from the other side of the door. It was probably time to get out of the tub. She stood up and stepped out of the tub, dried off, and dressed, then came out into the kitchen.

"Eva, papa said he told you I could go with you. I can't wait to go into town."

"Yes, he did, but I have to empty the water out of the tub and bring some food to the family in the barn, then we will go."

"OK, I will get ready." She ran back to their room, closing the door behind her.

"Sabina, come back. You need to eat," Fabien called after her. There was no response from the bedroom. "That girl, she is way too excitable. Would you please keep an eye on her in town? I don't like her going there anymore, now that…." he trailed off.

"I understand; I will keep a close eye on her." She lightly touched his arm to reassure him.

After breakfast, she emptied the tub of water and took some food to the barn for Ezra, his sister, and her children. She peeked her head in through the open barn door. "Hello?"

"We are here," she heard Ezra say.

She followed the sound of his voice to the back of the barn. He was sitting in the hay with his sister and her two children, who were playing in the hay and laughing.

"Good morning. I brought you some food. I hope it is enough for the four of you."

"It will do fine. Thank you, Eva," Rachel said. She told the kids to come and eat.

The boy ran over and sat in the hay between her and Ezra and crossed his legs. The girl sat on her lap and looked up at her mom with a large smile on her face.

"They are so well-behaved," Eva said.

"Not always. This is one of their good days."

Eva handed them the plates of food. "I'm going into town today; do you guys need anything?"

"Some yarn and knitting needles would be nice. I need to make the kids some hats and gloves for winter. They did not have any last winter, and I would like to have them made before the cold comes. I know that is a strange thought now because it is so hot outside, but I might not have them done in time if I don't start working on them soon. I will have to work on them a little every day to make sure I finish them in time."

"I will see what I can do about getting you some yarn and knitting needles. Is there a certain color that you want?"

"I know the choice of colors is limited, so just bring whatever you can get."

Eva watched as they ate their food. She felt bad that their portions were always so small, but there wasn't enough food to give them more. No one got much food these days except for the Germans.

"So, Ezra tells me you helped him milk the cows this morning."

Eva looked at Ezra and furrowed her brows. She could not believe that he had told her about that. His knowing was bad enough.

"He told me it went well, that you are a natural."

She realized that Ezra must not have told her about the incident. "He is being generous. I was not very good."

"I'm going to take Uri out in the fields and start teaching him a little about farming. Would you like to come?" Ezra asked.

"I can't go today. I will probably be gone until late. Perhaps another day. Maybe tomorrow, if that's alright?"

"It's all right. We can go tomorrow."

"I feel bad because I've been gone so much this summer that I have been little help to Fabien. I need to do more to pull my weight around here. He gives me a roof over my head, a bed to sleep in, and food to eat. I feel like I do so little to repay him."

"You are but one person, Eva. You don't take up much room, and you don't eat much. I've seen you eat. You give him more than you take. I've watched you with his daughter, and she seems quite taken with you. I know the two of you spend a lot of time together, and you do a lot with her. I'm sure that in itself is enough for him to see his daughter happy and looked after. But there are four of us, and we are much more of a burden." Rachel's words were kind.

"I know that there are four of you, but when times are hard, every person you have to feed and house becomes a burden, even me."

"Don't worry yourself too much about it. He knows what he is doing. They will be OK. Besides, you are not eating their food and taking up room when you are not here, so don't worry about being gone."

She was not sure how much she would be gone in the future. She, of course, would go to see Madame Blanc, but not as often as she thought she would, now that he was gone. Deep down, it still bothered her that he had simply disappeared and hadn't even tried to contact her, but she kept telling herself that it was for the best.

"Have you figured out what you will do about your living situation?" she asked.

With a look of defeat, Ezra diverted his eyes to the stables. "I am thinking at this point we are going to have to stay here for at least another winter. Fabien has been unsuccessful in finding us a place to stay or a way to England."

She knew this meant that the chances of them being found out and captured just increased considerably. "Ezra, I am sorry. I'm sure Fabien did all he could. We will keep trying, OK?"

"I know, Eva. It's all right. We will not lose hope and help Fabien as long as we are here under his roof and generous hospitality."

"I looked to see if I could get back to England, but there was no way for me either. While the Germans control Europe, no one is going to go to England. I am stuck here just like you."

"True, but your life is not at risk like mine, my sister, and her children."

She knew he was right, but it still felt like he was trying to downplay her situation. "I know I'm not the only one who's fallen on hard times, and I wish I could do more to help you. I do. I have no one here, and I wish I could go home. I feel like my life is flashing by me, and I can't do anything about it. I miss my family and my friends. I miss when life was simple, and I didn't have to worry about my safety every second, and I didn't have to be cautious of everything I said and every move I made. I can't even get word to them that I'm OK. We are all stuck in the middle of this terrible war, and none of us can do a damn thing about it. I didn't even have to be here, but I chose to come and help, and look how that has turned out for me."

"I'm sorry; I wasn't trying to say that your situation wasn't bad. I was just stressing the fact that you aren't being hunted. So, though you are stuck here too, you are, for now, safe. Your country isn't even at war with Germany, so they consider you a neutral party in this war. If you keep your head down, you should be fine."

He knew so little about her situation that it was pointless for her to even argue with him. He didn't realize that even if she survived the war, she might be stuck here in this time for the rest of her life. Ezra did not know what Bauer was about to do to her. If he did, he might have a different opinion.

This whole time, his sister sat quietly. Maybe it was a Jewish thing that women weren't to contradict or disagree with a man. Either way, Eva did not want to continue this conversation any further.

"I really have to go now. Sabina is waiting for me." She walked towards the front of the barn, and when she was almost to the doors, she could hear fast-approaching footsteps behind her.

"Eva, please wait."

She stopped right in front of the door and turned to look at him. She knew he was going to apologize to her, but she didn't feel the need for one.

"Eva, I'm sorry if I have upset you. We really appreciate everything you have done for us, and I know that this is difficult for you."

"Oh, you mean risking my life to go into Belgium and get the stuff you needed?" She wondered if she was being too harsh but felt he didn't truly appreciate her or what she had done for them.

"Eva…."

She turned back to the doors. "I do need to go now." She walked through the one-opened door and back towards the house. "Sabina, are you ready?" Eva asked as she entered.

"Yes, yes." She skipped through the kitchen towards her and stopped by her side. "Are you OK, Eva? You look upset, and your face is red."

She smiled at Sabina. "Of course, I'm fine. There is no reason for you to be worried about me. Now, let's go get this cast removed."

For now, Sabina seemed satisfied with that answer, so she smiled back and took Eva's hand.

They looked for new flowers that they had not picked before as they walked into town. She could not have asked for a better day for a walk. The sky was blue with no sign of rain clouds. The trees near the road offered them shade, and a slight breeze kept them cool from the never-ending heat.

"Look, Eva." Sabina ran over to the side of the road and picked a small white flower. "What is this one?"

"I don't know. I haven't seen that one before. Let's hang onto it, and maybe we can ask someone in town if they know what it is."

"That's a good idea." She put it in the pocket of her light blue dress. "I hope we find more flowers."

"Keep looking, and you might."

Sabina looked up at her. "Eva?"

"Yes?"

"You don't seem happy like you used to. Is it because that German man hasn't been around?"

If it was that obvious to a ten-year-old, then other people must have noticed it, too.

"No, there have just been a lot of things on my mind, like getting my cast off and the news I got in Paris about not being able to go home, that is all. I'm better now. I have accepted what is. I promise I will try harder to be more like myself so we can have fun."

Sabina frowned as she continued to look up at her. "I don't believe you. That's not the only reason you are different."

Eva stopped walking and looked down at her. "What are you talking about?"

"I know it's because of him, but don't worry, I won't tell Papa."

"Why do you think it is because of him?"

"Because you seem happy when you are with him, and since you met him, you are off in a faraway place in your head when he isn't around. I think you think about him."

She had no idea how she was going to deny all of that. "Look, the only people I enjoy spending time with now are you and your family. You guys are the ones that I concern myself with, and how do you know what I think about?"

"Because you started doing it after you met him, just sitting on the porch staring out at the trees for a long time."

"Fair enough… but I think about my family a lot too. That is probably what I am thinking about when you see me."

"I still think you are thinking of him. You have not said no. You just said you think about other people too."

"I did, but not anymore."

"Why did you think about him then but not now?"

"No more questions."

"Fine," she drew the word out in defeat.

Eva tried to help her find more flowers for the rest of the walk to keep her busy. She didn't want her asking any more questions.

"Sabina, I bet I can make it to the first building before you can." She gave Sabina a daring smile as they reached the edge of town.

"No, you can't. No one can run faster than me."

"Prove it. Words mean nothing. On the count of three."

Sabina got an intense look on her face, wrinkled up her nose, squinted her eyes, and then put her right foot forward.

Eva couldn't help but chuckle at how silly she looked. "Ready?"

Sabina nodded her head.

"One… two… three."

As soon as she said three, Sabina took off running. Eva took off too but hung back, not trying to pass. When Sabina reached the first building at the edge of town, she started doing a happy dance.

"I beat you. See, I told you I was faster."

"I guess you were right. You are the reigning champion and a faster runner than me."

She did a congratulatory bow, then reached her hand out, and Sabina gave her a high five.

"You know what we should do after getting your cast off?" Sabina said.

"No, what?"

"We should get ice cream."

"Really, we should get ice cream, huh?"

Sabina beamed with delight. "Yes, we should."

"All right, as a reward for you winning the race and me getting my cast off, I guess we can get ice cream."

She quilled. "Yesss."

They entered the lobby of the small hospital.

"Do you want to wait in the lobby, or do you want to go back with me?"

"I want to go back with you?"

"You can, but just stay seated and don't get in the doctor's way or ask questions."

"I won't. I'll sit just like you said."

"All right then, let's get this taken care of."

She walked up to the front counter. The nurse was a short, round woman with a gray bun on top of her head.

"Can I help you?"

"Yes, I'm here to have my cast removed."

"Sign in here, and we will call your name."

Eva signed her name on the clipboard and then sat in the lobby with Sabina to wait.

"Will it hurt when they remove the cast?"

"No, I don't think it will hurt."

"That's good. Will you be able to use your arm right after?"

"I believe so, but this is the first bone I have broken, so I'm not sure."

They called Eva's name from the other side of the room. She looked up to see a woman standing near a curtain that led to the back of the building. It was the town hospital, but Eva thought it looked more like a clinic; it was so small she could hardly think of it as a hospital.

She took Sabina's hand and followed the woman behind the curtain, who led them to a bed.

"Sit there. The doctor will be here shortly."

Eva sat on the bed with Sabina, but they didn't have to wait long when a tall skinny man with black hair in a white lab coat approached her.

"Are you Eva?"

"Yes."

"And you are here to get your cast off?"

"I am."

"How long have you had it on?"

"Seven weeks."

He took her arm and examined it. He moved it around and lifted it up and down. "Does any of this hurt?"

"No, it doesn't hurt."

"Good, let me get the tools, and I will be back to take it off."

"OK."

Eva was eager to get it off. She was so tired of having it on. It would be nice to do everyday things again and have full use of her arm.

The doctor returned with the same nurse who called her back; she held a shiny metal tray with some tools. She sat it on the bed next to Eva, then looked at Sabina. "She will have to move off the bed while we do this."

"Of course." Eva looked at Sabina. "Why don't you sit on the bed next to us."

Sabina hopped off the bed and sat on the one Eva told her to.

"Is it alright if she sits on that bed?"

"It's fine. She is welcome to sit there," the nurse said.

The doctor rolled a small table over to the side of the bed. "Put your arm on here. I don't want you to have it on your leg in case the shears slip. We can soak the cast if you want, but it will take hours to remove it that way."

"We can try the shears. Will it hurt?"

"Not if you stay very still. It shouldn't."

She put her arm on the table and watched as the doctor got a large pair of stainless-steel shears with a curved blade. They looked scary, but she knew most things seemed worse than they actually were. The nurse came to the side of the table to assist the doctor. Eva tried to relax and not tense her arm as he stuck the shears under the end of the cast. He used both hands to squeeze the handles of the shears, and she could see by the strained look on his face that it took a lot of effort to cut through the plaster. Every time he squeezed the shears, he would clench his jaw, and the blood veins and ligaments protruded in his neck and hands. It was good for him and her that the cast was on her wrist and not her leg. It would be even harder to cut. He reached up halfway through cutting with his left hand to wipe his forehead. There were red lines across his palm from the handles of the shears. She felt a little bad that he had to remove her cast that way, but she really wanted it off, and she couldn't leave it on forever. If only the plaster saw had already been invented.

When he continued cutting the cast, she could feel the blade of the shears pushing into her arm. It didn't hurt, but it didn't feel good either. When he got to the end of the cast at the palm of her hand, it made a snapping sound as he cut the last piece. He laid the shears on the table next to him and pulled the cast apart and away from her arm. It made a cracking sound as he applied pressure to it, and then the whole thing snapped. The air in the room felt cold on her arm, and as he removed both sides of the cast, she held her breath just in case it smelled.

"Does it smell bad?"

"I can't smell anything," the doctor said.

Eva looked down at her arm. "Oh my gosh, there is so much dry skin, and my arm is pasty white and thin. And why does it look hairier than the other arm? The hair on it is so dark, thick, and long. It looks nothing like my other arm."

"That is common for a leg or arm that has been in a cast. Your arm should return to normal after a few weeks. The loose skin will slough off on its own pretty quickly, but the hair will take longer. It possibly could take months for it to return to normal, but there is no way of telling. Everyone is different."

Great, so I might have to shave my arm, she thought. *And if I did that, I would have to shave the other one to make them look the same.*

"How long will it take before I can use this arm?"

"It should be feeling pretty normal in about a week, but let's look at it now without the cast." He lifted her arm out to the side, then straight up. "Does any of this hurt?"

"No, but my arm feels a little stiff."

"Good, it feeling stiff is perfectly normal, but we don't want there to be any pain. Don't overuse it during the first week and it should be fine. The nurse will help you get some of the loose skin off." He washed his hands at a sink in the room, then left down the corridor and turned a corner.

The nurse got a damp cloth and rubbed it up and down on her arm with slight pressure. Eva could see the skin coming off onto the fabric; it was one of the grossest things she had seen. She could not believe this was how her arm looked now. And it felt strange and was more sensitive than the other arm.

"That is all we are going to get off right now. Too much rubbing will make your arm sore. You can try getting more off tomorrow, but I wouldn't recommend doing it more than twice a day." She put the cloth back in the metal tub with water. "We are all done."

Eva got off the bed, and Sabina hopped down, coming to Eva's side.

She took Eva's hand and looked at her arm. "Gross, it looks weird."

"I know it looks funny."

"Does it feel funny too?"

"It does, actually. The skin is sensitive, and my arm feels smaller than the other arm. It also is dry and itchy."

Sabina touched her arm with her fingertips. "Ewwww, it even feels strange."

Eva laughed. "Now you know what will happen if you break a bone, so be careful and don't do anything silly. That means no more climbing trees or doing the other things your dad tells you not to."

She rolled her eyes. "Papa only says those things because he is scared, not because I will get hurt."

"No, Sabina, he tells you those things because you could actually get hurt doing them."

Sabina looked down at the floor. "Maybe he is right."

"He is right. Your dad worries about you because he loves you and doesn't want you to get hurt."

"I know that Papa loves me."

Eva put her arm around her shoulders. "Come on, let's get the things for Rachel and go home."

"No, you said we can get an ice cream on our way home."

"That's right. I did say we could get ice cream. How could I forget that."

Sabina looked up and smiled. "I knew you would like that idea."

"You were right, Sabina. I do like that idea."

She held Sabina's hand as they walked along the street; it felt so good to use her hand again. She smiled at the thought of no longer being limited to the things she could do, and it gave her a new sense of hope. Today, she would try to be happier, and tomorrow, she would begin working on new plans for a way home.

There were more people out than usual today. Some were shopping, while others just seemed to be enjoying the nice weather. A few shop owners were out cleaning windows or changing signs, and some were sitting near the fruit and vegetable baskets that they had on display in front of their shops. At the end of the street was the only café in town, the one she went to with Gerhardt, which was also the only place to get ice cream. Eva stopped in front of the general store next to the café, where she would get Rachel's knitting things.

"Would you wait outside for me? I will only be a minute."

"Yes, I will sit on the front step."

Eva kissed her on the top of the head. "I will be right back."

She hurried into the store and found the small yarn selection that they had. She grabbed some green yarn for the boy and yellow for the girl. They did not have any pinks, purples, or even blues, so this would have to do.

"Are you taking on a new hobby, mademoiselle?" the man at the front desk asked.

"No, this is for someone else. I told them I would pick it up while I was in town."

"That's nice of you."

She gave a smile and paid the man. He handed her the change with the yarn and needles he had wrapped in brown paper and tied with a string.

"Take care."

"Thank you."

She took it from him and met Sabina out front.

"Are you ready?"

"Yes, but can I stop and throw something in the fountain for luck first?" Sabina asked.

"I suppose. What will you throw in?"

"I want to throw in the flower I found today."

"We never did get to ask what kind it was. I guess throwing it in the fountain for luck is better than letting it wilt at home in your room."

They went to the fountain, and Eva sat on the edge.

"OK, throw it in."

"I want to make a wish too."

"Even better," Eva told her. "Make it a good one. We could all use some luck right now."

Sabina sat on the edge of the fountain next to Eva and closed her eyes as she held the flower in her palm. As Eva waited for Sabina to make her wish, she felt a certain calmness in the air that settled over her. It felt familiar, and she knew she had felt it before.

Eva turned her head away from Sabina and looked out over the fountain. Across the square was a man standing with the sun to his back, which shadowed his face. She could tell he wore a German officer's uniform as he stood perfectly still, holding his gloved hands together in front of him. She did not need to see his face; she knew who he was.

Chapter Twenty-Four

She stood. “Sabina, I will be right back. Stay here.”

Eva walked towards him without waiting to see if Sabina responded. He unfolded his hands and walked towards her, stopping only when they were a few feet apart. They quietly stood looking at one another, and a wash of emotions flooded her at this moment. She didn’t even know what to say. She was feeling so many different things right now, and she didn’t know which one was more appropriate to respond to.

He reached out and touched her arm. “I see you got your cast off.”

“I… I did. Where did you go, Gerhardt? You left the opera that night, and then you just disappeared. Another officer told me you went to Berlin.”

“I did. I had meetings there and realized I needed to take care of some other things while I was there.”

"So why did you never mention that you were going to Berlin that night?"

"Because I didn't know. A car came to my hotel early that morning and picked me up. We left right after I packed my things."

"And you couldn't have written me a letter."

"I did. I wrote you several, but then I threw them all away. I didn't know exactly what to tell you or if you were even expecting a letter from me."

"Of course, I wanted a letter from you. Gerhardt, you are my friend."

"Come now, Eva. You and I both know we are not just friends. We will never be just friends."

She had told herself that the lying about them was over, and she meant it. "You are right, Gerhardt. We will never be just friends. We have gone beyond that now." She smiled up at him, and it was the first time since he had left that she smiled, and it wasn't faked.

He gently brushed her cheek with his fingers. "I see your face whenever I close my eyes," he said, returning her smile. "I believe your love is the purest I will ever know."

Did he just tell me that he loved me? she thought. *I mean, that is not exactly what he said, but then what would he have meant if not that?*

He moved his hand back to his side and looked over her shoulder. "I think you have someone who is impatiently waiting for you."

She turned around and saw Sabina standing beside the fountain, watching them. She turned back to Gerhardt; she felt like if she left to go back to Sabina, he would disappear again.

"What are you guys doing in town?"

"I got my cast off today, and I planned to take her to the café for ice cream."

"Oh, it was today that you got your cast off?"

"Yeah, that was the reason I came into town."

"I will walk with you. The ice cream is on me, my treat."

She knew by now that arguing with him wouldn't do any good. He would buy it for them, anyway. They walked over to Sabina.

"Sabina, Gerhardt is going to have ice cream with us. Is that all right?"

She looked up, eying him curiously. "I guess."

"Thank you, Sabina. I will make sure yours has the biggest scoop," he said.

She smiled brightly. "Now I know why Eva likes you. You must buy her big scoops of ice cream too."

He couldn't help but laugh at her childish assumptions. "I don't buy her ice cream. I buy her other things, things adults like more than ice cream."

"Like what?"

"It is a secret that only Eva can know, but someday when you grow up, someone will buy you these things too."

That greatly excited Sabina. "I can't wait to grow up now. Do all grown-ups get these things?"

"No, just the girls."

"Who will give me these things?"

"Someone who respects and appreciates you. They will give you these things to show they care, especially if it is not possible for them to do so any other way."

"Why couldn't they just tell me they care?"

"Well, sometimes that is not always possible. Maybe other people won't like it if they know this person cares about you, or maybe it is easier for you to accept that someone cares for you if they show it in the form of a gift. You will understand someday."

"I hope I will because I don't really understand now. But I know that Eva is OK with you caring about her."

He looked at Eva. "Does she? Well, I am glad to hear that."

"People are staring at us. We should go to the café now," Eva said, her cheeks feeling hot.

He looked around at the shops and saw that most people on the street had stopped what they were doing and were now watching them. "You are right. Let's go to the café, and I will explain what happened in Berlin."

She could feel the people's eyes on her as they walked through the street, making her uneasy. This was not the first time people in town had seen them together. What must they think of her now, she could only imagine? There were other Germans on the street who had been going about their day, but unlike the townspeople, their gazes were not of contempt but more of curiosity. She heard whispers of people around her and knew some merely wondered why she was with him, and others no longer viewed her as a friend to the French but as a friend of the Germans.

He held the door of the café for her and Sabina. "Do you want to sit at the bar or a table?"

"Why don't we let Sabina eat hers at the bar, and we can eat ours at a table." She bent down in front of Sabina. "Gerhardt and I need to talk about some grown-up things. I want you to sit at the bar for now while you eat your ice cream."

"You have to stay close."

"Don't worry. We will be in a booth not far away."

He ordered three cups of chocolate ice cream, with Sabina's having two scoops. After they got their ice cream, Gerhardt and Eva sat at the booth closest to Sabina. Eva figured she would let him take a bite of his ice cream before she began asking questions. She took a bite of hers, too, and the ice cream tasted so good as it melted in her mouth; she had not had any since she had left her own time. Ice cream was quite expensive now during the war because it was a luxury item, and milk was scarce with the rationing.

"So, what did you do in Berlin?"

He took in a deep breath and put his spoon in the bowl. "Mostly, what I did was work-related, and of course, I saw my family while I was there. They still have had no word from Hans. My mother fears the worst, and she is probably right. My dad has remained optimistic and thinks there is a chance he will return, either now or after the war. He thinks that maybe he was taken as a prisoner."

"And what do you think?"

He didn't respond immediately but sat silently, looking at his bowl. "I want to believe that he is still alive like my father, but inside, I know he is not."

She could feel the sorrow radiating from him and the grief inside that he was not showing. She was going to ask about his fiancée, but it now seemed trivial. She wasn't going to burden him with that question. She did not know the pain that might be associated with her and didn't want to bring up a subject that could cause him more pain than he was already feeling. "I am so sorry, Gerhardt! I don't even know what you must be going through."

"It's OK, Eva. He knew the risks. We all did. Someday, I will be able to think of him and mourn him, but right now, I can't."

She couldn't even imagine the torment that must be going on in his mind right now. It would literally drive her to insanity; he must have a strength that she didn't possess.

"What will you do now?"

"Eva, I will be transferred from here to Berlin at some point. I don't know when that will be exactly. Maybe a few months, a few weeks, a few days. If I had to guess, I would say sooner rather than later. They are assigning me to a different position, one in Berlin."

Eva couldn't believe what she was hearing. Was he really leaving again, and this time for good? This changed her thoughts on going home and where she would go from there. What would become of them… maybe he was going home to be with his fiancée, but then why lead her on? Was she just a source of entertainment for him because he had no choice but to be in France and needed something to occupy his time while he was here? The thoughts raced through her mind.

"Eva, did you hear what I said?"

"Yes, I did. I guess I don't know what to say."

"Eva, I want you to know that I didn't choose to go to Berlin, but I would have just been transferred somewhere else if they hadn't sent me there. Regiments never stay in the same place. They are always moving."

OK, so he isn't going there for his fiancée, she thought. It made her feel happy even though it shouldn't, so she felt guilty about feeling happy. It was all so confusing. Although he wasn't going back for his fiancée, that didn't mean he wouldn't get back with her when he returned to Berlin.

"Can I ask what you will do in Berlin?"

"You can, but I can't tell you much about that. I can tell you that I will be working at the FHQ, which is the military headquarters in Berlin. But that is about all I can say. I can't disclose anything I will be doing there. I'm sorry."

"It's OK. I understand the need for secrecy."

"I wanted to ask, what will you do when I am gone?" His words were cautious.

"I don't know. I want to find a way home, but that probably won't be easy. So, while I am waiting for that to happen, I can perhaps do what I came here to do and help people in need. I can think of no better way to use my time."

"That is a noble cause. Just be careful. And don't lose yourself while trying to help others. You must know that helping some people would come at great personal risk to you, not to mention it is illegal. Eva, I hope I can say with absolute certainty that you would never put your life at risk like that, not even for someone else. There is a behavior and a mindset you should adopt. We do it in the military, 'never be weak and always obey rules.' It will keep you alive, Eva. I'm not saying that you are weak by any means. I'm telling you to follow the rules."

It took her a little by surprise that he was telling her not to help people, but it shouldn't. She did not know what his personal views of Jews were, but no matter what they were, he had to follow the Nazi's views of them. It made sense that he would tell her to stay clear of them, no matter how cruel it might sound to her.

"I understand."

What he said confirmed to her that she needed to be very careful about the family they had in the barn. She was sure he would be angry if he found out she was hiding a Jewish family. No matter what he might feel for her, he still had a duty to uphold.

"I know that the time I have remaining here will not be our last time together. We will see each other again. Maybe you can come and see me in Berlin sometime?"

"I don't know if I can. What I mean is I don't know if I'm allowed to travel there without a compelling reason."

"Just give them my name when asking for a travel pass and tell them you are coming to see me. They will give you the pass."

"You seem very certain of that."

"Because I know how it works. If I were just an enlisted, it would be harder, but it is easier when it comes to officers."

"I don't know what the rest of this year will bring, so I can't tell you yes, but I will try," she said.

"I can't ask any more than that." He looked over her shoulder to see Sabina turned in her chair, facing them, an empty ice cream bowl on the counter. "It looks like Sabina is done with her ice cream, too. May I walk back with you?"

"Yes."

They strolled side by side as Sabina ran ahead, looking for flowers.

"She seems to be a very content child," he said.

Eva watched as the mere sight of a flower on the side of the road brought her such joy. "She is. If only we could all be like that. Unfortunately, life becomes more burdensome the older we get."

"True, it does. But part of me wonders if we adults don't try hard enough to see the joy in the small things and simple pleasures, like Sabina. She has reasons to be unhappy, but still, she looks for joy, and if she can't find any around her, she makes it up." He watched as she picked flowers on the side of the road a few feet ahead.

"She finds joy in the smallest things. She is such a pleasure to be around."

"As are you," he said.

She looked at him and saw he was gazing down at her softly. "Thank you! You make this war more bearable too."

They turned down the narrow dirt road that led to the farm, bringing back a sense of déjà vu for Eva. It reminded her of the time they had walked down this very road and the feelings she was having as she walked next to him, but of course, she said nothing then, just as she would say nothing now. She always knew that this day would come, the day he would tell her he had to leave her, and the time with him would then be over. She dreaded the thought of it, so whenever it would come up, she would push it out of her mind, but always in the back of her head, knowing it was coming.

"I will walk you to the last field, and that is as far as I will go. I know it is best if Monsieur Dubois does not see us together."

"I don't know what he would do if he saw us together, to be honest. I know he would not be pleased with me. I would rather not have to deal with that. It's just better he doesn't know."

"Eva, now that you have your cast off, would you like to go swimming in the pond with me on Saturday?"

That was right; he had told her they should go swimming after she got her cast off. What reason did she have now to tell him no?

"I suppose there is no harm in going swimming. It would be easier for me if I stayed at Madame Blanc's, though, as it's a shorter walk, and there will be fewer people to explain my absence to. Madame Blanc will also be easier to hide from when we are done swimming, and if she happens to see me, a simple explanation would satisfy her."

"All right. I will meet you in the garden at noon on Saturday. I'm bringing food, so come hungry."

"Do I need to bring anything?"

"No, I've got it covered."

They stopped at the end of the last field before they got to the house. The cornfield Fabien owned sat in between his wheat and barley fields. It always brought a smile to her face whenever she passed it because it reminded her of the cornfields in America. Fabien only had three fields, and he sold the grains for the making of flour and beer, and he used the corn mostly to feed his cows, sheep, and chickens.

"I will see you—"

"Eva?" Ezra stepped out of the cornfield holding a straw basket filled with corn, his white undershirt covered in sweat and dirt.

Her heart skipped a beat, and her breath caught in her throat at the sight of him.

"What are you doing with him? Why is he here?" Ezra looked pointedly at Gerhardt.

She had to think of something quick. "I went into town to get my cast off, and he offered to walk us back in case we needed any help."

"Why would you need his help?" Ezra glared at Gerhardt.

"I didn't, but it was a nice gesture, so I accepted his offer." Eva's heart raced in her chest.

Gerhardt held out his hand to Ezra. "Hauptmann von Schulz."

Ezra looked down at his hand, then back to his face, but never moved a hand from the basket. “They don’t need your help.”

Gerhardt put his hand down to his side and looked at Ezra closely. “I don’t believe I have seen you before. How do you two know each other?”

She couldn’t believe Ezra showed his face to Gerhardt, much less opened his mouth. He was such an idiot. The more he talked, the deeper he was digging himself in, and the harder it was going to be to back up anything he said.

“I work for the Dubois.”

“When did you come into their service?”

“A few months ago.”

She knew she would have to step in and put an end to the conversation quickly. She couldn’t allow him to say anymore.

“So, you came here about eight weeks ago?”

“Yes, he came seeking employment, and frankly, we needed the help, so we hired him to do this and that around the farm. Fabien can’t pay him much, so we give him food and a place to stay in exchange for his work,” Eva hurried and said to keep Ezra from speaking.

“Is that so, and where is it that you come from? Not France.”

“He is from Belgium,” she pipped up again before Ezra could speak.

“Belgium, hmm. I didn’t catch your name?”

“Shane Peeters.”

“And why did you come to France from Belgium, Shane?”

“There is more work here than in Belgium.”

“And you are registered?”

“I am.”

She watched the conversation closely and the way they interacted with one another. Ezra was tense and on edge, and Gerhardt was suspicious. He would be more believable if he would calm down. She knew Gerhardt didn't wholly believe Ezra. She could hear it in the tone of his voice. She needed to get them away from each other before Ezra slipped up or Gerhardt asked one too many questions.

"Shaner, Fabien will want that corn, and Sabina and I need to get home. It is getting late."

"Right, I will bring the corn there now. I'll see you back at the farm." Ezra gave Gerhardt one last look, then turned and walked in the direction of the house with the basket of corn in hand.

"I didn't know that you took on extra help. You never mentioned him."

"I guess it just never came up. It wasn't of any great importance."

"Do you know who he is? Do you know what kind of person you have let into the house?"

"He sleeps in the barn, not the house."

"That's better, but still not ideal."

"He is a good worker and has never given us any kind of trouble."

"I'm glad to hear it; however, I find it odd that he had to come to France to find work. The story he gave about there being more work here would only be true because France is a bigger country, but the truth is that farms in any of the countries need good workers. Food is more important now than ever. Every bit of it is used, and all farms are expected to produce crops."

"He checked out and has all of his papers, so I don't care why he left Belgium," she said.

"Just be careful. Sometimes, people aren't what you think or who they say they are. And you are right, it is late, and I still have a lot to do. I'll see you on Saturday." He kissed her hand.

She nodded. "Sabina, let's go."

They walked down the road towards the house as Gerhardt walked in the opposite direction.

"What is going on? Why did the German ask Ezra so many questions? I don't think he likes him."

"He has to ask. It is his job."

"I want to go swimming with you on Saturday."

"No, Sabina, you can't go this time. Just the two of us are going right now."

"Why, is it a date?"

"No, it's not a date. It's just two friends hanging out."

"You are friends with him?"

"Sort of. It's complicated."

"I hope he likes Ezra. We are friends now."

"You are?"

"Yes, when you were gone to Belgium, he did things with me. I went to the barn to see him, and we hung out together. We would go on walks like you and I do. And guess what?"

"What?"

"He taught me how to milk cows. Isn't that great?"

"It is. So, you did a lot with him while I was gone?"

"Yes. We would feed the chickens, goats, and sheep. We also planted some flowers on the side of the house. Did you see them?"

"No, Sabina, I didn't see them." She wasn't sure how she felt about Sabina getting close to Ezra. Her shallow side was jealous, but her motherly side was concerned for her safety. She felt like she needed to talk to him about it, just to make sure that he was aware of the risks he put her in and to find out why exactly it was that he decided to hang out with Sabina while she was gone.

"Yes, we had a lot of fun. It helped me not to miss you so much. He is nice."

"I'm glad you like him. Sabina, go into the house, and I will meet you inside. I need to talk with Ezra," she said when they were almost to the front door.

"Is it about what happened at the field?"

"That and some other things. Go to the house now, all right?"

"Fine. But please, don't be too long. Can I sleep with you tonight?"

"Yes, you can sleep with me if you stay in the house and don't go to the barn. Deal?"

She smiled. "Deal."

"OK, run along."

Sabina ran towards the house and didn't look back.

Eva walked to the barn. She could see the light shining from under the doors, so she opened one and called inside.

"Hello."

"We are in the back," she heard Rachel call.

She walked to the back of the barn and saw Rachel sitting on the hay with her kids. "Is Ezra here?"

"No, he went out to the south field about fifteen minutes ago. Is something wrong?"

"No, I just need to talk to him about something I need him to do."

The look on Rachel's face gave away that she did not completely believe her.

Eva took a lantern and went to the south field. "Ezra, where are you?" she called. She stood still to listen but didn't hear anything, so she called again as she entered deeper into the maze. "Ezra, are you out here?" There was a rustling close to her. "Ezra, is that you?" She heard the rustling again, but there was still no answer. Her heart began to beat faster, but she knew it was silly to worry. It was probably Ezra, and if it weren't, it would only be an animal.

She held the lantern high in the air to see farther and looked in the direction of the noise when she felt a hand on her shoulder. She screamed and whirled around, dropping the lantern, the flame going out as it hit the ground. She could not see who it was that touched her, just a silhouette standing in the dark. Should she run or ask who was standing there? Both made sense to her.

"Ezra, is that you?" she asked, breathless.

The person bent down and picked up the lantern, then lit a match and held it to the wick. Ezra was holding the lantern and looking at her. She could see all the contours of his face from the warm glow of the flame.

"What are you doing, Ezra? Are you trying to startle me?" she said, her breathing still labored.

"No, I'm just trying to figure out why you are out here."

"Looking for you, obviously."

"Why?"

"I wanted to ask you why the hell you showed your face today in front of a German. Are you insane? Do you have any idea what could have happened or what might come of this now? What were you thinking?"

"That maybe somehow you were in trouble and needed my help."

"Why would I need any help? And why would you just assume that I was in some kind of trouble?"

"Oh, I don't know, maybe because you were all the way out here, just you and Sabina with a German. I thought maybe he was asking you some questions or bothering you."

"Well, he wasn't bothering me or asking questions, but he might now, all because of your poor judgment and the rash, stupid decision you made. And here is another thing, my affairs are my affairs. They are none of your concern. I am the one that is supposed to be looking out for you, not the other way around."

"Is that so? Right, because you are so good at making wise decisions? Is that why I found you out here with a German, that you allowed him to walk you home knowing that my sister, niece, and nephew are in the barn?"

"That's not fair. This is not my fault. He would have never known about you if you had not shown your face. He was only walking me to the field. I would have never let him walk me to the house. If you had kept your nose out of my business, we would not need to be having this conversation now."

"Fine, next time, I won't offer my help."

"Good. I don't need your help, I didn't then, and I don't now."

"Eva, do you even know what kind of person he is? You do not know who you are dealing with."

"Well, I certainly know more than you."

"How?"

Eva looked away.

"Oh… I see. This is not the first time you have spent time with him. I don't care what he tells you, or if you think you know him, you don't. He puts on a show when you are around, Eva. He hides his true self because if you saw him for who he truly is, you would see that they are all the same. There is no difference between any of them. They are cruel and vile people. They only do things that benefit them, and they don't care how many people they have to step on to achieve their goals or how many they have to kill."

"You have no idea what you are talking about. Do you even know any Germans?"

"I don't have to. I got a good enough look at who they were when they were rounding up the Jews in my village. I can't believe you are sticking up for them."

"I'm not sticking up for them or justifying anything they do. I'm just saying that it is ignorant to say that they are all the same and that not even one of them is a good person."

"That is where you are wrong. It's not ignorance. It's in plain sight for everyone to see. They don't do a good job of hiding how bad they are. I think you are the ignorant one. You would have to be to socialize with them and stick up for one."

She was not going to change his mind, and he was certainly not going to change hers. There was no point in continuing this conversation with him.

"It doesn't matter what you think. Now, please, just stay put from now on."

"You want me to stay hidden in the barn while you bring your German boyfriend here? Well, I will not stay hidden while you frolic with that bastard."

Eva held her hands up. "I'm not going to do this with you, Ezra." She walked past him in the dark. She would have to just feel her way back.

"Does monsieur Dubois know?"

"There is nothing to know, Ezra. He walked me home, that is all," she called back over her shoulder.

"So, you are not fucking him?"

She stopped in her tracks but kept her back to him. Right now, she wanted to turn around and slap him right across the face.

"I am not, but even if I were, it is none of your damn business. I told you already. He just walked me home, that is all."

For the life of her, she could not figure out why he even cared. He would be one of those people at the end of the war who would shave the heads of the women they knew or suspected were sleeping with the Germans. It had been a long time since someone had talked to her that way. Right now, she wanted to run back to Gerhardt and tell him what had happened. She wanted to be told that it was going to be OK by the person who had caused all of this. It was funny what emotions could do to one's logic and sense of reason.

"Why did you ask that?"

Ezra came up behind her. "Take the lantern. I don't need it."

She noticed he didn't answer her question. She wanted to tell him no, just out of spite, but she really needed the lantern. She turned around and jerked it out of his hand, almost putting the flame out again, and began walking as fast as she could back to the house. When she was sure he could not see her anymore, she started running. Tears were spilling out of her eyes, trailing down her cheeks and blowing off into the wind as she ran. Why did everything and everyone have to make life so darn hard? Everything had to contradict and fight against one another, people, opinions, countries…! She knew right after she asked him why he asked that he was not going to answer, and the truth was, it didn't matter why he asked.

She sat on the steps of the porch, not wanting to go in with her face looking the way it did. She had to be sure that no one could tell she had been crying. She wiped the tears from her cheeks and her nose on the back of her hand. She sniffed a few times, took a few deep breaths, and released them slowly to lower her heart rate and control her breathing, the breeze helping to dry her face and cool her cheeks. She stood up and looked in through the window; she didn't see any lights on. Maybe everyone was in bed; she could only hope. She blew out the flame in the lantern and opened the door slowly, but it squeaked; she froze and held the door still for a moment, listening. She did not hear any signs of movement in the house, so she pushed the door open a little more, just enough for her to squeeze through. She closed it behind her, sat the lantern on the table, and tiptoed to her room. The door was open, and she could see a hump in her bed, but it didn't move. Sabina was asleep, and she wondered if she should just sleep in Sabina's bed and not disturb her, but Sabina would be upset in the morning if she did. She resigned to the fact that she was going to have to wake Sabina up to move her over. She pushed Sabina to the side of the bed near the wall as gently as she could, hoping that there was an infinitesimal chance it would not wake her.

Sabina began moving under the blankets. “Why are you pushing me?”

“I have to get in bed, and you are in the middle. You have to scoot over if you want me to sleep with you.”

Sabina scooted to the wall without saying anything, then fell still again. Eva gently crawled into bed and curled up beside her. She closed her eyes, and the world quickly disappeared, but not the thoughts that raced through her head the rest of the night.

Chapter Twenty-Five

Now that Eva had her cast off, she could do more things, so she volunteered to hang the laundry for Brigitte. It was nice to help again and feel useful, finally, and it allowed her to be by herself and think. Tomorrow was Saturday, and she was going to meet Gerhardt at the pond, and she did not know how that was going to be. She had already informed Fabien that she was going to spend the weekend with Madame Blanc. She would leave after she was finished with the laundry and the other chores. She told Madame Blanc that she would eat dinner with her.

"Eva?"

She tensed at the sound of Ezra's voice. "I have nothing to say to you."

"Please, allow me to speak."

She reached into the straw basket and pulled out an item of clothing to hang on the line. She clipped one side of the pants to the line, then reached into her apron pocket for another wooden clothespin.

"Eva, please…!"

She took a deep breath. "Say what you have to say, then go."

"I wanted to tell you that I'm sorry for last night, more like most of yesterday. I wish I could say that I don't know what came over me, but that would be a lie. You asked me why I asked that question. The truth is that I was hoping you would give me an answer, and it would be no, which you did. It didn't take me long after asking that I realized I should never have asked it and that I had crossed a line."

She turned around to face him. He was holding his hat with both hands in front of him, looking at her in search of what she might be thinking, hoping that her face would give it away.

"Why do you care what the answer is? It doesn't affect you."

"But you see, Eva, it does. I wanted the answer to be no because I had hoped you did not give yourself to him. He does not deserve you. You have been so kind to my family and me, and I have noticed how you treat everyone around you. It has always been the same, with love and compassion. That is what I want—"

"Ezra, I don't—"

"Please, I have to finish saying this. Since I have been here, I have noticed you, Eva, and I have grown fond of you. I don't think you notice me or pay attention to me the way I do you. Before the war started, I was supposed to marry a Jewish girl from a good family. Back home, my father and the father of a girl named Abigail, who lived in my village, had arranged for us to marry. That is how things are done with my people. I had only met her once when I found out I was to marry her. She wasn't the girl I would have chosen, but I believed I could learn to love her in time. Then all of this happened, and I met you. You were so nice to me even when others weren't. You were willing to help my sister and her children as well as me and be my friend when I was hated and despised just for being a Jew. So, I grew fond of you without someone telling me I had to or feeling obligated to. I didn't know how you felt about me when I realized my feelings for you, and I don't know now. I wasn't planning on telling you how I felt, at least not anytime soon, until I saw you with that German. I don't know if anything is going on between the two of you, but if there is, it is a mistake. Noting, but pain and suffering could come of it. He is not a good person, Eva. I could make you happy and give you a wonderful home and a family, something he never could."

She felt like her knees might give out. This was the last thing she expected him to say. How could this be happening? She could not lead him on. She had to tell him how she really felt about him, and she needed to do it now.

"Ezra, I don't even know how to respond to that. I did not know you felt that way for me, but Ezra… I don't feel the same way. You are a wonderful person. Don't waste your love and energy on me. There is an amazing girl out there somewhere that is right for you, just waiting for the perfect man to walk into her life, and that man is you. I'm sorry if I ever gave you cause to think that I cared for you in that way, but please don't think for a minute that I am not still your friend."

He looked at his hat, toying with it in his hands. "Forgive me for speaking my mind. I could not keep it to myself any longer. But please, Eva, tell me that you don't have feelings for that German?"

"I… I am not sleeping with him if that is what you mean."

"Oh, Eva, why? Why would you choose a German of all people? Why not a French man?"

"I didn't choose anything. You say that I am kind to you, but that is how he is to me."

"Do you love him?"

"Yes, I think I do."

"I will not say anything to monsieur Dubois, but if I see him or any other German near my sister or her children, I will not hesitate to do what is necessary to protect them. It would be best if he stayed away from the farm and you. I know that you don't love me, but that doesn't change my feelings for you. I know he is bad for you, even if you can't see it. If he is here again with you and I witness it, I will hurt him." Ezra put his hat on and walked past her towards the barn.

She had a bad feeling about all of this. Ezra was going to do something stupid, and she would not be able to talk him out of this time. It would be a one-way path that would most likely lead to him dying.

She hurried and hung up the rest of the clothes and ran inside with the basket. She laid it on the table, went to her room, and grabbed her bag off the bed. She had packed that morning before she helped with the laundry but wasn't planning on leaving until around four, but she couldn't wait any longer. She had to get out of here now. She threw the bag over her shoulder and went outside to look for Fabien. She wanted him to give her a ride now and not later; she looked on one side of the house for him, and when she saw he wasn't there, she went to the other side. When she peered around the right side of the house, she saw the flowers that Sabina and Ezra had planted. The sight of them gave her a strange sensation in the pit of her stomach. She shook off the feeling, called Fabien's name, and heard him call back from the barn. *Really, that is where he is?* she thought.

She walked to the barn. "Fabien, can I talk to you please?" she called, just outside the doors.

"Yeah, come on in."

Well, that didn't work out as she had hoped. She walked into the barn. Fabien and Ezra were sheering some of the sheep from his small herd. Ezra gave her a strange look when he saw the bag over her shoulder.

"I was wondering if you could take me to Madame Blanc's now?"

"Now, I thought you weren't going until later?"

"I was, but I decided to go now. Brigitte doesn't have any more things she needs my help with, so I thought I would leave earlier. Is that all right with you?"

"Sure. Let me finish sheering this sheep, and then we can go."

"Thanks, Fabien. I'll go wait at the truck."

She went to the truck, put her bag in the back, and sat in the passenger seat to wait for Fabien. There was no way she was going to remain in the barn, not with Ezra there. She didn't know how to act around him anymore or what to say to him. It did not surprise her that he did not speak to her either while she was in the barn. He probably was unsure how to act around her now, as well.

The truck door opened, and Sabina crawled up into the driver's seat and sat next to Eva. "Why are you leaving now? I thought you weren't leaving until later? I was hoping you would help me finish building my house out of sticks before you left."

"I'm sorry, Sabina. I would, but I need to leave sooner. Something has come up, and I just have to get away from the farm for a while."

"Is it because of Ezra?"

"Ezra and I need some time apart, that's all." Eva continued to be surprised at how perceptive Sabina was sometimes.

"Why?"

"It's just something we have to do. You wouldn't understand." She leaned over and kissed her on the cheek. "I'll see you in a few days, and we can build that house."

"All right," Sabina said, sounding sad as she looked at her hands.

"You all ready?" Fabien said as he came around to the open driver's door.

"I am."

"Come on, little one. You have to get out." He lifted Sabina out of the truck and climbed in.

Eva waved at Sabina as they pulled out onto the dirt road.

"Are you all right? You seem like something is bothering you," he asked.

"I'm fine. I'm just excited to get away for the weekend and see Madame Blanc. It's been a while since I've seen her."

He glanced at her with that 'all right, don't answer' look. Today, she was supposed to go out to the fields with Ezra and Uri as she had agreed the day before, but after her conversation with him, she realized it would be better if she didn't. She knew he could not possibly still expect her to at this point. Gerhardt also did not know that she was going to spend Friday night with Madame Blanc. He thought she would be coming on Saturday. She wondered at his reaction when he saw her. The thought of it gave her a feeling in the pit of her stomach, but not like the one she felt today when seeing the flowers. It was the butterflies people talk about, a sensation she was unaccustomed to.

Fabien pulled around in front of the house and stopped next to the door. “Are you going to be OK?”

“I’ll be fine. Why wouldn’t I be?”

He pointed to three cars with Nazi flags parked in the grass at the far end of the house.

“Oh…” she said. What was going on? Why were they there? Gerhardt must be there too, having some kind of meeting. “I didn’t know that more of them were here. I will stay out of their way and keep to my room until they leave.”

“All right, but if you need to come home for any reason, don’t hesitate to let me know, and I will come and get you.”

“Thanks, Fabien. I think I’ll be OK.”

She got out of the truck, pulled her bag from the back, and waved to Fabien as he drove away. She walked up to the front door, stopped, and then decided that going through the kitchen’s side door would be a better idea. It made her less visible, and she could sneak up the stairs and wait until they left. She went around to the side of the house, gently opened the kitchen door, stepped in, and closed it softly behind her. She could hear talking coming from the dining room. They were all men’s voices, and the language spoken was German; it did not sound like a party, but there was the occasional laughter that echoed through the house.

Because the entryway to the dining room and the kitchen were offset, it made it impossible to see from the kitchen into the dining room and vice versa. From the kitchen, she would turn right and walk down the hall to the stairs, which faced the front door. If she had come in through the front, she would have had to walk right in front of the dining room to go up the stairs. She tiptoed through the kitchen towards the hall but bumped into someone coming in the kitchen just as she got to the doorway. She made a yelp and dropped her bag on the floor. She took a step back and put her hand on the counter for support. There was a man she didn't recognize in the doorway, staring at her with a surprised look on his face. He was a very tall man with dark brown hair cut short around the sides and longer on the top, similar to how Gerhardt kept his. He had blue eyes and was on the slender side, which made him appear even taller. He wore a German officer uniform but was not one of the Germans she had tea with in Paris; she had not seen him before.

"I am so sorry, Madame." He bent down, picked her bag off the floor, and held it out to her. She slowly reached up, took it from his hand, and put it back over her shoulder. Another man walked through the doorway into the kitchen behind the first man and said something to him as he entered until he saw her. SS Obersturmbannführer Bauer, the one man she was hoping was not there and hoped not to run into if he was.

"Miss Abrams, I did not expect to see you here. I didn't hear you come in or see you go past the dining room."

She knew that he knew she didn't come in the front door but wanted her to say it. There was no point in denying it. "I came in through the kitchen. I didn't want to disturb whatever you guys are doing in there."

"You would not have disturbed us, Miss Abrams. We had already finished up and were just having some drinks. Come and join us."

"Ummm, are you sure? You guys probably will talk about things that I know nothing about. I should probably just go to my room and leave you guys to it."

"Don't be silly. We will talk about things that you can take part in. Come, I'll walk you to the dining room."

"You two know each other?" the other man asked, surprised.

"We are acquainted with one another, yes," Bauer said. "Where are my manners? This is Oberleutnant Müller," he said, pointing to the tall man she had run into. "And this is Miss Abrams," he said, gesturing towards her.

Oberleutnant Müller held his hand out to her. "It is nice to meet you, Miss Abrams."

She took his hand. "Nice to meet you."

"Miss Abrams and Hauptmann von Schulz are also acquainted."

Müller focused on Eva. "Really, he has never mentioned knowing a girl here."

"Now that is strange," Bauer said slowly as he turned back to look at her.

She did not know what he was playing at, but he was definitely playing at something.

"Oberleutnant Müller and Hauptmann von Schulz have known each other for over half their lives, along with two other men in the dining room with him," Bauer said. "Let us go into the dining room and introduce you to everyone."

"I will take your bag for you," Müller said. "Do you want me to take it to your room?"

"Sure, it is the room at the top of the stairs, the door to the right."

He took the bag from her and disappeared through the doorway into the hall.

Bauer held his arm out for her to take. "Shall we?"

She reluctantly took his arm, and he led her to the dining room. The closer they got, the faster her heartbeat and the deeper her breathing became. When they walked into the dining room, she saw the table was full of German officers. At the head of the table, facing the doorway, was Gerhardt. When he saw her, he was writing something on a piece of paper, showing it to one of the other men. His hand stopped moving, and his eyes focused on her. He furrowed his brows and had the most confused look on his face.

"Everyone, this is Eva. She has come to spend a few days with Madame Blanc and will join us for the rest of the evening," Bauer announced to the others.

What? She never agreed to that. She only agreed to have a drink with them. She looked up at Bauer with a horrified expression on her face, and he looked down at her with a malintent smile.

"Here, come and sit next to me."

He led her to a chair next to the empty chair at the head of the table, opposite Gerhardt. It felt very deliberate that he was seating her at the opposite end of the table from him. There were empty chairs close to Gerhardt at that end of the table, but for some reason, only known to Bauer, he was keeping them separated. She sat in the chair he had pulled out for her, then he took the chair at the end of the table to her left.

"Eva, I didn't know that you were coming to spend tonight with Madame Blanc?" Gerhardt said.

"Yeah, I haven't seen her in a while, so I thought I would come and spend the weekend."

"She met Oberleutnant Müller in the kitchen, and he took her bag up to her room. If I am not mistaken, her room is right next to yours, is it not?" Bauer said.

"Yes, that is the room she always stays in. When I arrived here, Madame Blanc put me in that room unbeknown to Miss Abrams. It was quite a surprise when she first came to stay after my arrival and saw me in the room next to hers."

"But you are OK with it now?" Bauer asked, looking at her.

"Sure, Hauptmann Schulz does not bother me; he leaves me alone, and I leave him alone. We have a mutual understanding," she said, looking into Gerhardt's eyes. She knew he would understand her meaning.

"Interesting. Schulz, why don't you introduce her to your other two friends."

"Eva, this is Oberleutnant Meyer." He pointed to a man with dark hair who sat two chairs down from him. He was on the shorter side but had a muscular build. "And this is Oberleutnant Wagner." Like the other man, he was on the shorter side but had lighter brown hair and was not nearly as muscular as the first.

She nodded her head to each of them. "It is nice to meet both of you," she said in French.

"Eva…" he said in a more hushed voice. "They don't speak French."

"Oh, I'm sorry." She felt silly assuming that they could speak French, though they were German. Because they were here in France and knew Gerhardt, who could speak French well, she thought they could. "It is very nice to meet both of you," she said to them, this time in German.

Oberleutnant Müller came back into the room and sat down next to Gerhardt. "So, who is this, Gerhardt? You never told us you had such a lovely friend."

"It just never came up, but now that she is here, this is Miss Eva Abrams."

"Will we be seeing more of you in Berlin, Miss Abrams?" the one he introduced as Meyer asked.

"Uhh, I don't know. I wasn't really planning on going to Berlin."

"Oh, well, we hope you change your mind. You are not European, so how did you end up here?"

She did not want to go into all of that. It would take all night. "I came from America to work in France, then it was invaded, and I guess the rest is history."

"And how do you find the Europeans?" Bauer asked.

"Ah… that is such an open-ended question." She chuckled out of nervousness. "I like them very much."

"Even the Germans?"

"Sure," she said, glancing at Gerhardt. "I mean, I like some Germans."

Bauer laughed. "Relax, Miss Abrams. I'm only teasing."

As the evening progressed, Gerhardt spoke little to her but kept a close watch on her interactions with the men around the table.

Several conversations were going on simultaneously, and everyone was not so focused on her now.

"What will you do when Gerhardt leaves here and goes to Berlin?" Bauer asked.

"I don't know. Stay here, I guess. I don't understand why that would determine what I do?"

"I had assumed that you two were more than just friends, that there was something going on there."

"Why would you think that?" she asked, giving him a sideways glance.

"There just seems to be a connection between the two of you, something unspoken."

"You could not be more wrong. We are only acquaintances."

"I could have sworn that there was something else going on."

"There isn't, but why do you care?" she said through her teeth.

"I'm just curious. You are probably aware that he is engaged, right?"

"Yes, I am."

"I believe he got engaged just to make his parents happy, and it would be of the same if he got involved with another woman. Something is exciting until he has it; it's all about the chase for him, and he won't quit until he gets what he wants without regard for the other person."

"May I ask how you know this?"

"Because I've seen it. I was there when he did just that to a girl in Poland."

"What are you talking about?" Eva looked at him, astonished.

He smiled and leaned forward, putting his elbows on the table. "I am not surprised that he has not told you about this, but why would he."

She turned and looked at Gerhardt sitting at the end of the table, totally unaware of what she and Bauer were talking about. He was in a conversation with his three friends but would always take a second to glance at her.

She looked back to Bauer. "So, tell me then."

"Hauptmann Schulz and I met right at the onset of the war when they sent us both to Poland. It was his first assignment, and the first place we both saw action. It didn't take long to break through the Polish defenses, and within weeks we advanced on Warsaw, and the war for them was over. They had lost. The men were elated that we had won, and they could rest for a few days. The officers got billeted with families there like we are here. The family that Hauptmann Schulz and I were staying with had a teenage daughter that he took a liking to, but the father disapproved. She seemed to like him, too. He led her on for a while but then lost interest in her. She must have told her father that he mistreated her out of anger because of his rejection. Late one night, when Hauptmann Schulz came into the house, the dad took a swing at him with a lamp. That is how he got the scar by his eye."

She remembered seeing the scar on his face and wondered how he got it but didn't dare ask him about it. "I have seen it, but I assumed he got it from fighting."

"No, he has other scars from being hit by shrapnel, but they are not on his face. A tank he was riding behind ran over an anti-tank mine, and when it exploded, he was hit in the chest and stomach with some of the shrapnel. He was in the hospital for almost four months because of it."

She had no idea. There was so much about him she didn't even know, but to be fair, there was a lot she wasn't telling him, either. "I didn't know. He has never mentioned that."

"Well, he wouldn't. He doesn't talk a lot about his life. Most of what I know is because I've known him since this war started. We seem to keep finding ourselves in the same countries."

"But you're SS, and he is Wehrmacht. How have you two been together since the start of the war?"

"Because the Gestapo always go to the new places to weed out the unwanted after occupation."

Eva knew who he meant by 'unwanted.' She did not want to talk about that now; she wanted to learn more about Gerhardt. "So, what happened after he got hit in the face?"

"Of course, there were retaliations. I left right after that happened, but that night, when I got back, I heard screaming coming from inside the house. I didn't go in, but I looked through the window. I couldn't see well because of the dirt on the glass, but I could see enough to know what was happening."

Eva was holding her breath, staring a hole in him as he talked. She wasn't sure it was a good idea to hear the rest of the story, but she couldn't stop him now; she had to know.

"I could make out the two people in the middle of the floor, and I could see that there were people in the room standing around them, but I could not make out any of their faces."

"Who was on the floor…?" her voice catching in her throat as she asked.

"I saw Gerhardt on top of the girl. His pants were down, and her dress was up. She was screaming and crying as he held her hands above her head. I watched him have his way with her, and she was powerless to do anything about it."

"He raped the girl as punishment for what her dad did?"

"I don't know. We left not long after that, and he never spoke of it, and I never asked."

"Why did you tell me this story?"

"Because he is not who you think he is, and I wanted you to know that."

"Why do I need to know that?"

"You are not being honest when you tell me that you two are just acquainted. I don't know you well, but you seem like the kind of person who would be upset by this kind of thing. Something like this would leave scars. I tell you this for your own good. But of course, you don't have to listen to me. It is no skin off my back."

Why would Bauer tell her something for her benefit? Why would he care enough to? He must have some ulterior motives because she knew he hated her. She stood up from her chair and hurried out of the dining room.

She closed the door of her bedroom and locked it when she got to her room. Tears welled up in her eyes. All the things that had happened today were weighing on her. It was almost more than she could bear; it was too much for one day. She held out her hand and caught some of the tears that fell. Perhaps Bauer was right. Maybe she had too weak a constitution for this kind of thing. She saw her bag on the bed, went to it, and pulled out her gown; she would just change and go to bed; she had her fill of this day and was ready for it to be over. She now wondered about tomorrow. Should she still go swimming with Gerhardt? The thought of telling him she couldn't go upset her. He was an intense person, even more so than Kevin. But Bauer was scarier and more intimidating than anyone she had ever met. As far as she was concerned, he was pure evil. The knowledge of what Gerhardt did to that girl and the thought of the power he held over her made her think of herself and the fact that with just one slip up on her part, he could have her arrested and her life as she knew it would be over, possibly even her life itself.

She heard the doorknob on the joining door turning and ran to brace it. Just as it started to open, she put both of her hands on it and pushed it closed. She stayed there with her hands pressed to the door.

"Eva, what are you doing?" she heard Gerhardt's voice say from the other side.

"I don't want to see you right now. I'm tired and was just getting ready to go to bed."

"Eva, what is wrong? What did he say to you?"

"It doesn't matter. Just leave me alone."

"Please don't be like this. Open the door."

She was going through her thoughts rapidly, trying to find what to say to him next, when she felt pressure on the door from the other side. She backed up, and the door swung open. Gerhardt was standing in the doorway but did not attempt to come in. They stood like that, looking at one another. But she could not read his expression. She was not sure what he was thinking or what he was going to do.

"Eva, please tell me what is wrong. What is it that he told you to make you act this way?"

The tears were collecting in her eyes again, threatening to spill over. "He told me you raped a girl in Poland. How could you do that?"

He clenched his jaw, and his nostrils flared. "Is that what he told you?"

She nodded her head.

He came into the room, shut the door behind him, then went to the chair in the corner and sat down. "I never wanted you to know about this, but now that he has told you, I need to explain. It is probably not the way he told it. What exactly did he say?"

"He said that you liked a girl in Poland, you were staying at her family's house, but the dad did not approve, and that you later lost interest in her. The dad hit you, and you took it out on the girl by raping her."

He was covering his eyes with his right hand. "Eva, that is not at all what happened."

"Then tell me, Gerhardt, what did happen?"

He kept his hand over his eyes as he spoke. "When we moved into the house, I realized it was a nice family. I did anything I could to make our stay with them easier, so I helped in any way that I could. The girl took my efforts to be nice the wrong way. I can see how that would happen. She was just seventeen and didn't have any experience with men. It didn't take long for her to realize that she was living in a fairytale, a fantasy, so when I told her I did not think of her in that way and that I thought she was just a child, well, let's just say it did not go well. She told her dad that I had made advances toward her and was doing inappropriate things to her. One day, when I got back for the evening, her dad hit me in the face with a lamp as I walked through the door. What he didn't know was that right behind me were eight other Germans who had not come in yet, and one of them was my commanding officer. Assaulting a German officer is punishable by death. My commanding officer wanted to line the whole family up against a wall and shoot them. I pleaded for him to spare them, but he insisted that they had to be punished for what they did. He asked the man why he hit me, and he said because I did inappropriate things with his daughter. He asked me if that was true, and I told him it wasn't, that the girl just said those things because she felt rejected after I turned down her advances. My commanding officer… Eva, you have to understand that he was not a very nice man. He told me that if their lives meant so much to me, then he would spare them if I raped the girl in front of them, but that was the only way. The dad began pleading with him to kill him instead and spare the rest of his family and save his daughter from shame, but he wouldn't budge. He left us with only those two options. I could not let an entire family be killed because the dad attacked me. I told my commanding officer I would do it but asked that the family not be there. He agreed that the mother and the other children did not have to be there, but the dad did because he was the one who brought all of this upon his family. He wanted to show that man that nothing you do goes unpunished. The intent was to make an example of him and remind his daughter that what was happening to her was all her dad's fault. I was allowed to tell the girl what was to happen beforehand in her room, but when I did, she cried. I told her that if she just lay there, it would be over quick to not look at the other people in the room, to just look at me and focus on my face. I knew if she could mentally block out all the other people, it would not seem as bad. And I explained to her that it would hurt, but only for a minute. When I agreed to do it, I understood that I would be the first one she had ever been with. I told her how sorry I was that all of this was happening and that I wished to God that it wasn't, but it was the only way to save her and her family's lives. I asked for her forgiveness, but she never gave it. I hope she has forgiven me, or at least one day she can find it in her heart to do so."

Eva sat on the bed with tears streaming down her face. "So, she went with you, and it was over quick?"

He removed his hand from his face and leaned his head on the wall behind him, looking up at the ceiling. "Unfortunately, no. She was in such hysterics that she would not follow any of my advice. When I told her it was time, she freaked out and tried to run. I grabbed her and had to carry her to the living room. She was screaming and punching me in the chest, the arms, and the head the entire time, but I didn't blame her for any of it. I would have done the same thing in her position. All the others were already waiting in the living room, including my commanding officer, who was losing his patience. I realized I needed to make it happen quickly before he changed his mind and shot them. She would not calm down even when I repeatedly told her to, so I had to pin her on the floor and held her hands. She sobbed uncontrollably while looking around the room at all the men who were staring at us, watching what was going to transpire. I kept saying to her, 'Look at me, not them,' but she wouldn't listen. For both of our sake, it was over quick, and when I let her up, she ran to her room. I don't know who I felt sorrier for, her or her father. He had tears running down his face and kept saying, 'My baby, you have defiled her.' The look on his face, he was a broken man."

Eva squeezed her eyes shut, and the tears dripped off her chin onto her lap. She felt the bed go down as he sat next to her, but he didn't touch her. She opened her eyes and looked at him; there was nothing but remorse on his face.

"I am sorry that you had to hear that story, Eva. Once you know something, you can never unknow it, and that is something about me I hoped you would never know. I don't want that to be what you think about when you look at me, and now that is probably all that will come to your mind."

"I feel bad for you, too. I can't even imagine having to do something like that to someone, what you must have been feeling at that moment."

"It was something I thought I would never do, and I hope it is something I never have to do again. I don't want to talk about this any more unless you feel you need more answers."

She shook her head. "No, I don't need any more explanation."

He stood up. "I will let you go to bed now." He walked to the joining door and opened it.

"Wait," she called.

He turned to her. "Yes?"

"Are we still going swimming tomorrow?"

He smiled. "If that is what you want?"

"It is."

"After everything that has happened this evening, I figured you had probably changed your mind about being alone with me tomorrow or any time."

She shook her head. "I don't blame you for it."

Her reaction to what happened surprised him. He expected her not to want anything further to do with him, but not only did she not hold it against him, she felt bad for him. Her non-judgmental attitude towards him, even after she heard what he had done, made his feelings for her even stronger. He could no longer deny his attraction to her. It was difficult before, but now there was no way he could, and he wasn't going to try. He smiled at her and disappeared behind the door as he shut it.

Chapter Twenty-Six

July 30th, 1940

"Where are we going?"

"Don't worry. We are almost there."

"I thought you said we were going to the pond?" Eva pressed.

"We are," he chuckled.

"But this isn't the way to the pond."

"It is to the one I'm taking you to."

"So, we aren't going to the pond near the house the enlisted soldiers are staying in?"

"No."

"Well, I don't know of any other pond near here."

"I do, and I'm leading, so that is all that matters."

Eva had her doubts about a mystery pond out in the woods. He could easily be pulling a prank on her.

"How much farther?"

"You ask a lot of questions. We should be able to see it here any minute."

"Because you aren't telling me anything."

She noticed the trees were thinning now, and through them, she could see what looked like a small meadow. They stepped into a greenfield as the last few trees ended at its edge. The tall grass was dancing in the breeze, and there were small patches of flowers throughout. In the middle was a lone tree providing the only shade in the meadow. Just beyond the tree was a small pond, maybe half the size of the one she thought they were going to.

"How did you find this?"

"I take a lot of walks, and I stumbled upon it one day. You are not the only one who likes to go on walks, Miss Abrams. Afterward, I asked some locals about it," he said with a smile. "They told me an interesting story about that tree." He pointed to the lone tree. "They said there are rumors that long-ago lovers would meet here in secret, and if they could not meet, they would leave each other notes in a hole in the tree."

She looked at the tree. "Where is the hole?"

He walked to the tree and nodded his head to the side that faced the pond. "It's on that side."

She went around to the side of the tree, and in the middle was a hole, just big enough for a hand to fit or a small animal. "That is a nice story," she said, staring at the small opening.

"It is," he said, watching her. "Why don't we put the blanket and the food under the tree, then we can swim or eat. Which one do you want to do first?"

"I think we should swim first, then come back and eat when we get tired, and maybe we can swim again if we are feeling up to it."

"I think that sounds like a fine idea."

After laying out the blanket, he took off his jacket, pulled his suspenders down over his shoulders, and then started undoing his pants.

Eva quickly looked away, somewhat surprised by her embarrassment and by his brazen action. Her cheeks felt hot, and she knew they must be red. She glanced back over at him to see that he was now in his underwear and was removing his undershirt. He pulled it over his head and threw it on the ground next to the rest of his clothes, the sun reflecting off his sweaty muscular back. He was tanner than she had expected, and while he was removing his shirt, she could see his muscles flexing. She knew he was a big man, but with his clothes on, it was hard to tell just how muscular he really was; she had never seen him without a shirt before. He was fit with little fat. *So unfair,* she thought, then remembered him saying he was an avid swimmer before the war. But by the way he looked, he did a lot of other physical activities.

He turned around after he had removed his shirt. "Why are you just standing there? Are you planning on swimming in your dress?" he chuckled. "You know what I look like with minimal clothing. Now it's your turn."

She hesitated for a second, then grabbed her dress on both sides and pulled it over her head. He stopped smiling but didn't look away.

"What, am I fatter than you expected or something?" she asked, looking down at her body self-consciously.

"No, of course not! I knew you weren't fat."

"Then why the change in expression?"

"Because that," he said, pointing to her body, "is not what I expected.

"What do you mean?"

"I mean that your body matches your face."

"How so?"

"It is just as beautiful," he said unashamedly, looking her over.

"So, you thought I only had a pretty face that did not match my body because my body wasn't pretty…?"

"No, that is not what I meant at all. That came out all wrong. What I'm trying to say is that I have never seen your body before now, so I could not compare it to your face. You have one of the prettiest faces of any woman I have ever seen, and now I can say that you have one of the most beautiful bodies I have ever seen."

"And how many bodies have you seen?"

He smirked. "Up close, a few."

"What constitutes a few?" She usually would not pry when she could tell that someone did not want to talk about something, but this she really wanted to know.

"Like five…?"

He raised an eyebrow. "You are not going to let this go, are you? All right, very well. I will tell you, but you have to tell me how many you have seen naked, and you have to tell me first."

Her mouth dropped. "What, that's not fair."

"That's all you are going to get. Take it or leave it."

"Fine."

She thought of how she could lie and count women, but she knew that wouldn't be right. Plus, he might ask her about it. She had seen naked men on the TV, but he did not know about TV's yet. They had not been invented, so she couldn't use them either. The truth was, she had never seen a man naked in person. The closest she ever got was Kevin. She had seen part of his butt. He had made a move on her, and when she told him no and that he had to leave, he left only after shoving all the things on her dresser off in a fit of rage.

"I…" she paused, "I have never seen a man naked before," she said, looking at the grass.

He seemed taken aback by this. He gestured to himself. "But you have seen them like this before, right?"

"Yes, of course. I mean, I've never seen them with all of it off."

He nodded his head. "Well, I guess that doesn't surprise me too much."

"Why do you say that?"

"It just doesn't."

"Now you," she said. "How many?"

He laughed, seeming a little embarrassed. "Give me a second, let me think."

"You have to think about it…?"

"I do." He stared out into the distance. "Fifteen."

"Fifteen? You have seen fifteen women naked?"

"No."

She furrowed her brow in confusion. "But you just said you did."

He started laughing harder now. "No, I said up close, I have seen fifteen."

He was such a confusing man; couldn't he ever just say what he meant? "OK, I think I'm missing something here."

"Eva, I have slept with fifteen women. That is what I meant when I said up close."

"Oh. But you have seen more naked than just those fifteen?"

"I have. I know you are going to ask, so I will just go ahead and tell you. As we have traveled across Europe, sometimes the guys would go to these places where women would dance and take their clothes off on stage. I don't know what you call it in English or French."

"I think you are referring to a striptease show," she said to him in English.

"That sounds like it would be correct. Anyway, I went with them, but it was always their idea. I have to say that the food and drinks at these places were usually exceptional, so whenever they would invite me to one, I would go for the food. Now, I am sure that doesn't sound very believable to you, a man going to a place where women dance and take their clothes off just for the food, but it is the truth. I won't deny that I would watch and like what I saw. I'm human and a man, but that is not the kind of place I would go to on my own."

"I see. And what about the fifteen, who were they?"

"How do I answer that, Eva?"

"Well, how did you know them?"

"I wouldn't say I knew all of them. Some I had only met that day, but I needed an escape, a release, and so did they. We needed something at that moment and found it in each other's company. A few I dated, and of course, there was my fiancée."

"That's right. You are engaged. I almost forgot. I wanted to ask you about her."

"If you mean, are we still together, the answer is no. We broke up when I was in Berlin because we had grown apart during the war. It started when I left. Our relationship was not strong enough to survive the distance, I guess."

"I'm sorry."

"It's all right, don't be. I think the only reason we got together in the first place is that our parents wanted us to. When I was in Berlin, Eva, I missed you like I've never missed anyone in my life."

She had finally admitted that she loved him to Ezra; she would tell him at some point because keeping it from him was too hard. "I didn't know that you felt that way about me."

"I didn't either, actually. Or maybe I just told myself I didn't. I'm pretty good at keeping my emotions in check. My feelings usually stay beneath the surface. Eva, you have set my world on fire, and now I can't seem to put it out."

It was the first time a man had ever said something like that to her or spoken to her that way. Kevin would have never been so honest with her or have said something so kind. If Kevin ever said something like that to her, it would only be because he thought that was what she needed to hear so that she would go all the way with him. But Kevin probably would not have said anything that nice to her even then. And here she was now with a man who had been nothing but kind to her, honest and sincere, yet she could not be with him. Sometimes, life can be so cruel. It wasn't possible, and it could be dangerous for her in the current situation they were in.

"Gerhardt, I don't know what to say. I had no idea you even cared for me, much less missed me."

"Don't take this the wrong way, but I wish I didn't. I wish I didn't need you so bad. Honestly, you are distracting. You make it harder to focus on my work and what I need to be doing. Until now, my life had always been simple in the sense that I was a man who knew what he wanted and where he was going. I was always in control. I chose when, where, how, who—until I met you. You have stolen my heart, and I say stolen because it was not being offered when you took it. My heart was not given to you freely. None of this makes sense because I wasn't looking for anything or anyone, but then I met you, and you were exactly what I needed. But like you said in Paris, how could this possibly work? There are too many things working against us. I know you will go home the first chance you get, and I don't blame you. If you add up all the factors against us, it makes little sense."

It seemed he was telling her how he felt without actually telling her how he felt; it was frustrating.

"How do you know I will run back to America the first chance I get? Perhaps it depends on what you say next. I want to know the truth about how you feel but this time spelled out for me."

"If I said you are the last thing I think about when I fall asleep and the first thought I have when I wake, or if I told you how much I love you, would it make a difference?"

"Yes, it would," she breathed.

"How?"

"Because it would help me admit how much I love you, which would give me a reason to stay."

"Eva, it makes me happy to hear you say that. But I think it would be easier to always have you at arm's length than to truly have you only to lose you later. At least then, I wouldn't know what I had lost because I would have never had it. I know you will go home, and that's OK. I want you to. And I want to thank you for showing me what life could be with you in it. You gave me a glimpse into that world, and it has been the best part of my life!"

Tears welled in her eyes as she searched his for any sign of insincerity but found none. She reached up and put her hand on his cheek, feeling the roughness of his whiskers from the skipped shave that morning. He put his hand over the top of hers and moved it to his mouth, kissing her palm, then put her hand back on his cheek and held it there. He smiled down at her, and she could see a kindness in his eyes and a warmth in his smile that would only occasionally shine through.

"I have fallen in love with you, but I did not mean for it to happen," he said.

She sat down on the blanket. She suddenly felt lightheaded.

He knelt beside her. "Are you OK?"

"Yeah, all of this is just a lot to take in at once. And now you are going back to Berlin. I don't even know how this all fits together. It's an emotional overload."

He sat on the blanket next to her and took her hand. "We don't have to figure it out today. Let's forget about the world, this war, everyone else and just enjoy each other today."

She would love to forget about the war and all the complications in her life right now, except for him. He was a complication that she wanted. "OK. Let's go swimming," she said.

He stood and pulled her up by the hand he was holding and did not let go as they walked to the pond, stopping at its edge. "Right, which one of us is going to check the temperature of the water first?" he said with a smile on his face.

"I will." She stuck her foot out, put a toe in the water, and then jerked it back. "It's a little on the cool side, actually."

"What, that is not how you test the water. This is."

He wrapped his arms around her and leaned towards the pond until they lost their balance and fell in. She screamed, then held her breath as they hit the water. He let go of her after they went under so that she could get back up. She emerged just as he was coming out of the water. It was shallow enough to stand in but went up to her shoulders and his stomach.

When he stood up, there was moss stuck in his hair.

She laughed. "You have a plant in your hair."

"I do?"

"Yes. Do I?"

"No—not yet."

She at first was confused until she saw the ornery smile on his face. "Gerhardt, no, don't you dare."

She turned to run in the water as he grasped for her but missed and grabbed the back of her bra. As she fell forward, she could hear the tearing of fabric, then didn't feel her top anymore. She stood up out of the water and realized that her bra was gone entirely. She quickly wrapped her arms around herself. She was glad that her back had been facing him.

"Gerhardt… what the heck? Where is my bra? I need that?"

"I will give it back, but I don't think it will do you much good at this point." He held it in front of her. One strap had been torn completely off, and the back clasp was broken.

Her face was so red she was sure she could not look at him again today. "Gerhardt, I need something to put on."

She could hear him walking in the water and turned her head to watch. He went back to the tree, picked his shirt up off the grass, and then walked back. His wet underwear gave her more of a view than she had expected. She was not prepared for that. Her breath caught in her throat, and she hurried and looked away. *I think I know why he looks like that, oh God.* She wasn't sure she was ready for what might happen today while they were together.

He walked back into the water, stopped next to her, and held out his shirt for her to take.

"Why didn't you bring me my dress?"

"Because I thought you would want something dry to wear back to the house, so I brought you my shirt instead."

She carefully took it from his hand, not wanting her other arm to slip. He faced the other direction while she put it on. She touched his arm, and he turned to her.

"Why don't we go eat something now and sit for a bit?"

"All right."

They sat on the blanket, and she reached for the basket with food, but he hurried and snatched the handle, pulling it towards him before she could get it.

"Gerhardt, what is in the basket?"

"Food," he said with a smile

"Really, that's all that is in the basket?"

"I didn't say that."

"You said food."

"Yes, but I didn't say that was all that's in the basket."

"You…." She picked up her torn bra and threw it at him, immediately wishing that she hadn't.

He leaned to the side, and it missed him, landing in the grass.

"So, besides food, what else is in the basket?"

"You threw your bra at me. Maybe you don't deserve to see what's in the basket."

Why did he toy with her all the time? She was going to have to just take the basket from him. She stood up, walked over to him, and reached for the basket, but he grabbed her wrist, stopping her before she could touch it.

"If you sit down, I will show you what is in the basket."

"All right, but I'm going to sit right here." She lowered herself next to him and crossed her legs and arms.

He opened the basket, and all she could see was food. He took some of it out, then stuck his hand down to the bottom of the basket, pulled out a small brown box, and held it out to her. She took it from his hand; it was a little wooden box with gold hinges on one side. She lifted the lid, and music began playing; it was a tune she was unfamiliar with.

She looked up from the box and smiled. "What song is this?"

"It is an old medieval love song called Mein herz in steten treuen."

"It is lovely, thank you?"

"I brought it back for you from Berlin. It was my mother's. She had given it to me and told me that someday, when I fall in love, I was to give it to the woman who had captured my heart."

"And you didn't give it to your fiancée?"

"No, it didn't feel right giving it to her."

"Won't your mom ask you about it if she sees it missing?"

"She might."

"And what, you will tell her you gave it to an American woman you met in France?"

He chuckled. "Something like that. Oh, I have this for you too."

He pulled out a white flower with yellow in the middle from the pocket in the basket's lid and handed it to her.

"A pimpernel. Where did you find it?"

"I saw it in some shrubs while I was walking yesterday. It caught my eye just as I passed by. It was the only one I could find. I searched for more, but that was the only one."

"Oh, Gerhardt. Why do you have to be so kind to me? Sometimes, I wish you were like all the others."

He seemed confused. "Like the others?"

"The rule and not an exception."

"What do you mean the rule and not the exception?"

"You are not mean and cruel like the others, which is the rule for them."

"They are not mean and cruel. If you are referring to the commanding officer I had in Poland, most of the German soldiers are not like that."

"No, I don't think that is true. I think the rule is that they are cruel and heartless, but you are not like them, and that is why you are the exception."

"Eva, I think you speak of things that you don't know enough about, so why don't we not discuss this anymore."

"Don't know enough about? I know enough, more than you think. I have heard stories from other people about the atrocities your people have done and the awful things they have inflicted on others. Oh, I know all too well. Have you forgotten about SS Obersturmbannführer Bauer?"

"This is why I said, let's not discuss this. We will not agree, and I don't want to fight with you. And I do remember what SS Obersturmbannführer Bauer did to you; it was cruel and unfair, but he does not represent the whole of the German people."

"You are right. Let's not ruin a perfectly lovely day. On a somewhat unrelated topic, why do you think Bauer told me about Poland?"

"Who knows. I don't think his reasons for doing things are always clear to other people."

"He suspects me of something, but I don't know why. I have never given him any reason to."

"I don't always agree with him or the things he does, but he is a very loyal soldier. I believe he would do just about anything for his country. It would have to be something pretty remarkable to sway him."

"Yes, I believe he would do anything for his country."

She watched as he ate the fruit he had brought but looked away whenever he looked in her direction; she did not want him to see her staring. She looked at him again, but this time, their eyes met; he laid the strawberry down on his plate and scooted over in front of her. He took the strawberry from her and put it on her plate, then placed a hand on each side of her and brought his face to hers.

"You are the person I am like, Eva, not them. You are a good person, and I want to be like that. I want to be deserving of your love. I don't think I will ever get there, but I have to try. I hope you believe me when I tell you that I love you, and right now, this is the best I can do."

He leaned in closer, and she felt his lips on hers; she sucked in a breath and held it. He lightly bit her bottom lip as he reached his hand up and cupped her right breast over the shirt. His breaths began to come faster and deeper as he moved his hand down.

Her whole body was on fire, and she couldn't catch her breath; she panicked and jumped up, stepping off the blanket onto the grass. She stared at him, her hands balled into fists to her sides, trying to steady her breathing. She could still feel the tingling in her breast from his touch. It was like his hand was still there. He got up from the blanket and came over to her.

"Gerhardt, I'm sorry, I didn't expect that. You took me by surprise," she said breathlessly. "I don't know if I can do that. I'm not sure I'm ready. I have never…."

He brushed a piece of hair out of her face. "I know," he said softly. "It's getting late. We need to get you back before it's dark."

She wondered if he was upset with her, and that was why he really wanted to go back now.

"I'm sorry, Gerhardt."

"Why are you sorry, Eva? You don't owe me anything. You have no obligation to me." He went back to the blanket and started putting the food in the basket. "You can keep my shirt for now. I know you probably don't want to take it off to put your dress on. You can return it to me later."

She picked the blanket up after he had all the things off and folded it. "I'll have it washed first before I return it."

"You don't have to." He put his gray army jacket on over his white undershirt and buttoned it up. He held his hand out for the blanket.

"I can carry it," she said

"You can carry it part of the way. I will let you finish the rest of the way on your own when we get close. I will come back to the house a little later so they don't think we were out together."

"Yeah… that's a good plan."

She couldn't help but feel that he was upset with her now. She thought she was ready, that if or when he made a move, she would be able to go through with it, that her body would know what to do and would relax, letting him take the lead as he knew far more than she did. But of course, instead of listening to her body, she listened to her head and gave in to fear. She understood that the fear wasn't there without reason; it was there because of the uncertainty of what the first time would be like. How would it change them? How would it change her? And the thought of what would happen if anyone were to find out. Being with him would be bittersweet. She completely understood why he felt he should not have her. He knew it couldn't last, and she knew that better than anyone. But no matter what she knew, it didn't change the fact that she was now immersed in circumstances far beyond her control.

His silence did not go unnoticed as they walked home. She no longer had any doubts that he was upset with her.

"Are you angry with me?"

He stopped walking but did not look at her. "Eva, I am not mad at you. I am upset with myself for doing what I did without your permission. I should have let you make the first move. That should have never happened, and it will not happen again."

"Gerhardt, it's not like that. I'm not—"

"Shhhh," he said, putting a finger over his lips. "Someone is close."

She listened and could hear two different women's voices.

"You need to go now. Give me the blanket," he said, holding out his hands.

She handed him the blanket. "I guess I will see you tomorrow then."

"I should imagine so. Now go."

Chapter Twenty-Seven

Eva remembered that she was still wearing his shirt. *Crap, I can't go in wearing this.* When she could no longer see Gerhardt, she stepped behind a tree and exchanged the shirt for her dress. She rolled the shirt up and stuck it under her arm, hoping no one would notice. It was less visible that way than her wearing it. As she got closer to the house, she could see Adele outside, bringing things inside from the car. She must be one of the voices they heard.

Adele looked up from the trunk of the car. "Eva, where did you come from?"

"I was on a walk."

"That was a long walk."

"Yes, it was." What Adele didn't know was that she wished it could have lasted all night. She did not want it to end.

"You hurried off so quick today before lunch without saying where you were going."

"I didn't know anyone wanted to know."

"It would have been nice to know how long you were going to be gone so I could have planned dinner better."

"I'm sorry. I didn't think about that. I guess from now on, unless you know for sure that I will be here for dinner, just plan it without me."

"If that is what you want."

"Do you need help carrying anything in?"

"No, this is the last bag."

"OK." Eva walked past her to go inside.

"Why is your hair wet, Eva?"

She stopped and stood facing the house, trying to think how she would explain this to her. She turned around. "I saw a pond when I was out and went for a swim. It was a nice day, so it seemed like a good idea."

"But you were not alone."

"I didn't say anything about that."

"I wasn't asking, and you didn't need to. Hauptmann von Schulz has been gone all day, too, then you leave before lunch and don't come back until almost dinnertime, and your hair is wet. Also, it looks like a man's shirt under your arm."

She honestly did not know what to say. It wouldn't do any good to deny it. She walked back to the car and stood next to Adele. "And what if I was with him? Are you going to chastise me for it and tell me what a silly girl I am, and how could I be with such a bad person?"

"No, I have told you that already. I don't believe it would do any good to tell you again. You are a grown woman, and you are going to do what you want. I can't stop you; I just hope you know what you are doing."

"Why do you want to think of him as bad because he is German?"

"Because they all are, Eva. It worries me you can't see that."

"I am not saying that some of them don't do bad things. I know they are not all good people, but he is not like the others. You say it saddens you that I can't see that he is bad, but it saddens me that you can't see that he is good. You can't see him the way I can," Eva's voice was impassioned.

"Are you being careful?"

"Careful… what?"

"Don't tell him anything. The more he knows, the more dangerous it is for you. And because you have his shirt, I'm guessing that something happened when you were out with him? So, I'm asking if you are careful in that way too? The last thing you need is to get pregnant with his baby."

Eva's face turned fiery from embarrassment and anger. "No, nothing like that happened. My bra got torn while we were swimming, so he offered me his shirt so I wouldn't get my dress wet."

Adele closed the trunk and started walking towards the house.

"I hope you don't think less of me, Adele. I am not trying to be disrespectful to you."

"You are not being disrespectful to me. It is to yourself that you are disrespecting. He is going to ruin you, Eva."

Eva watched Adele go into the house, still standing by the car, in shock over what had just happened. Finally, she went to her room, wanting to wait there until dinner was ready. She did not think she had it in her to argue with Adele anymore tonight. But what did she mean, "he is going to ruin you?" She could not understand her meaning.

She realized she had not heard Gerhardt come back. She went to the joining door and cracked it open, then peered inside, but the room was empty. There was no sign that he had been back. *I guess I have time to shower before dinner.*

She unfolded his shirt and laid it out on her bed. It still smelled of him. Its scent caused a wave of emotions to hit her, and her eyes teared up. She must be the reason that he had not come back. Did he feel rejected by her? She had already done that to him so many times before. Maybe this was the last straw, and of course, it had to come after she admitted to herself, Ezra, and him that she loved him. It was so hard for her to come to that realization just to have it smothered before it ever really got started. People weren't kidding when they said love died hard.

She put the shirt on top of her basket of dirty clothes, then went into the bathroom to shower. It felt good to wash the day off. She reached up and cupped her right breast, the one he touched. She could still remember everything about his touch, how his hand covered her whole breast, the feel of his hot, clammy palm on her. She used her other hand and touched her lips, remembering the feel of his lips there; she traced a finger along the bottom lip where he had bitten. She didn't know her body could feel like that. Just the thought of it made her breath quicken as butterflies and knots formed in the pit of her stomach again. She quickly dropped her hands to her sides. *Stop it, Eva, just don't think about him.*

She finished showering quickly, put her hair in a bun, and hurried down for dinner. When she got to the dining room, Madame Blanc was already at the table with a plate of food.

"Eva, I am so glad you decided to join me for dinner. I feel like I have hardly seen you since you've been here."

"I know, it has been so crazy. The days go by so fast." Eva sat in the chair at the other end of the table from her.

"I heard about yesterday how you got roped into sitting at a table with a bunch of Germans. I am so sorry about that. I would have come to save you from them if I had known you were here."

"It's fine. I survived it." A*nd learned a lot,* she thought.

"Besides that, how has your stay been?"

"It has been good, Renée. Thank you."

"You know, I was thinking we should go back to Paris sometime again soon. I had such a lovely time there."

The thought of the opera with Gerhardt came into her head. "I did too. It was an experience I shall never forget."

"Oh, I am so pleased that you enjoyed it so much. Sometimes, I don't think Americans know how to truly enjoy Paris for what it is."

"So, has Hauptmann von Schulz been giving you trouble?" Eva asked.

"You know what, he has actually been quite easy to live with. He leaves early in the mornings and comes home late in the evenings. He does not require much, and we hardly talk. I think that is the best kind of arrangement you can have. The only thing I have noticed is that he still plays his violin a lot, but never too late. He is even gone a lot of the weekends."

"Hmmm…" Eva murmured.

"How have you found him? Is he nice to you when you two see each other?"

"He is, actually. He has always been very polite to me, except the first time we met and when he caught me in his room."

"Of course, I wouldn't have expected him to be then. I noticed that he talks to you more than anyone else when you are here and how he seems to light up when he is around you. He is not his usual stern self when you visit."

"Well, he is an enigma," Eva said, sipping her wine.

Renée laughed. "He does seem like a hard man to figure out."

Eva heard the front door open, and it made her jump.

"Don't be startled. It is just Hauptmann von Schulz coming back for the evening, not one of the others."

"Right."

She watched the entryway into the hall, waiting for him to pass by. He walked right in front of the dining room but barely glanced in her direction as he passed. She heard his boots on the stairs. They creaked under his weight, and then his door opened and closed.

After fifteen minutes had passed and Eva had eaten all that she could stomach, and most of the food on her plate was gone, she knew she was close enough to being finished to excuse herself.

"I am feeling quite tired. I think I will turn in early tonight if that's all right?"

"Of course, dear. Are you feeling all right?"

"I am. It has just been a long day, and I was in the sun a lot, that's all."

"All right… well, I'll see you in the morning then."

"OK. Goodnight."

Eva stood up from the table and went into the hall. She looked up the stairs and listened for any movement in Gerhardt's room but heard nothing, so she tiptoed up one step at a time and stopped at the top to listen again. She did not see any light coming from under his door or hear any sound from inside.

Could he already be in bed? she wondered.

She went into her room and sat on the bed without turning on the lights. Even with her lights out, she could not see any light coming from under the joining door. She took her shoes off to walk quietly, went to the door, and put her ear to it, but still no sound. Either he was not in there, or he was in bed. She went back to her bed and sat back down. Well, she would not get to talk to him tonight, so she might as well go to bed, too. She took her dress off, slipped her gown on, then crawled under the blankets, resigned to being confused without hope of an answer tonight.

She lay awake in her bed, listening to the sounds of Adele cleaning things up in the kitchen, Renée coming up the stairs for bed, then later Adele, and finally the silence, but sleep still escaped her. Thoughts were swirling in her head, one after another, and wouldn't stop. She sat up, looking at the colors of the moon on the wall and the shadows it cast there. She threw the blankets off and got out of bed. She went to the window and looked out down at the garden, remembering being there with Gerhardt. It seemed so long ago as all things did anymore. The moon's light reflected on something white, catching in the corner of her eye. She looked to the side and saw Gerhardt's shirt still lying on the top of her laundry hamper where she had laid it earlier. She walked over to the basket and looked at the shirt. She reached down, picked it up, and held it out in front of her. She looked over at the joining door, then back at the shirt. She laid it back down on top of the basket, then pulled off her nightgown and underwear. She picked up the shirt and slipped it on over her head, feeling the material caressing her naked body as it surrounded her.

She walked over to the joint door, put her hand on the doorknob, and paused, resting it there. Then, wrapping her fingers around it, she squeezed and turned it. The hinges protested slightly at first but then became quiet. She looked inside. The room was dark; only the light of the moon coming in through the window allowed her to see. There was a hump in the bed, and as she focused her eyes on it, she could see Gerhardt lying on his back under the sheet with his arms on top of it. She went into his room, closed the door behind her, and then again walked on the tip of her toes to the side of the bed. He seemed to be in a deep sleep, lying motionless, with shallow breaths coming and going. She looked back at the joint door, wondering if she should just go back to her room and go to bed; she was feeling a little crazy for doing this. Was she going to make a fool of herself and really go through with this? She looked back down at him. He looked so peaceful lying there, sleeping. She looked back at the door, then back at him. Her heart was beating so fast in her chest, and her palms were sweaty. It was now or never. She either had to just do it or go back to her room. She could not have him waking up, seeing her standing over him like a creeper.

Alright, let's do this, she told herself.

She slowly tugged at the sheet. When she pulled it out from under his arms, he moved, and she froze, holding the sheet in her hand. He only changed his sleeping position slightly, then was still again. She realized that she was holding her breath and released it slowly, then continued pulling the sheet down. She pulled it to his knees, then laid it softly across his legs. She got closer to the bed and put her right knee on the edge at his side, then swung her left leg to the other side, mounting him. Getting on top of him was something she had never done before to anyone, ever. She couldn't believe she was doing this. She had not sat down yet but was on her knees, holding up her weight. Then she took a deep breath, held it, closed her eyes, and lowered her weight on him. There was a sudden jerk beneath her, and he grabbed onto her shoulders and closed his fingers tightly on them. Her eyes flew open, and she saw him looking at her with a confused and startled expression, though he didn't say anything, nor did he release her. She could feel his whole body tense beneath her. His stomach tightened under her as hard as a board.

"Eva, what are you doing?"

The adrenaline was pulsing through her like thousands of tiny needles poking her all over, and her palms were even sweatier. For some reason, she had not thought of what she was going to do once he woke up, though she knew this would happen when she sat on him. She had to think of what she would do next and fast before he turned on the light and told her to leave. She reached up and tried to remove one of his hands from her shoulder. When he felt her hand on his, he released his grip on her. As he moved his hand from her shoulder, she kept a hold of it, brought it under the shirt, and placed it on her breast. She took his other hand and slid it up her leg to her inner thigh. She noticed there was no resistance from him as she moved his hands like a marionette doll and wondered if he was in shock that she was even there.

It was apparent she was not wearing any underwear, and she could feel his cool hand on the inside of her thigh, which was hot and damp. He moved his hand slightly farther up until he could not move it any farther. Her face was so hot and flushed, and she was happy for the veil of darkness. She reached down to his pajama bottoms and began untying the strings so she could pull them down.

He moved his hands from her and took hold of both of her wrists, overlapping his fingers around them. He held firm but not tight enough to hurt. "Eva…?"

She tried to pull her hands away, but he tightened his grip.

"Gerhardt, please!" she breathed.

To her surprise, he let go of her. She reached back down to his pajama bottoms and pulled on them until they exposed him. She took her hand and wrapped it around his penis. It felt different than she had expected. It was hard and smooth at the same time. Because it was erect, she knew the reason he had tried to stop her at first was not that he wasn't interested. She felt up towards the tip of it, and he took in a breath. She then lifted herself slightly off him with her knees and slipped him inside of her. There was a sharp, brief pain, and then there was the moment in which pain and fear mingled with pleasure. Once she had him inside of her, she rested her hands on his chest and began to roll her hips slowly.

As she moved on him and their bodies joined, it was a strange sensation for her, something that went beyond the simple pleasure of sex. He gripped her forcefully by the hips, and it sparked something inside of her that she had until now only been semi-aware of, and at that moment, the fear she felt was replaced by desire.

He pulled down on her hips and rose his up to meet hers, and she cried out. She knew she risked being heard, but right now, she was beyond caring. She bent down and lightly bit his shoulder. She did not want to let him down or humiliate herself; she did not want to seem like a poor choice compared to the other women he had been with. Before she knew it, in one swift, athletic move, he had laid her on her back and was on top of her. Although his arms mostly supported his weight, she was still pinned down and a little breathless beneath him. Even if his weight was not on her, she suddenly felt like she was imprisoned under him.

He stroked her body with skillful fingers; her arms, chest, stomach, legs. He followed along the curvature of her sides and hips with his fingertips, and brushed his lips across her neck down her collarbone, then to her nipples as he put one in his mouth, and after he spent a few minutes there, he let go, and his lips found hers. He bit her bottom lip again, this time not as soft as he did in the meadow. He moved from her mouth and began kissing her body again and doing things with his tongue that she did not know were possible. She could feel his strong yet gentle hands begin to stroke and caress her again. It all felt so loving. It didn't frighten her any more, although it was hard for her to understand what she was feeling. The touch of his hands doing things to her, Kevin's hands never did.

Knowing precisely what he was doing, he caressed the top of her opening with his finger, and she rose as a gasp escaped her lips, startling her. She did not expect her body to do that.

"Shhh," he whispered.

Everything he did was so slow, rhythmic, and gentle. Then she felt it, one finger at first, then two. She moaned, and he reached up with his other hand and covered her mouth to muffle her cries. She bit one of his fingers, and he groaned, then began moving his fingers in her faster when a sweet spasm went through her. While he kept one hand between her thighs, he removed the other one from her mouth and rose up to replace it with his mouth. He kissed her like she was the very air he breathed. When he moved his lips from hers, she threw her head back to offer her throat to him, and he began kissing her there. He put more of his weight on her, and she could feel his erection against her thigh. He then took his fingers out of her right before she climaxed again and settled between her legs; then, he pushed her knees up higher, completely exposing her. And like a cork being pushed into the neck of a wine bottle, he entered her again.

"Oh," she breathed.

She could feel the sensation again that was there when he had his fingers in her, except this time it felt different. It was like a spark deep inside of her. She felt his fingers tangle in her hair as the strength of his hips pressed into her. She put a hand on the wall to help push back as he drove harder into her. She felt like she was swimming against a current that was pulling her under, but it was bliss, so she took a breath and let herself go. She let the current take her.

"Oh, God."

Her breath shuddered, and she clenched the sheet in her fist as she arched up, turned her head, and buried her face in the pillow to smother her cries. Her moans and screams were now only muffled sounds. She writhed about on the bed beneath him, and after what seemed like forever and yet only seconds, his whole body tensed, and he buried his face in her shoulder as he muffled his release, too. His tensed body quivered several times before he relaxed and laid his full weight on top of her. His breaths were deep and long, and she could feel it on her neck, but her breaths were fast and shallow because of his bulk. She put her hands on his back, which was damp from the sweat. She slid them down to the round curve of his butt and rested them there. Like his back, she could feel the muscles beneath the skin. It felt so different from hers. It was much harder, and his skin was not as soft.

He continued to lay on her, heaving, so she explored more of his body with her hands. She rubbed the tips of her fingers up and down his back, along his spine, his sides, through his hair, then back down to his back, tenderly caressing as much of him as she could reach. She could feel the goosebumps on his skin now from her touch.

He rose onto his elbows to look at her. "Why did you come to my room tonight?"

How was she going to answer that? "Because I wanted you in the meadow. I was just afraid. I knew it would change everything, and you had surprised me, and I didn't quite know how to act or what to do. There were just a lot of emotions in that moment that I didn't know how to deal with or even what they all were. Before that day, I had never even felt some of them."

She caressed his face, admiring his masculine features that were still shadowed by facial hair, letting her hand rest on his cheek. She thought nothing in the world could have prepared her for tonight, for what she was feeling now.

"You mean more to me than anything. I want you to know that." He planted a tender kiss on her forehead before rolling off onto his back beside her.

She slid out of bed, and he caught her hand before she could leave.

"Don't go. Stay with me tonight?"

“I’m just going to the bathroom. I’ll come back.”

He released her hand, and she went to the bathroom, closed the door behind her, and locked it. She hadn’t realized that the act they just did was that messy, but it made sense if she had given it a little more thought. After she cleaned herself up, she sat on the toilet. She needed just a moment to compose herself. She did not know that it would be this emotional. She felt taxed. She looked out the window at the night sky and the stars that cradled the moon, and she knew she would often think about this night—the sweat, his touch, the way her body felt in his shirt, the moment his hands caressed over her body for the first time, the feeling of him underneath her and the sense of being underneath him. The pain, the pleasure, the smells, the noises, the feel of him inside of her, and his hard body would be with her forever. A tear escaped her eye and ran down her cheek. She reached up and wiped it away, but more fell. She felt somewhere deep inside of her that this, being with him, was already over, and she never wanted it to end. She would probably never be able to hold another without seeing his face, and there would be so many things that would always remind her of him now. How could she avoid them?

She heard a knock on the door.

“Eva, are you all right?”

She quickly wiped her eyes and cheeks. “I’m fine. I’ll be right out.”

He didn’t say anything, but she could hear his footsteps on the floor, then the springs on the bed as he climbed back in. She took several deep breaths, then opened the door and returned to his room. He was sitting on the edge of the bed waiting for her, so she came and sat next to him. She looked at the clock next to his bed.

It was three-thirty in the morning, but strangely, she didn't feel sleepy. She knew she needed to get some rest. He had more than her because she had not been asleep at all that night.

He laid down on the bed and scooted over by the wall. "Come here," he said in a soft voice.

She laid down next to him and put her back against his chest and her butt in his groin as he spooned her.

He wrapped his arm around her and nestled his face in her hair, taking a deep breath. "I love the smell of you."

Chapter Twenty-Eight

July 31st, 1940

Eva could see red through her eyelids as the sun shone through the window. It just clicked that it was daylight outside and that his arm was no longer around her. She rolled over, and the other side of the bed was empty. She sighed and put her arm across the spot he had been lying when she felt a piece of paper under her hand. She sat up and saw a folded piece of paper on his side of the bed. She picked it up and unfolded it.

Eva,
There are some things I must take care of this morning. I should be back before lunch. I'm sorry that I had to leave before you were up, but I couldn't bring myself to wake you. I want to talk about

what happened last night when I get back. As you said, it changes things. I don't think you know the joy I had in discovering you last night. Also, leave my shirt, but don't wash it.

-Gerhardt

She smiled and folded the letter back up, then threw the blankets off to get out of bed when she saw some of last night on the sheets.

Oh, God.

She hopped out of bed and looked at it. The spot was bad enough that there was probably no chance of saving the sheets between the small amount of blood and what came from him. She pulled the blankets off the bed onto the floor, then pulled the sheets off, rolled them up, carried them to her room, and poked them in the bottom of her bag. She would have to take them back with her and dispose of them there.

After she hid the sheets, she got in the shower to wash the rest of last night off. As she cleansed, she noticed how sore she was. She had not noticed it last night. Her legs hurt. Actually, most of her body seemed to hurt a little, especially down there, but that part was to be expected. But the other surprised her.

After she dressed, she tiptoed to the linen closet and looked in both directions to make sure she was alone. She opened the closet door and got one of the less nice sets out, ones that she was sure Adele would put on Gerhardt's bed. She closed the wooden door to the linen closet and hurried back to his room. She made the bed, then checked for any evidence that she had been there but found none. She took the shirt that she wore last night and laid it on his bed. She thought she knew why he did not want her to wash it. She picked it back up, put it to her nose, and inhaled deeply. It smelled of him and her, their sweat, her perfume, detergent, his cologne. But the most pungent scent was the smell of their bodies last night. It smelled of sex. She laid it back on the bed for him as he asked.

She knew it was too late to eat breakfast with Madam Blanc, so she went to the kitchen to find food on her own.

"You missed breakfast."

She jumped. Adele was standing in the doorway, watching her search for food. "I know, I didn't sleep well last night, so I decided to sleep in."

"I know, I knocked on your door this morning, but you did not answer."

"You did?" She was growing concerned that Adele might have heard them last night.

"Yes."

"I'm sorry, I must have been in a deep sleep. I didn't hear it."

"Eva, I've said it once, and I'll say it again. I sure hope you know what you are doing."

"You mean with Gerhardt?"

"Yes, I'm talking about him."

"And like I have said before, we are just friends."

"Friend or lover, he is still dangerous. And I know the latter is what he is."

"How…?" she said, almost stuttering.

"I have known that he was not just a friend to you for a while. And I told you in Paris. He is in love with you."

"For a while, I didn't want to believe you, even though I knew it was probably true. He has, however, told me himself that he loves me, so I can no longer deny it, not even to myself," Eva finally admitted to her.

"And you, did you tell him back?"

"I couldn't lie anymore, Adele."

She nodded her head and looked at the floor. "As I said, he will ruin you, Eva, and I can't help you. I am so sorry for that. I just hope he was worth it." She turned and walked out of the kitchen.

Did she know about them last night? Eva could not tell if she knew or not, but she was loud last night at times. Eva took her food to the kitchen table, and just as she pulled a chair to sit down, she saw Fabien pull up in front of the house. She left her food sitting on the table and went to greet him at the door. She opened it before he had a chance to knock.

"Fabien, what are you doing here?" The look on his face alarmed her. Something was wrong. "Fabien…?"

"Eva, you need to come back to the farm."

"Why, what has happened?"

"Two German soldiers came by yesterday looking for Ezra. Luckily, he was out in the field, so I told them I did not know which field he was in and that he would not be back until dark. We need to get them off the farm today, for our sake and theirs. I can only hope that this doesn't lead back to you. They already know I'm involved, but I don't know if they suspect you yet."

She knew exactly why they were looking for him. If he had not shown his face, they would not be. Gerhardt must have sent them. Was that what he was doing yesterday morning, and what he was doing right now?

"I think one of them suspects me already," she told him. "Let me grab my things. It will only take me a minute."

"Hurry. I'll wait in the truck."

She ran back to the kitchen and put her food in a dishtowel, then ran up the stairs to her room. Running was more painful than she would have thought, but there was no time to waste. She had to help Fabien get them out of there. She knew they most likely had little time. She grabbed all of her things and poked them in her bag however they would fit. She then went to his room, got a piece of paper and pen, and quickly jotted down that something had come up, and she had to go back to the farm early. She closed the door between the two rooms, grabbed her bag and food off the bed, and ran down the stairs. She threw her bag in the back of the truck and climbed into the passenger seat.

"Let's go."

Fabien started the engine and pulled away from the house. She looked at it in the mirror, not knowing when she would be back. For all she knew, she might have to go with the Schullers to their new place, wherever that might be.

"Oh, here. This came for you." Fabien held out a letter to her.

She took it from him and immediately noticed they had stamped it from the Red Cross in London. Her breath caught in her throat. Could it truly be a letter from Jon? She ripped the envelope open and unfolded the letter. He was still in England; he had not returned to their time. She was stunned.

Eva,

I could not believe it when I got a letter from you. The thought that you had died had crossed my mind, but I refused to believe that you were dead until I had some kind of proof. I knew something had happened when you did not return to England. I am so sorry that I suggested you ever go to France. I knew it could be a risk, but I was sure that you would be all right and make it back in plenty of time. I can only imagine what it has been like for you there, having to live in occupied France and amongst the Germans. I have been trying to find a way to bring you home, but so far, I keep coming up short. I won't give up, don't you either. Please don't lose hope. There is a way, and I will find it. The address the letter came from is the address you can reach me, that is where you should send any more letters you write. Please don't do anything that would bring attention to yourself. Stay low and follow all the rules. Write to me again and let me know what has happened since your last letter. I will write you as often as I can.

-Jon

She held the paper to her chest, hardly believing she finally got a letter to him and received one from him after all this time, and the fact that he waited for her and did not return home made her happy, so happy she could cry.

"Was that the letter you had been waiting for?"

"Yes, it was. He says that he is trying to get me out of France and that I should be patient. I can't believe it. I might go home soon. I can hardly remember what home is like."

He smiled. "I am happy for you, Eva."

"Thanks."

They pulled in front of the house, and he turned the engine off.

"Shit!"

"What?" Eva asked, looking at him before scanning the farm for what he had seen.

"We are too late. They are already here."

He pointed, and she followed his finger. The front of a German car was sticking out from the side of the barn.

"I really thought we would have more time."

Her anxiety spiked, and her heart raced. They got out of the truck and could hear yelling from the barn, men's voices, and shouts. Then, a gunshot came from the barn, and a woman screamed. She looked at Fabien for a fraction of a second before they both started running towards the barn. Fabien got there first, but when Eva rounded the corner through the open doors, she saw Ezra with blood on his shirt standing over a man in a German uniform who was lying in the hay near an empty stable. He, too, was covered in blood. Ezra looked up at the two of them and threw the gun in the hay next to the dead German soldier.

"Ezra, what have you done?" Eva yelled.

"He was trying to pull Rachel out of the barn. She was still holding Esther, Eva. I saw what he was doing and ran to help her. I knew what he was going to do with her. He tried to shoot me, so I took the gun and shot him first."

There was shouting in German behind them, and they turned just in time to see another German soldier coming into view, pointing his gun at Ezra.

"Please don't, I beg you!"

Eva knew that voice. She turned away from the soldier and looked towards the back of the barn. Sabina rushed out of one of the stables, right for Ezra.

"Sabina… noooo! Stop!"

Her warning came too late. Just as Sabina wrapped her arms around Ezra's waist, the soldier pulled the trigger. The sound of gunfire echoed through the trees and rang in Eva's ears. It felt like she had gotten shot, too. Her chest hurt, and she could not catch her breath. She put her hand over her mouth and collapsed to her knees. The tears came so fast she could hardly see. Eva crawled on her hands and knees to the small body lying in the hay, as a puddle of blood was forming around her. Sabina tried to say her name, but no sound would come out, so Eva lifted her and pressed her tiny body to her chest, touching their foreheads. A tear rolled down Sabina's cheek and dropped to the ground as she tried to speak again, but only a breath of air came out, and then nothing. Her eyes went blank, and her body was limp in Eva's arms. Eva hardly noticed the screaming from Fabien behind her, telling Ezra to leave, and then the sound of fighting, the sound of knuckles cracking on a skull. All she could focus on was the tiny body in her arms. She would never again see her sweet smile or hear her laughter. Eva brushed Sabina's blond hair back from her face, getting blood on the golden strands from her hand. She tried to wipe it away with her shirt, but it smeared in her hair. She touched her cheek to Sabina's, who was already cooling on the surface. She did not know it was possible to feel that hollow, that sad, that empty. Her crying was so intense now that she could not catch her breath. Fabien's hands pulled her out of her grief as her arms were torn away from Sabina.

"No, I won't leave her."

"Eva, she is gone. Take my truck and go. Now! More Germans will be here any second. There is no need for them to know that you were ever here today."

She looked at him through the blurriness of the tears and the shudders of her crying and managed to get a few words out. "It… doesn't… matter now."

"Yes, it does. She would not want you to die because of her."

Eva looked down at Sabina's lifeless body, still lying in the blood-stained hay. The blood was already drying in the thinner spots, and a few flies were now buzzing around the body. She felt sick and could no longer keep what remained of last night's dinner down. She turned away and threw up. She was glad now that she did not get to eat her breakfast.

"We will shed many tears for her, and she will get a proper funeral, I promise."

Eva wiped her mouth with the back of her hand, still tasting the acid. "But I won't get to be there. I can't say goodbye to her at her final resting place."

"Maybe someday you can, but you got to hold her in your arms for her last few seconds on this earth. That is a better goodbye than any you can give her now. You will miss her funeral so you can live. She understands why you cannot be there. I believe she would want you to think of her and be happy, not sad. So, remember those times that you two had together and cherish them."

"But whenever I think of her, it will make me sad. I cannot think of her and not see her like this." She took Sabina's hand and cradled it in hers.

"You have to, Eva. Listen, you don't have much time. You need to leave now!" He was growing frantic.

Fabien was telling her to leave, but she wanted nothing more than to stay with Sabina. But she knew he was right. If she stayed, she would never go home. She could not bring Sabina back or help her now.

"Eva, go get your things from your room and go back to Madame Blanc's."

"Where are Ezra and Rachel?"

"I told Ezra to leave. He cannot stay here any longer. They would catch him here if he did, anyway."

"And Rachel and the kids?"

"I don't know. They must have fled into the fields before we got here. Now go."

She suddenly felt the urgency in what he was telling her. She turned and ran as fast as she could from the barn, passing the beaten and bloody body of the other German soldier lying outside the barn, up the steps to the house, and into her bedroom. She pulled her suitcase from under the bed, and threw it on top, then grabbed her things and tossed them in it. She didn't care how. She saw the red teddy bear that Sabina would sleep with every night lying on top of the quilt of her neatly made bed. She picked it up and hugged it as if it were her. When she turned to put it in her suitcase, she saw on Sabina's dresser all the dried flowers they had collected while she was living there. She scooped them up and put them in her suitcase along with the bear. She got the music box and the Wizard of Oz book Gerhardt gave her, put them in the bag, closed the lid, and snapped it shut. She looked at her hands as she closed her suitcase and, for the first time, noticed that they were covered in dry blood—Sabina's blood. She looked down at herself and saw that it was all over her; she was covered in it. She started to feel dizzy and knew if she did not leave now, she would never get the chance to. She huffed her suitcase off the bed, carried it to the truck, and threw it in the back.

Fabien was walking back to the house. He, too, was covered in blood, but she could not tell whose it was. He was covered with the blood of multiple people.

She ran and embraced him. "Thank you for everything. I am so sorry, I am so sorry!" she cried again and again, feeling that nothing she said would ever be enough. She looked into his bloodshot eyes and saw that he had been crying and felt his emptiness mix with her own.

"Eva, you need to go." His voice cracked as he spoke.

"I know." Here was a strong man who had been pushed almost to the breaking point. He was fighting to keep it in but she could see him cracking at the seams.

She released him, ran back to the truck, climbed into the driver's seat, and looked at Fabien, knowing it would be the last time. She would never see him again. The tears began again as she drove away. Wiping them away with her hands every few seconds was all she could do to see and not run off the road. It must be past lunchtime now, Gerhardt would be home soon, but she hoped he would be late this once.

She pulled in front of the house and turned off the engine. She opened the door and almost fell while trying to get out. She felt like she was drunk, going through the motions in a haze. She walked in the front door, and her nostrils were flooded with the smell of lunch.

"Eva, is that you?" she heard Renée call from the lounge.

She did not want to talk, so she kept walking toward the stairs.

"Eva?" she heard again from the lounge.

Then Renée stepped into the hall and stopped in her tracks when she saw Eva. She screamed and put her hand over her mouth. Adele came running from the kitchen to see what was happening. She could not see the blood-covered dress and hands that Renée could. All she could see was the back of Eva and Renée standing in front of her, covering her mouth and staring with horrified eyes.

"Madame, what has happened?" She walked past Eva next to Renée and turned, then gasped. "Oh my God, Eva. Why are you covered in blood? Is it yours?"

Eva cried and slowly sank to the floor. "No, it's Sabina's," she said through sobs. "She is dead. They killed her. I felt the life leave her body as I held her, and I could do nothing to save her." Eva moved her arms in the same position she had while cradling Sabina. "She is gone, Adele, gone."

Adele looked horrified, and Renée started crying.

Adele knelt next to her and put a hand on her shoulder. "Who killed her?" she asked urgently.

Eva could hardly talk; tears and snot were running down her face. She tried to wipe them away as she spoke. "The Germans."

"Why did they kill a little girl?"

"Because she got in the way; they were trying to kill someone else."

"Who?"

"A Jewish man. She was trying to protect him."

"What Jewish man?"

"It doesn't matter. I don't want to talk about it anymore. I want to clean her blood off me," Eva said, hiccuping through her sobs.

"All right, let's go run you a bath."

"My things, they are still in the truck."

"I'll get them. Just go get in the tub," Adele said.

Eva climbed the stairs. Her body felt like it weighed hundreds of pounds. She went into the bathroom and closed the door but didn't lock it so that Adele could bring her clothes. She plugged the tub and turned on the water. She pulled the stiff dress over her head, dropped it on the floor, and removed her slip with blood on it and then her undergarments. She stepped into the tub and sat down, wrapping her arms around her knees. She sat like that until Adele came in with her clothes.

"Oh my," Adele said and turned the water off before it overflowed onto the floor. Adele took the sponge from the edge of the tub, stuck it in the water, and squeezed it as she rubbed it over Eva's back. She dipped it in again and repeated the process over her arms, shoulders, hair, and face.

Eva looked down at the water. It appeared almost crimson in the dim bathroom lighting. She stood up quickly, splashing water out of the tub onto the floor. "I can't be in this water," she said, almost in hysterics. She stepped out of the tub and took a step back, looking at the blood-soaked clothes on the floor and the red water. "Adele, please drain it."

Adele reached her hand in and pulled the plug; the water began swirling near the drain until it was all but gone. "I will fill it up with some fresh water."

Eva nodded her head as she stood in the middle of the bathroom with her arms wrapped around herself. When the tub was filled again, she stepped back in and sat down, leaning back.

"Thank you, Adele."

"You are welcome, Eva. I could not just leave you there in the hall when I saw you broken and only resembling a shell of your former self."

"I feel so empty."

"It will take some time to get through this, but it will get better, I promise."

"It doesn't feel like it will ever get better." Eva shook her head, looking at the wall in front of her. "How do I fill this hole I have in my chest?"

"You will find something else to fill it with. I had to, and you can too, but it won't be easy. With every passing day, you will feel the pain a little less and a little less until it isn't there anymore. You will never forget her, but life will go on. It will be the same with every other loss you have."

Eva looked at her. "Other loss?"

"You think Sabina is the only loss you will have in your life?"

"I guess not."

They could hear the slamming of the front door and talking echoing from downstairs. Renée was talking to a man, and Eva was pretty sure that she knew who it was.

"I need to go see what is going on. Will you be all right?"

Eva nodded.

Adele left the bathroom and closed the door behind her. Eva heard her shoes on the stairs, then, more talking. Finally, there were footsteps coming up the stairs, but they sounded heavier than Adele's. Then, there was a knock on the bathroom door.

"Eva?"

She heard Gerhardt's voice on the other side of the door. She did not think she could face him right now. "What do you want?"

"Can I come in?"

"No."

The door opened, and he came into the bathroom and closed the door behind him.

"What are you doing? I said no." she covered her breast with her arm and bent her leg that faced him to hide the rest of her.

"I know, but I will not leave you like this. Renée told me what had happened. She said that you were there." He looked down at the blood-stained clothes on the floor. He picked her dress off the floor and inspected it. "God, Eva, I can't believe you were there. Why were you there? You were supposed to be here. When I left, you were still asleep in my bed."

She squeezed her eyes shut, and the tears ran down her cheeks.

"Eva, look at me," he said fervently.

The intensity of his words made her open her eyes. She turned her head to face him.

He knelt beside the tub, touched her cheek with the back of his hand, and wiped a tear away with his knuckle. "I am so sorry about Sabina. That was not supposed to happen. I have no words for what you must be feeling right now. I would wrap you in my arms and hold you there until you felt safe again, and I would tell you that everything would be OK. But the truth is it's not. I can't bring her back, and I can't change what will happen next."

"What is going to happen next?" Eva asked, fear rising in her.

He pursed his lips. “Eva, Fabien, and the man I saw come out of the field have been arrested. Fabien killed the soldier that killed Sabina, and the other man also killed a German soldier. They are to be shot in the square today.”

She felt like she was going to have a heart attack. “No, please, Gerhardt, you can’t let this happen. I have already lost someone I loved today. I can’t lose someone else. I can’t. I don’t think I could take it.” Her voice quivered from the shock.

Gerhardt’s eyes teared up, and he reached into the tub and pulled her to him, not caring that he was getting his uniform wet.

“Eva, please forgive me. I am so sorry, but there is nothing I can do.” He held her tight in his arms. “They say everyone has to be there, but I’m telling you not to go.”

She pulled away from him. “I need you to leave.”

“Eva!”

“Get out!” she yelled. “I don’t want to see your face ever again. I don’t want to see any German. They are all the same. I thought you were the exception, but it turns out I was wrong. You are just like all the others. You have no heart. You are a monster. Now get out!” she screamed again.

The things she said shocked him. He knew she was hurting, but she could never take back what she said.

He stood, walked to the door, and paused. “I know you hate me now, and frankly, if I were you, I would too, but I hope that someday you can forgive me. I… goodbye, Eva,” he said, not finishing his sentence, then opened the door, stepped out of the bathroom, and gently closed it.

Once again, she was alone. She heard his heavy steps on the stairs, in the hall, then the front door opened and closed. She got out of the tub, dried off, and put on the clothes that Adele had brought her. As she was picking up her dirty clothes, the bathroom door opened, and she half expected to see Gerhardt. The anger she felt when he was in the bathroom was subsiding, and the guilt and realization of what she said to him were starting to set in. It was almost like she had no control over what she was saying at that moment. She was seeing red, and the anger and hurt had taken over.

Adele came into the bathroom and held out her hand. "I'll take those. I will take them down to the fire and burn them."

Eva put the clothes in Adele's hand.

"I heard you up here yelling at him; don't feel sorry for him. He deserved everything you said and more."

Eva sniffed. "I know."

"We have to go to the square. Everyone is supposed to be there."

"Gerhardt said I don't have to go."

"Why would he do that?"

"Because Fabien is being shot along with the Jewish man."

"You can't be serious?"

"I am. They took Sabina, and now they are taking Fabien. They have taken everything from me."

"I will dispose of these. Go lie down."

Eva lay on her bed. She could hear Renée and Adele leave to go to the square. She stayed curled up in a ball, looking at the joint door, and remembered the events of last night. So much has happened since then. Last night would not have happened if she could have seen the things that were to take place today.

She heard multiple guns being fired in the distance, then a single shot, followed by another. She jumped with every shot. She knew it was done, that Fabien and Ezra were now dead. And Rachel, her, and her kids were out there somewhere, hiding, but they wouldn't be for long. It was only a matter of time before they were caught and sent to a camp, which meant instant death for the children. She closed her eyes and gave in to the exhaustion she could not hold at bay any longer.

She was jolted awake when she felt someone shaking her.

"Eva, wake up. Eva!"

When she opened her eyes, the first thing she saw was Gerhardt's blue eyes looking down at her. She gasped and scooted away from him, looking at him as if he was going to pounce on her.

"Eva, you have to get out of here now."

"What are you talking about? Why do I have to leave?"

"Because they have ordered us to pick everyone up for questioning who lived on the farm, including you."

"Questioning?"

"Eva, listen to me. When they say questioning, they mean torture until you talk. If you think last time was bad, it is nothing compared to what it will be like now." He held out a piece of paper. "This is a travel pass. Go to Paris and find a way to get home. You are not safe here anymore."

"You mean in La Chapelle?"

"I mean in France."

"I have to warn Brigitte."

"There is no time. It is too late for her but not for you." He took her hand and put the pass in it.

"I have to at least try."

"Don't be naïve, Eva. Listen to me. You have to go now. There is no time."

She looked at the pass in her hand and back to him. She was still trying to get all of this to register—the fact that in just one day, she would have lost everybody. Some of them had died, and she now had to leave the others. She would be alone soon—entirely and utterly alone. She could not fathom it.

He grabbed her and pulled her off the bed, forcing her to stand. "Eva, what the hell. You have the pass, and your bags are right there on the floor. Now take them and run."

She had never imagined that he would ever be so forceful with her.

He took her small bag off the floor, draped it over her shoulder, and then picked up her suitcase. "Eva, run, damn it!"

She did not want to find out what he would do if she did not move this time. She hurried out of the room and ran down the stairs, listening to his footsteps close behind. When she got outside, she saw that the truck was still parked in front of the house, and the sun was coming up from over the horizon. She honestly had no idea what time it was, except that it was early in the morning. He put her suitcase in the bed of the truck and opened the door for her, and she threw her bag on the passenger side and turned to look at him. They stood staring at each other for a few seconds, but neither spoke. She thought he might kiss her, but he didn't move. He just stood a few inches away, taking in her face. The sun was now higher in the sky, and she could see beams of yellow and white from behind him, and the birds were chirping as they flew overhead.

“You better leave now.” He stepped back so she could get in the truck.

She felt like she needed to say something to him, but she didn’t know exactly what that was, so she got in the truck and shut the door. She started the engine and looked at him through the door window, his short dark blond hair that was combed to one side, his piercing blue eyes, his chiseled jaw, and perfectly pressed gray uniform. She turned away from him and looked ahead. She put the truck in gear, and it jerked forward as she tried to get it moving. She had never learned to drive a stick, but she was going to have to try and learn today.

Eva peered back through the mirror one last time to see him turn and face the truck as it drove away. She watched until she could no longer see him. She did not know what would happen now or what the future held for her. The only thing she was sure of was that she still loved him, no matter what she said.

About the author

J.L. Robison is an American author who currently lives in western Pennsylvania with her husband and two daughters. She has recently finished the fourth and final book in the Edelweiss series and is now working on a new story in the world of dark fantasy. Before becoming a writer, J.L. Robison taught English as a second language. She has had the opportunity to live in many states and has been to over fourteen different countries, experiencing their unique cultures. She writes in multiple genres, spanning historical fiction, literary fiction, romance, and fantasy. When she is not sitting on the couch with her laptop, she is outside working in her garden, playing tennis, bowling, ice skating, traveling, or doing things with her kids. She also enjoys going on walks with her husband or drinking a glass of wine to relax in front of the TV. Most of her inspiration comes at night when she can't sleep, is listening to music, or when on a walk alone in nature.

Printed in Great Britain
by Amazon

56870944R00300